Behind Those Blue Eyes

Rebecca Lange

Published by Rebecca Lange, 2022.

BEHIND THOSE BLUE EYES

First edition. August 20, 2022.

ISBN: 978-1957089256

Written by Rebecca Lange.

Table of Contents

Prologue.. 1
1 | Sharper Than Barbed Wire 7
2 | Thrown Over His Shoulder 17
3 | He Picked the Wrong Woman 39
4 | A Kiss in the Hayloft 57
5 | Stolen for a Stranger's Scheme 67
6 | A Cowboy's Last Ride 89
7 | Where Grief Met Grace in Kneeland 103
8 | Screams in the Empty Field 131
9 | More Than a Close Call 149
10 | Inheritance Written in Blood 163
11 | An Heiress in the Crosshairs 179
12 | Not a Real Kidnapping 191
13 | A Few Swats Short of a Revelation 207
14 | Dynamite in a Dress 225
15 | Caught Beneath the Hooves 251
16 | Words That Can't Be Taken Back 265
17 | Untangling a Cowgirl's Heart 283
18 | Watching Him Ride Away 307
19 | Breathless with Heartbreak 327
20 | Just Gone 339
21 | From Kidnapper to Protector 361
22 | When Blood Begs for the Truth 375
23 | Too Late to Pretend Anymore 387
24 | Braver Than They Bargained For 403
25 | The Making of a Monster 421
26 | The Cost of Their Silence 431
27 | The Hug She Dreamed Of 461
28 | Will You Marry Me, Leah Johnson? 471

29 | Behind Those Blue Eyes 489
30 | True Love Always Wins! 501
A Note from the author..509

For anyone who treats spiders like vengeful gods of doom—

may your fearless, broad-shouldered hero eternally smite those miniature spawns of darkness while you stand on a chair screaming like you just saw the Devil himself.

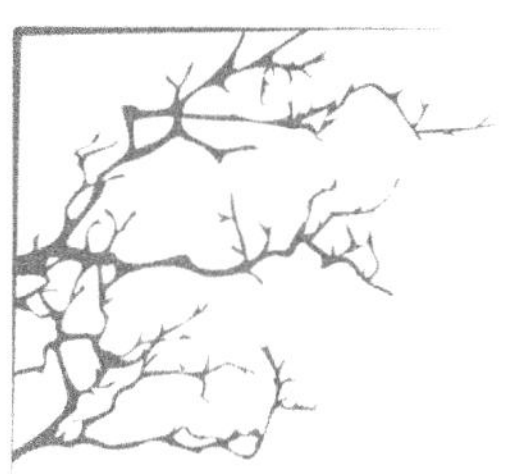

Prologue

"Sheriff Bailey? Aunt Mildred? What brings you here?" Leah Johnson asked the moment she stepped into the house. Doug Cashley, her father's best friend and the ranch's foreman, followed closely behind her. She kept a polite smile in place, though every muscle in her body ached from spending the entire day in the saddle checking fences across their vast property. All she wanted was a long, scalding bath. But with her father away visiting his closest friend, her godfather, in Sacramento, welcoming unexpected visitors fell to her.

Mildred stood beside Patricia Johnson, whispering urgently into her sister's ear. Sheriff Scott Bailey turned toward Leah. He didn't get a word out before she saw it: the grim heaviness in his eyes. Her heart lurched. She glanced toward her mother, but Patricia had turned away, her shoulders rigid.

"Mom? What's going on?" Leah's voice wavered as she stared at her mother's trembling back. Patricia didn't respond. Mildred only tightened her arms around her sister.

"Sheriff?"

Sheriff Bailey exhaled slowly. "There's no easy way to say this."

Leah's heart plummeted. "Just tell me."

"I received a telegram from David Smith. Your father never arrived in Sacramento. The sheriff there sent men to investigate. They found the stagecoach near Clearlake. It appears it was attacked, possibly robbed, and then set on fire. The horses panicked, lost their footing, and the whole coach went over the mountain bridge into the water. There were... no survivors."

Leah went white as linen. She gasped. Doug looked just as stunned, but he reacted first, pulling her into his arms. Her mother's quiet sobs filled the room, but Leah couldn't move. Couldn't think. Thankfully Mildred was there to hold Patricia upright.

Leah forced down a hard swallow. "So... they found everyone's body?"

Sheriff Bailey shook his head. "No. But the telegram said no one could've survived that fall. Part of the coach shattered on a rock before sinking into the lake." His voice softened. Leah refused to meet his eyes.

"Then that means," she said shakily, "that right now my dad is considered *missing*?"

The sheriff grimaced. "Leah, I don't want you getting your hopes up. They're searching for the bodies as we speak."

Doug stepped closer, worry clouding his features.

"Leah, sweetheart... you're not making this easier for your mother. Pretending won't help anyone."

Anyone who truly knew her, especially Doug, who had been like a second father, could see she was seconds from breaking. She tried to stay strong for her mother, but the thought of losing her father gutted her. Leah and Mitchell Johnson were inseparable. She adored him. She idolized him.

"Pretending?" Leah snapped, jerking out of Doug's hold. Her blue eyes flashed like lightning. "As long as they haven't found his body, Dad is *missing*. And I'm not giving up on him."

Sheriff Bailey reached toward her, but she turned away just as Patricia finally faced her. Her mother stepped forward and wrapped trembling arms around her.

"Sweetheart," Patricia whispered, voice breaking, "from the sound of it... there's no way your father could have survived something so terrible. We can't cling to false hope."

Leah bit hard into her lip as she eased out of her mother's arms.

"No, Mom. Dad is alive. I know he is. And I will never, ever stop believing that." Before anyone could stop her, she spun, bolted out the front door, and sprinted toward the stables. She saddled her horse with shaking hands, mounted, and kicked hard into a gallop. She didn't slow until she reached her sanctuary: the waterfall at Willow Creek.

Leah managed to hold herself together only until she slid from her horse and sank onto the broad fallen tree trunk beside the creek. When her boots touched the damp soil and the tumbling water wrapped around her, the walls she'd fought to hold up finally cracked.

She bowed her head, fingers digging into the rough bark, and let the emotions she'd shoved down surge free. It couldn't be true. It couldn't. God wouldn't take her father from her, not him. Not the one person who had always stood between her and the world's cruelty, who had taught her to be strong, to ride fearlessly, to trust her instincts, to speak her mind.

He wasn't just her father; he was her favorite person in the world, the steady anchor shaping the woman she was becoming. A choked sob escaped her. The creek's rhythmic rush, usually so soothing, only magnified the hollow ache in her chest.

Her mother had never been the strong one. Patricia was gentle to the bone, shy to a fault, and fragile in ways Leah only began to understand as she grew older. She had been abused for years, tormented by her stepfather and stepbrother, until the day Mitchell Johnson and Mildred stepped into her life like lifelines. It took years of tenderness and patience to draw Patricia out of the shell she'd built for survival.

Mildred, too, carried her own scars. Their parents divorced when the sisters were young, splitting them apart: Patricia with their mother, Mildred with their father. They hadn't reconnected fully until around the time Leah's parents met. By then, they were strangers learning to be sisters again.

Then Mildred's husband died suddenly, leaving her a widow with a broken heart and a suitcase full of responsibilities. She returned to Hoopa Valley, rebuilding her life piece by piece, teaching school in town by day, tutoring wealthy families' children by necessity. No matter how far she traveled, she always came home when Patricia needed her. Or when Leah did. And Leah had needed her more than ever today.

She scrubbed at her face with trembling hands. Her father had always known Patricia's insecurities ran deep, so he had prepared Leah from the time she was barely tall enough to grasp a saddle horn. He taught her livestock, land management, bookkeeping, everything she would one day need to run the ranch.

But that time was supposed to be years away. She was only nineteen. She still relied on his steady voice, his broader experience, his unwavering belief in her. He was supposed to be there to guide her. To stand beside her. To grow old watching her become the rancher he believed she could be. Her breath hitched. The idea of facing the world without him felt unimaginable.

"No," she whispered fiercely, the word catching on a sob. "You're not gone, Dad. I know you're not." The waterfall roared on, indifferent, as if daring her to keep believing. And she did. With everything she had left.

The sobs tore out of her with such force that her knees buckled. She dropped to the ground, clutching the damp earth as her breath hitched and broke. It felt as though the world had cracked open beneath her. She wasn't ready to let her father go, not now, not ever.

Her chest tightened painfully, her breaths coming fast and sharp, until she was gasping like someone drowning on dry land. Panic blurred her vision. The waterfall's roar faded beneath the pounding of blood in her ears. Then, warmth. Two strong arms wrapped around her from behind, lifting her off the ground and pulling her securely against a broad, familiar chest. She didn't need to look. She knew that embrace. Knew the steadiness, the strength, the scent of leather and pine from long hours on the trail. *Jaxon.*

"I just heard, Leah," he murmured, his voice rough with emotion. "Cash told me. I'm so sorry."

She clung to him desperately, pressing her forehead against his shirt as her breath shuddered out. Held in his arms, the spinning in her head slowed just enough for her lungs to remember how to work, but the tears kept coming, hot and relentless.

"He's not dead, Jaxon," she choked, her voice trembling with stubborn conviction. "He can't be."

Jaxon's grip tightened. He eased back just enough to lift her chin with gentle fingers. His dark eyes searched hers, those deep blue eyes now swollen and swimming with grief.

"Leah," he said softly, "look at me."

She tried, but her gaze faltered. He brushed away a tear with his thumb before speaking again.

"Whatever happens... you're not alone," he whispered. "You have people who love you. Family. Friends. Me. We're not going anywhere. I'll be right by your side, no matter what comes."

She swallowed hard, blinking through her tears, a tiny flicker of steadiness rising in her chest, not hope about the nightmare unfolding, but comfort. The comfort of knowing she wouldn't face it alone.

1
Sharper Than Barbed Wire

Patricia, their foreman Doug Cashley, and Leah stepped down from the stagecoach, stretching their stiff legs after the long ride. It had been years since any of them had set foot in Eureka. Mitch had always handled their business trips, and only Cash accompanied him now and then. Today, the small town felt unfamiliar, too loud, too busy, too full of faces that didn't know their grief. But with Mitch gone, at least in the eyes of the law, they had no choice. They were here to meet with Mitchell Johnson's attorney and discuss the future of the ranch.

Four months had passed since Sheriff Bailey had stood in their parlor with a telegram in hand and sorrow in his eyes. Four months since they learned Mitch had never reached Sacramento. Despite search parties, official inquiries, and desperate efforts to find remains, his body had never been recovered.

Leah refused, steadfastly, fiercely, to believe he was dead. Her mother, however, had surrendered to despair. Patricia had wrapped herself in mourning like a shroud, withdrawing deeper into the fragile shell, she had worked so hard to climb out of. Leah had known this would happen. Her mother had always been delicate, easily overwhelmed, and prone to collapsing inward when life pressed too heavily.

Patricia could hardly bear to look at Cash. Though he tried to be the loyal friend he had always been, she avoided him whenever possible. He reminded her too much of Mitch. His voice, his mannerisms, the way the two men had joked like brothers... every glimpse seemed to tear another hole in her heart.

Fortunately, Cash's sister, Ruby, had stepped in. She served as the Johnsons' cook and housekeeper and had a remarkable gift for navigating the emotional storms of both Patricia and Leah. The two women couldn't have been more opposite. They shared the same golden hair and blue eyes, but everything beyond that was night and day.

Where Patricia was timid, soft-spoken, and tender-hearted, Leah was fire, feisty, outspoken, stubborn as a mule. She loved fiercely and worked tirelessly, with a will as sharp as barbed wire and a tongue that could cut when someone deserved it. But she had never inherited her father's boundless patience, especially not for the constant tears and emotional neediness her mother clung to like a lifeline.

Leah tried—she truly did. She loved her mother. But listening to Patricia spiral into despair day after day wore her thin. Leah didn't understand why someone needed to talk and cry about every feeling. Leah handled pain the opposite way, she stuffed it down, locked it up, and pushed forward. The only people who had ever coaxed her into opening up were her father and Cash, usually sitting beside her at the waterfall until she finally broke.

Cash loved Leah as though she were his own daughter. Like Mitch, he had always encouraged her to stand tall, speak her mind, and never let anyone walk over her. Most ranchers in and around Hoopa Valley respected her, some even feared her just a little. She was sharp, quick-thinking, and impossible to deceive. More than one cowboy had tried to cheat her on livestock prices or land deals. All of them had walked away with their pride bruised and their wallets lighter. Leah was a fighter. Always had been.

And she never hesitated to call out dishonesty when she saw it. That unfiltered honesty, combined with her beauty and fierce independence, was probably one of the reasons she hadn't found a suitor yet. Plenty of young men admired her from afar, but she needed someone who could match her wit, challenge her stubborn streak, and not shrink at the first spark of her fire.

Someone strong enough not to be intimidated by her spirit. Someone who could go toe-to-toe with her and not flinch. Someone... rare.

And as she followed Patricia and Cash toward the attorney's office, Leah couldn't help but wonder if she'd ever meet a man like that, or if her father's disappearance had already changed the course of her life forever.

The secretary opened the office door and gestured them inside. Patricia, Leah, and Cash stepped in and found Walter Richardson rising stiffly from behind his desk. He forced a polite smile and motioned for them to sit.

"Mrs. Johnson," he began solemnly, folding his hands, "I'm afraid I have unpleasant news. Your husband accumulated a significant amount of debt over the past year. I've received multiple complaints claiming their bills were never paid."

Patricia nodded silently, her eyes already glazing with defeat, but Leah exchanged a sharp look with Cash. Neither of them believed a word of it. Mitch Johnson had been many things, but careless with money was not one of them.

"What would you suggest we do?" Patricia asked timidly, staring down at her hands.

"I recommend you transfer ownership to the individual named in Mitchell's Will."

Leah stiffened. She glanced at her mother, who looked ready to nod along with anything this man said, and felt her patience snap.

"Excuse me, Mr. Richardson," Leah said, keeping her tone cool but firm, "but I don't believe my father got into debt. He was meticulous with our finances and worked closely with the banker in town. I'd like to see these unpaid bills."

"There's no need for a girl," he began dismissively, Leah cut in at once.

"I'm nineteen years old," Leah snapped, her glare sharp enough to slice through the desk, "and I would appreciate it if you didn't treat me like a child."

The lawyer blinked, taken aback by the steel in her voice.

"Well," he tried again irritably, "this is a matter between your mother and me. There's no reason for you to involve yourself."

Leah leaned forward, unflinching. "I am involved, whether you approve. My father intended for me to take over the ranch.

I've been running it alongside him and our foreman for years. So, I'd appreciate it if you stopped talking down to me simply because I'm a woman."

Richardson gaped at her. Cash, standing protectively behind her, looked one breath away from leaping over the desk. The attorney cleared his throat.

"Regarding you taking over the ranch... your father did not leave it to you or your mother. According to his Will, the property goes to a man."

"Oh, really?" Leah lifted a brow, her voice dripping skepticism. She heard Cash suck in a furious breath through his teeth. "And what man would that be?"

"Let me check..." Richardson shuffled through a stack of papers and pulled out a page. "Milton Rowland."

Patricia flinched violently, dread flashing across her face. Leah and Cash reacted with instant disbelief.

"Is this some kind of sick joke?" Cash snapped before Leah could speak. "Why would Mitch leave his ranch to that man? A man who hasn't contacted the family in years, and who doesn't know which end of a cow is the front?"

"Mr. Cashley—" the attorney began, only for Leah to slice over him again.

"This is ridiculous. My father would never put anyone from my mother's family in his Will. Who gave you that document?"

"Your father," Richardson insisted defensively. "He signed it himself."

"Show me the signature," Leah demanded.

The man stared at her, stunned by her audacity, clearly unaccustomed to women who spoke with such force. His hesitation only fueled her determination.

"There's no need—"

"Show. Me. The. Signature." Her voice was low, steady, and unmistakably dangerous. "And stop trying to manipulate me just because my father isn't here to stop you."

Cash stepped closer, a silent warning of what would happen if the attorney refused. Finally, Richardson fumbled through the papers and slid the Will toward them. Leah examined the signature, instantly recognizing the shaky, unfamiliar scrawl for the forgery it was.

"Just as I thought," she said coldly. "That is not my father's signature. Did you fabricate this yourself, or did someone else hand you this mess?"

"How dare you?" Richardson sputtered, flushing red.

"How dare *I*?" Leah shot back. "You're the one telling lies. There are no outstanding bills. My father taught me every aspect of our operations, and we've always dealt in honesty. If there were problems, our business partners would have contacted us directly. Every one of them knows me and works with me. I meet with our banker regularly, and Cash also knows everything that crosses that ranch."

Richardson blinked, mouth twitching, but Leah wasn't done.

"Oh, and before I forget, my father didn't trust you anymore. He started involving our family attorney in all work-related matters and made sure copies of his *actual* Will were kept in multiple safe locations."

That struck home. Richardson's face drained of color. If he'd expected to railroad a grieving widow and a young woman, he had badly miscalculated.

Leah stood and turned to her mother. "Come on, Mom. We're done here."

Patricia rose slowly, nodded stiffly at the stunned attorney, and followed Leah and Cash out the door. Behind them, Walter Richardson remained frozen in place, mouth agape, sweat beading at his temples, as the truth of his shattered scheme settled over him like a winter frost.

Walter Richardson had never encountered a woman quite like Leah Johnson. She wasn't merely spirited, she was a force of nature, sharp-tongued and unyielding, the kind of woman who could slice through deceit with a single look. Even as she stormed out with her mother and Cash in tow, he sat in stunned silence, equal parts rattled and genuinely impressed.

The office had barely settled into stillness when a side door creaked open. Another man stepped inside, tall, cold-eyed, radiating displeasure like heat from a forge. Walter straightened instinctively, throat tight. The newcomer didn't bother with greetings.

"Richardson," he snapped, "that was beyond pathetic. You were supposed to control the meeting. Instead, you let that little beast run circles around you. I told you to focus on Patricia, not Leah."

Walter swallowed hard. "I tried, sir. But that girl... she understands business better than half the ranchers in

California. She sees through every trick. And she knows her mother is a pushover. Leah Johnson won't go down without a massive fight. She's smart as a whip and takes feistiness to an entirely new level."

The man scoffed with open contempt.

"You're too easily impressed. Even that girl has weaknesses. Everyone does." He paced once, jaw clenched, then flicked his hand dismissively. "I'll report this," he said coldly. "But I doubt our boss will be pleased. Consider yourself fired, Richardson. We'll find an attorney with more backbone, and far less incompetence." He turned on his heel and stalked out.

Walter didn't move. Oddly enough, he wasn't even upset. His stomach had twisted with regret since the day he agreed to this arrangement. He had known it felt wrong, felt dirty. And after facing Leah Johnson, after seeing the fire in her eyes, he wished he had never signed his name to any part of this scheme.

One thing was certain, though: he would never forget her. Leah Johnson had inherited far more than just her father's ranch. She had inherited his iron spirit. And she would be hell to reckon with.

"Maybe we should have listened to Mr. Richardson. I'm sure he meant well." Patricia looked uncertainly at her daughter, but Leah shook her head without a shred of hesitation. Across the table, Cash and his sister Ruby glanced over as they finished supper. Ruby had just pushed back her chair to fetch dessert when Leah spoke again.

"No, Mom. Walter Richardson wasn't trying to help us. He's working with someone, someone who wants our ranch and everything we own. Men like him think that because we're women, they can manipulate us. Dad warned me countless times about men who prey on widows, thinking they're easy targets who can't manage business on their own." Her voice trembled with indignation.

"I won't let that happen. This is our ranch and will stay our ranch. Dad and Cash worked too hard for anyone to waltz in and take it just because they're too lazy to build something themselves."

"Leah's right, Patti," Cash added, leaning forward. "You always want to see the good in people, and that's admirable. But some folks are nothing but dishonest vultures. Richardson tried to trick us, and he failed spectacularly. You should be proud of your daughter for seeing through that scheme before any of us."

Patricia glanced toward Leah, her eyes softening with pride before filling again with worry.

"I am proud of her. Of both of you. But I don't want to lose my daughter because criminals don't like being challenged."

"That's the only way to stop them, Mom," Leah said firmly. "The men who hired Richardson don't think we're a threat because we're women. They think they can invent lies about Dad and our business, and we'll just... hand everything over. They need to learn that women aren't stupid, and we can outplay them just as easily."

"Leah—"

"Trust me, Mom." Leah leaned forward, her voice gentle but unwavering. "I know what I'm doing. Dad may be gone, but I still have Cash as my mentor. He loves this place just as much as Dad did. And as much as I do."

Cash nodded with a warm smile. "Yes, ma'am. Every word of that is true."

Patricia sighed, shoulders sagging with a mixture of relief and lingering dread. Ruby stood and brushed off her apron.

"Don't worry so much, Patti. We'll all look out for each other. And you know the ranch hands adore Leah. Hoopa Valley is full of good people who'd do anything for this family. Even the Hoopa Tribe has taken a shine to your daughter. Mitch did a great deal for this community, and nobody's forgotten it. You've got plenty of folks watching your back."

"I know," Patricia murmured. "I'm still worried, though."

A sudden, sharp knock at the door made everyone freeze. Cash got up and crossed the room.

"Scott! What brings you here?" Cash asked as he opened the door. "You're just in time for dessert. Want to join us? Ruby always cooks enough to feed half the valley."

"Come on in, Scott," Ruby called with a grin. "I've got plenty."

Sheriff Bailey stepped inside, hat in hand.

"I don't want to trouble you. I came to see if Patricia might like to take a walk with me."

All eyes shifted to Leah's mother. Patricia turned the shade of a ripe strawberry.

"I—I'd love that," she stammered. "But please have dessert with us first. Ruby always makes something delicious."

The sheriff smiled and accepted the invitation. After dessert, he offered Patricia his arm, and the two slipped out into the cool evening.

2
Thrown Over His Shoulder

Leah walked to the window, watching them disappear down the road, her teeth worrying her bottom lip. Cash stepped beside her and draped an arm gently over her shoulders.

"Penny for your thoughts?"

"My thoughts?" Leah tilted her head. "It just feels strange. Sheriff Bailey keeps coming by so often lately. It almost seems like he's trying to court her."

Cash chuckled softly. "You've got to remember. Scott and your parents were close for years. Maybe he's just looking out for her, trying to be there the way any good friend would."

"Maybe," Leah murmured, still watching the dark shape of them moving down the path.

"But something about it feels... off."

Cash gave her shoulder a gentle squeeze but said nothing more. Sometimes, Leah's instincts were sharper than anyone gave her credit for.

"Engaged? You can't be serious." Leah stood rigid in front of her mother, outrage and disbelief blazing across her face. Cash lingered nearby, arms folded, silently observing every word, every movement, as though preparing to intervene if necessary. Patricia tried to reach out and touch her daughter's hand, but Leah stepped back as if the gesture burned.

"Is this some kind of sick joke?"

"Leah, please," Patricia whispered, her voice trembling. "Try to understand."

"Understand?" Leah's voice cracked, rising with emotion. "Mom, Dad hasn't even been gone five months. They never found his body. We don't even know if he's dead!"

"Your father is dead, Leah," Sheriff Scott Bailey interjected gently. He gave her a sympathetic nod, as though that alone could soften the blow. "I know this is hard, but it's time to accept it."

Leah's expression turned to ice. "You don't understand anything, Sheriff. It isn't your father who's missing. And no, I don't have to accept anything."

Patricia wrung her hands nervously. "Scott and I have talked this over, and we feel this is the right step."

"No!" Leah's voice rang through the room. "How can you move on so quickly? Why are you rushing this?"

"We need a man in the house again, Leah," Patricia said softly. "The ranch is suffering."

Leah's jaw dropped. "We need a man in the house. Really, Mom? What does Cash look like to you, a chicken?"

Ruby snorted behind them, unable to help herself. Cash shot her a warning glare, but even that didn't entirely hide the corner of his mouth twitching.

"Besides," Leah continued fiercely, "the ranch is not suffering. Cash and I have been running it just fine. The ranch hands are loyal, hardworking, and supportive. We're doing well."

"Cash can't do it all by himself," Patricia insisted, though her voice wavered. "And you're just a girl, Leah."

Those were the wrong words. Everyone in the room saw the explosion coming. Before Leah could unleash her fury, Cash stepped forward, wrapped his arms firmly around her, and pulled her back against him, more to shield Patricia than protect Leah.

"That's not fair, Patti," Cash said calmly, though his voice held an edge. "Leah's been running the ranch for a long time now. Yes, Mitch and I were there to help, but she's perfectly capable of doing it on her own." He held Leah still, hoping Patricia understood the warning in his steady gaze: *stop now*.

Patricia sighed and lowered her eyes.

"We're not getting married right away. We thought... maybe in a few months. Perhaps by the end of the year."

Leah jerked out of Cash's arms, her anger rekindled.

"I don't have time to listen to this." She spun around and stormed toward the door.

"I'm not trying to replace your father, Leah," Scott called after her, reaching out as though he could hold her with words alone. "I'm trying to help."

But Leah didn't slow. She didn't look back.

"Leah, please," Patricia cried, tears spilling down her cheeks. Scott wrapped an arm around Patricia's shoulders and drew her gently against him.

"Give her time," he murmured. "You know how much she loved her father. We can postpone the wedding if she's not ready."

Patricia nodded weakly, but the pain in her eyes said she feared she might lose her daughter long before she ever gained a husband.

Not knowing what else to do with the storm raging inside her, Leah stomped into the stables, her boots striking the packed dirt floor like warning shots. The smell of hay and horses usually calmed her, but not today. Not when anger was licking up her spine like wildfire.

Jaxon and two other cowboys were mucking out stalls. They paused when she marched past, grabbed a shovel and a pitchfork, and started attacking the nearest stall as if it had personally offended her. Without a word, the men shared a look. Everyone on the ranch knew that when Leah moved like that, trouble was brewing.

Jaxon approached first, cautious as if she were a wild mare ready to kick.

"All right," he said slowly, "what's wrong, Leah?"

She didn't even look up. "Why do you think something is wrong?"

"Just a hunch," he replied lightly. "That, or it's the steam rising off your end of the barn." He leaned on his pitchfork. "You want to talk about it?"

Leah shook her head sharply.

"It might help," he continued gently. "And I don't think that pitchfork will survive much longer if you keep stabbing that straw bale like it owes you money. It looks about ready to beg for mercy."

The two cowboys across from them snorted into their sleeves. Leah did not find it amusing. In fact, she felt an alarming urge to hurl the pitchfork directly at Jaxon's smug grin.

"I'm not in the mood for your jokes, Jaxon," she snapped. "Don't make me stab you next." Her glare made it abundantly clear she wasn't bluffing. Jaxon straightened, all humor vanishing.

"Okay. That's enough. Put down the pitchfork and follow me."

"No."

"Leah—" His voice dropped into a deep, no-nonsense growl that vibrated straight through her chest. "You're too wound up to be doing this. Someone's going to get hurt, and I'd rather it not be you. Hand me the tool. Come outside."

She tightened her grip. "No!" She heaved a load of dung and straw into the wheelbarrow with such furious force that half of it splattered onto the ground, and onto Jaxon's boots. The cowboys stared. Jaxon closed his eyes for a brief second, muttered something under his breath that suspiciously sounded like a prayer, and prepared to wrangle the most stubborn woman in all of Hoopa Valley.

"I'm not telling you again." Jaxon's glare was fierce enough to stop a bull in its tracks, but Leah continued ignoring him, stabbing at the stall as if she intended to dig her way straight to China. He stepped closer, jaw clenched. "If I have to carry you out of here, I will."

He knew he was pushing her farther than he should, but reasoning with Leah Johnson when she was this stubborn was like reasoning with wildfire. Still, he hadn't expected what came next.

She dropped the pitchfork, snatched up the nearest bucket of water, and flung it at him. Jaxon barely jumped out of the way in time.

"Oh, you're in big trouble now, young lady."

Before she could reach for another bucket, he charged forward, spun her around, and tossed her over his shoulder like she weighed nothing. Her furious kicking and shrill protesting didn't bother him in the slightest. He'd wrangled angry steers that put up less fight.

He strode out of the stable and headed straight for the creek behind the ranch house.

"I recommend you calm down now," Jaxon warned, his voice low and vibrating through her body. "Before I lose it too. I swear, Leah, I'm this close to putting you over my knee and giving your backside some attention."

"You wouldn't dare!" she raged, pounding her fists against his back.

"Yes, he would dare," another deep voice chimed in. Leah craned her neck enough to squint at Cash, who had followed them outside. "And if he doesn't, I'll be next in line."

Leah froze mid-wiggle.

"Are you ready to calm down?" Jaxon asked when she finally stopped thrashing. "Or do I need to make my threat come true?"

She rolled her eyes dramatically and scoffed. Jaxon lowered her back to the ground, but he didn't let go, his hands remained firm around her arms.

"So," he said, staring directly into her eyes, "what's going on with you?"

"Nothing."

"You just tried to drown me in the barn, young lady. 'Nothing' isn't the word I'd use."

"Fine," she snapped. "It's none of your business. There, better?" Her blue eyes still sparked with fury, but a hint of sass glimmered beneath it now. Jaxon held her gaze, unmoving. Leah pressed her lips together stubbornly, and Jaxon exhaled slowly. This girl could test the patience of a saint.

"Leah," Cash said, stepping closer, his voice gentle. "I know this is a shock for you, but your mother's decision is out of your control. If Patricia wants to marry Scott, there's nothing you can do. It's only a matter of time before you'll get married too."

"Patricia and Scott Bailey are getting married?" Jaxon blurted out, eyes widening. Suddenly, Leah's fury clicked into place.

"Not right away," Cash said. "Scott told her they'd wait until Leah's ready."

"I'm never going to be ready," Leah hissed. "How can she move on so fast? We haven't even had a funeral for Dad."

Cash sighed. "Your mother is lonely, Leah. After what she went through growing up, she clings to strong men. She's scared. With your father gone and Scott taking an interest, she's going to choose what makes her feel safe. Just try to understand her."

"I'm sorry, Cash," Leah shot back, "but I'm done trying to be understanding. I know she's insecure. I know she had a rough childhood. But this isn't just about her. Dad did everything for her. Catered to her every need. And now she's throwing herself at the next man who looks her way. She needs to grow up."

Jaxon and Cash exchanged a look, equal parts sympathy and concern. Cash finally pulled her into his arms, letting her rest her forehead against his chest.

"Your mom isn't built like you," he said softly. "She doesn't have your fire. Your father tried to nurture that fire in you because he didn't want you to live your life afraid like she always did."

Leah pulled back, eyes flashing.

"You know very well Dad and Ruby practically raised me. Mom did nothing. Ruby was hired because she couldn't handle chores or take care of a baby. Your sister did everything. Honestly, maybe Ruby should've been Dad's wife."

Cash barked out a laugh.

"Ruby and your father?" He shook his head, amused. Leah lifted her chin defiantly. "She was a child when Mitch married your mother."

"I know. But I saw the way she looked at Dad sometimes. She liked him."

"Well," Cash conceded with a grin, "your father was a handsome man."

"Yes," Leah agreed, then added with utter seriousness, "but so are you. Maybe you should marry my mom."

Jaxon burst into a wide grin. Cash nearly choked on his own spit. Leah's ability to pivot a conversation faster than a cutting horse never failed to stun both men.

"I don't feel that way about your mother," Cash managed.

"But don't you get lonely?" Leah asked innocently. "What about Jaxon's and Robyn's mom?"

Both men coughed violently. Leah caught the faint blush on Cash's neck, and her eyes gleamed with mischief.

"Lisa Finlay is about your age, isn't she? I bet if you asked, she'd court you in a heartbeat. She's beautiful. Peter died two years ago. Jaxon and Robyn are grown. Robyn will find a husband soon, and if Jax ever went to town, he'd find a pretty lady too." She flashed the men an exaggeratedly sweet smile.

"Leah..." Cash warned, eyebrows drawing together. "You're walking on thin ice."

"Why? I care about your happiness. I want you to be loved. Is that so wrong?" She batted her eyelashes dramatically and cast him the most innocent sideways glance she could muster. "I'm sure you wouldn't mind Cash becoming your stepfather, right, Jax?"

The look on their faces told her everything she needed to know. Leah squeaked, spun around, and sprinted. Jaxon had her in three strides. He scooped her up, slung her over his shoulder again, and marched straight to the creek. Before Leah could come up with another outrageous idea, he dropped her into the cold water. Of course, she managed to splash the two men hard enough that they were soaked from boots to hat.

Robyn Finlay wrapped her arms around Leah the moment she climbed into the hayloft. The familiar, dusty sweetness of hay wrapped around them, creating a private cocoon high above the noise of the ranch. The hayloft had always been their refuge, a place to talk freely without worrying about wandering ears or unexpected interruptions.

Robyn settled back against a thick pile of hay, strands clinging to her skirt, while Leah dropped down beside the wooden beam near the ladder and pulled her knees to her chest.

"How are you holding up?" Robyn asked gently. "Jax told me your mom got engaged to Scott Bailey." She grinned when Leah immediately rolled her eyes heavenward.

"Don't get me started," Leah groaned. "Half the time I still can't believe it myself."

"Have you tried telling your mom how you feel?"

"She doesn't listen," Leah muttered, plucking at a loose piece of hay. "I never thought of my mom as selfish, but right now she's only thinking about herself. If it were up to her, she'd marry him tomorrow. Scott's the one slowing things down."

Robyn's brows lifted. "Really? I've always thought of him as a good guy."

"He is," Leah admitted reluctantly. "I like him a lot. Under different circumstances, I wouldn't mind at all. But this," her voice tightened. "This feels wrong. We don't even know if Dad is dead or just... missing. What if the robbers took him? What if he's being held somewhere and they're trying to figure out who he is so they can demand ransom? And Mom just throws herself into a new relationship a few months after learning Dad never made it to my godfather's."

Robyn exhaled softly. "I get why you feel that way. But... not everyone is the same. Take my mom, for example. She's finally ready to think about another man, but it's taken her years."

Leah snorted. "Honestly, I'm surprised it took her that long, considering your father wasn't exactly a saint."

Robyn's lips tightened, but she nodded.

"Part of it was fear. Fear she'd end up with someone even worse. Father wasn't physically abusive, but he made our lives miserable with his drinking, the gambling, the yelling... the way he tore her down every chance he got. It takes a long time to believe you deserve better." Her voice softened further. "I really hope she finds a good man this time."

"I know one," Leah said slyly. She wiggled her eyebrows, and Robyn burst into giggles.

"Jax told me what you said." Robyn shook her head, amused. "I'm not sure he loves the idea, but honestly? Cash would make a great stepdad. And Mom and Cash would make a beautiful couple. He'd never treat her the way my father did."

"No, he wouldn't," Leah agreed. "Cash might not be shy, but he's cautious. He takes his time." A mischievous spark lit her eyes. "Which is why we may need to help him along."

Robyn squealed and slapped a hand over her mouth to smother it.

"We're matchmaking now?"

Leah winked. "Oh, absolutely. Someone has to make sure good men end up with good women around here."

"We might have to do some matchmaking for Jaxon too. That boy is a hopeless case," Robyn sighed dramatically.

Leah snorted. "I don't even get it. Jax is a good-looking guy. I'm surprised the girls in Hoopa Valley aren't lining up for him."

"Oh, they are," Robyn said with a smug little smirk. "I heard Miriam Henderson and Mia Collins at the store the other day. You should've heard them." She lifted her chin and adopted an exaggeratedly breathy tone. "'I don't understand why I can't get him to notice me, Miri. He's so handsome. If he asked me to court him, I'd say yes in a heartbeat.'"

Leah burst out laughing. Robyn wasn't finished. She fluttered her lashes, fanned herself, and switched to her second impression.

"'Why, I know just what you mean, Mia. Every time he smiles at me, I could swoon. His broad shoulders, those muscular arms, and don't get me started on those dreamy eyes—'"

Leah doubled over, clutching her stomach as laughter overtook her.

"Stop! You sound just like them!"

Robyn rolled her eyes. "They're ridiculous. I swear, the man can sneeze and half the town faints."

"Well," Leah said with a half-shrug, "he's just waiting for the right one."

Robyn gave her a slow, meaningful look.

"Funny you say that... because several girls are jealous of you."

"Me?" Leah blinked. "Why? Jaxon and I are friends, nothing else. He's your big brother, so we grew up together. That's all."

"Mmhmm," Robyn hummed knowingly. "But you get his attention. You spend more time with him than any other girl. People notice."

Leah rolled her eyes. "He works here. I work here. Jaxon is second in line to Cash. Of course, Jax and I are around each other. There's nothing to it."

"The gossips of Hoopa Valley say otherwise," Robyn sing songed. "If they had their way, you two would be getting married tomorrow."

Leah gasped, heat flooding her cheeks so fast she was sure she turned scarlet. Jaxon? Marrying her? His lips on hers? Absolutely not. No way. Her stomach flipped traitorously at the thought. And thank goodness he wasn't—

Two strong arms wrapped around her waist from behind, lifting her clean off the hay. Leah nearly rocketed out of her skin. She squeaked, actually squeaked, before twisting to look over her shoulder.

Jaxon stood there, his handsome face far too close, his smile far too devastating. Worse... the feel of his arms around her waist made her stomach drop straight through the floorboards.

"So," he drawled, voice low and smooth enough to melt butter, "you and I are getting married tomorrow? Why didn't you tell me? I could've gotten myself a decent suit for the occasion."

Leah opened her mouth, but nothing came out. His tone was serious. Dead serious. And in her panic, she completely missed the wicked sparkle in his eyes. Robyn, however, saw it instantly, and the grin spreading across her face could have lit the entire hayloft.

"Shouldn't I propose first?" Jaxon asked, his tone innocently earnest, his eyes dancing with mischief. Leah stared at him, utterly speechless. Her face felt like it was on fire. When Robyn started giggling behind them, Leah shot her a lethal glare that only made Robyn giggle harder.

Jaxon gently turned Leah fully toward him, his hands warm on her waist. Her breath hitched when he tilted her chin upward, forcing her to meet his deep brown eyes.

"We haven't even kissed yet," he murmured, leaning in far too close. "Should this be the moment?" His voice was low. Smooth. Dangerous. Leah swore her heart stopped. Heat surged through her cheeks until they burned. Jaxon's face was inches from hers, so close she could feel the warmth of his breath. And just when she thought he might actually do it, panic flared.

She scooted back so fast she nearly slid off the hay pile. Jaxon caught her effortlessly and pulled her right back against him.

"J-Jaxon," she finally managed to gasp. "This is not funny. Robyn and I were talking about the ladies in town gossiping about us."

"Who said I was joking?" His tone shifted, just enough to sting. Something earnest flickered in his eyes. "Let me show you how serious I am."

Before she could protest or run, he tossed her over his shoulder again with infuriating ease and started down the ladder. Robyn followed, laughing so hard she nearly missed a rung.

Once they reached the barn floor, he set Leah on her feet and caught both her hands in his. Unfortunately for her racing pulse, Cash and a few ranch hands were stacking straw bales nearby with front-row seats. Leah looked like she might faint on the spot.

When Jaxon started to lower himself onto one knee, Leah shrieked and yanked him back up so quickly it nearly dislocated his shoulder.

"Jaxon, stop this nonsense immediately!"

"What nonsense?" he countered, eyes wide with wounded innocence. "Are you seriously rejecting me to my face like that?"

The guilt rolled through her like a wave. His gaze had that effect, deep, soulful, and piercing enough to unravel her defenses.

"Oh, I get it now," he said with a thoughtful nod. "This isn't a romantic spot for you. You want something more scenic. Let's find one." He tightened his grip on her hand, ready to drag her off for a proper proposal.

Leah let out a strangled sound and tore herself free, spinning around and bolting for the ladder. She was one rung up, one, when his arms locked around her waist again. He lifted her clean off the ladder and set her firmly on the ground.

"I'm only teasing you, Leah," he chuckled, lowering his voice as he leaned close again. "No need to run away from me." His grin hit her square in the chest like a bucking horse. Her heart somersaulted. She slapped his arm, but the heat in her cheeks betrayed her.

"Why would you do that to me? I nearly had a heart attack!"

"A heart attack?" Jaxon's voice dropped to a low, seductive rumble. "Hmm... because you were hoping for a proposal?"

Her jaw fell open. No sound came out. Not one word. Jaxon's grin deepened. He leaned in, brushed a kiss over her burning cheek, and whispered, "Thought so," before winking at her. Leah's heart thudded wildly as he stepped back. She shook her head, but her pulse refused to calm. It was official: Jaxon Finlay was going to be the death of her.

It was a hot, suffocatingly humid day, the kind that clung to skin and turned every breath into thick, heavy air. Everyone from the Johnson Ranch was drenched in sweat and thoroughly miserable, but the work had to be done. They needed the cattle gathered and driven to Eureka for sale.

It was early September, still weeks before the rush to move livestock, but the Johnsons always prepared for winter long before the first frost. With herds scattered across their vast land, early planning was the only reason they survived the harsh months year after year.

They reached Pecwan Creek three hours after leaving the ranch. Though it was still morning, the sun blazed down like midday fire. Horses were lathered with sweat, cowboys wiped their brows with soaked bandanas, and even the cattle looked irritable.

"You've been awfully quiet today," Cash said, casting Leah a sideways look filled with concern. "You all right?"

Leah let out a long sigh and pushed damp strands of hair away from her face.

"I'm fine. Just... restless." She hesitated, fingers tightening on her reins. "I can't shake the feeling that something bad is about to happen. Nothing's wrong, not that I can point to anything, but the feeling's been gnawing at me since we left Hoopa Valley."

"Maybe it's the weather," Jaxon offered. He pushed his hat back and wiped the sheen of sweat from his forehead. "This heat is downright miserable. I'd welcome a thunderstorm at this point, anything to cool us down." His tone was light, joking, but the tightness around his eyes betrayed his own discomfort. Fall couldn't come soon enough.

Leah shook her head. "No. It's not the heat. I can't explain it... but ever since we rode out, I've had this sense that someone's watching me." She swallowed, her eyes scanning the tree line. "It's unsettling."

Cash straightened in his saddle. Jaxon's shoulders tensed. She knew these men better than most people in her life, and she saw the worry flash through both pairs of eyes. Cash's gaze swept the creek bank and the surrounding forest.

"Did you see anyone? Track anything unusual?"

"No." She bit her lip. "And I feel ridiculous even saying it. Maybe I'm just tired and letting my imagination run wild."

But neither Cash nor Jaxon looked convinced. And Leah's heart beat a little faster, because deep down... she wasn't convinced either.

"So, what's the plan?" Jaxon asked, glancing between Leah and Cash as he adjusted the reins in his hands.

"If we can locate the whole herd quickly enough," Leah replied, scanning the broad valley stretching out before them, "we might be able to head back this afternoon."

Cash nodded in agreement, his expression focused and thoughtful. Jaxon tipped his chin toward the grazing land.

"How many should be in this area?"

"We drove up five hundred head when we brought them here in the spring," Leah said. "And there should be at least fifty calves added since then. Maybe more—the grazing is ideal out here."

"Good-sized group," Jaxon murmured, glancing across the open field where dust shimmered in the heat.

"Okay, let's spread out," Cash decided, his voice carrying the authority of a man who'd worked the land for decades. "I'll take a few of the men and check the hill behind us. That area curves down toward the creek, stragglers drift over there sometimes." He pointed toward the sloping ridge where pine trees shaded the ground.

"You two," he continued, looking at Leah and Jaxon, "take the rest of the boys and start driving the ones already in the field. Push them toward that narrow gap between the hills. It'll funnel them together and make gathering easier."

Leah nodded, already turning her horse toward the meadow. Jaxon mirrored her movement, though not without a quick, searching look, still thinking about her earlier unease.

Within moments, Jaxon and Cash were shouting instructions. Cowboys peeled off in groups, hooves thundering as they rode toward their assigned spots. The organized chaos of ranch work unfolded, men whistling, horses snorting, cattle bellowing as the herd began to shift. Leah nudged her horse forward, Jaxon riding close beside her.

"Ready?" he asked quietly. She drew in a deep breath, shook off her nerves, and nodded.

"Let's get to work."

Together, they rode out across the sunbaked field, unaware that the uneasy prickling under Leah's skin was about to prove itself right.

Jaxon had just driven a group of cows and their calves back toward the main herd when Leah spotted several strays grazing on lower ground down the hill. She clicked her tongue, turned her horse, and headed after them.

It was quiet there, too quiet. The stillness wasn't peaceful. It felt watchful. Heavy. Every instinct inside her tightened. Even the cattle seemed uneasy, shifting their weight and flicking their ears nervously as she approached.

"Easy now," Leah murmured, though her own heart was beating faster. She quickly rounded the animals together and began pushing them back up the incline toward the others. Halfway up the hill, the eerie silence shattered. A sudden explosion of crows burst from the nearby trees, wings beating furiously, their shrill cries slicing through the air like alarms. Leah jerked in the saddle, nearly losing her seat.

"Easy," she breathed, though the tremor in her voice betrayed her. She urged her horse forward, trying to get the cattle moving faster, but they kept drifting apart, resisting her attempts to keep them corralled. Something had them spooked, and now she was too.

She angled her horse toward the narrow trail beside another stand of trees, hoping to guide the cattle around it. She never made it. A figure exploded out of the shadows, fast and silent as a striking snake. Before Leah could react, a pair of strong hands grabbed her, yanking her violently out of the saddle. She didn't even manage a scream. A rough, calloused hand clamped over her mouth, smothering the sound in her throat. Panic shot through her like lightning.

She kicked, clawed, twisted, anything to break free. The man was strong, but Leah had grown up on a ranch. She fought with every ounce of strength she possessed. In the struggle, they lost their footing. The ground beneath them gave way. They tumbled down the steep slope. Leah felt branches scrape her skin, rocks slam into her ribs, and then her head struck a large boulder with a sickening crack. White-hot pain flashed across her vision. And then, everything went black.

He darted behind a tree and snatched up a burlap sack hidden in the brush. The moment his fingers loosened the knot, the bag came alive, violent, writhing, hissing movement. The rattles started before he even opened it fully, the dry, deadly buzz slicing through the air like a warning from the devil himself.

With a sharp shake, he released several rattlesnakes onto the ground. Leah's horse squealed in terror, rearing up and bolting. The calves scattered first, then the cows followed, breaking into a frenzied stampede as the snakes slithered between them. Dirt flew in clouds, hooves thundered, and chaos erupted across the hillside.

He didn't bother watching for long. The animals were doing exactly what he wanted, running far, far away from the unconscious girl. Satisfied, he turned back to Leah.

She lay motionless where she had fallen, her golden hair tangled across her face, her breathing shallow. Blood trickled from a cut near her temple. He crouched, scooped her up with ease, and slung her limp body over his shoulder. With practiced steps, he carried her down the steep slope, moving between jagged rocks and thick trees as though he had memorized every inch of the terrain.

Within seconds, the terrified cattle were gone. And the man, along with Leah Johnson, vanished into the shadows of the wilderness.

"Leah? Leah?" Jaxon's voice cracked with rising panic as he scanned the hillside. She had been right behind him minutes ago, driving cattle, steady in her saddle, and now she was gone. A cold, hollow feeling opened in his chest. Then he spotted Cash hurrying toward him, leading Leah's horse by the reins.

Jaxon's heart dropped. He spurred his own horse forward and met Cash halfway.

"Where's Leah? How did her horse get to you?"

Cash's face was grim, lined with worry.

"I don't know. When we drove the cattle back toward the creek, her horse came barreling toward me, riderless. Spooked bad." He shook his head, jaw tightening. "I circled the area, checked the brush and the hill. No sign of her."

Jaxon's stomach twisted painfully. Leah would never leave her horse willingly. Something was wrong, terribly wrong. They began shouting her name, voices echoing across the hills and returning to them empty.

"Leah!"

"Leah, answer me!"

"Leah!"

Cowboys nearby heard the urgency and joined the search, spreading out over the terrain, scanning the ground, calling for her, listening for any cry or rustle. Nothing. No movement. No shout. No sign of her. The silence that followed was suffocating.

Jaxon's pulse hammered in his ears. Cash's expression hardened into raw fear. Something had happened to her. And whatever it was, it wasn't an accident.

3
He Picked the Wrong Woman

Leah drifted back to consciousness in a haze of pain. At first, everything was muffled, the world tilting, her stomach churning, her head throbbing with a deep, unbearable ache. Then she felt hands on her, rough and impatient, trying to hoist her upward. A wagon. He was trying to lift her onto a wagon.

A fresh spike of pain tore through her skull, white-hot along the edges of the wound she'd gotten when she hit the rock. But instinct surged up and took over. She fought.

"No—stop! Let go of me!" Her voice was hoarse, cracked, but sharp enough to carry her panic. "What are you doing? Who are you? What do you want from me?" She twisted violently in his grip, striking whatever part of him she could reach. Her nails raked across cloth and skin. Her elbow caught his ribs. She kicked blindly.

Her sudden burst of strength startled him enough that he lost his grip. Leah dropped to the dusty ground with a painful thud, gasping as the impact sent another shockwave through her skull.

But adrenaline shoved her forward. She dug her palms into the earth, ready to push herself up and run. She never got the chance.

A dark shape loomed above her. Metal flashed in the corner of her vision. Before she could even turn her head, the cold, solid butt of a gun slammed into her temple. Right over the wound. Agonizing pain exploded through her skull, white, blinding, searing. Her breath caught, the world spun violently. Then everything dissolved into darkness again.

It was nearly dark when Heber's wagon finally rattled into the small, weather-worn farm just outside Kneeland. Shadows stretched long across the yard, and the last streaks of daylight were fading behind the hills.

Colt stepped out from the barn, wiping sweat and dust from his brow.

"Heber, where have you been all day?" he called, irritation edging his voice as he approached the wagon. Heber rolled his eyes dramatically.

"Ain't nothin' but my work, Colt. Don't you go worryin' none."

That tone, arrogant, dismissive, made Colt's stomach tighten. Heber hopped off the seat and strutted to the back of the wagon, yanking the canvas cover aside. Colt froze.

Lying motionless inside, bound and bloodied, was a young woman, barely older than twenty. Her blonde hair was matted with dirt and dried blood, her face pale beneath the grime. She looked like she had been dragged through hell.

"Who is she?" Colt demanded, disbelief rising in his voice. "And what is she doing here?" He turned his glare on his older brother, fury simmering just beneath the surface.

"Ain't your affair, all right?" Heber barked. "She'll be stayin' on with us awhile. That's all you gotta know." He climbed into the wagon and began untying her wrists. But when he bent to lift her, Colt shoved him aside and scooped the young woman into his own arms. She was frighteningly light, her head lolling against his chest. Up close, the injury looked worse, an ugly, swollen gash at her temple, dried blood covering half her face.

"What did you do to her?" Colt spat, barely keeping his temper in check.

"She tried boltin' on me and cracked her head on a damn rock," Heber replied with a shrug. Colt's jaw clenched.

"That looks like more than a fall on a rock. Did you hit her too?"

Heber smirked, completely unashamed.

"She woke thrashin', so I gave her a good whack with my gun butt." He grinned, wicked and proud. Colt felt his stomach turn. There were vile men in the world, but his brother... his brother was something worse. Without another word, Colt carried the unconscious woman into the dimly lit house.

"Haul her to your room, Colt," Heber called after him. "She can be your plaything for a spell."

Colt stopped walking. For a heartbeat, his rage was so strong he couldn't move. Then he stalked into his small bedroom, laid the girl gently on his bed, and spun around. He grabbed Heber by the shirt and slammed him against the wall.

"You're nothin' but prairie coal, Heber," Colt muttered, fury tremblin' in his voice. "I ain't hurtin' that girl, and I ain't dishonorin' her. I'm goin' for the doctor and the sheriff. You'll rot behind iron for this."

Before Heber could respond, his Indian woman stepped into the room carrying a bowl of water and cloths. The moment she saw Colt pinning Heber to the wall, fear flickered in her eyes. Heber jerked free of Colt's hold, grabbed the woman by the wrist, and shoved the barrel of his gun against her head. The bowl slipped from her hands and shattered on the floor, water splashing across the boards. She gasped, trembling.

"You listen close," Heber growled, "you tell a soul, and Sarah and Cora both die. I'll make damn sure of it."

Colt's blood ran cold. He knew it wasn't an empty threat. Heber had crossed plenty of lines before, but threatening the lives of the two innocent Indian women was too much. Colt breathed hard through his teeth. His brother wasn't just cruel. He was one of the worst human beings alive.

Heber was fifteen years older than Colt, old enough to have been more of a shadow than a brother throughout Colt's childhood. He and their older brothers had moved out when Colt was barely five, leaving home with nothing more than a knapsack and a trail of trouble behind them. Their parents rarely spoke his name after that, and Colt didn't see him again for years.

Then, the previous week, Heber rode back into his life without warning, grinning like he owned the world, with two Indian women walking behind his horse like frightened shadows. One of them, Cora, was little more than a child, fifteen at most. The older woman, Sarah, perhaps in her late twenties, was thin and wary, her eyes hollow with fear and exhaustion.

Colt had wanted to throw Heber off the property the instant he saw them. But he didn't. Not because he wanted his brother there, Heber was the last man he would willingly host, but because he didn't want to put the women in even greater danger.

Heber's life had always been a trail of immorality, crime, and selfish destruction. Yet Colt had made a promise, a dying promise, to their mother. On her deathbed, she had clutched Colt's hand and whispered through fading breath: "Only turn your brother in if you can keep yourself, and others, safe."

Colt had lived by those words. Barely. He knew full well Heber would never change. But as long as those two girls lived under his roof, he couldn't risk provoking Heber into further violence.

And now, seeing how Heber had treated this new girl, the blonde woman he'd dragged in, bloodied and unconscious, Colt felt that promise twisting around his heart like barbed wire.

He didn't know where Sarah and Cora had come from. He suspected the truth, though, Heber had either snatched them from their tribe or 'bought' them from someone equally vile. The thought made Colt's stomach churn.

Heber finally released his grip on Sarah's wrist. The terrified woman scrambled out of the room to fetch fresh water, her feet slipping in the spilled puddle on the floor. Colt's jaw tightened, fury burning through every nerve in his body. Someday soon, he promised himself, his mother's words or not... Heber was going to answer for all of this.

Leah stirred when something cool and wet touched her forehead. The faint dabbing sent a flash of pain through her skull, pulling a low groan from her throat. Her eyelids fluttered, heavy and swollen, and when she finally pried them open, she found a young Indian woman leaning over her with gentle, careful hands.

The woman was cleaning the wound at Leah's temple. Her dark eyes filled with sympathy and worry. Panic shot through Leah like lightning. She tried to sit up, tried to run, but the sudden movement made her head explode with agony. She gasped and fell back against the pillow, dizzy and disoriented.

"Where... where am I?" she whispered, her voice trembling. "Who are you? How did I get here?"

The woman set down her cloth and placed a calming hand on Leah's shoulder.

"Shh... you are safe. Please, don't move too quickly. What is your name?"

Leah opened her mouth, then froze. Her mind felt like a blank, endless fog. No names. No faces. No memory at all.

"I... I don't know," she stammered, breath hitching. "I don't remember."

A man stepped closer, tall, broad-shouldered, worry shadowing his features. He looked younger than the other man lingering in the doorway.

"Do you know where you're from?" he asked softly. "Who your family is?"

Leah tried. She really did. But nothing came. The more she reached for the memories, the faster they dissolved like smoke. She shook her head helplessly. Before he could say anything more, the older man shoved past him. He was rough, hard-eyed, with a coldness that made Leah's stomach twist. Something about him, his voice, his presence, felt wrong. Unsettling. Familiar in a way that made her skin crawl.

"Ain't no need to worry none, Leah," he said, all honeyed smoothness. "Your memory'll trot on back before long." He gestured around the room. "Name's Heber. That there's Sarah," the Indian woman flinched at the sound of it, "an' this fella's my brother, Colt."

Leah's gaze flicked toward Colt. He looked tense, like he wanted to say something, interrupt something, but his eyes darted toward Heber, then Sarah, and the words died on his tongue. Heber continued, far too casually, "You're Colt's wife."

Leah's breath caught. His voice was too smug. Too controlled. Too cold. Even without her memory, she could sense the lie coiling through his words like a snake. Colt stiffened visibly at Heber's declaration, his jaw locking tight, but he didn't refute it. Leah didn't know why he held back, but the tension radiating off him was palpable.

"Yep," Heber continued, voice slick as oil, "you're Colt's wife, an' you walloped your head on a beam in the barn. Two good hits. We found you out cold."

Leah squeezed her eyes shut, trying desperately to summon even a flicker of memory, her home, her family, her own name, but there was nothing. Only darkness. Her heart thudded painfully. Nothing. Not a single thing.

Seeing Heber press a cocked gun to the back of Sarah's head told Colt everything he needed to know. Now was not the time to argue, not unless he wanted the terrified woman dead.

"We should get a doctor," Colt said, forcing his voice to stay steady. "Her wound looks bad."

"No." Heber's reply was sharp and immediate. "Sarah can handle it." And with that, he turned and stalked out of the room. The sound of his boots faded down the hall, and Colt finally let out the breath he'd been holding. He muttered a curse under his breath but stayed close, standing near the doorway like a silent guard in case Sarah needed protection.

Leah still lay on the bed, eyes closed, her breathing shallow. Colt could see each tiny flinch. Every slight movement of her head sent a wave of pain through her body. Her skin had gone pale, her lips colorless, and she looked moments away from vomiting. When she finally opened her eyes again, she focused on Sarah. She didn't speak until the Indian woman finished cleaning and stitching the wound, her hands gentle, practiced, careful.

"What tribe do you belong to?" Leah asked quietly as Sarah began wrapping a clean bandage around her head. Sarah's fingers paused. She glanced toward the doorway, open just an inch, and fear flickered across her eyes. Leah noticed immediately.

“I don’t belong to a tribe anymore,” Sarah whispered.

Leah frowned. “Is Heber your husband?”

This time, Sarah said nothing. Her silence was answer enough.

“Sarah isn’t an Indian name,” Leah said softly.

Sarah flinched at a noise from the other room, a chair scraping, Heber muttering to himself. Each time she reacted, Leah’s brow creased a little deeper. She followed Sarah’s anxious gaze toward the door, then leaned in slightly and lowered her voice.

“Are you scared of Heber?”

Sarah did not hesitate. She looked directly into Leah’s eyes, and tears filled her own. She nodded. Colt’s hands curled into fists by his sides.

“Did... did he capture you?” Leah asked gently.

Sarah shook her head.

Leah swallowed. “Did he buy you from someone who captured you?”

Slowly, painfully, Sarah nodded.

Leah’s breath hitched. “Sarah isn’t your real name... is it?”

Sarah met her gaze again and shook her head.

“He doesn’t allow you to use your real name?” Leah whispered. Another nod, small, broken, full of shame and fear.

Colt felt something inside his chest twist. Leah didn’t remember who she was, where she came from, or the family searching for her, but even in her state, her instincts were sharp. Sharp enough to sense danger. Sharp enough to know Heber was not to be trusted. She was asking all the questions Colt had been too afraid, or too watched, to ask. And Sarah... Sarah was finally answering.

"What tribe did you belong to?" Leah asked softly, her eyes fixed on the young woman's face with gentle insistence. Even in her weakened state, there was something steady and anchoring in her gaze, something that made it impossible for Sarah to look away.

For a long moment, Sarah's lips didn't move. Her hands trembled slightly against the bandages, her breath uneven. She hesitated, glancing once toward the open doorway as if expecting Heber to barge in at any second. Then, almost too quietly to hear, she whispered, "Choctaw."

The word was barely audible, little more than breath, but Colt heard it. His chest tightened. He was stunned, not only by the revelation, but by the fact that Leah had managed to coax the truth out of her. Sarah rarely spoke at all. In the week he'd known her, he could count her spoken words on one hand.

But with Leah, this stranger who couldn't even remember her own name, Sarah had opened up in minutes. Colt found himself staring at Leah, struck by the ease with which she had broken through the terrified woman's silence. It wasn't force. It wasn't demand. It was something else, something warm, steady, quietly determined. Even injured, confused, and barely conscious, Leah possessed strength, others instinctively leaned toward. And it was becoming clearer with every passing moment.

Leah reached out and gently squeezed Sarah's hand. The gesture was small, but full of warmth, and her heart ached for the woman. Even in her foggy, fractured state, she felt Sarah's fear, her loneliness, her quiet desperation.

She wasn't sure how she knew it, but something deep within her stirred with familiarity. A sense of connection. A sense of protectiveness. The Indigenous people of this land... she cared for them. Deeply. It felt like a truth rooted in her bones. And then, just for a moment, something flickered across her mind, not a full memory, but flashes. Sensations. Images.

She remembered herself as a young girl, sitting cross-legged in a schoolroom, devouring every lesson she could about the tribes of the country. She remembered staying after class to ask questions her teacher struggled to answer.

Another image surfaced: smiling Hoopa elders watching, while Indian women showed her how to weave a basket. Children painting her cheeks with tribal symbols. A soft drumbeat echoing through a clearing while the scent of woodsmoke curled through the air.

And then sharper memories, heated arguments, her voice raised in fierce defense, fists clenched at her sides as she stood up to people who mocked the tribes. Faces blurred by fog, but the feeling was unmistakable. They were pieces of a puzzle scattered across her mind, but they were hers.

Her voice softened as she spoke again, eyes still on Sarah.

"I… I think I've known many of your people," she whispered. "I can't remember everything, but I know this, I've cared about the tribes for a very long time."

And despite the fear clouding her mind, a spark of determination flickered beneath it. If Heber wanted to break Sarah's spirit, he had picked the wrong woman to bring into his home.

"You've come a long way," Leah murmured, studying Sarah's face with gentle curiosity. "You're from Mississippi, aren't you?"

Sarah's eyes widened slightly in surprise. Then she nodded, slowly, cautiously. A small, fragile smile touched her lips, as if Leah's recognition meant more than expected.

"Is your family still alive?" Leah asked softly. Tears welled instantly. Sarah pressed her lips together, but she didn't need to speak, the grief in her eyes said everything.

"I'm so sorry," Leah whispered. "Did they… kill everyone?"

Sarah nodded once, and Leah felt her heart squeeze painfully. She reached for Sarah's hand again, the instinctive gesture offering comfort, and silently buying more time. She needed Sarah to keep talking. She needed answers. And most of all, she needed to understand how much danger they were all in.

"Are you the only one here besides Heber and Colt?" Leah asked quietly. Her senses sharpened, every floorboard creak, every shuffle in the hallway made her muscles tighten. Sarah shook her head.

"There's another."

Leah's breath caught. She didn't need Sarah to say more, though she asked anyway.

"Is she Choctaw too?"

"No." Sarah swallowed hard. "She belonged to the Sioux. She doesn't speak much English. She was captured a few months ago when we were traveling through Montana."

Leah's stomach twisted. "Can she understand you?"

A nod.

"What's her name?"

"Mr. Thatcher calls her Cora," Sarah murmured. "But her real name is Aponi. It means... butterfly."

Leah's expression softened. "That's beautiful. What's your real name?"

Sarah hesitated, then whispered, "Tallulah. It means leaping water."

Leah smiled, despite the terror in her chest.

"Tallulah... that's beautiful too." She swallowed hard. "How old is Aponi?"

"Fifteen."

Leah gasped. Pain and fury surged through her.

"And... has Heber... violated her? Has he forced—" She couldn't finish. But Sarah understood. She flicked her gaze downward and nodded. Leah's hands curled into tight fists against the blanket.

"And his brother? Is he like that too?"

This time Sarah's eyes drifted sideways, toward the doorway, before she shook her head.

"No. He's kind. We've only been here a week, but he tries to protect us."

A soft sound, a deliberate clearing of a throat, made both women jump. Leah turned her head and gasped. Colt was standing in the doorway. Her cheeks flushed with embarrassment, expecting anger or judgment, but instead, Colt's expression was gentle. He offered Sarah a small, reassuring smile and shook his head, silently telling her she wasn't in trouble.

Sarah still flinched.

"Please don't let Mr. Thatcher know, I told you so much," she whispered. "I don't know what he'll do if he finds out..." Her voice cracked, fear twisting every syllable. The sight of it tugged at Leah's heart until it nearly broke. Leah leaned forward and squeezed her hand again, her eyes warm with empathy.

"I won't say anything," she promised softly. "I swear it." And in that moment, memory or no memory, Leah knew one thing with absolute certainty: She would protect these girls.

No matter the cost.

Leah kept her movements small and careful, doing everything she could to avoid triggering the sharp, pulsing pain in her head. When Sarah slipped back into the room carrying a supper tray, she wasn't alone this time. A beautiful girl followed behind her, balancing a warm blanket in her arms. Her long black hair fell in soft waves down her back, and her big brown eyes lifted shyly when Leah reached out and took her hand. So much sorrow lived in those eyes that Leah felt something inside her crack. Leah pointed gently at herself.

"I'm Leah."

The girl stared for a breath, then whispered, fragile as a leaf in the wind, "Aponi."

Leah opened her mouth to say something more, but a sudden crash, a chair hitting the floor, made all three of them jump. The doorway filled with a looming figure. Heber. His expression was a storm of outrage and cruelty.

Aponi instantly cowered, shrinking back like she was trying to disappear. It didn't matter. Heber lunged forward, grabbed her by the arm, and shook her violently. Aponi whimpered in terror.

Colt was already moving, charging into the room with fire in his eyes, but Leah got there first.

On pure instinct, she forced herself out of bed, fighting through the dizzying pain that nearly knocked her on her knees. She reached Aponi, yanked her out of Heber's grip, and shoved herself between them.

The room spun. Her head pounded. But Leah stood her ground like a wall of iron.

"Why are you treating her that way?" she snapped, her voice cracking with fury. The pain in her skull threatened to blind her, but she glared at Heber with every ounce of strength she had. He took an involuntary step back.

"Name is Cora," Heber barked.

"If her name is Aponi," Leah shot back, "then we should call her Aponi."

Heber's eyes narrowed. "She needs to pass easy when we're among folks. Her Indian name riles people up."

Leah scoffed, lifting her chin with proud defiance.

"Look at her," she said. "She's a beautiful Indian girl. A new name doesn't change that. People aren't stupid."

Colt smirked from behind Heber, unable to hide his appreciation for Leah's bluntness. Even Sarah turned away to hide a smile.

"And besides," Leah added, fire burning behind her eyes, "we aren't around people right now."

"Leah," Heber snarled, moving in close enough for his sour breath to hit her. "You mind what I say. I gave those women new names for a reason, and you'll use 'em. Every time."

Sarah and Aponi quickly retreated to the other room, disappearing like frightened birds. Leah wished she could reassure them, but Heber blocked her path.

"No!" Leah's shout echoed off the walls. Her fury flared, hot and bright. "I'm part of this family, am I not? I'm your brother's wife, so you don't get to boss me around. Why are Sarah and Aponi here instead of with their families? Why are you treating them like this?"

"Ain't your damn business, so back off," Heber roared and shoved her hard. The sudden jolt sent agony shooting through her skull. Her vision blurred, dizziness twisting her insides. Her stomach lurched violently. Before she could stop it, before anyone could move, Leah doubled over... and vomited all over Heber.

The silence that followed lasted only a second, but the look on Heber's face promised a storm. And Leah, trembling, pale, and aching... still lifted her chin, ready to fight again if she had to.

For a moment, Colt just stood there, frozen between two impulses. Part of him wanted to haul Heber out by the scruff of his neck and throw him straight into a ditch. The other part, surprisingly, wanted to laugh at the sight of his brother covered in vomit.

But then Heber's foul mouth erupted, cussing loud enough to shake the rafters, and Colt's decision was made. He grabbed Heber by the shirt, shoved him backward out of the room, and slammed the door hard enough to rattle the frame.

The moment Colt turned back to Leah, her eyes fluttered closed and her knees buckled. She sank toward the floor in a slow, helpless collapse.

"Whoa—easy," Colt breathed as he lunged forward. He caught her just in time, scooping her into his arms before she hit the boards. She felt so small, so fragile, and yet so fierce and stubborn only moments earlier.

He carried her back to the bed and laid her down gently. When her eyes opened again, they lifted to his face, full of dazed pain, confusion... and trust. That trust hit Colt like a blade between the ribs. He hated lying to her. Hated every second of it. But if she believed—for now—that she belonged in this house, under his roof, she might be safer than if she realized she was a stranger with a firecracker spirit and no memory to anchor her. He gave her a soft, reassuring smile.

From beyond the door came Heber's voice, furious, slurred with disgust, gagging between curses as he berated Sarah and Aponi for something that wasn't their fault. Colt's jaw clenched, heat rising beneath his skin. Every foul word scraped across his nerves like a knife.

He wanted to stay beside Leah, wanted to make sure she didn't pass out again. Wanted to put cold cloths on her forehead and keep her safe in the only way he knew how. But the cries and whimpers from the next room reminded him he wasn't the only one she had rescued tonight. With fists tightening at his sides, Colt forced himself to stand.

"I'll be right back," he murmured to Leah, though she was already drifting into a half-conscious haze.

He stepped into the hallway, fury simmering just beneath the surface. He found Heber shoving Aponi aside, still covered in vomit, still shouting. That was the last straw. Colt grabbed him by the back of his filthy shirt, spun him around, and shoved him through the open doorway.

"Get out," Colt growled, pushing him off the porch. "And don't take one step back in here until you've cleaned yourself up at the creek."

Heber sputtered, cursed, threatened, and gagged all at once, but Colt didn't flinch. He stood in the doorway like a wall of stone. For the first time all day, Heber backed down and stomped toward the creek, dripping and swearing as he went.

When he disappeared into the darkness, Colt exhaled a shaky breath and rubbed a hand over his face. Then he turned back toward the house, toward Leah, Sarah, and Aponi. He couldn't save them all. Not yet. But he would do everything in his power to keep them breathing until he found a way.

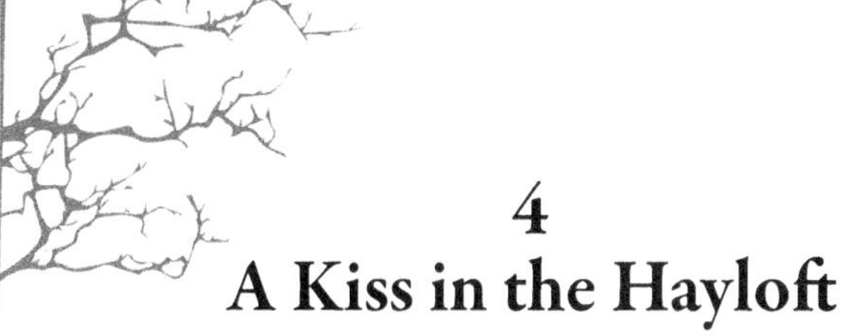

4
A Kiss in the Hayloft

Sarah and Aponi helped Leah wash up as gently as if she were made of glass. Sarah brought a cup of warm tea and a piece of dry bread so Leah could rid herself of the vile taste lingering in her mouth. When Sarah returned with a nightgown, Leah was too exhausted to protest. She let the older woman guide the soft fabric over her head and down her aching body. It fit her perfectly, as though it had been sewn just for her.

With Aponi's help, Sarah eased Leah back beneath the covers, placed a folded dress on the dresser for the following morning, and, without a single word, slipped quietly from the room with Aponi close behind her.

Leah nestled into the blanket, muscles slowly unclenching. The darkness wrapped around her like a cocoon, warm and heavy, and she felt herself drifting, eyes closing, breath softening. She hovered on the edge of sleep when she heard the door creak open. Her lashes lifted sluggishly.

Colt stepped inside. Her heart lurched, painfully. He walked toward her with quiet, heavy footsteps, and before she could process it, he moved as though to climb into the bed with her. Panic hit like a lightning strike.

"No—no, don't—" Leah scrambled, instinct swallowing reason. She rolled toward the edge of the mattress, trying to slip away, but Colt caught her around the waist and pulled her back. She shoved at him, panic blurring everything, but he pinned her arms with his weight leaning over her.

"What are you doing? Let go of me!" Her voice cracked with fear. His face was too close, far too close. Leah twisted, fought, and willed herself free. "Stop, let me go!" Her heart was pounding so violently she could barely breathe. They had told her he was her husband, but she didn't remember him, didn't remember anything. And now he was—

His lips pressed against hers. Tears flooded her eyes. Just as a strangled cry caught in her throat, Colt suddenly shifted. His head dipped to her ear and a large, calloused hand covered her mouth.

"Listen," he whispered, urgent but controlled. "I'm not going to hurt you. I swear it. I'm trying to protect you from my brother. He's watching us right now. He won't hold back if he snaps, not for anyone."

Leah's breath trembled beneath his hand. Slowly, very slowly, he drew it away. His eyes searched hers, apologetic and fierce all at once, then he rose from the bed, strode to the door, and shoved it shut... right in Heber's face. A harsh click followed as he turned the key in the lock.

Colt lingered there for a moment, forehead resting against the door as if steadying himself. Then he returned and sat on the edge of the bed, careful to keep distance. Leah pulled the blanket tight around her shoulders, staring at him with wide, frightened eyes.

"He... he would even touch his brother's wife?"

Colt nodded grimly. "Yes. And just so you know, we aren't married. I don't know who you are. I don't know where you came from or why my brother dragged you here."

Leah studied his face, those earnest brown eyes, the gentle lines of worry carved into them, and something warm flickered in her chest. Instinct whispered a single word: *Trust.*

Colt offered a small, heartwarming smile.

"But listen to me, Leah. You must pretend you believe the story he told you. You must act like my wife. We have to share this bed, or he'll know something's wrong." His voice dropped, darker. "And he already told me he'll 'take care of you' if I refuse."

Fear prickled the back of Leah's neck. "If he's that dangerous, why haven't you turned him in?"

Colt scrubbed a hand over his face. "Because he threatens Sarah and Aponi every single time I step out of line. He's unpredictable, and he uses them as leverage. Every time he leaves the farm, he takes one of them with him to make sure I can't go to the sheriff." He exhaled hard through gritted teeth. "Promise me you won't interfere when he scolds or hurts them. Let me handle it."

Leah's eyes filled with stubborn fire.

"I don't think I'm the kind of person who steps aside when someone else is mistreated. I might not remember my life, but I know this much, I can't keep quiet when someone is being hurt. I think it's part of who I am."

Colt gave a breathy, resigned laugh, the kind that held equal parts admiration and dread.

"I figured as much." He shook his head. "After the way you stood up for Aponi tonight... I knew I'd have my hands full with you. Looks like I'll just have to make sure I'm close by whenever Heber's about to explode."

When Colt climbed into the bed again, Leah tensed. He noticed. At once, he shifted to the far edge, creating as much space as possible.

"Don't worry," he murmured gently. "I'll stay on my side of the bed. I promise."

She swallowed hard, knowing she had no choice but to trust him. To survive, she had to. They whispered goodnight, voices soft in the dim room. Leah turned away, facing the opposite wall. Even with fear twisting inside her, exhaustion eventually tugged her toward sleep, closer than before, but never fully at peace. Not with a monster in the next room. And a stranger she might have to trust with her life lying inches away.

Colt couldn't sleep, not at first. He lay on his back, staring up at the shadowed ceiling, listening to the rhythmic rise and fall of Leah's breathing. Every time he closed his eyes, his mind dragged him back to the one thing that never let him rest: Heber.

Colt didn't know everything his older brother had done, but he knew enough. Heber and their other two brothers had spent their youth drifting across the country like a storm cloud, leaving trouble, fear, and broken lives in their wake. The other two hadn't made it far. Both were shot during a bank robbery gone wrong. Heber, the only survivor, had been arrested and thrown into prison.

Colt didn't know how long he'd served, but sometime after his release, Heber had acquired Sarah... and then Cora. Colt didn't know if he had bought Aponi, stolen her, or threatened someone into handing her over, but every option made his stomach twist.

Heber wasn't hiding at the farm for family. He wasn't there because he cared. Colt knew the truth with painful clarity: Heber was hiding from the law. And the women were leverage. Shields. Tools to keep him safe. Colt exhaled slowly, forcing the knot in his chest to loosen.

His thoughts drifted to a different part of his past, one far gentler than Heber's violence. After their father died, Colt and his mother had moved to this place, his grandparents' homestead. His mother had tended to the aging couple, until they passed one after the other. She'd been ready to sell the land and move to Eureka for a fresh start... but fate hadn't given her the chance. One quiet afternoon, a rattlesnake had struck her while she was gathering herbs near the well. With no doctor anywhere close, she didn't make it.

Colt closed his eyes, hoping the pain would dull. It never did. She had been a good woman. Tender-hearted. Wise. Strong in the ways that mattered. He missed her more than breath sometimes. His gaze slid to the woman lying beside him. Leah.

Even injured and lost, even stripped of her name and past, she radiated something fierce and pure, kindness wrapped in fire. Innocence wrapped in grit. She stood her ground without hesitation, yet there was softness beneath all that iron. A softness Heber didn't deserve to be near.

A good woman, Colt thought. Something he'd always longed for but never dared imagine he would have. He forced the thought away. It was dangerous, foolish, unfair to her. She wasn't his, not her memories, not her trust, not her future. She didn't even know her own name. And until she did, he had no right to think about her that way.

With a hard swallow, Colt rolled onto his side and willed sleep to take him. The farm would not slow down simply because he'd had a restless night. The animals would need feeding, the fences mending, chores completed before the sun climbed high. Tomorrow would be long. And with Heber under the same roof, every day there was a step through a minefield.

Colt finally closed his eyes, hoping, praying, that when morning came, he'd still have the strength to protect everyone in his house. Especially the young woman breathing quietly beside him.

Leah woke with a violent shiver, the kind that rattled through her bones. Cold air seeped through the thin walls like icy fingers creeping across her skin. A steady rain pattered against the roof, soft, miserable, and relentless, adding a damp chill to the already frigid room.

She tried to burrow deeper beneath the blanket, willing her body to warm itself, but her teeth chattered uncontrollably. Every muscle felt stiff and sore, likely from lying perfectly rigid on her side all night, terrified of moving too close to the stranger beside her.

Finally, unable to bear the cold any longer, Leah shifted and rolled toward her other side. She gasped. Colt's face was inches from hers. His breath stirred the loose strands of her hair, warm against the cold morning air. For a heartbeat she lay frozen, unsure if she should move or if movement would only make things worse.

Colt's eyes fluttered open. He blinked, still half-asleep, and focused on her. Leah hugged herself tightly, her shoulders shaking, her teeth clacking in a rhythm she couldn't control. He didn't know if it was fear or cold causing the trembling, maybe both. Without hesitating, Colt reached out and pulled her toward him. Leah nearly fainted from shock.

"N–no... please..." Her voice stuttered as she tried to pull back. "You promised."

Colt stopped immediately, his arms loose, leaving her space. His voice was low, gentle, steady.

"It's all right, Leah. I'm not breaking my word. You're freezing." He paused, meeting her frightened eyes with calm reassurance. "Will you let me hold you? Just to warm you up? Nothing else. I swear it."

She searched his face, his expression, his eyes, the way he held himself still, as if one wrong move might send her running. Nothing threatening. Nothing demanding. Just quiet concern. He gave a small nod, confirming the honesty behind his offer.

Leah hesitated a moment longer, breathing hard through the cold. Then slowly, very slowly, she loosened her grip on her arms and let her tense shoulders drop. Colt gently pulled her closer, gathering her into the breadth of his chest. His arms wrapped around her with cautious strength, warming her immediately. Heat seeped through her chilled skin, easing the stiffness in her muscles and calming the tremors.

Her cheek rested against the rough fabric of his shirt, and she realized she could hear his heartbeat, slow, steady, grounding. In less than a minute, his breathing settled into the soft, even rhythm of sleep.

Leah's eyes fluttered shut. The cold ebbed away, replaced by warmth she desperately needed. For the first time since she'd been dragged into this place, she felt something close to safety. Wrapped in the arms of the man she barely knew, she let herself drift back into sleep, if only for a little while.

Colt insisted that Leah stay in bed for a few days, at least until the pounding in her head settled and the dizziness eased. Leah hated every moment of it. She wasn't built for lying still, not when her instincts told her danger lurked behind every thin wall of the farmhouse. But Colt was firm, and Sarah checked on her so frequently that Leah barely had time to stew in her impatience.

Sarah brought her simple meals, changed her bandages, and talked with her in quiet, soothing tones. Leah found herself looking forward to those visits. Despite the pain and fog in her mind, she and Sarah formed a gentle, unexpected bond, one built on shared fear and a growing, unspoken trust.

Whenever Colt finished his chores for the day, he came to check on her as well. Leah couldn't deny he was a handsome man, broad-shouldered, steady-eyed, likely somewhere in his early thirties. Something about his presence grounded her. Calmed her. Made her feel safer than she had any right to feel in a house that also held a monster.

By the third day, Leah could no longer stand being trapped in the small bedroom. Her restlessness gnawed at her until finally, right before supper, she pushed herself to her feet and decided the world outside her door wasn't going to terrify her into staying hidden forever.

At supper, she joined Colt, Sarah, and Aponi at the table. The food was simple but warm, and for a moment, eating together almost felt like a family, until Heber spoke, snapping sharply at Sarah for dropping a knife, and the illusion shattered. Leah's hands curled into fists beneath the table. If Colt hadn't nudged her foot gently, silently reminding her to stay calm, she might have thrown something at Heber's head.

After the dishes were cleared, Colt glanced her way with a quiet smile.

"Would you like me to show you around the place?" he asked.

Leah nodded eagerly. She followed him outside, grateful for the evening air. Colt walked her through the small property, past the vegetable patch, the chicken coop, and the pair of old but sturdy horses in the pasture. A handful of cattle grazed lazily in the fading light. The creek behind the house sparkled between the trees, full of trout Colt often caught for supper.

Leah couldn't deny it was a beautiful place. Peaceful. Gentle. A slice of the world she could imagine herself happy in... if only Heber weren't poisoning every shadow with his presence. His fake politeness from the first day had long since worn off, replaced by cruel snapping, muttering, and vicious glares he reserved for Sarah and Aponi. Every time he raised his voice at them, Leah felt fire rise like it lived beneath her skin.

Colt must have noticed her clenching jaw, because he cleared his throat softly and pointed upward.

"Up there is our hayloft."

Leah followed his gaze to the ladder leading to the loft. Something tugged at the back of her mind, a brief flicker of memory, laughter echoing in a different barn, the smell of summer hay, a teasing voice she couldn't quite place. It vanished before she could grasp it.

She sighed. "I love the smell of fresh hay."

"Go on," Colt encouraged. "Climb up if you'd like. I brought in some fresh bales yesterday."

His grin was warm, inviting. Comforting. He didn't have to tell her twice.

Leah placed her hands on the rungs and climbed upward, the familiar scent of dried grass growing stronger with every step. The loft glowed softly in the early evening light filtering through the gaps in the boards. For a moment, just reaching the top felt like breathing again. Colt followed behind her, the ladder creaking under his weight as he ascended after her.

5
Stolen for a Stranger's Scheme

They had a lovely view from the small loft window, rolling pasture bathed in moonlight, the creek glinting silver, and the sky stretched in a sweeping blanket of stars. Leah leaned out slightly, bracing her hands on the rough wooden frame as the cool night air brushed her cheeks. The glow of the full moon illuminated her features in soft, ethereal light.

Colt settled behind her, close enough to feel the warmth of her body but not touching. He watched her take in the night, the rise and fall of her breathing, the way her hair glimmered wheat-gold in the moonlight. Something tightened in his chest. She was stunning, and far too good to be tangled up in Heber's darkness.

Colt still loathed his brother's cruelty, his crimes, and every violent decision he'd ever made. But bringing Leah here... that he could almost forgive, if only Heber would explain why he'd taken her in the first place. What made her worth risking so much?

Something in the hay rustled beside Leah. Colt's lips twitched. Any second now...

Leah glanced down, and a moment later, a tiny mouse poked its head out of a stray pile of straw.

"Oh," she breathed softly. "Aren't you a cute little thing? Come here." Her voice was warm, coaxing, almost musical. But the mouse took one look at her outstretched hand and vanished. Colt chuckled.

"You're not afraid of mice?" he asked in that deep, gravelly voice. Leah jumped, hard. Colt let out a full, rich laugh. Before she could steady herself, he slipped his arms around her waist and tugged her against him. "Yet you get scared when I talk to you?" he teased.

Color bloomed across her cheeks. "I forgot you were here," she said quietly.

Those blue eyes lifted to his, big, innocent, and full of something that tugged at him in ways he wasn't prepared for. Something electric threaded between them. Colt felt it pulling him forward, slowly, instinctively, until he was leaning down, lips inches from hers... and she suddenly shrieked.

Leah leapt to her feet, swatting frantically at her hair.

"Get it off! Please, get it off!" she cried. Colt blinked, baffled, until he spotted the giant spider clinging to one of her blonde curls. Her expression said it all: terror, disgust, panic. Despite himself, Colt burst out laughing and stepped forward quickly. He plucked the spider from her hair and tossed it out the window.

Leah shuddered violently and darted toward the ladder, ready to flee. Colt caught her hand and gently pulled her back.

"You're safe, Leah. I won't let any spider harm you," he said with a playful grin. But she wasn't smiling. Her eyes darkened, and her voice trembled.

"It's not funny. I was bitten twice as a child. Both times I nearly died." A memory, another fragment returning to her.

Colt's smile vanished. "I'm sorry," he murmured, sincere and tender. "I didn't know."

Her breathing slowed. Her rigid shoulders softened. Then she looked up at him, really looked, and something unspoken passed between them. He moved without thinking.

Colt cupped the side of her face, leaned down, and pressed his mouth to hers in a kiss that stole both their breaths. Leah's lips parted beneath his, soft and hesitant, and for a heartbeat, just a heartbeat, she kissed him back.

When he finally drew away, she lowered her gaze, flustered, with color rising high across her cheeks. She stepped away from him, as if putting distance between them could calm the storm he'd awakened. Colt swallowed hard and forced himself to speak.

"Let's head back to the house. It's getting late." His voice was rougher now, edged with the lingering heat of the kiss. "I'll lock the barn and check the enclosure. You go on ahead. I'll follow in a bit."

Leah nodded, unable to form words. She turned toward the ladder, her hands trembling slightly as she climbed down into the shadows below. She didn't look back, but Colt watched her go, with the sinking suspicion that the kiss had changed something for both of them.

Colt woke to the sound of his brother shouting, vicious, sharp, the kind of anger that made the walls feel thinner. Aponi's frightened whimper followed, slicing through the morning stillness. Leah was still nestled in his arms, her head tucked against his chest, her breath warm on his shirt.

For a single precious moment, Colt forgot the world outside that room. His heart kicked hard. He could get used to this, waking with her in his arms, her soft weight against him, the quiet peace she brought simply by existing. It wouldn't take much longer before he fell for her completely.

Then Heber shouted again, louder this time, and reality slammed back into him. Leah's eyes snapped open. Confusion flickered, then sharpened into recognition. Without hesitation, she scrambled out of bed, yanking the blanket around her shoulders like a cloak, and stormed into the hallway. Colt cursed under his breath and followed her.

They entered the main room just in time to see Aponi cowering in a corner, tears streaking her cheeks. Sarah was pressed into the opposite corner, trembling, eyes wide with fear. Heber towered over Aponi, arm raised, hand pulled back to strike.

Before Colt could reach them, Leah hurled herself between Heber and the terrified girl, stopping his swing mid-air.

"How dare you?" she snapped, eyes blazing. "What's wrong with you?"

Heber's lip curled, breathing through his teeth like a bull ready to charge.

"Stay out of it." He grabbed her arm and tried to yank her aside, but Leah planted her feet. She didn't budge.

"You're a horrible excuse for a human being," she shot back. "A monster. What did this girl do that you have to terrorize her every single day?"

"Ain't none o' your damn business!" Heber barked. "Move!" He tried to pull her again. Leah shoved him backward, hard.

"No! You're the one who needs to go away," she shouted, fury shaking her voice.

Heber's face darkened. Colt saw the warning signs, the twitch of his jaw, the flex of his fingers. He stepped in just as Heber's temper detonated.

"Leah's right, Heber," Colt said, his voice low and deadly calm. "I've told you a hundred times, stop torturing the girl. She doesn't understand you. She's terrified."

Colt met Heber's glare head-on. He was several inches taller, and the burn of rage in his stomach steeled his expression. He wanted nothing more than to rip his brother's head clean off.

"You nor her got any place in this, none!" Heber roared, lunging forward and swinging his fist.

Colt caught his wrist mid-air. In one swift motion, he grabbed the front of Heber's shirt, dragged him through the doorway, and threw him into the dust.

"How dare you?" Heber sputtered.

"I have every right," Colt snapped, chest heaving. "This is my house, not yours. Keep your filthy temper in check. Go hack some wood and get it out of your system." He slammed the door before Heber could answer.

When Colt turned back, Leah was kneeling beside Aponi, murmuring softly.

"I'm so sorry he treats you this way. I promise, I will get you away from him someday."

Her voice was gentle, but her expression was fierce, full of fire and compassion. Sarah stepped forward to translate, and Aponi lifted her tear-filled eyes to Leah. She whispered something, and Sarah nodded.

"She asks how you'll do that. We both tried running many times. He caught us every time."

Leah swallowed, her voice steady. "Then we'll find a way together. I promise."

Colt stepped forward, took Leah's hand, and gently but firmly tugged her back toward his room. Once inside, he shut the door and turned her toward him. His expression was tight, shaken, and threaded with fear.

"Why did you do that?" he demanded softly. "Why jump between Heber and Aponi like that? He could have hit you."

Leah lifted her chin, unrepentant. "I told you. I won't look the other way. He tortures her. She doesn't deserve it."

"I know," Colt said. "And I agree. But you shouldn't put yourself in danger."

"Then why don't you throw him out?" she fired back. "If this is your house, you don't have to let him stay."

"It's not that simple," Colt replied, frustration simmering beneath his words.

"Isn't it?" Leah stepped closer, fierce as a storm. "You're allowing him to terrorize the entire household. He's evil, Colt. Those girls need you protecting them all the time, not just when you can."

"I do what I can," Colt snapped, glowering.

"That isn't enough." Leah's voice shook, but not with fear, with outrage. "They shouldn't be here at all, especially not as slaves to your brother. Stop protecting that demon."

Colt's jaw clenched. "You don't know anything about me. Or why I'm tolerating what I'm tolerating." His voice rose. "It's easy to judge when it isn't your family misbehaving. Your temper's almost as bad as my brother's." The words left his mouth before he could stop them. The second they landed, he saw it, hurt, sharp and raw, flashing across her blue eyes.

"I use my temper to defend those who can't defend themselves," she said quietly, her voice trembling with fury and pain. "If I had a brother like yours, I'd rather see him in prison than watch him abuse innocent people." She turned abruptly, yanked open the door, and vanished down the hall.

Colt stood frozen for a moment, the silence heavy around him. Then he drew a slow, ragged breath through his teeth, as though he could somehow close the wound her words had carved straight into his chest. But he knew the truth. What she had said hit so hard... because deep down, he believed it too.

Leah didn't know where she was going. She only knew she needed away, away from the shouting, away from Colt's wounded glare, away from Heber's cruel voice echoing through the house. She didn't want to hear another argument, another excuse, another reminder of how little she truly understood about her own life.

Barefoot and still dressed only in her nightgown, she stepped out into the cold morning without a second thought.

The chill bit her skin, but she was too angry, too hurt, too exhausted to care. For once, the cold felt honest, sharp, biting, and real.

The rhythmic thud of an axe striking wood echoed from behind the house. Heber was hacking at logs, spilling his rage into splintered bark. Leah let out a shaky breath. At least he was directing his temper at something that couldn't bleed.

She hurried across the yard and ducked into the barn. The familiar scent of hay embraced her, a small comfort in the chaos. She grabbed the nearest horse blanket, heavy and warm, and wrapped it around her shoulders like a makeshift cloak. Then she walked. She followed the creek, its soft murmuring guiding her deeper into the quiet.

The world felt calmer here, gentler, the way she imagined her life must have been before everything shattered. After a few minutes, she spotted a fallen tree trunk, worn smooth by weather and time. She sank onto it with a sigh, pulling the blanket tight around her body. The morning air stung her bare legs, but she didn't flinch. She rested her elbows on her knees and pressed her palms to her eyes.

Why can't I remember? The question burned inside her, a wound with no bandage. She forced herself to think, really think, trying to claw her way back into the fog that had swallowed her identity. She reached, stretched, strained for anything solid, anything familiar. Nothing came. Nothing except useless fragments, distant faces with blurred edges, flickers of sensations with no meaning, flashes of heat or laughter or anger with no origin: A child learning tribal stories.

A classroom full of shadows. A drumbeat. A kind smile. Heat on her cheeks. Cold water running over her hands.

Nothing she could grasp long enough to form a memory. No name. No home. No past. She felt like a ghost wearing a stranger's skin.

Her throat tightened, and she pulled the blanket higher, burying her face in its coarse fabric.

"Who am I?" she whispered into the wool. The creek murmured back, soft, but without answers. Leah closed her eyes, willing her mind to offer her something, anything, to anchor her. But all she felt was the hollow space where her life should have been.

"That's precisely what I was afraid of," Patricia sobbed, her voice breaking as tears streamed down her cheeks. Scott Bailey pulled her into his arms, holding her with all the tenderness he could muster. "Leah should never have talked back to that lawyer in Eureka," she cried into his shoulder. "Now I've lost my husband and my daughter."

"Oh, Patti..." Mildred stepped in gently, though her own eyes were bright with unshed tears. "You know Leah. She's stubborn as a mule. She fights back, stands her ground, and never bows to anyone. You can't protect her from everything."

Patricia shook her head helplessly. Cash crouched in front of her. His face lined with worry and exhaustion.

"We're not giving up," he said firmly. "Mayor Jessop already put together a group of volunteers, and half the valley is out searching. We'll keep going until we find her, Patti. Not a single person in Hoopa Valley is going to stop looking." He spoke with conviction, but even he couldn't hide the tremor in his voice.

Across from them, Ruby sat with her apron bunched in her hands, tears slipping down her cheeks. She hadn't stopped crying since the moment she heard Leah hadn't returned from the cattle drive. The shock of it, of seeing Cash, Jaxon, and the rest of the cowboys ride back without Leah, had been a blow none of them were prepared for.

Cash swallowed hard, trying to steady his voice.

"Jaxon is beside himself, Patti. He's already saddled his horse again. That boy won't sleep, not even an hour, until Leah's back on this ranch."

Patricia pressed trembling hands to her mouth, her shoulders shaking with grief and fear. Mildred squeezed her hand, voice soft but resolute.

"Leah's strong. She's out there somewhere, fighting to come home. And we'll fight just as hard to bring her back."

In that quiet, grief-filled room, every person felt the same truth settle like a weight in their chest: Hoopa Valley might not rest until they found Leah Johnson, but none of them would truly breathe again until they did.

Jaxon stood rigid in the middle of his mother's sitting room, breathing hard, anguish carved into every sharp line of his face. The walls felt too close, the air too heavy, like the whole house was suffocating under the weight of Leah's absence. Without warning, he slammed his fist into the door frame. The crack of impact echoed through the room, and both his mother and sister jumped, tears streaking down their cheeks.

"I swear I'll find her," Jaxon choked out, his voice thick with fury and fear. "I'll find her and bring her home. I don't care how long it takes." He ran a trembling hand through his hair, pacing like a caged animal.

"We should've listened. She told us she felt like she was being watched. Cash and I should've checked the area. Maybe we could have—" He broke off, chest heaving. His mother stepped closer and took his hand gently, grounding him.

"Jaxon," she whispered, "this wasn't your fault, nor Cash's. Nobody could have foreseen this. Nobody."

Robyn wiped her eyes and moved to her brother's side.

"Maybe... maybe Leah just got hurt," she said through broken sobs. "Maybe she fell off her horse, or fainted, or... something. And that's why they were separated."

Jaxon shook his head firmly, his jaw clenching.

"We looked everywhere," he said hoarsely. "Every ravine, every tree line, every patch of brush. If she'd been hurt and lying somewhere close, we would have found her. She wouldn't wander off on her own. She'd never leave the area without letting one of us know."

The hopelessness in his voice made Robyn break down again, burying her face against his arm.

Their mother cupped Jaxon's cheek with her trembling hand.

"You'll find her, Son," she whispered, trying to steady her voice. "Or she'll find her way back to us. Leah is one of the smartest, strongest women I've ever known." She paused, smoothing her thumb over his cheek the way she had since he was a little boy. "God will protect her," she said firmly. "We must believe that. We must have faith."

Jaxon swallowed hard, blinking rapidly as if holding back tears of his own. Faith. Right now, it was all they had. But he would not rest, not tonight, not ever, until he brought Leah Johnson home.

"Leah, you're going to catch your death if you don't get dressed soon." Colt's voice was soft but strained with worry. He had been standing behind her for several minutes, watching her sit there, half dressed, shivering, staring at nothing as the chill of the morning crept into her bones. She didn't acknowledge him. Didn't move. Her damp hair clung to her neck, and goosebumps rose on her arms. He stepped around her and lowered himself into a squat so he could meet her eyes.

"Listen," he said gently, "I'm sorry about what I said earlier. I shouldn't have gotten upset with you. Not after what you've been through."

At that, Leah finally lifted her gaze. Her eyes were tired and shadowed from pain, but they still held fire, a fire he admired more than he should.

"I'm sorry too, Colt," she whispered. "I shouldn't have attacked you like that. I know my temper can be awful." She swallowed, emotions tightening her voice. "But it makes me so angry when I see someone abuse the people in their care. I can't stand it. I never have."

Colt nodded slowly, a muscle feathering along his jaw.

"I understand," he said. "And honestly?" He let out a breath, almost a quiet laugh. "It's refreshing to see someone besides me putting my brother in his place. He deserves that, and more."

His smile softened, warm and unexpectedly tender. He reached for her hands and helped her rise to her feet. She swayed slightly, and he steadied her instantly, his hands strong around her arms.

"Come on," he murmured. "Let's get you warm again."

There was something about the way he said it, gentle, protective, that wrapped around her like a blanket all on its own. And for the first time since waking in that strange house, Leah didn't feel entirely alone.

The outbursts from both Leah and Colt had changed things, dramatically. Heber, though still dangerous, now reined in his temper far more than before. Whenever his anger began to spike, he stormed outside to hack wood instead of unleashing his rage on Aponi. And he kept his distance from Leah entirely, which allowed her a small sense of peace she hadn't felt since waking in this house.

Leah proved to be an extraordinary asset to the homestead. She worked with quiet confidence, tackling every chore as if she had been doing it her whole life. She moved with instinct and skill, mending fences, tending animals, gathering eggs, cleaning, hauling water. Whatever needed doing, she simply did it. And she and Colt became... a team. A natural, seamless team.

They understood each other's rhythms without speaking. They often reached for the same tool at the same time. Their hands brushed. Their shoulders bumped. Their eyes lingered longer each day. And Colt, he was falling hard.

Three weeks after Heber kidnapped Leah, Colt invited her to join him in catching wild horses before fall, a task he had always done alone. But once he realized how skilled she was in the saddle, how fearless and sure, he wanted her by his side. Needed her by his side.

They spent the entire day under the wide northern sky, galloping across open fields, whooping after mustangs, laughing when their horses kicked up dust clouds behind them. The exhilaration of the chase left them breathless and windblown, cheeks flushed and eyes bright. And by sundown, they had managed to drive a good-sized herd into the enclosure.

After they closed the gate, Leah climbed onto the fence, perching there as she watched the wild horses circle, toss their manes, and adjust to their new surroundings. The heat of the day still clung to her skin, and the fading sunlight turned her golden hair into a halo.

Colt stepped up behind her. Close. Very close. He wrapped his strong arms gently around her waist and pulled her back against him. The moment their bodies touched, Leah's breath hitched, just slightly, but Colt felt it. His voice brushed warm against her ear.

"Leah," he murmured, "will you marry me?"

She stiffened, stunned. She twisted enough to look at him over her shoulder.

"Marry you?"

He nodded, a grin tugging at the corner of his mouth as her cheeks flushed pink.

"Yes."

"Colt," she whispered, shaking her head, "we just met. I still don't know anything about myself."

"I know." His arms tightened around her just a little. "And I'm not asking you to marry me tomorrow. Or even next month. But I needed you to know..." His voice grew huskier, more vulnerable. "I care for you. Deeply. And every day I spend with you... I'm falling more and more in love with you."

Her gaze dropped to the fence rail beneath her feet, her breath trembling.

"Colt..."

He angled his head, searching her eyes. "Aren't you attracted to me, too?"

Her blush deepened into a fiery red.

"Y—yes. I am. More than I want to admit." She swallowed. "But I need to know who I am before making a decision like that. What if I already have a beau? Or I'm promised to someone else? Or... worse... already married?" Her blue eyes lifted to him, full of honest fear and confusion.

The words punched the air from Colt's lungs. *Married.* The idea sliced through him with unexpected sharpness. He brushed his fingers along her cheek.

"I'd hate it if that were the case," he admitted softly. "Hate it more than I can say." His gaze roamed her face with reverence. "But I wouldn't be surprised if someone had already claimed your heart. You're a beautiful girl, Leah. Anyone would be lucky to have you."

Her breath caught. He leaned closer, voice barely above a whisper.

"But if you are free... if you get your memories back, will you at least consider marrying me?"

This time, her lips curved into a radiant, heartfelt smile.

"Yes. I will."

Joy flashed through his eyes, pure, boyish joy. Colt didn't hesitate. He pulled her gently but firmly off the fence and into his arms, then lowered his head and kissed her.

It was not tentative. It was a full, passionate, hungry kiss that poured out everything he couldn't say yet. Leah's arms slid around his neck, her body melting into his. She kissed him back, with surprising heat, a spark of longing that had been building between them since the day she arrived.

For the first time since losing her memory, Leah felt something clear, powerful, and unmistakably real: She wanted him. And she wanted that kiss to never end.

When Leah woke the following morning, she found herself cradled securely against Colt's chest, his arm wrapped firmly around her waist. For a moment she simply lay still, absorbing the warmth of him, the steady rise and fall of his breathing, the sense of safety she hadn't felt in far too long.

Her heart beat a little faster, shy, startled, yet undeniably moved. It astonished her how a man who had been nothing more than a stranger mere weeks ago was now quietly, steadily taking over the spaces of her heart she once believed were closed forever.

Colt stirred, his lashes lifting as he looked down at her. A soft smile eased across his rugged features, and he bent to press a lingering kiss to the crown of her head.

"It's still early," he murmured, his voice gravelly from sleep. "Try to rest a bit longer."

She wanted to protest, to tell him she felt safer with him awake, but exhaustion tugged at her. Colt brushed his thumb gently across her shoulder. "I need to get up and have a word with my brother," he continued. "But you stay right here. Get some more sleep."

Leah nodded, her eyes drifting closed again as his warmth slowly slipped away. She heard the faint rustle of clothing, the quiet tread of his boots, the soft click of the door as he stepped out. Wrapped in lingering warmth and the echo of his affection, she drifted into drowsy half-dreams, comforted by the knowledge that Colt would be close.

Leah didn't know how much time had passed before raised voices jolted her awake. At first, her groggy mind struggled to place the sounds, low, rough, unmistakably male, but within seconds she recognized them clearly. Colt. And Heber. And they were shouting.

Her stomach tightened. She scrambled upright, heart thudding, and hurried to dress. She had just reached for the doorknob when the sharp edge of their argument carried clearly down the hall.

She froze.

"She ain't yours to marry, Colt," Heber barked, voice full of grit and irritation. "I don't even know what the hell we're supposed to do with her, or if she's got any chance o' goin' back home."

Leah's breath caught. Her fists curled at her sides.

Colt fired back, furious. "Then why'd you drag her here? Why rope me into this fool charade? I care for her, Heber. I want her in my life, not as some damned game you cooked up."

A pause, long enough for Leah's pulse to hammer painfully against her ribs, then Heber's voice rose again, louder and nastier than before.

"I told Leah she was your wife so you could have yourself a little fun with the girl! You should've taken the chance I handed you, instead o' fallin' for her and tryin' to make her sweet on you."

Leah's vision blurred with shock and humiliation. Her nails dug into her palms. *How dare he?* How dare he speak of her like that, like she was nothing but a toy? Colt's reply cracked through the house like a whip.

"She's a beautiful human being, Heber! I could never take advantage of her, or any woman. Believe it or not, not everyone is as immoral and selfish as you. You're a sick man."

A heavy silence followed, thick with rage. Then a door slammed so violently that Leah flinched, breath shallow, heart hammering as the echoes faded into an awful, shuddering quiet.

Leah waited until she heard the front door open, then close again. Only when the house fell quiet did she finally step into the hallway. Through the open doorway she spotted Heber climbing up onto the buckboard seat. Sarah and Aponi sat next to him, stiff and silent, fear etched across their faces. Colt, jaw clenched and shoulders rigid with anger, stalked toward the barn.

"Where you ridin' off to, Colt?" Heber barked. Leah held her breath, straining to hear Colt's reply. "Goin' into town for some damn fresh air, and get us some grub," Colt shot back. "Unless you'd rather the whole lot of us go hungry?"

The sharpness in his tone made Leah shiver. Colt was furious, beyond furious. And despite her own turmoil, she didn't envy him. Being tied to a man like Heber, trapped in whatever mess Heber had created... no one deserved that burden. Least of all Colt.

She stood perfectly still until the wagon rolled away in a clatter of wheels and hooves. Only when it vanished around the bend did she move. This was her chance. Heart pounding, she rushed down the hall and slipped into Heber's room. The door clicked softly behind her. She moved quickly, rifling through the closet, the drawers, the shelves, desperate for anything that would tell her who she was, where she came from, and why Heber had wanted her.

Nothing. Not a scrap of handwriting. Not a ribbon or trinket that felt familiar. She was heading toward the door when her boot caught on the edge of a rug. She stumbled, grabbed the dresser to steady herself, and the rug bunched beneath her feet. That was when she saw it: a loose floorboard.

Leah's pulse spiked. She pushed the rug aside, pried up the plank, and uncovered a narrow cavity stuffed with folded papers. She gathered them all and sat on the edge of the bed, hands trembling as she sorted through the stack. Bills. Names she didn't know. Ledgers. Supply records that meant nothing to her. Then, papers about Sarah and Aponi.

Her stomach dropped. She folded those and shoved them deep into her pocket. At the bottom of the pile, she found a letter, older, creased, stained. She unfolded it. And everything inside her stopped.

Heber,

Pa an' me get loose come October. Still ain't sure yet if we need that girl, Leah Johnson, for the plan or if we can pull it off without her. Fetch her anyway, 'fore we ride up to the Johnson Ranch, and keep her hid till you hear from us again.

You gotta catch her when she's alone. She's near always workin' alongside that foreman o' theirs, Cash, or one o' the Johnson hands. Cash's been playin' the father-figure since her pa passed, and he'll be mean-protective of her. Make damn sure he ain't anywhere 'round when you take her.

They're fixin' to drive their cattle back from Pecwan come the first o' September. That's likely your best chance. Pa an' me'll send word once we know more.

Milton Rowland

A sharp, stabbing pain shot through Leah's chest. Memories slammed back into her mind with terrifying clarity, her father's face, his laughter, the night he didn't come home... and the crushing knowledge that he never would again. Her breath hitched. Her vision blurred. She pressed a trembling hand to her mouth. She needed to get back to her room. She needed to think, to breathe.

A hand clamped around her from behind. Leah gasped as she was yanked violently to her feet. Instinct surged. She kicked, twisted, clawed, but the grip only tightened.

"You sneaky little witch," Heber hissed at her ear. "Creepin' about like that... I knew you weren't to be trusted." He flung her onto the bed. Rope bit into her wrists before she could scramble away. Another loop snapped tight around her ankles. In seconds she was trussed, helpless, shaking. He slung her over his shoulder like a sack of grain. Leah screamed, kicked, thrashed, but his hold never budged. He carried her down the hall, shouting over her muffled cries toward Sarah and Aponi: "You so much as think 'bout runnin', I'll put her in the ground. You hear me?"

Leah's heart lurched. The women froze where they stood, terror widening their eyes. Heber marched outside with her and dumped her into the back of the wagon before striding back toward the house.

"I'll lock 'em in my room," he said, voice rough as gravel. "Ain't no window in there, so don't go lookin' for 'em for savin'."

Panic clawed up Leah's throat. She twisted her bound wrists, inching toward the wagon's back end. She managed to hook her heel on the boards and began sliding herself over the edge. Heber saw her. He cursed viciously, grabbed her by the waist, and yanked her back with brutal force. Pain shot down her arm. Leah cried out. This time he tied her to the front seat, tight, cruel knots that burned her skin.

"Stop, let me go!" she begged, fighting until her muscles trembled.

He ignored every word. Instead, he shoved a rag between her teeth, knotting it behind her head. Then he climbed onto the seat, snapped the reins, and the horses lurched forward. The wagon rattled down the road. Leah's world narrowed to fear, the sting of rope, and the terrible realization that she was utterly trapped with the man who planned to use her as a pawn in something she didn't yet understand.

6
A Cowboy's Last Ride

As soon as Colt reached Kneeland, he tied off his horse and strode straight toward the sheriff's office, each step quick and hard with urgency. The bell above the door jingled as he pushed it open. Sheriff Craig Townsend looked up from the papers on his desk. A friendly smile touched his weathered face.

"Good morning, Colt. What can I do for you?"

Colt removed his hat, running a tense hand through his hair.

"Morning, Craig. I need help. Do you know if a young woman has been reported missing? I don't know much about her, just that her name is Leah." His voice tightened. "And my brother kidnapped her."

The sheriff's expression transformed instantly. The smile vanished.

"Leah?" he repeated, sitting straighter. "We received a telegram from Hoopa Valley about two weeks back. They asked for help searching for a Leah Johnson." He exhaled slowly. "Since we're quite a distance from there, I didn't put much weight on it, but we kept our eyes open. Anyone we didn't recognize, we questioned." He lifted a brow. "Can you tell me what she looks like?"

Colt described Leah, the blonde hair, the frightened but determined eyes, the small scar near her temple, every detail he'd memorized without trying. The sheriff nodded along thoughtfully.

"Listen, Craig," Colt continued, voice dropping to a grave tone. "My brother's dangerous. He showed up at my place about a week before Leah did. He had two Indian women with him, Sarah and Aponi." He swallowed. "I don't know if he kidnapped them or bought them, but I'm sure it wasn't legal. He keeps them close so he can threaten me. Reminds me constantly that if I report him, he'll hurt them."

Sheriff Townsend leaned back, studying him carefully.

"Then what made you decide to come forward today?"

Colt hesitated, jaw working. Honesty pressed against his ribs until he let it out.

"Because..." He let out a shaky breath. "I care for Leah. And I don't want her to get hurt. Not another minute."

A knowing look softened the sheriff's stern face. He gave a short nod.

"I see."

"I left after an argument with Heber," Colt said. "Told him I was going into town for supplies. I'll pick up a few things at the general store to keep up the story, then head right back." He set his hat on the sheriff's desk, leaning in. "I need to get home before he suspects anything."

"Do you want me to come to the farm and arrest him?" Craig asked.

"Yes," Colt said without hesitation. "But I need to make sure the women are safe first. If I can get him away from them, I'll try taking him down myself. But if I haven't come back with him by this evening—"

"I'll gather a few men," the sheriff promised. "We'll head out to your place. Quietly. Last thing we want is to spook him into doing something rash."

"Thanks, Craig." Colt reached for his hat again, then paused at the door. "And... could you send a telegram to Hoopa Valley? Let Leah's family know we found her. Or at least where she's been."

"Will do," the sheriff said with a firm nod. "You just get home safe, Colt."

Colt stepped out into the morning sun, chest heavy with worry, but for the first time in days, he felt a sliver of hope. He was going back for Leah. And this time, he wasn't letting Heber get anywhere near her again.

"Cash, a telegram just came for you." Chuck Foster handed the folded slip of paper to the foreman, his eyes wide with hope. Cash, Jaxon, and a group of exhausted volunteers had just ridden back into town after yet another fruitless search for Leah. Dust clung to their boots and shirts, and the weight of worry sat heavily on every man's shoulders. Jaxon looked nearly as worn down as Cash felt, pale, tense, and desperate for any sign of good news.

Cash opened the telegram with rough, trembling fingers. The moment his eyes skimmed across the first line, something shifted in his expression. His shoulders straightened, and for the first time since Leah had gone missing, a faint but unmistakable smile tugged at his lips.

"She's on a farm near Kneeland," he breathed. Jaxon let out a long, shaky sigh, relief washing over him, like a wave.

"Is it from her?"

"No," Cash replied, reading on. His brow tightened again. "It's from Kneeland's sheriff. And it sounds like she's still in danger." He lifted his gaze to Jaxon's, the determination there sharp and immediate. "Let's go get her. We'll bring her home where she belongs."

Jaxon didn't need to be told twice. He spun on his heel and sprinted toward his horse, his movements fueled by urgency and fear disguised as adrenaline.

"Should someone let her mom know?" Chuck asked quietly behind them, cautious hope in his tone.

Cash shook his head firmly. "No. Not yet. I won't raise her hopes only to break them if something goes wrong." He turned toward the sheriff, Scott Bailey. "But Scott, sending a telegram to David Smith wouldn't be a bad idea. He and his family have been beside themselves. They deserve to know we have a lead."

"Sure thing, Cash," Sheriff Bailey replied without hesitation.

Within minutes, Cash and Jaxon were mounted and thundering down the main road, riding harder and faster than they had since the day Leah vanished. Townspeople stepped aside, watching them disappear in a cloud of dust, hope flickering anew in their hearts. Leah had been found. And now, nothing would stop them from bringing her home.

Colt pushed open the front door and stepped inside, his nerves already stretched thin. He paused, listening. The house was silent, too silent. The kind of silence that made the hair on the back of his neck lift.

"Heber?" he called out. Only an echo answered him. Then, from down the hall, Sarah's voice floated back, trembling.

"Colt? We're in here."

He strode toward Heber's bedroom door, the unease in his stomach tightening into dread. He twisted the knob. It didn't budge. Locked. Of course, Heber had taken the key.

"Sarah, Aponi, move back," Colt ordered, urgency roughening his voice. The two women scrambled out of harm's way just as Colt stepped back and drove his boot into the door. Wood splintered on the first kick, gave way on the second, and swung inward with a sharp crack. Sarah and Aponi hurried into the hall, their fear written plainly on their faces.

"Heber took Leah," Sarah blurted, wringing her hands. "He found her snooping through his things."

A groan tore out of Colt before he could stop it, the sound thick with guilt and fury. He should never have left her behind, not even for an hour. He knew Heber would never allow Leah to go anywhere with him except to do chores... but leaving her alone had been a mistake. A terrible one.

"Do you know where he's taking her?" Colt demanded. Sarah exchanged a glance with Aponi, then nodded slowly.

"He… he muttered to himself when we were driving back earlier," she said. "Something about how if his suspicions were right, and she was trying to find answers, he'd take her to a cabin on Fickle Hill."

Colt stiffened. That place was isolated. Remote. Dangerous.

"We stayed there one night before coming to your farm," Sarah continued. "It has a secure earth cellar. I think… I think he plans to lock her in there."

A string of curses slipped from Colt before he could rein them in. He didn't apologize. He didn't have the luxury.

"All right," he said, switching into action in an instant. "Gather your things. Both of you. Quickly."

Sarah and Aponi didn't hesitate. They rushed to their small room as Colt stormed outside toward the barn, fury boiling beneath his skin. He threw open the stall and began saddling his second horse with practiced, furious efficiency. His thoughts raced, fear for Leah, rage at Heber, regret that he hadn't protected her better, but above all was resolve. He had a chance now. A chance to get Sarah and Aponi to safety. A chance to alert the sheriff. A chance to stop Heber before he hurt Leah again. And Colt Thatcher was not going to waste it.

When Colt reached Kneeland a second time, he brought Sarah and Aponi straight to the sheriff's office. Sheriff Craig Townsend stepped outside before they had even dismounted, his expression tight with concern.

"I sent the telegram as soon as you left," Craig said. "Her family is already on their way to get her. Should I ride with you to Fickle Hill now, do you think?" He looked toward the tree-lined hills with a frown. "Or should I wait until they arrive this evening and follow you then?"

Colt shook his head immediately. "I think it's best if you wait."

Craig's brows rose. "You're sure?"

"If we all go now, we'll put Leah in even more danger," Colt said firmly. "Heber's skittish, mean as a cornered rattlesnake when he thinks someone's after him. If he sees a whole group of riders coming, he could panic, hurt her, or take off into the woods with her before we can stop him."

The sheriff exhaled sharply, the weight of the situation settled between them.

"All right. We'll do it your way."

Colt nodded once, jaw set, every muscle tight with urgency.

"I'll get her out. One way or another."

Craig placed a steady hand on his shoulder. "Just be careful, Colt. A woman's life is on the line."

"I know," Colt murmured, his voice low and grim. "Which is why I can't afford to make a single mistake."

When Heber finally reached his destination, the sun was high and unforgiving, the midday heat pressing down like a heavy blanket. The horses were lathered and blowing hard, the wagon wheels creaking as it came to a halt. Without a word, Heber climbed down, his boots hitting the dirt with a thud. Then he stalked toward Leah.

His grip was as rough as the calluses on his palms when he untied her from the wagon seat. Leah twisted, kicked, and jerked against him, anything to slow him down, but Heber didn't waver. He slung her over his shoulder once again, ignoring her muffled cries as he carried her toward a small, weather-beaten cabin nestled among the trees.

Behind it stood a half-hidden earth cellar with a slanted wooden door. Leah's stomach dropped.

Heber strode down the narrow steps and tossed her onto the packed dirt floor as if she were nothing more than a nuisance. Her shoulder hit hard, sending pain shooting down her arm. Before she could catch her breath, he ripped the gag from her mouth and sawed the rope from her ankles, only so she couldn't trip him on his way out. Then he turned and hurried back up the stairs.

"Heber—don't! Please—!"

The only answer was the slam of the cellar door above her and the scrape of a heavy bolt sliding into place. Darkness swallowed her. Leah scrambled to her knees, gasping. Her wrists burned where the rope had dug into them. Each movement made the fibers' bite flare anew. She winced but forced herself upright, blinking as her eyes adjusted to the dim, earthy gloom. She wouldn't stay trapped. She couldn't.

Taking a shaky breath, she climbed the narrow stairs and pushed against the door with all her strength. The wood didn't move, not even an inch. She tried again, pressing her shoulder into it this time, gritting her teeth until her muscles trembled. Still nothing. Her breath hitched, panic clawing at her chest.

She lowered herself onto the step beneath her, exhaustion and fear crashing over her like a wave. Tears pricked her eyes. How was she ever going to get out? And who would find her in a place like this?

She didn't know how long she had been sitting there, minutes, hours, maybe longer. Time dissolved in the darkness of the cellar. Her legs had gone numb, her back ached from the cold stone, and her eyes strained for any scrap of light. But when she heard footsteps and the thud of boots outside, her entire body went taut. He was coming back.

Leah pushed herself upright, bracing against the wall, ready to throw herself at Heber the moment the door opened. She would not go down without a fight. She had already let him overpower her once. Never again.

The cellar door creaked open, and a blast of blinding sunlight poured down the stairs. Leah raised a hand to shield her eyes, just as Heber's silhouette appeared... carrying a large burlap sack writhing violently in his grip. For a heartbeat she thought the heat and fear were making her imagine things, until the sack hissed. Rattlesnakes. Her blood turned to ice.

The moment Heber started down the steps, the bag writhed harder, the sound of rattles filling the confined space like a swarm of death. Leah's breath hitched, and she stumbled backward until she hit the far wall.

Heber's vile grin came into view first, sharp, gleeful, wicked. It made her stomach twist with fury and dread.

"Well now," he drawled slow, stepping off that last stair, "reckon you been waitin' on me, darlin'."

He dropped the wriggling sack onto the cellar floor, the impact making the rattles erupt into a frenzy. Leah flinched violently.

With a swift motion, he reached for his knife. For one dizzying moment she thought he meant to harm her, but instead he grabbed her bound wrists and sliced the rope clean through. Leah tore her hands away, rubbing the raw, bleeding skin. Heber just chuckled and returned to the sack. He loosened the knot, then tipped the bag over. Two rattlesnakes slithered out. One settled on the bottom stair, coiling and shaking its tail in warning. The other glided across the dirt floor toward the door, positioning itself directly beneath the opening, blocking any hope of escape.

The hissing grew louder, echoing off the earthen walls. Leah pressed a trembling hand to her mouth, her skin prickling with terror.

"There," Heber snarled, clapping his hands together like he'd just finished something worth bragging about. "That oughta keep you behaved." He stepped back, eyes glinting with a feverish thrill as the nearest snake lifted its head, tongue flicking like it already claimed her. Leah froze, breath catching in her throat. Heber let out a soft, jittery laugh, too bright, too pleased, too wrong.

"You really oughta thank me," he crooned, tilting his head like he found the whole thing entertaining. "Gave you a mite more room to stretch." His grin sharpened. "Course... if those snakes get curious, come slitherin' over to play?" He gave an exaggerated shrug, delight dancing in his eyes. "Well now, sweetheart... that's between you and them. I ain't gettin' in the way of nature havin' its fun."

"You're not getting away with this," Leah spat, even as she flinched when the snakes rattled louder at her raised voice. Her fear burned into anger. "Someone will find me. Colt will find me."

Heber threw his head back and laughed, long, cruel, triumphant.

"I already did get away with it."

Before she could move, he marched back up the stairs, two long, furious strides, leapt clean over the coiled snake, and slammed the door with such force that dust sifted down from the rafters like shaken flour. The iron bolt scraped harshly into place, sealing her in.

Leah froze, listening. Heavy footsteps pounded across the yard, each one echoing through the hollowness of her chest. Then came the creak of wagon wheels... a sharp snap of reins... and moments later, the horses trotted off. Their hoofbeats faded steadily, swallowed by distance until nothing remained but the faint rattle of her own breathing.

Silence settled thick and merciless around her. Leah swallowed. She was alone. Trapped. And two rattlesnakes lay between her and the only way out, coiled, watchful, and far too patient.

A sick, heavy feeling settled in Colt's chest the moment he reached the cabin on Fickle Hill. Something about the place felt wrong, too still, too quiet. Even the birds seemed to avoid this stretch of forest. His horse stamped nervously, ears flicking back as if sensing danger.

There was no sign of Heber. No wagon. No tracks leading away that he could see from a quick glance. But what unnerved Colt most was the silence, thick, oppressive, unnatural. If Leah was here, why couldn't he hear her?

He drew a steadying breath and approached the cabin, pushing the door open and scanning every corner with sharp eyes. Empty. A few overturned items, a chair skewed at an odd angle as the breeze slid through a crack in the wall, but no Leah. A cold jolt of dread stabbed through him.

He hurried around the side of the cabin to where Sarah had said the earth cellar would be. It was built halfway into an enormous, jagged rock, the wooden door reinforced with metal brackets. Colt reached for the iron latch. Locked. Not just locked, chained. Heber had wrapped a heavy chain around the handles and secured it with a thick padlock. Colt's pulse thundered.

"Leah!" he called, voice raw with urgency. For one breathless second there was no answer. Then he heard it, the rattling. A sound that made every muscle in his body go rigid. "Leah!" he shouted again, louder this time. "Leah, can you hear me? Are you in there?"

"I'm here," came her reply, soft, shaky, controlled, as though she feared even her voice might provoke whatever was inside with her. Relief flooded him so quickly his knees nearly buckled.

"Thank goodness." He pressed his forehead briefly to the wooden door before forcing himself to stay focused. "How many snakes are in there with you?"

"Two," she whispered. His jaw locked. His vision burned with fury.

"All right. Listen to me, Leah. Move as far away from the door as you can. Stay against the back wall. I'm going to break this thing open." He didn't wait for a reply. He didn't dare waste another second. Colt spun on his heel, sprinted to his horse, and yanked his rifle from the saddle scabbard. His hands shook, not with fear, but with the sheer rage coursing through him, yet he forced himself to steady the barrel as he aimed at the chain.

"Hold on, sweetheart," he muttered under his breath. "Just hold on."

He braced himself and fired once, twice, three times. Sparks flew. Metal splintered. On the fourth shot, the padlock shattered and fell to the dirt. But he wasn't done. Colt aimed again at the door latch itself. One deafening blast. Then another. The hardware bent, twisted, then finally snapped with a metallic groan. The cellar door jerked loose, ready to be thrown open. And Colt didn't hesitate a single heartbeat.

But Heber hadn't left. He had only moved the wagon farther down the narrow trail, just far enough for the sound of hooves to fade and Leah to believe he'd abandoned her. In truth, he had slipped into the thick line of trees bordering the massive rock, crouching low among the ferns and shadows. From his hiding place, he had watched everything. Watched Colt arrive. Watched him search the cabin, watched him discover the cellar. He had watched him call Leah's name with panic in his voice.

Heber's lips twisted into a cruel, triumphant sneer. The fool actually cared.

While Colt retrieved his rifle, Heber crawled along the jagged edge of the rock with slow, predator-like precision. He carried another burlap sack, larger and angrier than the first. The sack writhed, bulging and shifting, the rattling inside rising to an ominous chorus.

He pressed his back against the rock's face, inching closer to where Colt stood at the cellar door. He waited. Waited until the final gunshot shattered the lock. Waited until Colt leaned forward to wrench the mangled hardware aside. Then Heber struck.

With a vicious grin stretching across his face, he lifted the writhing sack high, untied the knot, and shook it open, sending a cascade of furious rattlesnakes straight down toward Colt's unprotected shoulders. The snakes hit his body and the ground inches from his boots, tails buzzing like deadly warnings. One struck immediately. Colt jerked back with a shout, stumbling as the sudden explosion of rattling filled the clearing. Heber's laughter echoed from the rocks, cold and feral. He had been waiting for this moment.

7
Where Grief Met Grace in Kneeland

The startled reptiles reacted instantly. The moment the sack split open, the rattlesnakes, already agitated and disoriented, struck with lightning speed. Colt barely registered movement before he felt the searing pain of fangs sinking into his arm... then his shoulder... then the side of his hand when he tried instinctively to swat them away.

He shouted, a raw, guttural sound torn from his chest, as he staggered backward. His rifle slipped from his grasp, clattering uselessly to the ground. The clearing spun. Another strike landed high on his forearm, fire exploding beneath his skin. He jerked violently, shaking off the first snakes, but their tails buzzed angrily as they coiled again, ready to lunge.

Disoriented and trying desperately to get away, Colt stumbled blindly toward the cellar. His boot caught the top step. His balance pitched forward. He fell. Hard. He crashed down the narrow stairwell, hitting one step, then another, before slamming onto the packed earth floor. The impact knocked the breath from his lungs and sent a bolt of pain shooting up his ankle. A hiss sounded inches away.

Before he could roll clear, Colt realized too late that he had landed on the very snake Heber had placed at the bottom of the steps. The furious reptile struck instantly, driving its fangs deep into the side of his calf.

Colt cried out louder this time as agony ripped through his leg. His body jerked involuntarily, and he clawed at the dirt, scrambling away as it rattled in warning. The pain came in waves, sharp, burning, unbearable, and his vision blurred at the edges. But even through the haze of venom and panic, one thought thundered through him: Leah was still trapped, and he had to get her out.

Leah's heart stopped. For one paralyzing moment she could only stare in horror as Colt tumbled down the steps and the rattlesnakes struck him again and again. Her breath lodged painfully in her throat, a scream rising, but she forced it back. Panic won't save him. That single thought steadied her.

She rushed forward, ignoring the shaking in her limbs, and snatched Colt's revolver from his holster. The rattlesnakes were already coiling to strike again. Leah lifted the weapon with trembling hands, aimed, and fired, one shot for each snake. The gun boomed in the confined space, echoing off the stone, but both snakes fell still. She sprinted up the stairs, hoping to catch Heber before he struck again, but the outside snakes had already slithered into the crevices of the rock. She scanned the trees desperately. Heber was nowhere. He had vanished again like the coward he was.

Leah ran back into the cellar, lungs tight with fear, and dropped to her knees beside Colt. Tears blurred her vision as she took his hand, his skin hot and damp.

"Colt," she whispered urgently, "do you think you can get up? I can help you inside the cabin. I'll take care of your bites, I promise."

He nodded, though pain carved deep lines across his face. Every movement sent another wave of agony through him, yet he tried to stand. She wrapped an arm around him and helped him climb the stairs, supporting most of his weight.

They rounded the corner of the cabin just in time to see Heber dart into the forest, disappearing into the trees like a wounded animal. Leah lifted Colt's revolver and fired, but the shot cracked harmlessly. He was already too far away.

There was no time to chase him. Colt was barely staying upright. She guided him inside and into a small back room where, mercifully, a bed waited. Colt collapsed onto it with a heavy groan, clutching the blankets as another violent wave of pain tore through him.

Leah's throat tightened. She wanted to sob, to fall apart entirely, but she couldn't. Not now. She searched the cabin, ripping open cupboards and drawers, praying for medicine, herbs, anything. But the shelves were bare except for spiderwebs and dust. Nothing to ease venom. Nothing to help him. Her frustration nearly broke her. She found an old cloth and a dented bucket and ran outside to a nearby stream, filling it with icy water.

By the time she returned, Colt was shaking uncontrollably, his breathing uneven and shallow.

She dipped the cloth and began washing the bite marks on his arms. Then she unbuttoned his shirt, breath hitching when she saw more punctures across his chest and shoulders. So many. Too many. Leah closed her eyes for a moment, gathering her strength, then dipped the cloth again.

But when she lifted her hand to wipe his chest, Colt grabbed her wrist. His grip was weak, barely a tremble, but it stopped her. His forehead glistened with sweat. His eyes, clouded with pain, still held a spark of stubborn determination. He shook his head faintly.

"No," he whispered. "Too late."

"You can't give up, Colt," Leah pleaded, her voice breaking as tears streamed freely. "Please don't. You can't leave me here. You can't... I love you," she whispered, gently caressing his cheek. She knew, deep down, she knew, there was no hope. The venom was too strong, the bites too many, help too far away. But her heart refused to accept it.

Watching him suffer tore her apart. Colt's body convulsed now and then, his jaw tightening as he tried to withstand the agony twisting through him. He tried to be brave for her, she saw it in the way he fought to keep his eyes open when they drifted closed, in the way he squeezed her hand each time the pain surged.

Hours passed. Long, unbearable hours of torment and helplessness. Colt was drenched in sweat, breathing in ragged, shallow bursts. Sometimes he gasped as if air wouldn't fill his lungs. His limbs trembled. His skin grew pale and cold.

Finally, he reached for her hand again. Leah leaned closer, her tears falling onto the mattress.

His lips moved, slurred and slow.

"I'm... sorry," he whispered. "Sorry I... couldn't get you away... from my brother. Back... to your family." His face was numb now, his speech fading into soft, broken murmurs. "Don't... let him win."

"I won't," she whispered, choking on the words as tears ran unchecked. "I won't, Colt, I promise..."

He lifted his hand, barely, and his thumb brushed her cheek in a ghost-like gesture, wiping away her tears. A weak smile tugged at his lips. Then another agonizing spasm seized him. He cried out, the sound raw, and Leah pressed her hand against his chest, helpless, shattered.

Colt fought for another hour. Another hour of pain, determination, desperate breath. Then his body stilled. He drew one last breath, thin and trembling. And then... nothing.

Leah's cry tore through the cabin like a wounded animal's howl, echoing off the walls, echoing into the trees outside. She collapsed over his chest, fingers clutching his shirt, her whole body shaking as grief crashed through her. She sobbed until her throat burned. Sobbed until she had nothing left. Sobbed as though her heart had shattered in her hands. And perhaps, at that moment, it had.

Heber stood in front of the cabin, hidden just beyond the tree line, listening to Leah's anguished cries echo through the weathered boards. The sound was raw, piercing, a howl of pure heartbreak, and it brought a twisted, satisfied grin crawling across his face. He felt no sorrow for Colt. Not an ounce.

His brother's death wasn't a loss. It was an opportunity. And the knowledge that Leah was inside that cabin, crumpled over Colt's lifeless body, shattered and drowning in grief... that delighted him. He wanted her to break. He wanted her to suffer for daring to defy him, for daring to show courage when he expected nothing but fear, for defending Sarah and Aponi when they should have been too terrified to speak. Every scream feeding his hatred. Every sob fueling his rage. But his hatred didn't start here. It had festered for years, decades, even.

Heber's thoughts drifted back to a time long before Leah was born. Years ago, he and his brothers had been drifting through Colorado on their way to California, taking odd jobs, wasting their pay on cheap whiskey, and leaving trouble in their wake. One night, stumbling toward a saloon in a half-drunken haze, he collided with a family who was also journeying west. And he saw her.

A young woman, barely more than a girl, whose beauty struck him so forcefully that he sobered for an entire heartbeat. Leah's mother. Those same eyes. That same face. Heber had stopped dead in the road, smitten and stunned. The next day, still hungover and smelling like whiskey, he approached her father and demanded, rather than asked, for the right to court her.

Leah's grandfather had looked him up and down with open disgust. Then he told Heber, in words that burned like acid, that he would never, ever, allow his daughter near a man like him. Heber had been seething. That night, he followed them. And the next day. And the next week. He tracked them all the way to Hoopa Valley, rage growing with every mile.

Once they settled, he tried again and cornered the family, begged and demanded in the same breath for another chance. Instead, he was threatened with the sheriff. Told to leave the young woman alone or face real consequences. And then Mitchell Johnson appeared.

Mitchell courted her openly. Respectfully. Honorably. And she accepted him, chose him. Heber had challenged Mitchell to a fight, thinking brute force would earn him victory. But Mitch beat him soundly, without hesitation. Without fear. The humiliation had burned deeper than any wound.

When Mitchell and the young woman married, something inside Heber twisted, the jealousy, the bitterness, the wounded pride until it hardened into hate. A corrosive, consuming hate. He promised himself that one day he would ruin them both. Tear apart the life they had built. Make them regret ever rejecting him.

Years passed, but the hate only grew. Then, not long after Mitchell died, a letter found Heber. A request. A job. Kidnap Leah Johnson. Revenge had fallen straight into his hands. He had never hesitated. He gathered men, planned routes, watched the Johnson ranch, waited for the moment she was alone. And when he saw her for the first time... it stunned him.

She looked exactly like her mother. Same hair. Same smile. Same eyes that made him feel something he couldn't name and didn't want to feel. But it also stoked the fury that had been festering in him for decades. He wanted to break her simply because she existed.

Hurting her was the closest thing he could get to hurting her mother. And since Mitchell Johnson was already dead, making Leah suffer felt like the perfect balance to the scales.

Colt dying in the process? That meant nothing to him. He would sacrifice anyone, family included, if it meant feeding his vengeance. And as he listened to Leah's sobs echo through the cabin, Heber felt only satisfaction. His revenge had finally begun.

Leah cried until her whole body trembled and she had no tears left to give. The grief hollowed her out... but beneath it, something else burned. Anger. Deep, fierce, soul-shaking anger. It combined with the pain until it felt like her chest was splitting open.

She wiped her eyes with the back of her hand and swallowed the sobs clawing at her throat. Colt didn't deserve this. None of it. And she refused, refused, to let Heber's cruelty be the final chapter in his life. With painstaking tenderness, she pulled a blanket over Colt's still form, smoothing it over his shoulders as though tucking him in for sleep. Her fingers lingered for a moment before she forced herself to stand.

Her eyes swept the room, cold, sparse, shadowed, and her fists curled tightly at her sides. She would not let Heber win. Not now. Not ever. She needed to get out of this cabin. She needed fresh air. She needed Colt's horse. If the animal hadn't bolted, she could ride, she would ride, back to Kneeland before dark. She didn't know the way, but she knew how to read tracks. And Heber's wagon tracks would be bold and obvious.

She crossed the main room, heading toward the door, determination building inside her with every step. But before she could reach it, the front door swung open. Heber stepped inside like a demon returning to his lair, his vile smile stretching wider when he saw her, red-eyed, exhausted, grief-stricken. He clearly expected her to be broken, defeated, barely standing. He thought he had destroyed her.

But the moment Leah saw him, saw the gloating satisfaction in his eyes, something inside her snapped. All the fear. All the grief. All the agony of watching Colt suffer for hours... it all transformed into something sharper. Hotter. Stronger.

Before Heber even realized what was happening, Leah lunged. She seized the front of his shirt with both hands, fingers curled like claws, and slammed him backward. His shoulders hit the wall with a heavy thud, dust shaking loose from the boards. Shock flickered across his face. Leah leaned in close, close enough for him to see the fire in her eyes. This time, she wasn't terrified. She was the woman he had pushed too far.

The attack caught Heber completely off guard. For a split second his eyes widened, stunned that the girl he believed he had broken still had enough strength, enough fury, to fight back. Leah's fists slammed into his jaw, his cheek, his chest, anywhere she could reach. She hit him again and again with the wild, desperate force of someone who had nothing left to lose.

Heber cursed and stumbled, trying to grab her arms, but she was too furious, too quick. She landed another blow to his mouth that split his lip. He lunged for her again, missed, then grabbed at her sleeve only for her to wrench herself away.

It took him several attempts, sloppy, furious, breathless, before his hands finally closed around her wrists. But even then, she didn't stop. With her arms trapped, Leah switched her attack, kicking him savagely in the shin, in the thigh, in the stomach, anywhere she could land a blow. The rage inside her was blazing, incandescent, stronger than her fear, stronger than her grief.

Heber snarled and forced her backward, slamming her down onto the settee. His weight bore down on her, pinning her legs, trapping her arms beneath his knees. Leah thrashed, twisting, jerking, trying to wrench free, but she was at a terrible disadvantage.

"You horrible, evil excuse for a human being!" she shouted, the words ripped from her throat. She spat directly into his face. "What kind of devil lets his own brother suffer like that? It should have been you, not Colt. He was a good person!"

Heber wiped her spit away with the sleeve of his shirt, his grin widening into something grotesque.

"Oh sure, sure... he was such a *saint*, wasn't he?" Heber drawled, his grin twitching at the corners, too wide, too pleased. "Fine man like that, oughta keep him safe, huh? Except it didn't." A snicker slipped out, sharp and ugly. "Should've kept his fool nose outta things that weren't his concern. But no... no, he just *had* to chase after you. Had to go pretendin' he was some kinda hero." He stepped in closer, shoulders shaking with a soft, off-kilter laugh. His breath hit her like something rotten.

"Poor little Leah," he crooned, voice dropping into a mocking whisper. "Bet you thought he'd save ya. Bet you fell head-over-heels for that noble, dead fool." He tilted his head, eyes gleaming like a rattlesnake's. "Tell me somethin', sweetheart..." His grin widened, unhinged. "Does it still hurt? Thinkin' 'bout how he died for nothin'?"

"Sweet victory," he breathed, voice gone dark as a storm cellar. "Soon as I drop my brother's rottin' carcass in a hole, we're headin' back to the homestead." He paused, letting the words settle like dust. "Now you listen close, Leah Johnson..." His voice slithered into a cold, rattlesnake hiss.

"You don't obey me, *every damn word*, and Cora's next. I won't just kill her." A twisted smile curled his lip. "I'll make her suffer. Slow." He leaned in till his nose nearly brushed hers, his breath rancid, his eyes wild with glee. "And I'll make you watch."

"No!" Leah screamed, a raw, desperate cry. Fueled by terror and fury, she tore one arm loose and began pummeling him again with her fists, striking whatever parts of him she could reach. This time Heber's control snapped. His face twisted, and with a roar he clamped both hands around her throat. Leah's world constricted in an instant. His fingers dug cruelly into her skin, cutting off her air. Panic exploded through her. She clawed at his wrists, kicked beneath him, thrashed wildly, but his grip was iron.

"You want me to torture you first?" he bellowed in her face, hot spit hitting her cheek. "You beggin' for me to do to *you* what I been doin' to Sarah and Cora these last months?" His grin twisted, stretching too wide, too pleased, pure rancid hatred warping every inch of it. "You ain't gettin' away, Leah," he hissed. "Whatever comes next, *every last bit of it*, that's on you."

She tried to gasp, tried to scream, but no air came. Spots danced in her vision. Her lungs burned. Her heartbeat hammered frantically in her ears, growing faint, then fainter still. Heber squeezed harder.

"I'll savor every damn minute," he growled.

Leah's strength ebbed. Her limbs weakened. Darkness tunneled around the edges of her vision.

She was seconds away from losing consciousness, seconds from death, while the monster above her tightened his grip.

Before Heber could inflict one more second of terror, the cabin door exploded inward with a violent crash. Boots thundered across the floorboards. A strong hand seized Heber by the back of his shirt and hurled him off Leah with brutal force. Several more men stormed inside behind the first, weapons drawn, voices raised.

Leah lurched upright, coughing violently as precious air rushed back into her lungs. Her chest burned. Each gasp felt like fire. She barely registered the chaos around her, Heber cursing, men shouting, because all she could focus on was breathing. *In—out. In—out.* Too fast. Too shallow. Her vision swam as panic threatened to swallow her whole.

Then two strong arms wrapped around her, warm and steady, pulling her against a broad chest that smelled faintly of saddle leather and pine. Leah didn't hesitate. She threw her arms around the man's neck, clinging to him with every ounce of strength she had left. She sobbed openly, her tears soaking into his shirt as she gasped for breath, her body trembling from shock and terror.

When her breathing finally steadied and her sobs began to subside, Cash tightened his embrace, holding her as though he would never let go.

"How can you be here?" she whispered, staring up at him with disbelieving, watery eyes. Cash brushed a sweaty strand of hair from her face, his own eyes red with emotion.

"The sheriff in Kneeland sent us a telegram this morning. We left as soon as we read it." His voice broke. "Goodness, Leah... it's good to hold you again. To see you alive. We've done nothing but search and worry since the day you disappeared."

"That's right," another voice said thickly. Leah turned, and the moment her gaze met Jaxon's, she burst into fresh tears. Her best friend, dusty, exhausted, terrified on her behalf, stepped forward and gripped her hand. Then, without hesitation, he pulled her fiercely into his arms.

She collapsed against him, weeping into his chest. The feel of his strong embrace, safe, familiar, unwavering, calmed her in ways she desperately needed. Jaxon buried his face in her hair, his grip tightening each time she sobbed, as though reassuring himself she was real.

When her tears slowed and the room exhaled in collective relief, Sheriff Townsend stepped toward her. Behind him, two deputies were dragging Heber out the door in handcuffs. They shoved him onto a waiting wagon, already prepared to haul him straight to the Kneeland jail.

"Miss Johnson," the sheriff said gently, removing his hat, "I'm grateful we arrived in time, and that you're finally safe with your family." He hesitated. "Did Colt ever make it here?"

At the sound of Colt's name, Leah's composure shattered. A strangled sob tore from her throat, and her knees buckled. Jaxon caught her instantly and pulled her back into his arms.

"H–he's dead," she cried into Jaxon's chest, her words broken. "Heber locked me in the cellar with two rattlesnakes... and when Colt tried to rescue me, Heber threw more snakes on him. H–he was bitten so many times." She gulped for air. "There was nothing I could do..."

The sheriff's face went pale. "So, you were with Colt the entire time... watching him die?"

Leah nodded, trembling. Cash let out a horrified gasp and wrapped both arms around her and Jaxon, pulling them close.

"Oh, Leah..."

"I wanted to save him," she sobbed. "I tried. After he fell down the steps, I shot the snakes that were near me, I got to his gun, but Heber stole Colt's horse. There was nothing here... nothing to help him." Her voice cracked with anguish. "It was too late..." Her breath hitched again as grief clawed through her. Every memory of Colt's suffering, his bravery, his tenderness, hit her like a tidal wave.

The sheriff cleared his throat. "Sarah and Aponi are safe," he assured her gently. "Colt left them in town before he rode here."

Relief washed through her, but it was faint, muffled beneath the crushing weight of her sorrow. A few moments later, the sheriff and two men returned from the back room carrying Colt's lifeless body on a blanket. They placed him carefully on the main wagon. Leah's tears fell anew.

"What are we going to do now?" Jaxon asked quietly. "It's too late to ride all the way back to Hoopa Valley tonight."

Leah lifted her head, her eyes swollen, her voice trembling.

"We can't stay here," she whispered. "I can't... not after seeing—" Her voice broke. She couldn't finish.

"We won't stay, Leah." Cash took her hand gently and pressed a kiss to her forehead, fatherly and tender. "We'll go back to Kneeland, stay at the hotel tonight, and head home first thing in the morning."

Leah nodded, leaning against him, her heart aching, but no longer alone.

It was fully dark by the time they arrived back in Kneeland. Lanterns glowed in windows along the street, casting soft golden pools across the dirt road. The exhaustion of the long, harrowing day hung heavily over all of them.

Cash secured two adjoining rooms at the small hotel. The moment Leah received her key, she slipped away without a word, her face pale and hollow. When Cash asked if she wanted supper, she only shook her head.

"I just... need to be alone," she whispered.

Cash watched her retreating figure with a worried frown. Jaxon's expression mirrored his concern.

"She shouldn't be by herself tonight," Jaxon murmured.

"I know," Cash replied quietly. "We'll give her space, but not too much of it."

They both understood too well the kind of grief that could swallow a person whole. Across the street, the sheriff found them and gave a brief update. Sarah and Aponi had refused the hotel rooms offered to them, they wanted nothing to do with Kneeland tonight, not when Heber remained in the same town. Even with the man locked securely in a jail cell, neither woman could bear the thought of sleeping anywhere near him.

The sheriff and his deputy had taken them back to Colt's homestead and returned the stolen wagon as well, assuring Cash that the women were safe and being looked after. Only once that was done did the two lawmen join Cash and Jaxon for supper.

No one spoke at first. The weight of the day made words feel heavy. Finally, Sheriff Townsend reached into his coat and slid a folded document across the table.

"I thought you should see this."

Cash frowned and opened the paper. His eyes widened. "This... this is a will."

The sheriff nodded.

"Sarah showed me where to find it. Turns out Colt wrote it recently, within the last few weeks, from what she said. He put everything he owned in Leah's name."

Cash stared at the paper, overwhelmed. It wasn't just a will. It was a declaration of trust, of protection, of affection Colt had never had the chance to voice aloud. Jaxon leaned in and read over Cash's shoulder, his expression somber.

"She'll need to see this," Jaxon whispered. "Not tonight," Cash answered. "She's suffered enough for one day."

The sheriff cleared his throat gently. "I also wanted to let you know... Colt's funeral will be held tomorrow. Around noon, out at the little cemetery behind the church." He hesitated. "I figured you and Leah might want the chance to attend before heading home."

Cash closed his eyes briefly, swallowing hard.

"Thank you, Sheriff. That means more than you know." He glanced toward the hallway leading to Leah's room, his heart twisting. She needed closure, needed to say goodbye to the man who had risked everything for her. And tomorrow, she would have that chance.

Leah was restless. Every time she drifted toward sleep, the nightmare dragged her back under. She heard Colt calling her name, desperate, breathless, followed by the sinister buzz of rattlesnakes' tails. She tried to scream a warning, tried to tell him Heber was behind him, but her voice was gone. Nothing came out but a strangled gasp.

In the dream she watched it happen all over again, the snakes striking, Colt stumbling, his body crashing down the cellar steps. She reached for his gun, but her fingers wouldn't close around it. She could only watch as he fell. A loud crash jolted her awake.

Leah bolted upright in bed, gasping for air, tears streaming uncontrollably down her cheeks. For a breathless moment she didn't know where she was, cellar, cabin, hotel, everything blurred together. But instinct took over before thought. Something had broken. Something needed to be cleaned before someone got hurt.

Her gaze darted around the dim room. Moonlight spilled through the window, pale and cold, illuminating the shattered remains of the lamp on the floor. Her hands trembled as she slid out of bed and knelt beside the pieces.

The pain in her chest was suffocating. She couldn't breathe without feeling like her ribs were splintering apart. The sobs she'd tried to hold down surged, breaking free as she reached for the glass. She couldn't unsee it. Colt's face, drawn with agony, sweat shining on his skin, eyes dimming, was burned into her memory. Every time she blinked, she saw him again. Heard him struggling to breathe. Heard him whisper, *don't let him win.*

The thought ripped through her. She grabbed the base of the broken lamp and hurled it at the wall. It shattered with a violent crack. Leah sank to her knees, sobbing so hard her entire body shook, the sound ragged, frantic, desperate. Without thinking, she reached for more glass, gathering pieces with trembling fingers. But the world tilted. Her vision blurred. She lost her balance and threw her hands out to catch herself. A sharp, slicing pain shot through her palm as a large shard buried itself deep into her skin.

She cried out, a small, terrified sound, and for a split second her mind transported her back to the cellar. *Snake. It's a snake bite. The venom is already spreading. I'm going to die like Colt did—*

The door burst open. Cash and Jaxon rushed inside, breathless and alarmed. Jaxon held a lamp aloft, casting warm light over the room. What they saw rooted them both in place, the broken lamp, the blood smeared across the floorboards, Leah kneeling against the bed, her hand bleeding heavily as raw, agonized sobs tore from her throat.

"Leah..." Cash whispered, horrified. He snapped into action instantly, dropping to his knees in front of her. "Sweetheart, look at me." His voice cracked but stayed steady enough to reach her.

Jaxon stood frozen for a moment, until Cash muttered tightly, "Go. Get the doctor."

Jaxon nodded sharply and vanished down the hall, leaving the lamp behind. Cash scanned the room. A towel lay folded on the settee, and beside it a small handkerchief. He grabbed both, then returned to Leah.

She looked up just as he gently took her injured hand, wrapped his own hand with the towel to protect it, and in one swift, practiced motion pulled the shard free. Leah gasped, and more blood spilled over her palm, but Cash was already pressing the handkerchief firmly against the wound.

Only after securing pressure did he slide his arms around her waist and lift her gently to her feet. Leah collapsed against him, trembling violently.

"I'm s-so sorry," she sobbed. "I tried... I tried to save him... I didn't mean to break the lamp—I didn't—" Her words dissolved into choking sobs. "I'm sorry, Cash... I'm so sorry..."

Cash tightened his hold, one hand stroking her hair, the other pressing the cloth to her wound.

"Shh... Leah, listen to me. None of this is your fault. Do you hear me? None of it." His voice was thick with emotion. "You didn't do anything wrong."

She cried harder, her face buried in his shirt. He held her through it, rocking her gently, whispering reassurance until her sobs finally weakened.

A few minutes later, Jaxon returned with the physician. They stepped inside quietly, their expressions softening when they saw Leah still clinging to Cash, her breathing shaky, her hand bleeding through the cloth. Only then, when help had arrived, did Cash finally loosen his embrace, though he kept his arm around her, steadying her as the doctor approached.

Jaxon's face was pale with worry as he watched Leah try to calm her sobs. His dark eyes followed every tremor in her body, every uneven breath, torn between wanting to comfort her and wanting to punch something on her behalf.

The doctor set his bag down and gently took Leah's injured hand. She winced, but didn't pull away. He examined the wound carefully, probing to ensure no hidden shards remained. Once satisfied, he disinfected it and wrapped it tightly in fresh bandages.

Her leg came next, scrapes and small cuts from kneeling among shattered glass. Nothing serious, but enough to warrant care.

"There now," the physician murmured. "You'll be sore, but you'll mend."

When he left, closing the door quietly behind him, Leah immediately stood and looked around the room.

"I need to clean the mess," she rasped, searching for a broom.

Cash stepped forward. "Leah, no. Get back in bed. Jaxon and I will take care of it."

She hesitated, habit, trauma, instinct telling her she needed to fix what she broke. But Cash's kind, firm tone left little room for argument. Exhaustion won. She nodded and sank back onto the bed while the two men searched the room.

It took longer than either expected to find a broom, but eventually they cleaned every shard from the floor, careful not to leave a single piece behind. When they finished, the room looked peaceful again, on the surface, at least.

Before leaving, Cash walked to her bedside and sat down gently. She wasn't sleeping. Her eyes were open, though she kept her face half-hidden in the blankets, as if hiding from the world, or her own mind.

"What's wrong, Leah?" Cash asked quietly. She turned her head just enough to glance at him, then buried it again. Cash's heart tightened. He reached out and gently lifted her chin. "Please tell me," he said softly.

Leah swallowed hard. When she finally spoke, her voice was barely above a whisper.

"I'm terrified to go back to sleep." Her eyes glistened, full of dread. "What if that horrible nightmare keeps repeating itself?"

Cash exchanged a glance with Jaxon, both men visibly moved. Then Cash gave her a warm, reassuring smile.

"I'll sleep on the settee tonight," he said firmly. "If I see you getting restless or scared, I'll wake you. You won't be alone."

Leah's breath hitched. She reached out and squeezed his hand, her eyes filling again, but this time with gratitude.

"Thank you, Cash," she whispered. And for the first time that night, she looked just a little less alone.

Both Cash and Leah were exhausted when morning came. Sleep had been fractured, fragile. Twice during the night, Leah's nightmare dragged her under again, each episode wrenching her awake in a delirium of fear. Each time, Cash rose from the settee to gently wake her, grounding her until her breathing steadied. But falling back asleep afterward had felt nearly impossible.

Now dawn had come, pale and cold. Leah dressed slowly, her hands shaking as she buttoned her blouse. Every movement felt heavy. She dreaded the funeral... dreaded standing beside Colt's grave... dreaded the finality she wasn't ready for.

If I start crying, she thought, *I won't be able to stop.* But she wasn't alone. Cash had been her anchor through the night, never leaving her side for more than a minute. And Jaxon was just as protective. She was grateful for them in a way she couldn't put into words.

They arrived at the church early. The morning was crisp, the scent of pine drifting through the air. Leah spotted two men in the graveyard through the window, working silently to finish preparations for Colt's burial. Her heart hammered. The pain inside her flared so sharply she pressed her hand to her chest. She was so lost in thought that when a deep voice spoke behind her, she nearly cried out.

"Miss Johnson?"

Leah turned quickly. A very young reverend, no older than twenty-eight, she guessed, stood there with gentle eyes and an earnest expression. She nodded.

"May I speak with you for a moment?" he asked softly. She nodded again. He gestured toward a nearby bench, and she sat. Cash and Jaxon remained close, quietly watchful. "I spoke with the sheriff late last night," the reverend began, tone warm and compassionate. "And again, this morning. He told me what happened, at least what he knew." He paused, sympathy deepening in his gaze. "I am truly, deeply sorry for your loss. My heart goes out to you."

"Thank you, Reverend," Leah whispered.

"If you need someone to talk to, please know I'm here," he continued gently. "You've endured something no young woman should ever have to face. Such experiences weigh heavily on the mind. Sometimes for a long time." His eyes searched hers, hopeful, but Leah remained quiet, her grief too raw to share.

"Don't keep it inside, Miss Johnson," he encouraged softly. "We must speak of our feelings if we're to heal." He studied her for a moment longer, then sighed and patted her hand kindly.

"I don't want to force you. But I don't want you to suffer alone either. Just remember, I'm here if you need me."

Leah nodded faintly.

The reverend continued, "The sheriff also mentioned that you intend to drive a herd of wild horses back to Hoopa Valley." His expression brightened slightly. "I grew up on a ranch. I'm happy to lend a hand if you need help." He smiled gently. "How many horses did you catch?"

"Thirty," Leah answered quietly.

"Thirty?" he repeated, impressed. "Would you like my help with the drive?"

Leah glanced instinctively at Cash. The foreman gave her a reassuring nod and stepped forward.

"Thank you, Reverend. That's very kind. We could use extra hands. Thirty head is no small drive."

"It's my pleasure," the reverend said warmly. "My name is Noah Olsen."

Cash shook his hand firmly, and they exchanged polite introductions before falling into brief conversation. Leah drifted back toward the window, staring out at the quiet graveyard as if trying to prepare her heart for what was coming. A moment later, Jaxon approached her silently. Without a word, he wrapped an arm around her shoulders. Leah leaned into him, drawing strength from his solid warmth, though she never looked up at him.

From across the room, Reverend Olsen watched them curiously.

"Are they courting?" he asked quietly.

Cash shook his head. "No. They're just friends."

"Are you sure?" Noah asked, raising an eyebrow as he studied the way Leah clung to Jaxon's side.

"Yes," Cash replied with certainty. "They've known each other since they were children."

Noah nodded slowly, though a glimmer of doubt lingered in his eyes.

Reverend Olsen delivered a touching, heartfelt sermon, soft-spoken yet full of compassion. His words drifted through the small cemetery like a prayer carried on the breeze. Leah hardly heard all of it. Her mind drifted between the present and memories of Colt's quiet kindness, his gentle smile, the way he had protected her without hesitation.

When it was time to pay their final respects, Reverend Olsen approached her with quiet reverence. He held out the shovel first, not because she was the youngest, but because Colt had no family left to stand at the grave. The gesture cut through her like a blade.

Leah stepped forward. Her vision blurred. Tears burned behind her eyes with vicious intensity. She clutched the shovel, but her hand shook so violently she couldn't lift a single scoop of earth. Her lower lip trembled, and she swallowed a sob that threatened to escape. She was losing control.

Before she broke completely, two familiar figures stepped behind her. Cash placed his large, steady hands over hers, guiding them gently. Jaxon stood close too, offering silent support. With Cash's help, Leah managed to tip a small cascade of soil onto the coffin below.

The moment the earth fell, Leah let out a broken gasp. She turned and collapsed into Cash's chest, pressing her face into his shirt as sobs tore from her throat. Cash wrapped both arms around her, holding her with the tenderness of a father comforting a hurting daughter. He guided her a step aside to give the others room to approach the grave, but he never loosened his embrace. He simply held her as she wept.

When the service concluded, the mourners drifted away one by one. Cash and Jaxon stayed with Leah, waiting patiently until she was ready to leave. She lingered at the grave for a long while, her hand resting on the fresh mound of earth, whispering a quiet goodbye only the wind could hear. But they couldn't remain in Kneeland forever. They needed to return to Colt's homestead first to gather the horses for the long journey home.

Jaxon lifted Leah onto his horse with careful gentleness, then swung up behind her, wrapping one protective arm around her waist. She leaned back against him, grateful for the support as her legs felt weak and unsteady.

The ride to Hoopa Valley was long, but for the first time in days, Leah found something that helped ease her thoughts. Herding the horses proved grounding, something physical, something real, something that kept her mind from spiraling into the painful memories she wasn't ready to face again.

Sarah and Aponi followed behind in the wagon. The two women had decided to join them, grateful for a chance at a new life.

"We'd like to live with the Hoopa people," Sarah had said earlier, her voice full of earnest hope.

"We want to be free again," Aponi added, her eyes shining with cautious joy. The thought warmed Leah's aching heart. After so much fear and suffering, the idea of these women finding a home, a true home, brought the slightest spark of comfort.

As the group traveled, weaving through forest and valley, the pain remained, but for the first time, it didn't consume her entirely. She wasn't alone. And somewhere deep inside, she clung to the quiet promise she had made to Colt: she would not let Heber win.

Leah kept mostly to herself on the ride. She rode stiffly, shoulders slightly hunched, her gaze fixed on the trail ahead. Even when Jaxon spoke quietly to her, she gave only short answers, then retreated back into silence. She seemed wrapped in her own thoughts, heavy, unspoken things that weighed down her usually bright spirit.

Reverend Noah Olsen guided his horse up alongside Cash's. He kept his voice gentle, respectful, as he nodded toward Leah's quiet figure.

"Is Leah always so reserved and quiet," he asked softly, "or is it because of what happened at the cabin on Fickle Hill?"

Cash let out a long sigh, watching Leah with a fatherly sort of ache.

"This isn't like her at all," he said. "She's the opposite, actually. Normally she's talkative, lively... always looking out for everyone else." His voice lowered. "I believe Colt was someone she trusted. Someone she felt safe with." He paused to draw a breath. "So, seeing him suffer like that, and dying with nobody else around..." Cash shook his head. "It was devastating for her. More than she knows how to talk about right now."

The young reverend nodded solemnly. He had suspected as much. No one could endure something so traumatic and remain unchanged overnight. Only time, and the people who loved her, could help her find her way back to herself.

It was already dark when they finally reached Hoopa Valley. The lanterns hanging outside the homes glowed softly, casting amber halos across the dirt road. The wagon wheels creaked to a stop at the reservation, and Sarah and Aponi climbed down.

A small crowd of Hoopa people emerged from the shadows, greeting the women with open arms and warm smiles. Their soft murmurs of welcome, their gentle hands on Sarah's and Aponi's shoulders, spoke of safety and belonging.

Leah watched from horseback, her chest swelling with gratitude. They were free. They were among people whose traditions and beliefs matched their own. At least someone's story was finding its way toward healing.

8
Screams in the Empty Field

When the group continued into town, Leah was stopped repeatedly. Townsfolk filled the street, shopkeepers stepping out of their stores, mothers holding children at their hips, elders leaning on canes, all of them calling her name with relief and joy.

"Welcome back, Leah!"

"We're so glad you're safe!"

"Bless the Lord, child, look at you!"

Leah blinked back sudden tears. She had missed her home, the warmth, the familiarity, the sense that she truly belonged somewhere. She offered smiles, nods, shy waves. Their kindness wrapped around her like a warm blanket.

She had just nudged her horse to move forward when a pair of strong arms suddenly wrapped around her waist and lifted her clean off the saddle. She gasped, instinctively tensing, then relaxed the instant she found herself staring into the familiar, loving eyes of her godfather.

"Uncle David?" she breathed.

He crushed her against his chest in a fierce hug, lifting her slightly off the ground. She could feel his shoulders shaking with relief.

"What are you doing here in Hoopa Valley?" she asked, giving him a small, breathless smile.

David Smith didn't let go. Instead, he hugged her tighter.

"What am I doing here?" he repeated, voice thick with emotion. "We were worried sick about you, sweetheart." He cupped her face briefly before pulling her close again. "Brooke nearly came with me when we got the telegram saying you'd been found. It is so good to hold you. To see you with my own eyes." When he finally drew back, he kept his hands on her arms and turned her slightly so he could look her over.

"What a stunning young lady you've become," he said softly, almost in awe. "I hardly recognized you. How long has it been since I last saw you?"

Leah's face softened. "I think three years. You and Aunt Brooke came for my sixteenth birthday."

David nodded, a smile tugging at his lips.

"I remember now. And look at you... all grown up. Stronger than you know."

Leah felt her throat tighten. For the first time since the nightmare began, she felt a small part of her heart settle. She was home.

Leah had barely swung her leg over her horse to dismount when the front door of the house flew open. Her mother rushed out first, Patricia's face blotchy from crying, her eyes shining with disbelief. Right behind her came Aunt Mildred, her hands pressed over her heart as if she still couldn't believe Leah was standing there.

Both women descended the steps quickly and enveloped Leah in a tight, trembling embrace. Her mother's arms were warm and familiar, and Aunt Mildred's hand cupped the back of her head, stroking her hair as though she were a child again.

"My baby..." Patricia whispered breathlessly. "I'm so glad you're back. These past few weeks have been torture." She pulled back just enough to look Leah in the eyes, giving her a trembling, grateful smile.

Aunt Mildred added, her voice thick with emotion, "Patti is right, Leah. We feared the worst. One day you were here, and then you were just gone. Everyone searched for you. Every day. Every night. It was agony not knowing what happened to you."

Leah felt her mother's hands tighten gently around hers.

"When we got Cash's telegram this morning," Mildred continued, wiping a tear from her cheek, "saying you'd been found in Kneeland and were on your way home... we just, oh, Leah, we cried. We prayed. We thanked heaven you were alive."

Behind them, Sheriff Bailey had stepped onto the porch, his hat held respectfully in his hands. He gave Leah a small nod, his expression soft with sympathy.

"Welcome home, Leah."

Leah nodded faintly but didn't meet his eyes, or anyone's, really. Her chest felt tight, her mind fogged, her emotions exhausted beyond words.

"It's good to be back," she murmured. But the moment the words left her mouth, a wave of crushing fatigue washed over her, physical, emotional, soul deep. She forced a polite nod. "Please excuse me. It's been... a very long day."

Before anyone could respond, Leah turned on her heel and hurried up the porch steps, her boots thudding quietly on the wood. She reached her room, closed the door behind her, and leaned against it, breathing hard as she tried not to fall apart all over again. Only for a moment. Then she allowed her knees to give out, sinking onto her bed as the weight of everything pressed down on her once more.

Leah was grateful to be home, grateful for familiar walls, familiar voices, and the comforting rhythm of ranch life, but the nightmares didn't loosen their grip on her. Every night they returned with brutal consistency, dragging her back into the darkness of the cellar, the rattling tails, the echo of Colt's voice fading as venom stole his breath.

Cash slept in her room for the first few nights, keeping vigil on the settee just as he had at the hotel. Each time she thrashed awake in terror, he was immediately at her side, steadying her, calming her, helping her catch her breath. But it took a toll on him. Leah could see the growing shadows beneath his eyes, the weariness in his movements. She couldn't bear to be the cause of that exhaustion.

"Cash," she said one evening, blocking the doorway with her injured hand pressed to the frame, "you can't stay in here anymore. I won't allow it."

He tried to protest, but she shook her head, hard, too hard.

"No. You need sleep. Real sleep. Not this half-rest you've been getting."

He relented only because she was adamant. But he refused to go far. From that night on, he stayed in the bedroom right next to hers, door cracked open, boots by the bed, ready to come running if she needed him.

Despite everyone's efforts, it was obvious to the entire ranch that Leah was unraveling. The dark rings beneath her eyes, the hollow look in her once-bright face, the way she startled at even small sounds, anyone could see she was sleeping only in fragments, if at all.

But no matter who tried to talk to her, Patricia, Aunt Mildred, Cash, Jaxon, Leah wouldn't open up. She listened politely, nodded when expected, but never let a single piece of her suffering slip through her tightly guarded exterior.

Reverend Noah Olsen began visiting Hoopa Valley often. He always asked after her, always stopped by the ranch to offer kind words or gentle encouragement. He had known Colt, too, and hoped that shared connection might coax her to speak. But Leah pushed him away just as firmly as she pushed away everyone else. Instead, she buried herself in work. She threw her entire body and mind into ranch chores, refusing to rest even when she could barely stay on her feet. She rode for long hours checking fences, scrubbed stalls until her hands ached, helped with branding and feeding, anything that kept her too busy to think, to remember, to feel.

Cash and Jaxon exchanged worried looks more often now. They watched her silently from the corral rails or across the pasture, their concern growing with every passing day. Leah had always been the heart of the ranch, warm, open, kind. But now she was distant. Closed off. Untouchable. Hurting far more deeply than she would admit. And both men knew: if something didn't change soon, she might break in a way no one could put back together.

It was the second week of October when Cash and Jaxon finally admitted to themselves that something had to be done. Leah's silence, her distance, her relentless work schedule, it wasn't healing her. It was hollowing her out.

"We can't keep letting this go on," Cash muttered one morning as he and Jaxon stood by the corral fence, watching the ranch hands saddle up. "She's headed for a breaking point."

Jaxon nodded grimly. "She's barely eating. Barely sleeping. She won't let anyone close. We've got to make her talk it out, Cash. Somehow."

Cash knew he was right. That morning, he sent several cowboys to Eureka to sell the herd of wild horses Leah had caught with Colt, horses she once would have been proud of. Now she didn't even look at them.

After sending the men off, Cash asked around the ranch and the reservation, trying to find Leah. But everyone gave the same answer: "We haven't seen her." His worry sharpened. Late that afternoon, one of the younger hands approached him, wiping sweat from his brow.

"Cash, I remembered something," he said. "Leah mentioned earlier today she wanted to check on some of the fences. Said she planned on repairing a few if they needed it."

Cash straightened, tension rippling through him. Repairing fences meant wandering across thousands of acres alone. He found Jaxon immediately.

"She's out somewhere on the property," Cash said. "Checking fences."

Jaxon grabbed his reins without hesitation. "Then what are we waiting for?"

They didn't waste another second. They mounted up and rode out, splitting off in opposite directions. They knew every inch of the land, every stretch of sagging fence, every remote corner where wire posts leaned crooked from weather or wandering cattle. And each of those spots was a place Leah might be, alone, exhausted, and hurting. They prayed they would find her before she pushed herself past the point of return.

Leah was cold and exhausted. Down to the marrow of her bones. She hadn't slept properly in weeks, not truly. Every time she drifted off, the nightmares clawed her back into the darkness of that cellar: Colt tumbling down the stairs, snakes striking, his face twisted in agony. Even endless labor couldn't keep the memories away anymore.

She lifted the hammer again, aim wavering, and drove the fence post deeper into the earth. Each strike sent another flash of memory slicing through her mind. Her stomach clenched. Her vision blurred. Sweat stung her eyes despite the chill in the October air.

Her hands were already raw, blistered, cracked, bleeding. The cold only made the ache worse, but she barely noticed anymore. Pain was familiar. Pain was grounding. But nothing, not the cold, not the work, not the mindless repetition, washed away the image burned into her soul. Colt... dying. Her breath shuddered. She grabbed the coil of barbed wire, not thinking, not caring. The moment the sharp edges bit into her palm, she hissed and jerked, but she didn't let go. The wire cut deeper, slicing across tender skin. Blood welled instantly.

Leah moaned, a small, broken sound she couldn't stop. The barbed wire slipped from her fingers, falling into the grass with a soft thud. And then her legs gave out. She collapsed onto the cold ground, trembling, her knees hitting the dirt hard. At first, she tried to swallow the knot in her throat, tried to blink back the tears pressing so painfully behind her eyes. But she couldn't. Not anymore.

Leah bowed her head and let the tears fall freely, hot, uncontrollable, wracking sobs that tore from her chest and echoed across the empty field. She curled forward, wrapping her bleeding hands around her arms as the pain she had been trying to outrun for weeks finally swallowed her whole.

Jaxon reined in his horse so sharply it skidded in the dirt. He saw Leah collapsed on the ground, sobbing, and his heart lodged in his throat. He dismounted in one swift movement and rushed to her, pulling her gently but firmly to her feet. She flinched at his touch. When he tried to wrap his arms around her, she shoved him so hard he stumbled backward a step.

"What do you think you're doing?" she snapped, tears streaking down her face. She forced herself to breathe evenly, forcing back her sobs. "Why are you even here? I thought you and Cash wanted to go to Eureka today."

Jaxon swallowed, his brow furrowed in pain at her words.

"I'm here because I'm worried about you, Leah. Everyone is worried about you."

"It isn't your job to worry about me, Jaxon." She turned her back on him, voice tight with exhaustion. "Focus on your work and leave me alone."

He stepped in front of her again, blocking her path. His hands grasped her arms, not roughly, but enough to stop her.

"You can't keep doing this. You can't keep shutting everyone out. Talk to me. Talk to someone."

"I have nothing to say. Now get out of my way."

"No," he said firmly, grounding himself. "You need to move on. It's time to let Colt go and be yourself again."

Hurt flashed across her face before she masked it with fury. She jerked out of his hold.

"Go away!" she cried. "I don't want to be around anyone right now, and you don't get to decide how long I must grieve! You weren't there when Colt died, so don't you dare tell me to move on!"

"Cash and I have spoken to Reverend Olsen many times these past weeks," Jaxon said softly, trying to reach her. "He told us a lot about Colt, who he was—"

"Oh, and that makes you an expert now?" Leah shot back, fists clenched, shaking with emotion.

"Leah... you're just a shadow of yourself. You can't work like this. It isn't healthy. You aren't healthy."

"No," she spat, voice cracking. "I'm not healthy because when nightmares haunt you every single night, you don't sleep well!"

"Then talk to someone. Open up. Let Cash help you at night."

"He did help," she said, breathing raggedly. "At first. But it was wearing him out. He needs sleep. And so does everyone else! I hate that my nightmares keep waking up the whole house." She squeezed her eyes shut and drew in a sharp breath, trying desperately to steady herself. The truth slipped out before she could stop it.

"I—I've been sneaking out after everyone falls asleep," she admitted quietly. "I sleep in the cabin near the creek, so I don't keep anyone up. Nobody deserves to suffer because of my nightmares."

Jaxon's eyes widened in horror. "Leah, do you know how dangerous that is? There are wild animals, and—"

"I don't need a lecture from you, Jaxon Finlay!" she snapped. "I've lived here all my life, just like you. I know the dangers. I'm careful. I always take my gun."

He raked a hand through his hair, frustrated, trying to reach her.

"Leah, no matter how much you fight me, something has to change. You're turning into your mother."

Her face drained of color the moment the words left his mouth. The volcano erupted instantly.

"How dare you bring my mother into this?" Her voice shook with rage and hurt. "How dare you say something like that? I'm nothing like her!"

"You're more like her than you want to admit," Jaxon said, voice soft but unwavering. "You're letting the grief fester. It's making you miserable and isolated. You can't outrun pain by working until you collapse. You have to face it."

"You don't understand anything," she whispered, voice trembling. "I can't control the nightmares. I don't choose them."

"No," he agreed. "But you can start talking about what happened. You can share what you went through. Let someone carry a piece of the weight with you." His voice gentled even further. "You can only overcome Colt's death by facing it."

"Stop bringing it up," she whispered fiercely. "I don't want to talk about him. Or how he died."

Jaxon saw fresh tears forming and exhaled slowly. He stepped closer, gently wrapping his fingers around her wrists and pulling her toward him.

"I know it's painful," he murmured, "but it's the only way."

"I don't want to talk about it, Jaxon," she cried. "Not with you. Not with Cash. Not with anyone." She tried to turn away again, but he caught her, stopping her escape a second time.

"You can't keep doing this, Leah," he said more forcefully. "Look at your hands. You're torturing yourself. Cash and I won't stand by and let you destroy yourself. We will step in every time we see you hurting yourself this way."

"Leave me alone!" she screamed, tears pouring down her face. "I don't deserve happiness. It's my fault Colt died. I'm to blame."

Jaxon froze. "What?" he breathed. "Why would you think that? None of it was your fault."

"Yes, it was," she sobbed. "I snooped. I went into Heber's room. He caught me. If I hadn't done that, he wouldn't have taken me to the cabin. Colt wouldn't have come looking for me. He wouldn't have—" She choked on the words. She tried to shove him away, but he held her, firm but gentle.

"Leah," he said, staring straight into her eyes, "listen to me. Colt's death. Was. Not. Your. Fault. Heber kidnapped you. He put you in that cellar. He set the trap. And the sheriff told us Heber's been bragging in jail about dropping those snakes on Colt." Jaxon's voice hardened. "Heber murdered his own brother. You played no part in that."

Before she could interrupt, he continued.

"Let me ask you something. If Colt, or anyone else you love, had been kidnapped the way you were, and they snooped around trying to figure out why... would you blame them?"

Leah's breath hitched. She stared at him, thinking hard. After a moment, she shook her head.

"No. I wouldn't."

"Then why," Jaxon said softly, "are you blaming yourself? We have to give ourselves the same compassion we give others."

Silent tears streamed down her face. For the first time, something inside her cracked, not with pain, but with recognition. She was being far harsher to herself than she ever would to another soul. Her thoughts drifted. And for the first time, she allowed herself to relive that terrible day, not with fear, but with honesty. She told him everything.

Jaxon listened without a single interruption, never looking away, never flinching at the emotions pouring out of her. He simply let her speak. Let her feel. Let her exist in her pain. But when her memories turned toward Heber, the cruelty, the terror, and the suffering, she stopped mid-sentence. Her fists clenched. Her jaw tightened.

She saw Cash approaching them in the distance. Panic flickered across her face, panic at the idea of opening up to anyone else. She stepped back immediately, walls snapping back into place. She turned to flee, but Jaxon caught her by the arms.

"Let me go," she hissed, struggling.

"No," he said gently but firmly. "You're holding something back. Let it out."

"It's none of your business!" she snapped. "Leave me alone!"

"Leah," he pleaded, "listen—"

"Go away!" she screamed. "I don't want you here! I don't want anyone here!"

Jaxon tightened his grip, not to hurt, but to anchor her.

"Let it out, Leah. Even the anger. Even the pain."

"It won't help!" she cried. "Nothing will bring Colt back!"

"No," Jaxon said quietly. "But it will help you. And you deserve that."

Her lip trembled. "No, I don't..."

"Yes," he insisted. "You do."

She looked like she might break apart again. Jaxon lowered his voice even further, his eyes never leaving hers.

"Leah," he said softly, "if I were Heber, if the man who hurt you was standing right here, what would you want to tell me?"

Leah stared into Jaxon's eyes. What he saw there made his stomach twist, a fierce and burning outrage and a depth of bleeding pain, he had never witnessed in her before. Her whole expression trembled with it. She looked like she wanted to hit him. Like she wanted to scream in his face until her voice gave out. Like she wanted to hurt him simply because he was standing here alive while Colt was not.

Her pain was so raw it nearly looked like hatred. But instead of letting those emotions loose, Leah tore herself out of his grasp with a violent jerk. She spun around, ran back to the fence line, and seized the heavy mallet she'd been using earlier. The way she lifted it, desperate, shaking, reckless, told Jaxon exactly what she intended. She meant to use it on the only thing she felt she could control. Herself.

"No, Leah!" he shouted. He sprinted to her, snatched the mallet from her hands, and whirled her around. Before she had time to react, he threw her over his shoulder. Leah exploded.

She kicked his chest so hard he grunted, raining her fists against his back as she writhed and fought.

"Put me down! PUT ME DOWN!" she screamed, but Jaxon ignored her, tightening his hold as he carried her away from the tools and the fence line. He didn't stop until he reached Cash, who had just dismounted and was already striding toward them with concern etched across his face.

Jaxon lowered Leah to the ground but didn't release her arms. Her anger had gone from simmering to blazing, and he could feel the tremor of it through her entire body. He was prepared to go as far as he needed, push as hard as he must, to get her to finally let it out.

When Leah tried to bolt again, Cash stepped directly into her path. His eyes met Jaxon's briefly, an unspoken agreement passing between them. Cash understood exactly what Jaxon was doing. And he agreed. Leah was seconds away from breaking.

"Why are you two cornering me?" she cried, voice shrill with emotion. "I want to be left alone! I don't want anyone near me!"

"Leah," Cash said softly but firmly, "stop holding it in. You'll destroy yourself if you keep this up."

"Maybe that's what I want," she snapped, her voice dropping into a guttural whisper. "It's my decision, not yours."

"We won't let you do that," Cash replied, stepping forward. "We love you too much."

His words cracked something in her. Leah tried to sidestep him, but Cash caught her around the waist and pulled her into a tight, immovable embrace. His arms were like iron bars, warm, familiar, unbreakable. And Leah snapped. Her scream tore through the air like lightning. Jaxon didn't rush to release her. Instead, he moved closer, grabbed her legs to keep her from kicking Cash, and held on tight. Leah's fury ignited like wildfire. She thrashed between them, her entire body, a storm of rage and grief. She pushed, kicked, clawed, fought, every buried emotion erupting at once.

For the first time since Colt died, she let out the screams she had been holding in for weeks. It was primal. It was heartbreaking. It was everything she had been too afraid to do and speak. She fought until her strength failed her, until her legs gave out, until her sobs drowned out her screams, until the weight of everything she'd carried alone crushed her. Only then did Cash and Jaxon slowly loosen their hold.

Leah collapsed forward, trembling violently, and Cash caught her instantly, pulling her against his chest. This time she didn't fight him. She simply melted into his embrace, sobbing with nothing held back. Cash held her tightly, rocking her gently, whispering soothing words into her hair while Jaxon stepped back, breathing hard, his eyes glassy with relief and heartbreak. Leah had finally broken open. And for the first time since Colt's death, she wasn't breaking alone.

Her sobbing deepened until it became a full, uncontrollable crying fit. Nothing could stop the flood of tears that had been locked inside her since Colt's death, nothing could dam the torrent of grief she had been choking down for weeks.

The sound was raw. Shattering. But necessary. Slowly, painfully slowly, the crushing pressure in her chest began to ease. Not completely, but enough that she could draw a full breath without feeling as though invisible hands were squeezing the life out of her.

She closed her eyes and let the memories come. Every image. Every scream. Every moment inside that cellar. She allowed her mind to relive the pain with Colt, his voice, his suffering, the helplessness she'd trapped inside until it nearly destroyed her. And when her body instinctively tried to tense up and shut the emotions out again, Leah forced herself to push past the instinct. She didn't want to suffocate in silence anymore.

Jaxon and Cash stood nearby, their expressions tight with worry, but they didn't interrupt. They didn't try to soothe or shush or restrain her anymore. They simply let her pour out every ounce of anguish until she was empty.

Almost an hour passed. Leah's knees buckled, and her breath grew faint. She was trembling violently, close to passing out. Cash reacted instantly. He guided her gently to a fallen tree trunk and sat her down, then wrapped his arm around her shoulders, letting her lean into his chest as if he were the only thing keeping her upright.

For several minutes she just breathed. Shaky, uneven breaths, but breaths that were finally her own. Not choked. Not trapped. When she finally gathered enough strength to look up at the men who had forced her through the storm she'd avoided for far too long, they both gave her warm, encouraging smiles.

"How are you feeling, Leah?" Jaxon asked quietly, his voice soft as a breeze. She gazed up into his handsome, worried face.

"I... I'm not exactly sure," she admitted. "It feels like that horrible pressure in my chest is gone." She touched her sternum lightly. "But now I just feel... sad. Sad and completely drained."

Jaxon nodded with gentle understanding. Cash squeezed her shoulder.

"That's perfectly normal," Cash said. "You just went through all your emotions at once. That would drain anyone. Let's get you home so you can rest. I'll have someone ride out to get Doc Carter. Your hands need treating."

Leah nodded, too exhausted to argue.

"And about your nightmares..." Jaxon added softly, watching her closely. "Let us be there for you, Leah."

She lowered her gaze. "I don't want to keep everyone awake again," she murmured. She tried to sound firm, but she suspected Jaxon could see how her stubbornness was beginning to crack. Cash exchanged a look with Jaxon.

"Then we'll stay with you in the cabin," Cash said simply. "All three of us. That way the others can sleep. We'll wake you when the nightmares start and talk you through them. They will stop eventually. But you're done fighting this alone."

Leah stared at him in shock. "You... you know about me sleeping in the cabin?"

Cash sighed and brushed a fallen strand of hair from her forehead.

"Of course I do. I followed you a few times when you snuck out. Then I stepped back, hoping you'd come to us on your own. It wasn't easy." He paused, voice thick with emotion. "But we can't let you face this by yourself anymore, sweetheart. It's too big for you. Too big for anyone."

Leah's throat tightened. She nodded slowly, letting out a long, trembling sigh as the truth settled in. They were right. She couldn't keep carrying this grief alone. And for the first time since Colt's death, she felt a fragile thread of hope weaving itself through the darkness. Maybe, just maybe, she would learn to breathe again. Maybe one day she could move forward without the weight crushing her. And maybe, with their help, she could finally begin to leave the terrible memories behind.

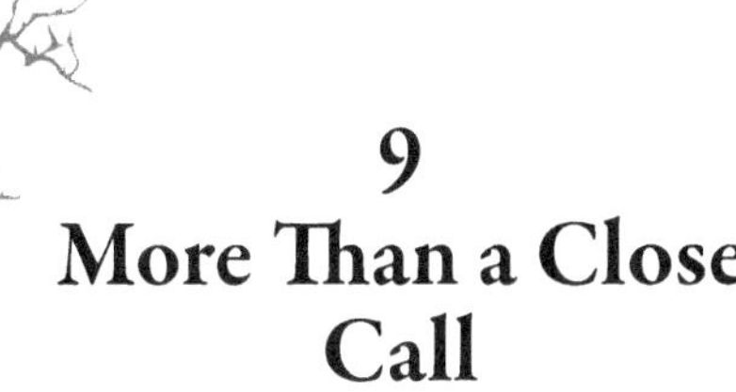

9
More Than a Close Call

"I can't believe how cold it's gotten over the last three days," Leah murmured, rubbing her gloved hands together as she sat atop her horse. Her breath fogged in the air, drifting away on a sharp mountain breeze.

"Well, we're in the mountains," Cash replied gently. "The temperature always drops faster up here."

Leah nodded, hugging her coat tighter around her. Cash scanned the fading light across the rocky slope ahead.

"We should make camp here for the night. It's getting dark, and we've still got a good three hours before we reach the cattle. The trees and rocks will give us some protection from the cold wind."

The cowboys agreed without hesitation. Within minutes, camp bustled, men gathering branches, others building a fire that crackled to life. Sparks drifted upward like tiny fireflies swallowed by the night.

Jaxon and Cash kept a careful eye on Leah as they worked, and she hated how aware she was of it. Hated feeling like she needed constant watching. She had made progress in her grieving, more than she ever imagined, but letting go of Colt... she wasn't ready. She didn't know if she ever would be.

After supper, the men built two more fires, spacing them wide enough for warmth but far enough to avoid catching grass. Leah settled near one, wrapped in blankets, watching the flames dance and pop. The cowboys drifted off quickly, most asleep within minutes, their snores blending with the whistling wind. Leah closed her eyes. Shifted. Breathed deeply. Tried. But she couldn't sleep. Even with the fire, the cold seeped through her layers. And something else, heavier, sharper, pulled on her chest.

With a quiet sigh, she stood, careful not to disturb the others. Wrapping her blanket around her shoulders, she walked away from camp, her boots crunching softly over frosted earth. She didn't stop until she reached the creek. Moonlight shimmered across the narrow stream, the sound of trickling water filling the silent night.

Here, this place, held memories. Her throat tightened instantly. This was where her father had brought her on her very first cattle drive. She remembered sitting on a log beside him, sharing beef jerky and stories as the sun dipped behind the mountains. It was the last place she'd ridden next to him before he passed, the last place she'd felt whole and safe.

A sob lodged in her chest, burning. She missed him. Not just as a father, but as her anchor, her steady voice, her example of strength and kindness. She had always struggled to connect with her mother, and recent changes only deepened the distance between them.

She clenched her eyes shut, trying, and failing, to hold back tears. Too much had happened. Too much pain. Too much loss. And here, alone in the cold, the weight crushed her again. The first tear fell hot on her cheek. Then another. And another. She buried her face in her blanket as sobs tore free, silent at first, then louder, trembling, choked.

She didn't hear the footsteps approaching. But she jerked when a warm hand gently closed around hers. Before she could react, Cash pulled her close, wrapping his arms around her in a fatherly embrace. Her sobs only intensified at the sudden comfort.

"It's okay, Leah," he whispered into her hair. "Just let it all out."

She clung to him, shaking, her tears wetting his coat. Cash held her as if he could shield her from every ache in her heart, rocking her gently the way her father used to.

"I miss Dad so much," she finally whispered, her voice trembling. Cash lifted her chin with gentle fingers, coaxing her to look at him. His expression was warm, understanding, carrying grief of his own.

"I know," he murmured. "I miss your father too, and I always will. He's not gone from our hearts, Leah. Not ever."

And in his embrace, Leah felt safe enough to believe it.

They broke camp at sunrise. The sky was a dull, heavy gray, promising the weather would turn. The cattle grazed in one of the highest pastures on the ridge, the last herd needing to be brought down before winter. If they didn't move them soon, snowstorms could trap them for weeks.

They hadn't ridden an hour before the first cold drops splattered against their coats. Within minutes, rain poured in icy sheets. Everyone pulled their collars high. Even wrapped in slickers, the rain cut like a blade. The wind rocked the horses. The world turned dark and slick.

Leah gritted her teeth. She loved ranching, but she despised storms, not just for the misery, but the danger. Swollen creeks. Mudslides. Flash floods. Storms meant vigilance. One mistake could cost a life.

Three long, freezing hours later, they reached the paddock. The cattle were restless, shifting, snorting, sensing winter's approach. While the cowboys herded them toward the slope, Leah, Jaxon, and Cash circled the area for strays. It didn't take long for Leah to spot a calf stuck deep in the mud near a thicket.

"Hang on, little one," she muttered. She looped her rope around its chest and braced herself. The mud released the calf with a wet, sucking pop, and it stumbled free. Leah wiped the muck from its coat and secured the rope to her saddle horn. She had just tightened the knot when Jaxon approached through the rain.

"Need help?" he called. She shook her head, pushing wet hair from her face.

"No. I'm fine." She swung back into the saddle—and froze. A deep rumbling vibrated through the ground. Not thunder. This traveled low, rolling, growing. Jaxon's head jerked up. Alarm flashed across his face. A flash flood.

"Jaxon!" Leah shouted. "Go help Cash and the others, get the cattle to higher ground!"

"I'm not leaving you alone!"

"We don't have time for this!" she snapped. "Go! I'll get this calf to safety. I'm right behind you!"

"Leah—"

"GO, JAXON!"

Rain hammered harder, drowning out whatever curse he barked back. Fury and fear warred on his face, but he finally turned and dashed toward the herd, shouting orders.

Leah kicked her horse forward, dragging the calf up the rising trail. Mud sucked at her boots each time she dismounted to help it climb. They were nearly level with the herd when the calf suddenly balked, planting its hooves, refusing to budge.

"Come on, we have to hurry!" Leah tugged hard. Nothing. She let out a frustrated cry and yelled a string of curses she hoped no one heard. The flood roar grew louder. Too loud. Like a train barreling toward them. She dismounted again, shoving at the calf's hindquarters. It barely moved.

"Oh, for goodness' sake—MOVE!" She grabbed a sturdy stick and smacked the calf sharply. It bolted. Leah yelled at her horse, who surged uphill after it. She grabbed the saddle horn and scrambled upward, slipping, clawing for purchase as the thunder of water closed in behind her. When she looked up, she saw Jaxon and Cash at the top of the incline, soaked, shouting, gripping her horse's reins while reaching desperately for her.

She pushed harder. Mud slid beneath her. She was almost there. Almost. Then the flash flood hit. Water exploded across the slope like a wall of fury, sweeping around her boots and dragging her downward. Leah gasped as her footing vanished. Her legs flew out from under her as the flood yanked her backward.

"Leah, NO!" Jaxon lunged for her hand, desperate to catch her before the floodwaters swallowed her whole. His fingers grazed her sleeve, but the force of the water ripped her out of reach in an instant. She was gone.

Cash and the other cowboys stood frozen for only a heartbeat, disbelief and horror carved into their faces. Then instinct kicked in.

"GO!" Cash roared.

Several men mounted their horses and charged after the roaring flood, hooves pounding the mud. Others stayed behind, forcing the panicked cattle higher up the mountain to safety. But Jaxon... Jaxon was already far ahead of everyone. Fueled by pure panic, he pushed his horse harder than he ever had, overtaking the floodwaters as they thundered down the ravine. His breath came in ragged gasps, his mind repeating the same plea over and over: Please, God. Not her. Not Leah.

At a sharp bend in the mountainside, where the water was funneled into a violent torrent, Jaxon leapt off his horse before it even stopped. He sprinted to the edge of the racing flood, mud splashing up his legs as he dropped to his knees beside the swollen creek. His eyes scanned the water wildly.

"Come on... come on... where are you?"

A flash of blonde hair. A pale hand. Leah's body surfaced for a split heartbeat before being dragged under again. Jaxon didn't think, he reacted. He plunged his arm into the icy water at the exact moment she was swept past him. His fingers closed around her forearm, and he snarled with effort as he hauled her toward him.

Her body was heavy, limp, terrifyingly limp. With a final, desperate heave, he dragged her onto the muddy bank and pulled her entirely out of the water, cradling her head in his shaking hands. Leah wasn't breathing. Jaxon's heart nearly stopped.

"Leah?" he choked out. "Leah!" Her chest didn't rise. Her lips were blue. For a moment, he froze, paralyzed by fear so sharp it felt like a knife to his ribs. Then instinct surged through him. He laid her flat, lowered his face to hers, and breathed for her, deep, urgent breaths, willing her lungs to respond.

Come on, Leah, come on. Please don't do this to me. Please don't leave me. His panic grew with every second that passed. Every moment felt like a lifetime. Then, she jerked. Coughed. Choked.

Jaxon rolled her onto her side as she retched up water, rubbing her back, whispering broken prayers under his breath. When her coughing eased and her breathing steadied, she slowly rolled onto her back again. Her eyelashes fluttered. Then those familiar blue eyes opened—and stared straight into his.

"Thank you, Jax," she whispered weakly. "I guess that was a close one."

Jaxon let out a choked laugh, part relief, part exasperation, part hysterical aftermath of terror.

"Really?" he said, half laughing, half scolding. "Those are your first words? 'That was a close one?'"

She gave him a tiny, sheepish smile. He shook his head and tried to calm his racing pulse.

"I almost lost you. Don't ever do that to me again."

She rolled her eyes.

"Oh no you don't," he said sharply. "Don't roll your eyes at me, Missy. This could've ended a whole lot worse."

Her expression sobered, and she sighed. "I know. It would help, though, if you didn't worry so much."

Jaxon nearly sputtered. His jaw worked as he swallowed several heated retorts. But before he could speak, Leah reached out and took his hand, her fingers trembling but warm. Her eyes softened, shimmering with gratitude.

"Thank you, Jaxon. I mean it." Her voice was quiet but sincere. "Thank you for rescuing me."

Those blue eyes, full of life and gratitude, hit him like a punch to the chest. All his fear, anger, and panic melted in an instant. He leaned down. And without hesitating, without thinking about anything except that she was alive, he kissed her. Fierce. Desperate. Unrestrained. A kiss born from terror, relief, and something far deeper he could no longer deny.

Leah nearly passed out a second time. Jaxon Finlay, her childhood friend, her constant thorn, her steady presence, was kissing her. Not some accidental brush. Not a desperate gasp-for-air contact. A real kiss. Fierce. Deep. Breath-stealing. She shoved him back with a gasp, her hand flying to her lips as though to make sure they were still attached.

"What are you doing?" she sputtered. "We're friends. You can't just—just kiss me like that!"

She scrambled to her feet, intending to put distance between them. Her legs wobbled like water-soaked twigs, and she pitched forward, straight back into his arms. He caught her easily, the corner of his mouth quirking upward with maddening confidence.

"Sorry," he murmured, not sounding sorry at all. "Guess I got a little carried away." He winked.

A wink. Despite the cold and shock, heat blasted up her neck and into her cheeks.

"Huh, you think?" she sputtered. "Darn it, Jax, you nearly gave me a heart attack! You gave me no warning whatsoever!"

"So..." he drawled, folding his arms. "If I gave you a warning first, kissing you would be allowed?" His grin stretched wider when her cheeks went from pink... to crimson... to full wildfire.

"I don't think I have to answer that," she snapped. She tried to give him her fiercest death stare, but unfortunately, it only made his grin widen. Before he could escalate his teasing, thunderous hoofbeats approached. Cash dismounted so fast his horse barely had time to stop. He swept Leah into a crushing hug.

"Thank goodness you're alive," Cash breathed shakily. "I swear you're the reason my hair is turning gray."

He lifted her chin, his rugged face softening, as he searched her expression. Leah gave him a watery smile.

"Sorry," she whispered. "I didn't mean to scare you."

"But you did scare us," Jaxon shot out suddenly, his voice sharp as flint. Leah spun around at the anger in his tone. His eyes stormed with emotion, fear, frustration, relief, and something fierce enough to make her breath hitch. "Why do you have to be so dang hard-headed?" he snapped. "We know you're tough. You don't have to prove anything by risking your life!"

Her irritation flared instantly. "I wasn't trying to prove anything, Jaxon Finlay. Being a rancher comes with danger."

"Why can't you let one of us men handle the risky jobs? Your pride is so out of control."

"That calf had nothing to do with pride! Ugh, you're impossible!" she exclaimed, glaring at him. Her frustration only seemed to set him further on edge. He grabbed her hand, tugged her toward him, and, with no warning whatsoever, tossed her over his broad shoulder.

"Put me down right now!"

"No."

"Jaxon Finlay, you put me down this instant!" She hammered his back with her fists, furious and mortified, as he marched toward his horse.

"You are the most stubborn girl I've ever met," he growled. "I already feel bad for the man who marries you someday."

That one hit harder than he realized. Leah stiffened. She forced herself not to flinch, but her eyes stung. She pushed out of his hold the moment her boots hit the ground.

"If you despise me so much," she said quietly, painfully, "why did you bother pulling me out of the water? Why didn't you just let me drown?" Her voice cracked. She blinked hard, but the tears came anyway. Jaxon froze, his face collapsing into regret.

"Leah, wait—"

She turned her back before he could speak.

"Okay, you two, that's enough," Cash interrupted, stepping between them. "We are not doing this out here. Leah nearly died, and we're all strung tighter than barbed wire. Let's not say anything else we'll regret."

Jaxon blew out a long breath. "Leah... I didn't mean what I said."

"It's fine, Jaxon," she mumbled, but she didn't look at him. Her voice was small. Tired. Raw.

She tried to mount his horse, but Jaxon gently caught her hand and urged her to face him. She refused, shaking her head.

"Leah," he whispered, "please look at me."

Her throat tightened. "I'm fine," she rasped. "Let's just get back to the cattle."

He cupped her chin and turned her toward him before she could pull away. Tears burst into her eyes instantly.

"I'm so sorry," he said softly, his voice thick with regret. "I never meant to hurt you."

"It's not your fault," she whispered, shaking her head as fresh emotion welled behind her eyes. "I'm sorry I'm such a silly goose, crying over everything lately." She tried to laugh, but her breath hitched instead.

Her chest tightened as old memories rose, unbidden, sharp.

"You just... reminded me of something," she murmured, pressing her palm lightly to her sternum as though steadying the ache beneath. "Dad and I had an argument on my last cattle drive with him. Almost the same words you used." Her voice wavered. "I said things I shouldn't have. Things he didn't deserve. I always meant to apologize, but..." Her throat tightened, closing around the words. "I never got the chance. And then he was gone." A trembling breath escaped her. "This... it just brought everything back." She blinked hard, as if fighting to stay present, to keep from drowning in the grief that still lived just under her ribs.

Her voice trembled, and she leaned into him, letting herself rest against his chest. He wrapped his arms around her gently, steadying her until she could breathe again. When she finally looked up, her blue eyes were glassy. Vulnerable.

"I wasn't trying to be difficult earlier," she whispered. "I just didn't want to lose a single one of Dad's cattle. This was the last herd he helped drive up."

Jaxon's gaze softened with tenderness so warm it almost broke her again. He brushed her tears away with his thumbs, then pressed a slow, reverent kiss to her forehead.

"I know," he murmured. "And I shouldn't have snapped. It just... scared me. The idea of losing you." He let out a shaky laugh. "Truth is, we've known each other our whole lives, Leah. So yeah, I know how stubborn you are."

Cash stepped forward and drew Leah into his arms, giving her a fatherly hug that steadied her heart.

"Leah, your dad knew exactly who you were and how you loved," he said gently. "There isn't a thing in this world you could've done to make him love you less. Not then. Not ever." He paused, his eyes twinkling. "Now, I'm not saying you should go around killing people in cold blood, but even that wouldn't have stopped Mitch Johnson from loving you."

Leah let out a trembling laugh, burying her face against his chest for a moment.

"Thank you, Cash," she whispered.

He kissed the top of her head before letting her go, leaving her standing between the two men who loved her in different, complicated ways. The tension faded, but a new, quieter heat sparked in its place, especially when Jaxon's eyes met hers again. Something had shifted. And they both felt it.

Jaxon watched her reach for his saddle, determined as ever, though her limbs trembled from exhaustion and cold. Her skin was pale, her damp hair clinging to her cheeks, and he could see the subtle shivers running through her body. She was weaker than she wanted anyone to notice, especially him. Before she could hoist herself up, he gently caught her by the arm.

"Leah," he murmured, "you're freezing." Without waiting for her protest, he shrugged off his coat. The instant he wrapped it around her shoulders, her breath hitched. Warmth enveloped her, and she looked up at him with a soft, grateful smile, small, but more beautiful than anything he'd seen all day. Something in his chest clenched.

Before she could turn away, he slid his hands around her waist. In one smooth, effortless motion, he lifted her completely off the ground. Leah gasped, her palms bracing against his shoulders in surprise.

"Jax—!"

"Just hold on," he said, voice low with a tenderness he didn't bother to hide. He placed her gently in the saddle, as though she were made of something fragile and precious. She blinked down at him, wide-eyed, cheeks warming beneath the cold. Jaxon swung up behind her, settling with practiced ease. His arms came around her naturally, not trapping her, but forming a protective barrier against the biting air. She felt the heat of him through her back, solid and steady, and a small shiver, not from the cold, moved through her.

Cash mounted his own horse beside them, his voice gruff with lingering worry. "Let's get her home. She needs warm clothes before the next storm rolls in."

Jaxon tightened his hold just slightly, his breath brushing her ear as he murmured, “Lean back if you need to. I’ve got you.”

Leah nodded faintly, resting more of her weight against him as they guided the horses down the trail, his coat wrapped around her, his arms steadying her, and his heartbeat a quiet, reassuring rhythm at her back.

10
Inheritance Written in Blood

"You were *so* lucky, Leah. If Jaxon hadn't gotten to you in time—" Robyn stopped short, her eyes widening at the look on her best friend's face.

"I know," Leah cut in quickly. "I'm aware it could've ended badly... but it didn't." Her tone was too dismissive, and Robyn's brows inched upward.

"I bet my big brother nearly lost his mind with relief when he saw you breathing again."

Leah gave a small, weak smile but didn't lift her gaze. She kept brushing her horse in tight, repetitive strokes, pretending to focus on a patch of hair that didn't need cleaning. Robyn spotted the faint pink rising in Leah's cheeks and narrowed her eyes.

"What?" she demanded. "Wasn't he relieved?"

Leah hesitated just long enough for Robyn to grin triumphantly.

"He kissed me," Leah muttered, barely audible. Robyn gasped so loudly the horse jerked its head.

"Jaxon *kissed* you? Like, a real kiss? On the mouth?" Her voice pitched into a squeak.

"Will you keep your voice down?" Leah hissed. Robyn only grinned wider, lit up like Christmas morning.

"So...?" Robyn leaned closer, eyes sparkling. "Is he a good kisser?"

"Robyn!"

"What? It's a valid question."

"I don't want to talk about it," Leah declared, firm and flustered.

Robyn scoffed. "Oh, please. You can't toss a stick of dynamite like that at me and then walk away. I want *details*."

"There are no details," Leah muttered. "He was caught up in the moment. He scared me half to death. I wasn't prepared, mentally or emotionally, and he shouldn't have done it."

"Why not?"

"Robyn..." Leah groaned. "Jax and I are friends. *Friends.* We've known each other since childhood. That's what we are. We're not courting, and I don't feel that way about him."

Robyn crossed her arms, unimpressed. "Are you sure? Because friends turning into more is... extremely common."

Leah shot her a look. "Stop."

"Why are you so stubborn about this?" Robyn pressed. "Are you scared of falling for my brother?"

"I am not falling for him," Leah snapped. "And I don't want to have this conversation. I already regret telling you anything. Are you buying into the gossiping tongues of Hoopa Valley?"

"This isn't about gossip," Robyn said calmly. "This is about the way your face turned pink the second I said his name."

Leah's eyes narrowed dangerously. "That means nothing."

"Mm-hmm." Robyn lifted a brow. "Then why not just admit you have feelings for my handsome brother?"

"Because I don't," Leah shot back. "Drop it. Please."

Robyn, of course, did not drop it. "What are you going to do if he falls in love with you? Turn him down because you're terrified of your own feelings?"

"I'm not scared."

"Leah."

"I'm not," she exhaled sharply, rubbing her forehead with the back of her wrist. "I don't know what I'd do. I don't want to lose his friendship. And if we tried something and it failed... we'd both get hurt."

Robyn's expression softened. "Or," she said gently, "you could gain something extraordinary."

Leah rolled her eyes, though her shoulders sagged.

"You'd have a man who already knows you," Robyn continued softly. "Someone who understands ranching, this land, this life. Someone who would stand beside you in everything. And... you'd be my sister."

Leah's throat tightened. "I'm not... We're not... Can we not do this right now?"

Robyn sighed. "Fine. But this conversation isn't over. I'm only postponing it."

"I know," Leah muttered. "Unfortunately."

Robyn laughed and slung an arm around her shoulders, while Leah tried very hard not to blush again at the memory of Jaxon's mouth on hers.

"Hello? Anyone home?"

"In the stable!" Leah called, brushing hay off her skirt as she stepped outside. Her face lit instantly when she saw the man leaning under the old oak tree, hat tipped back, grin warm and familiar.

"Uncle David!" She ran to him, and he caught her in a fierce, fatherly hug.

"Goodness gracious," David said, holding her at arm's length as if inspecting her for damage. "You get more stunning every time I see you." He turned her slowly. "Have the young men started lining up yet? Surely a girl as beautiful as you must have at least half a dozen suitors."

Robyn, wearing the smuggest grin in Hoopa Valley, chimed in, "No suitor she'll admit to."

Leah pinched her sharply.

David laughed. "Hello, Robyn."

"Good to see you again, David," she replied sweetly.

He turned back to Leah, eyes twinkling. "So... who, exactly, was your best friend referring to?"

Leah shot Robyn the deadliest glare of her life. "Nobody. There is no suitor. Robyn is teasing me. So, what brings you here?"

David exchanged a knowing look with Robyn at the swift subject change but let it go.

"Unfortunately," he said, humor fading, "I'm not here for a happy reason. Preston Burton is expected tomorrow. And he'll want to meet with you."

Leah frowned. "Who is Preston Burton?"

"A snake of a lawyer hired by Milton Rowland."

Leah's eyes flashed. "Is this about our ranch? Or are they planning to kidnap me again?"

"Kidnap you again?" David stared at her, stunned.

"Yes." Her voice was steady, cold. "I found a letter in Heber's room. Signed by Milton Rowland. Heber took it before I could show anyone, so I can't prove it... but I know what I saw."

David rubbed his forehead. "If they orchestrated your kidnapping, they won't try again so soon. Too risky."

"How did you find out Burton was coming?" Leah asked.

"I've been watching this situation for a while. Your father and I prepared for possibilities. He always expected trouble. Burton showing up fits the pattern."

"Will you stay with us tonight?" Leah asked hopefully.

David shook his head. "No, and don't tell your mother I was here. I don't want her panicking if Burton doesn't appear, or if Milton is pushing harder than we expected."

"Should I tell her about the kidnapping?"

"Have you told *anyone*?" he asked sharply.

Leah shook her head. "No. I actually forgot about the letter until you mentioned Milton's name."

"That's for the best," David murmured. "Your mother... Patricia has always been sensitive. Losing Mitch broke something in her."

Leah swallowed. "She's changed a lot since Dad died. And she's... engaged. To the sheriff."

David's eyebrows shot up. "Is she now? And how do you feel about that?"

"I don't like it," Leah whispered. "It feels like a betrayal. And the timing is strange. Too fast. Too sudden."

David nodded slowly. “I agree.” He squeezed her shoulder. “I’d better get going. I’ll be back tomorrow. And Leah, tell Cash everything I told you. He needs to know.”

She hugged him tightly before he mounted his horse and rode off. Robyn watched him disappear, worry etched across her face. When she looked at Leah again, her voice trembled.

“Be careful, Leah. I don’t like the sound of this at all.”

Leah exhaled. “It *does* sound scary,” she admitted. “But Uncle David will be here. And Cash. I’ll be all right.”

Robyn didn’t seem convinced, but she stepped closer, linking her arm through Leah’s.

“Just promise me you’ll be careful,” she whispered. Leah nodded, though a knot of unease had already begun to form low in her stomach.

The loud, insistent knock at the front door made Leah’s stomach tighten. It was time. She glanced at Cash. He gave her a slow, steadying smile, the kind he used whenever she was about to walk into something ugly.

Her mother sat stiffly in the armchair by the fireplace, hands twisting nervously in her lap. Patricia didn’t know the nature of the meeting, but she sensed its weight. Leah wished Mildred were home. Her aunt’s calm presence always steadied her mother.

Leah inhaled deeply and opened the door. A tall, rigid man stood on the porch, his polished black coat repelling sunlight like armor. His expression was carved from stone.

"May I help you?" Leah asked, feigning polite curiosity, pretending she didn't know exactly who he was and why he had come.

"Are you Miss Leah Johnson?"

"I am. What can I do for you?"

"My name is Preston Burton," he said, voice clipped and cold. "I'm here to discuss legal matters pertaining to this ranch, as directed by the Will of your late father."

Leah's jaw tightened. "The body hasn't been recovered. As of now, my father is missing, not deceased. And our family attorney is handling all matters concerning his Will."

A flicker of irritation cut across Burton's face.

"May I come in?"

Leah stepped aside without replying. He entered, eyes sweeping the room with calculated interest. Cash rose from the dining table, posture straight, alert. Ruby, pretending to dust a shelf, froze mid-motion. Patricia sat rigid, pale, white-knuckled.

"I believe introductions are in order," Burton said stiffly.

"Certainly," Leah replied, voice calm but firm. "This is our foreman and my father's business partner, Mr. Doug Cashley."

Burton shook Cash's hand with visible reluctance.

"This is my mother, Patricia."

"My condolences, Mrs. Johnson," Burton said immediately. Leah nearly snapped at the performative sympathy, but Cash's hand brushing her arm reminded her to hold back.

"And who is this?" Burton asked, gesturing at Ruby as if she were a misplaced object. Leah's temper flared, but Ruby beat her to it. She dipped into a crooked curtsy.

"Oh, don't fret 'bout plain ol' me," she chirped, sweet as honey on hot bread. "Just the housekeeper askin' somethin' for Mrs. Johnson. I'll be outta your hair quicker'n a jackrabbit." She winked at Leah before slipping out. Burton's lip curled in annoyance.

"Will Mr. Cashley stay?" he pressed.

"Of course," Leah answered coolly. "He's part of this ranch and the business."

"I was hoping to speak with just you and your mother. Privately."

"That's not going to happen," Leah said, too quickly. Patricia opened her mouth, likely to comply, but Leah cut her off. "If you have something to say, you'll say it in front of all of us."

Burton's nostrils flared. Before he could argue, another knock jolted the room. Leah opened the door and nearly sagged in relief.

"Uncle Dave," she exclaimed brightly. "What a pleasant surprise! What brings you here?"

David Smith laughed under his breath and pulled her into a warm hug.

"Passing through for business and thought I'd visit. You're looking well." He squeezed her hand, a subtle reassurance, then stepped inside. Patricia stared at him, stunned. Only then did Leah notice Sheriff Scott Bailey behind him. Her relief faltered.

"Sheriff Bailey," Leah asked carefully, "are you here to visit my mom?"

"No," David answered smoothly before Bailey could speak. "Scott told me they're engaged, and since we've all known each other for years, I invited him along."

Burton bristled. "Excuse me, but we are in the middle of a very important meeting."

David blinked innocently. "Oh? Am I interrupting?"

"Actually, no," Leah said quickly. "It's good you're here, since you're our family attorney." She turned to Burton, watching his expression twist. "Mr. Burton claims he's here on legal business. And you know everything concerning our ranch."

"He's your attorney *and* your uncle?" Burton asked, baffled.

"No," Leah replied. "He's my godfather."

"How fortunate," David added lightly. "And since this concerns the ranch, it's good Sheriff Bailey is here as well. Considering he's to be married to Patricia, he'll certainly need to be informed."

Cash, Leah, and David all watched Burton, waiting for the crack in his composure.

Burton growled, "Let's begin."

"Milton Rowland hired me," Burton began, "to inform you that he has received word he is to inherit this business and ranch. You are refusing to honor your late father's wishes."

"There is no inheritance for Mr. Rowland," Leah snapped. "My father's Will is secured in multiple locations. Mr. Smith and Mr. Cashley signed as witnesses."

Burton folded his hands, smirking. "Your father contacted Mr. Rowland and me last year. He signed an official document leaving the ranch to him."

Leah scoffed. "Fabricating documents, are you? Just like the other corrupt attorney did months ago?"

"How *dare* you?" Burton hissed, eyes flashing with fury.

"You expect us to believe my father, who trusted no outsider with important affairs, suddenly reached out to two men he'd never met?" Leah's voice sharpened. "Something tells me you've been paid handsomely to be here. But you're wasting our time."

"Miss Johnson," Burton sneered, "your arrogance is blinding—"

"My arrogance?" Leah shot to her feet. "You came here to steal what doesn't belong to you."

He leaned in, voice low and venomous.

"Be very careful. Not taking this seriously could become dangerous for you."

A cold shiver ran up Leah's spine. There was hatred in his eyes, and malice, but she refused to cower.

"Oh, threats now?" Leah retorted. "Because I won't bow to you?"

Cash and Sheriff Bailey stiffened, rage simmering. Before the situation exploded, David stood, voice calm but edged with steel.

"That's enough, Mr. Burton. You're out of line. Your reputation precedes you, intimidation, threats, manipulation. These tactics are unethical and illegal. If you continue, I'll take you to court myself. And before you try threatening me, remember, we are all witnesses. You won't win."

Burton's face reddened to a dangerous shade.

"We shall see about that," he spat. His gaze snapped back to Leah. "And you all might want to keep an eye on your precious little princess. My client does not play games." He stood abruptly. "And just so you know, Leah Johnson," he added cruelly, "your father is dead. I met with the sheriff in Sacramento. They pulled his rotting body from the bottom of a lake."

Leah's world collapsed. The blood drained from her face. Cash stepped closer, barely restrained from hitting Burton.

"You're lying!" Leah cried, voice cracking.

"Am I?" Burton snarled. He slammed a silver pocket watch, a signet ring, and a pair of cufflinks onto the table. The pocket watch flipped open with a sharp click, revealing her father's initials.

Leah's knees buckled. Cash caught her before she fell. Burton's smile turned monstrous.

"I suppose you're not as tough as you pretend. Did you think Daddy would come home and protect you from the bad men?"

"GET OUT!" Cash roared. Sheriff Bailey and David stepped forward, ready to drag Burton out by force.

But Burton moved first. He whirled, gun in hand. A shot rang out. Patricia screamed. Bailey fired at the same instant, his bullet slamming into Burton's leg. The man collapsed with a howl, dropping his weapon. Before he could reach for it again, Bailey had him on the floor, cuffed and helpless. Burton glared up at Leah with pure hatred. But for the first time since opening the door, she didn't look away.

Leah had followed the entire exchange with growing nausea, the room tilting as Preston Burton's poisonous words wrapped around her like a tightening rope. Her heartbeat thundered in her ears. Shock, grief, and fury churned in her chest until she thought she might be sick. Then the shot rang out.

A searing pain tore through her upper arm, sharp and hot. Leah gasped, a broken, ragged sound, and instinctively clutched the wound as warmth spread beneath her fingers. She swayed, vision blurring at the edges. Darkness pulsed at the corners of the room. Cash saw her falter first.

"Leah!" he barked, lunging toward her.

Her knees buckled. The floor tilted. With a faint moan she couldn't hold back, she collapsed against Cash, her body limp and trembling. He caught her instantly and lowered her onto the sofa just as the last threads of consciousness slipped away.

"Easy, sweetheart... I've got you," he murmured, pressing a steadying hand to her cheek before grabbing a nearby cloth. Sheriff Scott Bailey turned from where he'd cuffed Burton, his expression carved with fury.

"I'll take this coward to the jailhouse," he said, hauling Burton upright by the collar. "And I'm sending Doc Carter here immediately." His gaze flicked to Leah, sharp with guilt and anger. "I'll return as soon as I can."

David nodded tightly. Cash did too, though he never removed his eyes from Leah, already pressing a folded cloth against her bleeding arm.

Bailey shoved the limping, cursing Burton out the door with far less gentleness than the law typically allowed. The moment they crossed the threshold, silence fell, heavy, trembling, broken only by Leah's shallow breaths and Cash's panicked whisper: "Stay with us, Leah... stay with us."

Patricia hadn't moved since the gun went off. She sat rigid in her armchair, hands clamped around the wooden rests, her face devoid of color. Her eyes were wide and vacant, fixed on the doorway as if the horror were still unfolding there. She didn't blink. Didn't speak. Barely breathed.

Cash glanced at her, alarm tightening his jaw.

"Patricia," he called gently. No reaction. Not even a flinch. "She's in shock," he muttered, raising his voice. "Ruby! Ruby, get down here!"

Footsteps thundered overhead. Ruby flew down the stairs within seconds, braid half undone, face chalk white. She skidded to a stop in the doorway, eyes sweeping the chaos, Leah unconscious on the sofa, blood seeping into the cloth in Cash's hand, Patricia trembling silently, David pacing like a caged bear.

"Oh, my word," Ruby breathed. "What happened?" She rushed forward, hands shaking, expression torn between terror and fury. Her gaze kept darting to the open door as though expecting Burton to storm back inside. Cash shifted just enough to let her see Leah but kept firm pressure on the wound.

"Burton fired a shot. Leah's hit. Sheriff Bailey got him, but—"

Ruby gasped, hand flying to her mouth. "Oh no... oh, that wicked man!"

Cash shook his head. "Right now, Patricia needs you. She's not responding."

Ruby tore her gaze from Leah and turned to Patricia. The woman sat stiff as carved stone, fingers digging into the arms of the chair, breathing shallow and uneven. Ruby knelt beside her, placing a steadying hand over Patricia's white-knuckled grip.

"Patricia? Honey... look at me," she whispered softly. Nothing. No blink. No flicker. She was gone inside herself, swallowed by fear, grief, and the shattering blow of hearing her fiancé fire his weapon and her daughter get shot in her own home. Ruby swallowed hard and glanced at Cash and David.

"She's in full shock," she murmured. "We need to calm her before her mind fractures worse than it already has."

Cash nodded grimly. "Doc Carter will tend to Leah, but Patricia will need him too."

Leah groaned faintly, drawing their attention back to her. Ruby squeezed Patricia's hand again, determined.

"Come back to us, Patricia," she whispered. "We need you. Leah needs you."

Patricia's eyes flickered, barely, but it was a start.

Leah's sleeve was soaked through, crimson spreading down the fabric in a slow, frightening bloom. Cash and David worked quickly, steady hands and grim expressions, while Ruby focused on Patricia, speaking softly to keep her anchored.

The front door was still hanging open—that was how Jaxon and Robyn managed to burst in without knocking. Robyn froze only a moment, long enough to take in Leah bleeding on the sofa, before letting out a sob and rushing to her friend's side.

Jaxon skidded to a halt. His eyes locked on Leah, and the sheer panic in them made her chest tighten even in her haze. He looked like the ground had vanished beneath him. Cash grimly tore away the blood-soaked sleeve of Leah's blouse.

"Robyn!" he barked, a man hanging on by a thread. "Kitchen. Bowl of water. Clean cloth. Hurry."

Robyn nodded frantically and sprinted away. David leaned over Leah from the opposite side of the sofa, jaw clenched tight. Leah forced her eyes open. Everything hurt. Her arm throbbed with a deep, scorching burn, but the ache in her chest, the terror, the grief, the shock, was so much worse. Tears welled despite her effort to swallow them back.

Jaxon dropped to his knees beside her. He took her uninjured hand in both of his, gentle, but firm enough to anchor her. Then he bent and pressed his lips to her forehead.

"We're here, Leah," he whispered. "You're not alone." His voice trembled. That alone nearly undid her. Cash examined the wound, wiping blood away with torn fabric.

"Looks like an intense grazing shot," he muttered.

David exhaled sharply. "Thank goodness Scott reacted fast. I hope they hang that ba—"

"Here! Water and cloth!" Robyn burst in again, cutting him off. She handed the bowl to Cash, sloshing water onto the floor, then dropped to Leah's side, stroking damp hair from her forehead with trembling fingers.

Leah winced as Cash pressed the clean cloth to her arm. Jaxon didn't let go of her hand. Not once. David gently stroked her head, though his eyes burned with fury. The room fell quiet except for Leah's uneven breathing and Ruby's soft voice coaxing Patricia back from the brink.

Surrounded by trembling friends, furious protectors, and the fading smell of gunpowder, Leah realized one thing with startling clarity: She was loved. Fiercely. Unconditionally. And every person in that room would fight tooth and nail to keep her safe.

11
An Heiress in the Crosshairs

Doc Carter and Sheriff Bailey entered together, the door banging lightly against the wall as they stepped inside. The tension in the house was thick enough to choke on. Scott's expression was grim but composed. Doc Carter's face was tight with urgency.

"I've already contacted the authorities in Sacramento," Scott announced as he crossed the room. His voice was clipped and controlled, but the fury simmering underneath was unmistakable. "They've been informed about the incident with Preston Burton. They'll take it from here."

David and Cash nodded in acknowledgment. Doc Carter's attention was already locked on Leah. He moved toward her with brisk efficiency, setting his medical bag on the table beside the sofa.

"Gentlemen," he said firmly to Cash, David, and Jaxon, "I need space to work. Step outside for now."

All three men hesitated, unwilling to leave Leah for even a moment. It wasn't until Doc Carter fixed them with a pointed stare that they exhaled and complied, though reluctantly. Jaxon's hand lingered on Leah's for a heartbeat longer before he followed the others into the dining room.

Robyn stayed exactly where she was, one hand on Leah's uninjured arm, the other ready to assist. Ruby remained too, determined to keep Patricia from spiraling again. Patricia looked marginally better, less glassy-eyed, no longer frozen, but her complexion was still ghost-white. Her hands were clasped so tightly together it looked as though she were holding her composure in place by force.

Ruby knelt beside her, murmuring softly, "You're all right, Patricia. Leah's in good hands now. Breathe with me."

Doc Carter leaned over Leah, assessing the wound with a practiced eye.

"It's a deep, but clean graze," he muttered, relief slipping quietly into his tone. "Painful, but not life-threatening. Still, we're going to clean it and stitch it properly."

Leah tried to sit up straighter, but the dizziness returned, making her sway. Robyn steadied her instantly. Doc Carter glanced over his shoulder at Patricia, whose eyes were fixed on her daughter with a look torn between terror and disbelief.

"Mrs. Johnson," he said gently, "your daughter is going to be just fine."

Patricia blinked rapidly, swallowed hard, and nodded, though her voice remained trapped somewhere in her throat. The doctor turned back to Leah, rolling up his sleeves.

"All right, sweetheart," he said softly. "Let's take care of you."

Cash rubbed a hand over his face, looking from David to Jaxon to Scott. His expression was grim, more serious than anyone had ever seen from him.

"Leah can't stay here," he said quietly, though with absolute conviction. "My guess is that Patricia's brother and father will arrive within the next few days, and we should not play with fire."

Jaxon let out a humorless snort.

"You do realize she won't go willingly, right? To get her out of Hoopa Valley, we'd practically have to tie her up and toss her into the stagecoach ourselves."

David gave a grim nod. "He's right. Leah will fight tooth and nail. And I don't blame her."

Scott folded his arms. "What about Patricia? Won't she be in danger too?"

David answered before Cash could.

"No. They know she's... fragile. She'll hand over anything the moment someone pressures her. That's why Mitch put Leah in his Will. He knew Patricia couldn't stand up to men like the Rowlands." He paused. "Leah is the one they fear. The one who questions. The one who pushes back. She's the threat."

No one argued. A heavy silence settled until Cash cleared his throat.

"So... how do we handle this?"

David leaned forward, elbows braced on his knees.

"Leah can stay with me. I'll be in town for a few more days. If the Rowlands show up, I'll take her with me immediately."

Scott lifted a brow. "She won't agree to that."

David's lips curved into a wry half-smile.

"Which is why we're not giving her the option. Jaxon's right, she'll fight us. So, we have to surprise her. Gentle… but firm. We'll get her out before she knows what's happening."

Cash nodded slowly. "Patricia can be told afterward that Leah's safe, but not where she is. For her own protection."

Jaxon tapped his fingers against his thigh.

"We need someone who can convince Leah she's leaving voluntarily. Otherwise, we'll end up with a full-out wrestling match on our hands."

Cash snapped his fingers. "Robyn."

Everyone turned toward him.

"Robyn is desperate to keep Leah safe," Cash said. "She can convince her to take a short trip. Some time away from the ranch to clear her head."

David nodded. "And she can pack Leah's clothes without raising suspicion."

"That's smart," Scott agreed.

Jaxon straightened suddenly, eyes brightening.

"Robyn's birthday is next week. She could use that as an excuse. A girls' trip to Sacramento, celebrate, shop, relax. Leah wouldn't see it coming."

Everyone nodded, the plan taking shape.

Cash let out a slow breath. "Good. We'll do it that way." He glanced toward the sitting room, where Leah rested, pale and shaken. "Patricia will be fine here. Ruby and I will keep watch. The Rowlands won't see her as a threat."

David's expression hardened. "But they'll come for Leah."

Cash nodded. "And we'll be ready."

Dr. Carter opened the door a few minutes later and motioned for everyone to come back inside. His sleeves were still rolled up, and there was a faint sheen of perspiration on his brow from the work he'd just finished.

"Just like you said," he reported to Cash and David, "it was a fairly deep grazing shot. Painful, but not dangerous. Leah was lucky." He turned toward her with a warm, reassuring look, one meant to soothe after the horror she had endured, but Leah couldn't muster even the smallest smile. Her eyes were hollow, her breathing shallow, her mind miles away. Her voice came out barely above a whisper.

"May I get up?"

"Yes," Dr. Carter said gently, "but remember what we discussed, Leah." He gave her a firm, almost fatherly look. "No ranch work. No heavy lifting. No riding hard. No physical activity of any kind for several days. Let that arm heal."

She nodded, though her expression remained distant, numb. Robyn slid an arm around her, steadying her as she rose. The movement made Leah suck in a quiet breath, but she didn't complain.

"You did good," Robyn murmured softly. Leah didn't answer. She allowed herself to be guided toward the hallway, her steps slow and unsteady. Dr. Carter and the others watched her leave, Robyn at her side, ready to catch her if she wavered.

As the door closed behind them, the room fell into a heavy silence. Everyone knew Leah was walking away not just from the doctor's care... but from the shattering truth Burton had forced her to face.

"How the hell can something like that happen?" Riley Carter exploded suddenly, his normally calm voice echoing off the walls. "We can't have strangers waltzing into town and shooting at people!" His temper flared hot, jaw clenched so tightly the muscle jumped.

Scott Bailey exhaled a weary sigh, bracing a hand on the doorframe.

"The culprit is already in custody. He's locked up and not going anywhere. I told my deputy to tend to his leg wound until you can look at him, Riley."

The young physician took a deep breath, still rattled from everything he'd walked into.

"Leah didn't say much," he murmured, shaking his head, "but anyone with eyes could see she's suffering from more than a gunshot. She looked... broken."

David stepped forward, anger simmering in his eyes.

"Burton claimed her father's body had been found. Then he tossed Mitch's belongings onto the table like poker chips. No warning. No preparation. He hurled the truth at her and watched her fall apart."

"My word..." Dr. Carter's shoulders sagged. His brows knit with horror and sympathy. "Hasn't that girl suffered enough?" He let out a sharp breath. "That man is a real piece of prairie coal."

Scott arched a brow. "You'll still treat him fairly."

"Oh, I'll treat him," Riley retorted bitterly. "But perhaps making his wound treatment extra unpleasant will teach him some manners." Though the words held dark humor, no one missed the protective fury burning in his eyes. Burton had crossed a line, and Riley Carter had every intention of ensuring he regretted it.

"Do you want to talk about it, Leah?" Robyn's voice was gentle, but the worry in her eyes was unmistakable. She hovered close, hands twisting nervously. Leah didn't look up. She simply shook her head, slowly, weary, resigned.

"I have nothing to say," she whispered. "My hope that my dad might still be alive was crushed today... and the Rowlands are still after our ranch and land." Her expression didn't crack or tremble. It wasn't natural stillness, it was forced, rigid, held in place by sheer will. "Talking about it won't change anything."

Robyn's heart ached at the sight. Leah's face might have been carved from stone, but the shimmer in her eyes betrayed the storm beneath, grief, fear, exhaustion all battling for dominance.

"Would you please give me some time alone?" Leah continued quietly. "I just... I need some time to myself."

"Leah..." Robyn stepped closer, desperate to help somehow.

"I know you're worried," Leah said, finally lifting her head. Her blue eyes, usually bright with fire, were dull with heartbreak. "And I appreciate it. I do. But there's nothing you can say or do that will make this pain disappear." Her voice cracked just once before she forced it steady again. "Please, Robyn... just give me a little space?"

Robyn nodded, her throat tightening. She slipped her arms around Leah, pulling her into a soft, lingering hug. Leah didn't hug back at first, but after a few seconds, her fingers curled weakly into Robyn's sleeve, quiet gratitude for the only comfort she could bear.

"As much as I want to stay," Robyn murmured into her hair, "I understand."

Leah whispered a barely audible "thank you," and when Robyn finally stepped back, she did so slowly and reluctantly, granting Leah the space she'd asked for, without taking her love or concern with her.

As soon as Robyn disappeared from sight, Leah bolted. Ignoring Dr. Carter's strict orders, ignoring the throb in her injured arm. She didn't care. She had to move, had to run, had to do something, or her chest would burst open from the pressure strangling her heart. Every breath scraped like broken glass. The pain was too much. Far too much. She ran until the buildings disappeared behind her and the land and forest opened. The cold air stung her lungs, but she didn't stop. Her boots pounded across the uneven ground, carrying her toward the one place her feet always seemed to lead her when life became unbearable. The family cemetery.

The moment the small white fence came into view, her strength gave out. She slowed, stumbling the last few steps until she fell to her knees beside her aunt's grave. Soon, far too soon, there would be a marker for her father here. The thought cleaved her heart in two.

A raw, heart-ripping sob tore from her throat. Leah sank into the grass, her palms pressing into the earth as if she could anchor herself against the grief threatening to swallow her whole. She leaned back against the old wooden fence behind the grave marker, solid and cold against her spine.

Then she folded forward, burying her face in her arms, and finally let the tears come, violent, shaking sobs she had been holding at bay for hours, maybe for months.

"I can't... I can't do this," she whispered into her sleeves, though no one was there to hear. The wind carried her words away. She had never met the aunt whose name was etched on the stone before her, yet somehow, she had always felt connected to her, as if the woman understood her in ways others never could. Leah had come here countless times as a child, running from heartache she didn't have words for. And now she returned again, older, more broken, her world falling apart around her.

She didn't know how long she sat there, minutes, an hour, maybe longer, crying until she had no breath left, only empty trembling. Then suddenly, strong arms wrapped around her from behind and lifted her to her feet. Leah gasped, instinctively resisting before she recognized the familiar scent of leather and pine. Jaxon.

He didn't say a word. He simply pulled her against his chest, holding her with quiet, steady strength. His coat brushed her cheek. His heartbeat thudded against her ear, calm, constant, grounding. Leah's sobs returned at once, though softer now, as if her body had finally realized it no longer had to hold everything alone.

It amazed her, every time, that he always found her. No matter where she tried to hide, no matter how quietly she slipped away, he ended up beside her as if her pain itself called him. Despite wanting to be alone, she didn't fight him. She couldn't. She had no energy left for stubbornness. So, she leaned into his embrace, letting herself be held, letting his body shield her from the wind and the world and the crushing weight inside her chest.

Burton's words had shattered her heart, but now Leah felt the faintest flicker of safety, quiet, warm, and deeply unexpected.

Cash was already standing at Leah's shoulder when she opened the front door two days later. He had expected trouble, and trouble arrived on cue. Three men stood on the porch. The moment Leah saw who they were, the seriousness in her eyes hardened into open irritation.

"Jack. Milton." Her voice was ice. "What are you doing here?"

Jack Rowland's face twisted instantly, his pride clearly bruised.

"Rude and high-handed, just as I recall," he snapped. "I'm your grandpa, missy. Don't you go talkin' to me like I'm some nobody knockin' at the door."

"The title grandfather is earned," Leah replied evenly, though the spark in her eyes warned of the storm brewing beneath the surface. "And I don't recall you ever acting like one, Jack."

The old man's jaw flexed. His eyes narrowed with cold fury.

"The last time I saw you was nine years ago," she continued, "so don't pretend we've had some close, devoted family relationship. I'll ask one more time, what do you want?"

Milton, her mother's brother, stepped forward with the same smirk he'd worn the day he'd tried to force her father out of business.

"This is Preston Burton," Milton introduced curtly, motioning to him. "We're here to speak on ranch affairs and business dealings."

Leah let out a humorless laugh. "That's Preston Burton? Do you truly think I'm a fool?"

Milton blinked. "What the hell's that s'posed to mean?"

"Your attorney was here two days ago," Leah said, her voice sharp as a knife. "And he's currently sitting in jail for threatening me on your behalf, and for shooting me."

Milton's mouth fell open. For a moment, he looked genuinely stunned, too stunned, in Cash's opinion, to be completely innocent. Leah clearly didn't buy it either.

"I… I didn't have the faintest idea," Milton stammered. "Leah, I'm awful sorry. I give you my word, I wasn't mixed up in none of that." He pointed at the quiet man. "This here's the real Preston Burton. He'll tell you."

The attorney, an older, sharper-eyed version of the imposter, nodded briskly. He produced a business card, identification papers, and a polished metal case of credentials. Cash stepped subtly behind Leah, his presence solid and protective. He didn't trust a single soul on that porch, and he didn't trust the way Milton kept glancing at Leah's injured arm. Without turning her head, Leah felt Cash shift closer, creating a clear barrier between her and the men.

Meanwhile, Ruby, already instructed what to do, slipped quietly out the side door. Cash caught the faint tapping of her boots on the porch boards as she sprinted toward the barn. One of the cowboys would be on a horse within moments, heading straight for town to bring Sheriff Bailey and David Smith. For now, Cash stayed exactly where he needed to be: one step behind Leah, ready to intervene at the slightest sign of danger.

"And you thought you could just show up here and have a meeting without notifying us first?" Leah asked, her voice deceptively calm, but Cash felt the fury radiating from her like heat off a forge.

Milton lifted his chin. "We're here with Mitchell's attorney."

"David Smith is my father's attorney." Leah's tone turned even colder, ice with a serrated edge. Her jaw tightened, and Cash could almost feel her bracing to launch into a full-blown eruption. Milton's posture softened in a weak attempt at diplomacy.

"Mind if we come in and talk this over proper-like?"

Both Leah and Cash raised an eyebrow at the word proper-like, but after a beat, they stepped aside. Cash positioned himself strategically behind Leah as the three men entered.

12
Not a Real Kidnapping

Patricia was halfway down the stairs when she spotted them. All color drained from her face.

"Father... Milton... wel–welcome," she whispered shakily. Jack Rowland wasted no time. He stepped forward, his cane tapping sharply against the floorboards. His lip curled the moment his eyes landed on Leah.

"Your daughter's still as mouthy as I remember," he barked. "Why didn't her pa teach her, her place? Women need firm discipline if they're to act right."

A growl rippled in Cash's chest. Leah scoffed aloud, her blue eyes flashing dangerously, but Cash immediately squeezed her arm in warning. *Not until backup arrives*, he silently urged. *Not yet.*

Patricia wrung her hands, her voice trembling. "I—I'm truly sorry, Father." She didn't move closer. In fact, every line of her body screamed she wanted to be anywhere else. The old man noticed. He seemed to enjoy the fear he provoked.

Milton cleared his throat and gave his sister a stiff nod before turning back to his father.

"Enough jawin'. Let's get this meetin' underway."

Cash remained behind Leah, muscles coiled, his stance protective and ready, because this 'meeting' was about to become a whole lot more than Jack and Milton bargained for.

After everyone had taken their seats, Preston Burton and Milton began outlining their 'plan' in a calm, almost rehearsed cadence, words smoothed by practice and arrogance. Leah sat rigidly, hands clasped so tightly her knuckles blanched, and Cash could feel the heat of everything she wasn't saying. He himself had bitten his tongue so many times he suspected it might be bleeding.

The atmosphere was taut, until a sudden, heavy knock rattled the front door. The three visitors jerked in their chairs like guilty men caught in the act. Cash stood, his movements controlled, and opened the door.

David Smith swept in with Scott Bailey right behind him.

"Ah," David said loudly, not bothering with pleasantries, "another Preston Burton." He strode forward as though he'd been invited. "Tell me, Mr. Rowland, how many real and counterfeit attorneys have you hired so far?"

Jack Rowland stiffened, Milton sputtered, and the so-called attorney's jaw flexed with suppressed irritation. What followed was chaos disguised as a meeting.

Every time Leah or Cash countered their claims, the Rowlands insisted, louder each time, that Mitchell Johnson had personally gone to this Burton to draft and notarize a new Will. Their voices rose, their composure cracked, and Preston sat stone-still as though confident his performance would hold.

David finally slammed his palm on the table.

"This discussion is over. Not one word of your story is true." His voice was steel, ringing with authority. "Mitchell anticipated deceit long before today, and he took every measure to protect his ranch and business." He reached into his satchel and withdrew a crisp set of documents.

"This is an authenticated copy of the real Will. Signed by Judge Hudson in Sacramento. There are two other identical copies secured elsewhere. Don't bother attempting forgery, you'll fail."

Jack and Milton went pale. Preston, if that was even his real name, merely narrowed his eyes, looking more calculating than shocked.

"So," the man drawled, "according to that document, who inherits everything? I assume his wife, Patricia?"

David shook his head. "No. Mitchell knew Patricia would not be able to manage the ranch. His daughter will."

Patricia gasped softly, tears gathering in her eyes. Milton's head snapped toward her.

"So, she don't get nothin'?" he demanded.

"Patricia will want for nothing," David replied calmly. "Leah has a generous heart, and she'll see to her mother's comfort."

"That can't be all of it," Milton muttered. "Leah ain't even of age yet. Who's her legal guardian?"

"That," David said, "would be her mother, and me."

Milton leaned forward. "So, you're sayin' Patricia gets to call the shots on the ranch till Leah turns twenty-one?"

"Yes and no." David folded his arms. "Leah inherits immediately upon her father's death. If she is underage, her mother may make decisions regarding the ranch—"

Leah's head snapped up, panic flickering in her eyes.

"—but," David continued smoothly, "with Leah's eighteenth birthday, any major decision requires both Leah's signature and my written approval."

Milton's jaw dropped. "You can't be serious, no damn way."

David's smile was razor-sharp. "Dead serious. Mitchell wasn't about to let anyone manipulate Patricia or try marrying her for access to the estate."

Milton and Jack leaned toward their attorney, whispering urgently, but the man finally shook his head.

"Mr. Smith is correct," he admitted quietly.

Cash rose to his feet. "Then I guess that wraps up this meeting. I'll show you out."

"We ain't leavin'." Milton's voice was low, defiant.

"You're not welcome to stay here," Leah snapped, her tone icy enough to freeze a river. Milton ignored her, as he always had, and turned his attention instead to Patricia.

"Patricia," he said low, "you're tellin' me we ain't wanted in our own kin's home?"

Every pair of eyes in the room swung toward her. Patricia's face flushed a deep red. Her hands shook.

"Of—of course you are welcome," she whispered. "You can stay as long as you wish."

"Mom!" Leah's voice cracked like a whip, sharp, warning, but Patricia couldn't bring herself to meet her daughter's eyes. Milton gave a smug grin.

"Well then. Looks like we don't need no escort to the door, do we?"

Cash's jaw flexed, but he forced out, "Fine. The rest of us have work to do." He gave a curt nod and strode out through the kitchen door before his temper snapped. Ruby hurried down the stairs to begin straightening the sitting room. Scott and David moved toward the front door.

"I need to head out as well," David said, turning back. "Leah, may I have a word?"

She nodded stiffly and followed him outside, already bracing for whatever truth he felt she needed to hear next.

Robyn was at Leah's side the moment she stepped outside. "I have a surprise for you," she announced, practically bouncing. Leah's brows knit instantly. Robyn's 'surprises' usually came wrapped in trouble.

"What kind of surprise?" she asked warily, already bracing herself.

"You and I are going to Sacramento for a while!" Robyn declared, nearly squealing. "David invited us both to stay with him and his family. And since it's my birthday this weekend, and Mama's off visiting Aunt Lucy in San Francisco, it's perfect timing!"

Leah gasped, and not in delight. Jaxon and Cash stepped closer like two hulking accomplices.

"I'm sorry, Robyn," Leah said quickly, shaking her head. "I can't leave right now."

"It would be good for you to get away for a little while," David interjected gently, though his tone made it clear this was far from a casual invitation.

Leah stiffened. "We have far too much work to do. Winter is coming fast. Some cattle still need to be sold in Eureka, and we need every hand."

"But it's my birthday," Robyn whined, sticking out her bottom lip in an exaggerated pout. "You never miss my birthday."

Leah's eyes narrowed. And then she saw it, the guilty little flicker in both Cash and David's expressions.

"You guys set me up, didn't you?" she accused sharply. Cash and David didn't bother denying it. "You're trying to drag me out of here, so Mom's father and brother don't get the chance to force me into handing over the ranch." Leah practically hissed through her teeth.

"Yes," David said bluntly. "We want you to leave, because it's safer."

"And leave my mother alone with the men who tormented her for years?" Leah scoffed. "Not a chance."

"Your mother is no threat to them," David replied, his voice hardening. "And they know it. She won't fight. But you will, and you have. They're going to focus all their attention on the one person standing between them and everything they want." His expression grew darker. "We will not risk another kidnapping attempt. Not when they're desperate and cornered."

"I'm not going." Leah folded her arms tightly, jaw locking. Her expression was the same one she wore when facing a charging bull, unyielding, immovable. "I'm no coward. I'm not running just because things get a little dangerous."

"Young lady," Cash said, stepping closer, his voice carrying the weight of command, "this isn't about pride. It's about keeping you alive." His gaze locked onto hers, stern, unshakable. "You are going. That decision has already been made."

Leah's head snapped back. "I said I'm not going."

"Your godfather has full authority to decide what's safest for you," Cash reminded her. "And he has decided."

"You can't force me," she snarled. A slow, dangerous smile curved across Jaxon's face as he stepped forward.

"You want to bet?"

Before Leah could react, Jaxon grabbed her around the waist and hoisted her over his broad shoulder like she weighed nothing.

"Jaxon Finlay! You put me down this instant!"

"No," he replied cheerfully, tightening his grip as she kicked and pounded her fists against his back. "Robyn already packed your things. Cash and I are taking you to town to make sure you get on that stagecoach." His tone left no room whatsoever for argument.

"If you dare make a scene," he continued, "I'll march right down Main Street with you over my shoulder, and if I have to, I'll climb straight into that stagecoach and hold you in my arms the entire trip."

"You wouldn't dare!" she shouted, wriggling like an angry cat.

"Don't tempt me," he warned, though he sounded far too amused to be threatening. He carried her straight to the waiting buckboard, ignoring her outraged sputters. When he finally set her down, he didn't give her a chance to bolt, he slid into the seat beside her and wrapped his arms firmly around her waist.

"You can't do this," Leah snapped, trying to shove him off, to no avail. Her struggles only made him tighten his hold. David, Cash, and Robyn all watched with undisguised amusement. Robyn was practically glowing.

Eventually Leah's wiggling slowed, then stopped. She was still bristling, but exhaustion and reality were catching up to her. Her shoulders sagged. She didn't fight when Jaxon's arms stayed around her.

"I can't just leave," she muttered, voice cracking. "Mom will be worried sick. Especially after everything that happened before."

"We'll tell her you're safe," Cash said gently. "We'll make sure she understands you needed a break."

"We won't tell her where you're going," David added. "Not until the Rowlands are gone and the danger has passed."

Leah swallowed, her throat tight. She looked from Cash to David to Jaxon's unyielding grip around her waist. Three men she trusted. Three men determined to keep her alive, even if they had to drag her to safety. Finally, she exhaled a shaky breath and nodded once, defeated, though not entirely willing. But she wasn't alone. And she knew that, too.

"Leah Johnson, I hardly recognize you." Brooke's delighted voice filled the spacious entryway the moment Leah stepped inside. "What a beautiful young woman you've become. Truly. You were always a pretty girl, but these last three years..." She gestured up and down with a soft gasp. "You've bloomed even more."

Leah felt a shy smile tug at her lips. "Thank you, Aunt Brooke."

"I understand you'll be staying with us for a while?" Brooke asked, her tone both curious and sympathetic. Leah nodded, though her voice dipped into a quiet grumble.

"It seems that way. Not that I had any say in the matter."

Her godfather shot her a pointed look and nudged her elbow, *behave*, and Brooke tried, and failed, not to smile at the familiar dynamic. She opened her arms again, and Leah stepped into her warm embrace. Robyn was next, receiving an equally affectionate greeting. A moment later, footsteps sounded from the hallway, and a tall, handsome young man appeared. Leah straightened instinctively.

"Leah, do you remember our youngest son?" Brooke asked proudly.

"Of course." Leah's smile brightened. "Good to see you again, Chad."

"Welcome back," he said warmly as he crossed the room. "It's been years, but—wow. You've grown up since the last time I saw you. And honestly, 'stunning' doesn't even begin to cover it."

Heat shot into Leah's cheeks, and her voice wobbled slightly.

"Why, thank you. You don't look too bad yourself."

Chad's grin widened. Then, quite suddenly, his attention shifted to the young woman standing beside Leah, and his expression softened with unmistakable interest.

"And who is this?" he asked, his voice dropping into something smoother. Robyn, whose confidence rarely wavered, turned bright red from collarbone to hairline. Leah nearly snorted, she couldn't help it. The pairing made perfect sense: Chad with his green eyes, strong jawline, and easy smile. Robyn with her long black hair, striking green eyes, and fiery nature.

Chad had recently finished law school, eager to follow in his father's footsteps. Robyn was lively, pretty, and unafraid to match wits with anyone. Leah didn't need much imagination to picture the two together, and the vision sent a spark of amusement dancing in her eyes.

Since Chad had finished law school and temporarily had more free time than he knew what to do with, he made it his personal mission to keep the girls entertained. His father had quietly explained Leah's situation, and Chad took it to heart, planning outings, filling afternoons with laughter, doing everything he could to distract her from the heaviness she carried.

He even invited his closest friend, Michael, to join them. Michael, handsome, charming, wonderfully attentive, took an immediate liking to Leah. He tried, in subtle and not-so-subtle ways, to impress her: helping her mount her horse, offering his arm when they walked through town, telling stories meant to make her laugh. Leah liked him, he was kind, thoughtful, easy to talk to, but there were no sparks. No fluttering feelings. Her heart remained untouched, still bruised and too guarded.

Two weeks passed before the tension inside her grew too sharp to ignore. She paced more. Ate less. Woke early. Stared out windows for long stretches. Robyn noticed. Brooke noticed. David noticed most of all.

One morning, Leah found him in the library and stood stiffly in the doorway, wringing her hands.

"Uncle Dave... I'm sorry, but I can't stay here any longer." Her voice cracked, not from fear, but from longing. "I know you've all been trying to keep me busy, and I truly appreciate everything you've done. I've even enjoyed parts of being here. But city life is just not for me, and I can't stop thinking about home. Every day feels like I'm shirking my responsibilities. I need to return."

David set his book down, his expression immediately serious.

"Leah... I don't think it's wise to go home yet."

She crossed her arms. "Why not?"

"Cash wired me yesterday," he began gently. "Jack and Milton Rowland are still at the ranch. They've settled in, and Milton..." David's mouth tightened. "Milton is now attempting to 'work' with the ranch hands. Though from what Cash says, 'work' is a generous word. He's mostly swaggering around, ordering men twice as capable as he is, pretending to run things."

Leah's eyes flashed. "See? That is exactly why I need to return. I can't let them take over. They'll ruin everything my father built. They'll destroy the ranch."

Robyn, seated in a comfortable armchair, looked at her friend with open worry.

"Leah... listen to him. If you go back now, you'll be putting yourself right in their path. They want control, and you're the one thing standing between them and the ranch. You'll be in danger if you go home."

"I know," Leah admitted, hugging herself. "But I can't hide here forever. They're not going to give up. If I avoid them now, they'll just try again later. And I hate the thought of Cash and Jaxon dealing with all this alone. I trust them implicitly, but I'm afraid Milton and Jack will sabotage things or bully the ranch hands into obedience. They've only been there two weeks and already they're causing trouble." She shook her head, her fists were clenched.

"I want to go home," she mumbled determined. "I *need* to go home."

David studied her for a long moment, weighing her words. He clearly wasn't pleased about the idea of her returning so soon, but he also wasn't blind to her reasoning. Leah's resolve was iron, she meant every word, and he knew it.

"I need to find out what they're up to," she pressed quietly but firmly. "I need to know why they're doing this. I can't spy on them from Sacramento, but I *can* when I'm back home."

"Leah." David's voice was soft but heavy with worry. "I don't want you spying on anyone. That's dangerous, and you're the last person who'd be able to do it unnoticed. The minute you step foot on the ranch, they'll be watching you like hawks."

Leah straightened her posture, her chin lifting with that unmistakable Johnson stubbornness.

"You can't keep me here against my will, Uncle Dave. I know you're trying to protect me, and I appreciate it, but this isn't where I belong. And I owe it to Dad to protect what he built. I won't let anyone steal it out from under us."

"Then let one of your men spy on the Rowlands," David countered. But Leah shook her head instantly.

"They don't have time. Every hand is needed, and none of them know the whole truth about why the Rowlands are even there. They'd never know what to look for." Her determination filled the room. Robyn exchanged a worried glance with Brooke. David sighed deeply, and before he could reply, Leah went on.

"What if..." She hesitated, glanced around, then squared her shoulders. "What if I went back in disguise? Show up in Hoopa Valley dressed as a cowboy and get hired on."

Three jaws dropped. Robyn bit her lip to keep from laughing. Brooke's eyebrows shot up. David just stared at her.

"What?" Leah demanded. "You think I can't do it? I've done ranch work practically my entire life."

David lifted a hand, trying not to smile. "We're not doubting your skill as a rancher, sweetheart. But passing you off as a *man*? That's... another matter entirely."

"I'll bind my hair, wear men's clothes—that's all I need."

"It isn't that simple," Brooke said gently, though her tone carried seriousness. "Leah, honey, you're a beautiful young woman. You move like a woman. You speak like a woman. Your height alone will raise questions. And your hands—"

"My hands?" Leah looked down defensively.

"They're delicate," Brooke added delicately. "Cowboys are... not."

"I'll stay out of sight as much as possible."

David shook his head. "Brooke is right. You're petite, and there's nothing about you that reads 'boy.' Even with men's clothes, gloves, and a hat pulled low, you'd stand out."

"How about I go with her?" Chad suggested suddenly. His expression was serious, but Leah nearly snorted.

"Chad," she said dryly, "have you ever worked a day on a ranch?"

He shook his head.

"Exactly. We're trying to be believable, not suspicious."

Robyn perked up, mischief sparking in her eyes.

"Actually... Chad's idea might work. If he's a lousy cowboy, it'll make Leah look more competent. The ranch hands won't question her 'manliness' if she stands next to someone who's clearly worse."

Chad glared at her. "Thanks, Robyn."

"You're welcome." She grinned, unbothered. Leah sighed, but Chad faced his father.

"I could say she's my younger brother, fourteen, maybe fifteen. That would explain why she's shorter and more petite."

"That part could work," David said slowly. "But we'd need men's clothing, hats, gloves, jackets, and likely a wig for you. And you'll need to always wear gloves, so no one notices your hands. Maybe several loose shirts, a neck cloth, and a bulky coat to hide your shape as much as possible."

Brooke's concern deepened. "But what about sleeping arrangements? You can't stay in a bunkhouse full of men."

"We have a large cabin for full-time ranch hands," Leah explained, "but there are also several smaller cabins for temporary workers. Each holds two or three people. If Cash hasn't hired anyone new, Chad and I could share one."

"That's... highly improper," Brooke said firmly.

"Chad wouldn't do anything," Leah insisted.

"That's not the point. Even the appearance is inappropriate. And what about privacy? Dressing? Bathing?"

Leah opened her mouth, then closed it. Her face flushed. That was indeed a problem.

"I have an idea," Robyn said, brightening with excitement. "My mother is still gone for several weeks, and Jaxon lives on the ranch. Leah could slip away to my house to wash and change. She can visit me during her free time, and because we live on the outskirts of town, nobody would notice. And if someone does ask questions, I'll say she's my cousin staying with me for a spell."

Everyone looked at Robyn, surprised but impressed. Leah let out a breath she didn't realize she'd been holding.

"It... might work," David admitted reluctantly. "It's risky. Very risky. But it might work."

Leah lifted her chin again, resolve burning in her eyes.

"It *will* work. I'm going home."

Luckily, only Robyn, Chad, and Leah occupied the stagecoach from Eureka to Hoopa Valley. The bumpy ride was long, but at least Leah didn't have to pretend to be someone else until they arrived. She could sit comfortably in her men's clothes without worrying about lowering her voice or keeping her posture stiff and awkward.

"Remember what Dad told you," Chad reminded her as the stagecoach rattled over the last hill before descending toward town. "If you can convince Cash and Jaxon that you're a boy, you'll be able to fool anyone."

Leah—hair bound tightly beneath her hat and wig, face partially shaded, clothes hanging loose on her slender frame—shot him a dry look.

"Thanks for the vote of confidence," she muttered.

Robyn giggled. "Lucas," she corrected, using Leah's chosen alias with exaggerated seriousness, "don't speak unless you absolutely must. Deep voice, short answers, no smiling, and for heaven's sake, no sashaying."

"I do not sashay," Leah huffed.

Chad snorted. "You very much do."

Leah rolled her eyes so dramatically that both laughed.

"We've gone over all of this a hundred times," she grumbled, though her nerves prickled beneath the surface. "Keep my hat low, gloves on, speak little, and act like I'm miserable to be alive. Shouldn't be too hard right now."

Robyn nudged her gently. "You'll do great. And remember, Cash and Jaxon won't be expecting this. That's half the trick."

Leah pulled in a breath, steeling herself as the coach slowed and Hoopa Valley came into view.

"Ready, Lucas?" Chad teased.

"No," Leah whispered honestly. "But I'm going home anyway."

13
A Few Swats Short of a Revelation

As soon as the stagecoach jerked to a halt in the center of Hoopa Valley, Robyn practically leapt out. She grabbed her bags, waved a quick goodbye to Leah—Lucas—and hurried down the boardwalk with her head ducked low. Her heart hammered. If Jaxon or Cash saw her with or without Leah, everything would unravel before it even began.

She forced herself to breathe and kept walking, but the moment she rounded the corner toward Main Street, she froze mid-step. There, right in front of the bank, stood Jaxon, arms crossed, talking with Cash. Her stomach dropped to her boots.

Oh no. No, no, no. If either of them looked her way, they would immediately notice something was off. She wasn't supposed to be back yet, and certainly not stepping off a stagecoach without Leah in sight. Before panic could swallow her whole, Chad hopped out of the stagecoach behind her, slinging a bag over his shoulder.

"Go," he whispered under his breath.

Robyn didn't hesitate this time. She slipped behind him, using his broad frame as a temporary shield. Chad walked straight toward the two cowboys, drawing their attention and buying Robyn the few precious seconds she needed. As soon as their eyes shifted toward him, she darted off toward the alley behind the mercantile, heart pounding like a stampeding herd. She didn't stop until she was halfway home, breathing hard, clutching her skirts. That was far too close.

Leah had never felt more uncomfortable in her life. Standing on Main Street disguised as a boy, hat tugged low, collar high, gloves tight on her hands, while the two men who knew her better than almost anyone stood directly in front of her, was unnerving in every possible way.

Jaxon and Cash eyed her with the kind of suspicion that made her spine turn liquid. They kept glancing at her, Jaxon especially, and each time she felt his gaze linger, her heart slammed against her ribs. She kept her head down, chin tucked, pretending to study the dust at her feet while she stayed half-hidden behind Chad's shoulder.

"Isn't your brother a bit young for a job at a ranch?" Cash asked, his eyes narrowing as he looked her over. Leah bit the inside of her cheek so hard she nearly winced.

Stay quiet. Stay still. You're Lucas. Just Lucas.

"Lucas is fifteen," Chad answered smoothly.

Cash's eyes flicked back to her. "Why isn't he talking?"

"He's just shy 'round folks he don't know," Chad said without missing a beat. "But he works hard. That I promise."

Jaxon crossed his arms, expression skeptical.

"Tell me again why we should hire you two?"

"Pa wants us gettin' our hands dirty for real," Chad explained, sliding right into their made-up tale. "Says if we're takin' over the ranch someday, we gotta work under folks who won't coddle us 'cause of who we are. Folks in Eureka told us the Johnson place in Hoopa Valley hires temp help. So... figured we'd give it a go."

Jaxon's gaze slid back to Leah again. She felt it under her hat brim like a hot brand.

"You two don't look like you have a whole lot of cowboy experience," he remarked. Leah's blood ran cold. He definitely suspected something.

"I don't," Chad said easily. "Just wrapped up law school. Pa figures I oughta learn ranchin' from scratch." He nudged her shoulder with a grin. "But Lucas here? Boy's been helpin' on our spread since he could walk."

Cash raised an eyebrow, unconvinced. "He doesn't look strong enough for the work we do."

Don't react. Don't flinch. You're a boy. A small one, sure, but a boy.

"He's stronger'n he looks," Chad said quickly. "Takes after our ma, smaller build, but tough as rawhide. You won't need to fret over him."

Cash studied her for a moment longer, his jaw ticking. He still didn't seem fully convinced... but Leah knew Cash had always believed in giving even the most unlikely worker a chance. Finally, he nodded.

"We'll hire you for two weeks," he said at last. "If we like what we see, you can stay. If you disappoint us, or if you mess up too often, we'll send you packing early. Deal?"

Chad exhaled in relief and shook his hand. "Deal. We gonna need to rent horses in town?" he asked. Cash shook his head.

"No. We've got plenty back at the ranch. You can pick one when we get there."

Leah kept her head down, but her pulse was hammering. They'd bought it. At least for now.

"You'll be staying here," Jaxon said as he led them to one of the smaller cabins, exactly what Leah had prayed for. Relief fluttered in her chest, though she kept her head ducked so he wouldn't see the flicker of emotion. He pushed the door open and stepped aside.

"Our cabins are full at the moment, so you'll be sharing with another hand. We hired him last week, goes by McKay. Good worker. Keeps to himself."

Leah exchanged a quick glance with Chad. Someone quiet was exactly what she needed.

"You two can get settled," Jaxon went on, "and start work tomorrow morning. Supper's at the big cabin every evening at seven sharp. Don't be late." He leaned his shoulder against the doorframe and gave them a wry smile. "We're spoiled around here. The Johnsons hired a cook just for the bunkhouses. Terrence makes food so good even the cows would line up for a plate if they could. But cowboys are always hungry after a day's work, so if you stroll in late, you'll be staring at empty platters. Consider yourselves warned." He gave them both a curt nod, his eyes lingering, too long, on Leah, before turning on his heel and heading back down the path.

The moment the door shut behind him, Leah exhaled so hard she swayed.

"Phew," she muttered, collapsing onto the nearest bunk. "Not being allowed to talk is harder than I expected. My throat feels like it's full of swallowed words."

Chad chuckled. "You? Quiet? I knew this disguise would be a challenge." He plopped his bag onto the opposite bed. "But seriously, is the food here really that good?"

Leah nodded. "Terrence is incredible. He cooks for our family sometimes when Ruby is sick or needs a day off. Even my mom likes his food, and she complains about everything."

"That good, huh?" Chad grinned. "I won't miss supper, then."

Leah stood and looked around the cabin. It was small but clean, two bunks, one trunk, a table, a stove, and pegs on the wall. Exactly what she needed. Exactly what she feared.

"Which bed do you want?" Chad asked. "Top or bottom?"

"Normally? Top," she said. "But if I have to sneak in or out without being noticed..." She glanced toward the door. "Climbing a ladder would give me away. Or make too much noise."

"Bottom it is," Chad said. "I'll take the top."

Leah let out another breath, her heart slowing now that she had a moment to think, breathe, and exist without eyes scrutinizing her every move.

"This is really happening," she whispered, half to herself. Chad nodded, expression softening.

"It is. And you're gonna pull it off, Leah. Just remember, you're Lucas now."

"Lucas," she repeated quietly, tugging her hat lower. "Time to make everyone believe it."

Chad and Leah joined the rest of the cowboys as the bell rang for supper. The long tables inside the big cabin were already filling up. The air hummed with voices, clattering tin plates, and the rich smell of Terrence's stew. Leah kept her hat low, her shoulders rounded, trying her best to shrink into Lucas's persona. Jaxon stood near the head of the table and cleared his throat.

"Boys, we've got two new hands joining us for a spell, Chad and his younger brother, Lucas."

A chorus of nods, grunts, and halfhearted greetings followed. Typical cowboy welcome.

"And this here," Jaxon added, "is McKay, your cabin mate."

Leah glanced up—and nearly forgot how to breathe. McKay was... unfairly handsome. His build rivaled Jaxon's. Broad shoulders, strong arms, and a lean, capable frame. His blond hair looked sun-touched rather than pale, and his eyes, good heavens, were a vivid, clear green that seemed to take in everything around him. When he smiled, she could easily imagine women swooning.

Chad and McKay were swapping jokes within minutes, easy as childhood friends. Leah stayed glued to Chad's elbow, answering no one and keeping her voice buried in her throat. But of course, McKay eventually approached. He turned on the bench to face her, resting an arm casually along the back.

"So, Lucas," he said, voice friendly, "your brother tells me you've got a knack for breakin' horses?"

Leah's heart lurched. She had two choices: speak and hope he couldn't place her voice... or stay silent and seem suspicious. He was new—he wouldn't recognize her voice. She took a breath and replied, keeping her tone lower than usual.

"Yeah," she said with a small shrug. "Reckon I've got a knack for it."

McKay's eyes brightened with interest. "Your brother swears you can break a horse in two, three days. You really that fast?"

She nodded. "Mostly, yeah," she said. "Horse to horse, it's different. Some're mule-stubborn, some just need time." She stared down into her bowl, refusing to look up into those sharp green eyes. "My pa was the one who taught me. Every trick I got came from him."

"That's mighty impressive," McKay said, real admiration in his voice. "'Specially for a young'un like you."

Leah shrugged again, keeping her movements small and boyish. "Started young."

From across the table, Jaxon was watching her again, sharp gaze narrowed slightly, as though Lucas's voice tugged at a memory, he couldn't quite place. Leah's stomach tightened. McKay flashed her a friendly grin, unaware of the storm swirling in her head.

"Well," he drawled, cup lifted in a friendly toast, "can't wait to see what you're made of, Lucas."

Leah managed a stiff nod, pulse racing. She had survived her first real conversation. Now... she just had to survive everything else.

The next few days were packed from dawn until long after sunset, but Leah thrived under the work. It grounded her, kept her mind from spiraling into grief or fear, and slipping into the role of Lucas became easier with every chore she completed.

Chad struggled with most tasks, but he tried with admirable determination. His effort earned respect, even if his skill did not.

Cash and Jaxon watched the pair closely. Too closely, in Leah's opinion. But every time suspicion flickered in their eyes, she countered it with impeccable work. She rode hard, worked harder, and handled cattle better than half the seasoned hands. It impressed the men and startled them, especially when it came to her horse.

Leah had chosen a mare notorious for bucking off every rider except her. The mare practically melted under her touch, following her commands as if she understood every word. Jaxon noticed. Cash noticed. Even McKay raised a brow more than once.

"Animals've always taken a shine to him," Chad'd say offhand. "Boy's got a natural way with horses."

Leah kept her expression shy and humble, doing her best not to meet anyone's gaze for too long. It worked.

McKay proved to be a surprisingly easy roommate. He usually turned in early and slept like a rock until the morning bell. That gave Leah space to slip out unnoticed. She hid her wigs, clothes, and bathing supplies in the hayloft of the far barn, her quiet sanctuary, and changed there each day.

She knew every cowboy's routine, every shift rotation, every errand. Avoiding them wasn't difficult.

Her real challenge lay elsewhere. Milton and Jack still slithered around the ranch like snakes masquerading as ranch hands. Milton strutted through the yard barking orders like he was the foreman. Neither Cash nor Jaxon corrected him, they didn't need to. The cowboys ignored him so completely it bordered on comical.

But Leah didn't laugh. She watched. She listened. She lingered nearby whenever Milton or Jack spoke, sweeping barns, checking equipment, mucking stalls, doing anything to justify being close enough to overhear. She hadn't uncovered much, but she sensed something brewing. And then came the breaking point.

Milton swaggered into the yard one afternoon while the men were sorting cattle.

"You mule-brained fools, pick up the pace!" he barked. "Get them critters penned, and I mean now!"

No one even looked at him. Milton's face reddened.

"Do you hear me? I'm speakin' to you, dammit!"

One of the older hands finally turned, jaw tight and eyes blazing.

"We don't take orders from you," he said, voice level as bedrock. "We answer to Cash. We answer to Jaxon. And we sure as hell answer to Leah."

Milton's nostrils flared. "She's a child—"

"She's our boss," the cowboy snapped. "You ain't."

A hush fell. Milton trembled with rage, but no one gave him the satisfaction of reacting. They simply went back to work.

Standing off to the side in her Lucas disguise, Leah felt a strange mix of triumph and dread.

If Milton was furious now, what would he do next? Because one thing was certain, men like him didn't accept defeat quietly.

One early morning, just as the sky turned from charcoal to pale gray, Leah crouched in the hayloft preparing for another day as 'Lucas.' She reached for her disguise, only to watch both wigs slip through a narrow crack in the floorboards. They tumbled in slow motion. *Plop. Plop.* Straight into the massive water barrel below.

Leah clapped a hand over her mouth. Her heart dropped. Her third wig, her emergency backup, was still at Robyn's house, freshly washed and drying on the clothesline. Disastrous. She couldn't be seen in daylight with her own hair. She couldn't show up for breakfast without her disguise. Chad couldn't cover for her forever. She had to get to Robyn. Immediately.

Leah scrambled down the ladder, fished the drenched wigs out of the barrel, hurried back up, and laid them out in a dripping heap beside her bag. Should she take the bag with her? Instinct screamed *yes*. But walking across the yard at dawn with a travel bag was the fastest way to raise questions. *No*, she'd have to leave everything.

She shoved her long hair into the tightest bun she could manage, jammed her hat low to hide it, and climbed down again.

She was halfway to the stable when something stopped her cold. The guestroom window was open. And voices drifted out, two she recognized instantly. Jack Rowland. Milton Rowland.

Leah froze, instincts flaring. She should have walked away, her disguise was falling apart, but curiosity hooked into her and pulled her closer. She crept to the house, ducked into the tall bushes beneath the open window, and pressed herself into the leaves, heart thundering. She listened.

"Ain't got the faintest notion where Mitchell's will ended up," Milton grumbled. "Checked every corner of this house, not a scrap. Smith must've carted it off to Sacramento. And seein' as they made more copies, who can say where the rest're squirreled away?"

Jack huffed. "Oughta just made Patricia sign the will we wanted," he snapped, eyes cuttin' sharp toward his boy. Milton shook his head.

"That'd have been downright stupid," he snarled. "They'd jail us for fraud, easy as breathin'. We can't risk that. No, we sit tight. Leah won't stay holed up like a frightened rabbit forever. She'll come back. And when she does, we'll be waitin'."

Leah's jaw clenched. *Ready all you want, you devils... you won't take our ranch.*

"Have you contacted Wilson yet?" Jack asked.

Leah leaned in closer, breath held, waiting for Milton's reply, but she never heard it. A strong arm suddenly wrapped around her waist from behind. A hand clamped over her mouth, smothering her startled gasp. In one terrifying motion, she was yanked backward into the shadows, her boots dragging across the dirt. Panic exploded in her chest. She twisted, clawed, shoved, anything to break free, but whoever held her was far stronger. Her heart pounded violently against her ribs. She couldn't make a sound. She couldn't breathe. She was trapped. Helpless. Unseen. Her pulse thundered as the man hauled her farther from the house, her mind screaming one thing: Not again.

McKay yanked her into the cabin before Leah even had time to gasp. The door slammed behind them, rattling the walls, and in the next heartbeat he shoved her down onto his bunk, holding her firmly in place. Leah kicked, twisted, and bucked beneath him, but he pinned her easily with the weight of his legs and the strength of hands far too quick and far too sure.

In the scuffle, her hat slipped, just enough for a spill of blonde hair to escape. McKay froze. Only for half a second. Then he snatched the hat entirely off her head. A cascade of golden curls tumbled free. The sight wiped the breath straight out of him. A sharp inhale, a flicker of disbelief, and then a slow, dangerous smirk tugged at his mouth... only to vanish beneath a furious scowl.

"Well lookie here, Lucas," he spat, voice sharp with blame. "Or whatever your real name is. You sly little snake." His jaw bunched hard. "What business you got on this ranch?"

"It ain't your concern!" Leah spat, fightin' against his grip. "Let me go!"

“You here thievin’?” he growled, shovin’ his face nearer. “That ‘brother’ yours, he in on it too?”

“Leave me be!”

McKay rose abruptly, hauling her up with him. His hand clamped around her arm like a steel shackle.

“You’d best start talkin’,” he growled. “Or I’ll holler for Cash and march you straight to the sheriff.”

Leah lifted her chin, all fire and fury. “I don’t give a whit ’bout your threats. You’re just a ranch hand, not the man runnin’ things.”

His brows crashed down. Suspicion flared. Recognition followed. Something clicked behind those fierce green eyes.

“I swear, girl,” he muttered darkly, “you keep on with that sass, and I’ll haul you over my knee like any wayward young’un. You’re beggin’ for a good tannin’ of your backside. Pretty face don’t change a thing. Someone skipped teachin’ you manners, and I ain’t afraid to finish the job.”

Leah’s breath caught, not from fear, but rage.

“You’ve no right to touch me—none. No right to threaten me either,” she spat. “You don’t even know who I am. Let me go before you get yourself fired.”

He barked a laugh. “I found you skulkin’ about, eavesdroppin’ like a thief. You lied to get hired and played at bein’ a boy.” His fingers clamped harder. “That puts you square in trespasser territory.”

“You know nothin’,” she snapped, eyes sparkin’. “And I don’t answer to you.” She jerked hard, unexpectedly hard, and broke half free. But McKay was faster. His hand shot out, fingers brushing her chin, trying to force her to look at him—Leah bit him. Hard.

McKay swore, jerking back, but before she could bolt for the door, he caught her around the waist.

"You little beast—" One swift motion, one blur of strength, and he sat, hauling her across his lap and pinning her there. Leah gasped in shock, just before his palm landed sharply across her backside. Once. Twice. Again. Not hard enough to truly hurt, but enough to sting. Enough to humiliate. Enough to make her see red.

She kicked. She writhed. Her fists pounded the mattress. But McKay held her fast, delivering several more crisp swats before finally stilling his hand. Her face burned. Her pride blazed. And McKay's voice dropped low over her shoulder, rough with anger and something unreadably intense.

"Now," he growled, jaw tight, "you're gonna tell me who you are, and what sort o' mess you brought to this ranch."

The cabin door flew open with a bang. Jaxon, Chad, and Cash stormed inside like thunder rolling down a mountain, only to freeze mid-step. Leah was still draped across McKay's knees. Not Lucas. Not a boy. A girl. *A familiar girl.* Two pairs of eyes widened in perfect unison. The air went dead silent.

"What's going on?" Cash thundered, his booming voice shaking the cabin. Leah cringed. And McKay, reckless, maddening McKay, gave her two more sharp swats before releasing her. She shot upright like she'd been scorched.

"How dare you?" she snapped, eyes blazing, fury radiating off her like heat from a forge. Jaxon and Cash gasped together, because the voice that came out of her was unmistakably female.

She tried to bolt past them, but Jaxon lunged, catching her by the arm before she made it three steps. Cash bore down on her with an expression somehow worse than fury. It was disappointment. Deep, fatherly disappointment. The kind that dropped Leah's stomach to her boots. She couldn't meet his eyes. Not for long.

"Leah Amelia Johnson," Cash rumbled, "you are in a world of trouble, young lady. What are you doing here?"

"Shouldn't you ask him what *he* was doing?" she snapped, pointing furiously at McKay. "He spanked me!"

Cash didn't even blink. "You're lucky he already did," he said flatly. "Because you deserved it. And more. Now tell me why you're back here, pretending to be a cowboy."

"I don't think we should be discussing this in front of him," Leah hissed, jerking her chin toward McKay.

"You can speak in front of him," Cash said firmly. "We trust him."

"Well, I don't."

McKay stepped forward, arms folded, wearing an expression suspended between smug amusement and irritation.

"Reckon that's one memorable way to meet you, Miss Johnson," he said with a lazy grin.

"You plannin' to send me packin'?"

"You bet," she snapped.

"Nobody's getting fired," Cash cut in sharply. "Not yet. We need answers first."

"How do we know he's trustworthy?" Leah demanded. "For all we know, he could be spying for Milton."

McKay snorted. "Like I'd spy for that lump of prairie coal. Man walks around like he's king o' the valley and ain't done a lick of work since he showed up."

"And that should convince me?" Leah arched a brow. McKay stepped closer, too close. His green eyes locked onto hers, intense enough to make her cheeks warm, much to her annoyance.

"Leah," he murmured, "I swear to you, I ain't tied up with Milton Rowland."

"It's *Miss Johnson* to you," she shot back. His smirk returned, slow, aggravating, confident.

"Ouch," he murmured, hand over his heart. "Deep wound."

"Your godfather hired him," Cash added, nudging Leah to sit beside him on her bunk. "Now start talking. Did you run away from Sacramento?"

"No," she muttered. "I didn't run away."

"So, David approved this charade?"

Leah's lips pressed into a thin line. "He wasn't thrilled," she admitted, "but he knows I can't hide forever. That's why Chad came. He volunteered."

"You shouldn't have done this," Jaxon ground out. His brown eyes flashed, anger, fear, and something painfully vulnerable beneath. "This was foolish. And dangerous."

"What was I supposed to do, Jaxon?" Leah burst out, voice cracking. "Sit around knitting while the Rowlands take everything we built? Everything my father worked for?" Her chest rose and fell rapidly. Her eyes burned. "I won't let them win. I love this ranch. I'm not giving it up because there's danger."

Cash's jaw tightened. Jaxon exhaled sharply. Neither approved, but both understood.

"Will you at least promise to stay away from Milton?" Jaxon pressed.

"You know I can't. He's hiding something, and I'm going to find out what."

"Leah," Jaxon said through gritted teeth, "stop being so darn stubborn."

"Then stop trying to control me!" she shot back. "Now if you'll excuse me, I need to fetch my drenched wigs and get the dry one from Robyn."

"I'm coming with you," Jaxon declared immediately.

"I don't need a babysitter," Leah snapped, shoving her hair back under her hat with trembling hands. She marched out of the cabin with defiant strides, but Jaxon followed so closely she could practically feel his frustration radiating off him. He wasn't letting her out of his sight.

Not now. Not after this.

"Holy smokes," McKay breathed, still watchin' her storm off. "That girl's made o' dynamite and hellfire both."

Cash let out a long, weary sigh, the kind only years of Leah Johnson could produce.

"You have no idea," he muttered, rubbing the back of his neck. "She came out of the womb with a mind of her own and the temper of a cornered bobcat."

McKay huffed an incredulous laugh. "I'm starting to believe it."

Cash glanced toward the doorway, where distant raised voices, very likely Leah and Jaxon, echoed across the yard. He shook his head again.

"Chad," he said, turning to the young man shifting awkwardly by the bunks, "you'd better go with them."

"With... them?" Chad blinked. "Both of them?"

"Yes." Cash raised a brow in grim amusement. "If Jaxon shows up in town dragging Leah along, folks will start talking. If you're with them, it'll look like the three of you are just running errands."

McKay snorted. "Or like they're tryin' to keep David's powder-keg goddaughter from blowin' sky-high."

Cash gave him a look that was half exasperation, half resignation.

"That too."

Chad didn't argue. He grabbed his hat, nodded once, and hurried out the door, jogging to catch up with the pair already striding toward the horses.

The moment he was gone, Cash exhaled slowly, half prayer, half curse.

"Heaven help us," he muttered. "Between those two hotheads, we'll be lucky if the whole town doesn't hear them coming from a mile away."

McKay folded his arms, lips twitching. "Pure dynamite," he echoed with a grin.

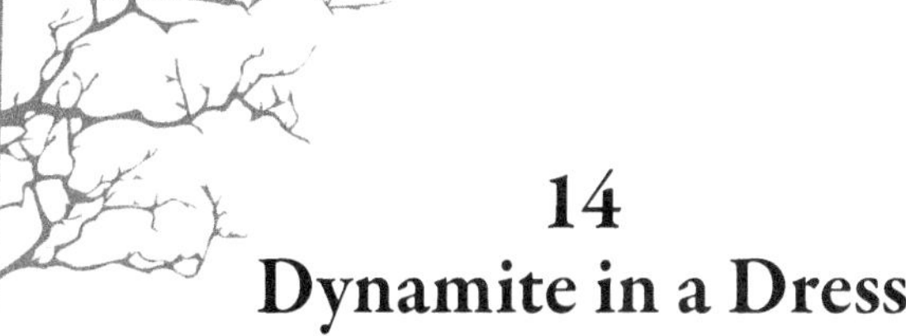

14
Dynamite in a Dress

"Jaxon, I told you, I don't need you following me. Now go away." Her tone could have cut through granite. Leah shot him a murderous glare and scrambled up the ladder to the hayloft, grabbing her bag and the sopping-wet wigs. She hoped the height would buy her a moment alone.

It didn't. Jaxon's boots hit the loft floor a heartbeat later.

"First," he said, voice low and edged with anger, "I want to know why McKay punished you."

She stiffened. "It's none of your business."

"Leah." That one growled word rolled through the dusty rafters, dark, frustrated, unmistakably warning. She ignored him, shoving the wigs into her bag, and headed toward the ladder. She didn't make it two steps.

An arm banded around her waist, strong, unyielding, and in one swift motion Jaxon hauled her backward and tossed her onto the big mound of hay. Leah gasped, breath knocked clean out of her, and before she could scramble up, he pinned her with his body.

"Let me go!" she snapped, breath trembling with equal parts fury and... something else. His face hovered above hers, too close. Far too close. A dangerous grin curved his lips.

"Remember how I made you talk when we were kids?" he murmured, voice infuriatingly smug. "I don't mind doing it again."

Her pulse leaped. "I'm not a little girl anymore," she shot back, twisting beneath him. "And you don't get to manhandle me."

He didn't budge. "If you won't talk, I have other ways."

"Don't you da—" Her protest dissolved into a startled yelp when his fingers dug into her sides. A shriek of laughter burst from her, helpless, involuntary, humiliating.

"Jax—stop—stop!" She writhed, laughing so hard she could hardly breathe. "Jaxon! I swear—don't—"

"I knew you'd cave." His satisfied chuckle vibrated against her ear. He released her only enough to pull her upright, settling her beside him in the hay. Her cheeks were flushed, her breathing rapid, half outrage, half the dizzying awareness of how close he was. His thigh brushed hers. Their faces were inches apart.

"That wasn't fair," she muttered, elbowing him sharply. "And you know it."

He only grinned and waited.

Leah huffed. "Fine. McKay found me while I was... eavesdropping on Milton and Jack."

Jaxon's expression darkened instantly. "Leah. You need to stay away from them."

"No," she said without hesitation. "I need to know what they're planning. Jack asked Milton if he'd contacted a man named Wilson. While I was gone, did he meet anyone by that name? Have you heard it at all?"

Jaxon shook his head. "No. But before you get any ideas," he caught her chin, turning her face toward his. His touch was gentle, thumb grazing her jaw, sending an unwelcome shiver through her. "I mean it. I'll do the investigating. You stay away from them."

She tried turning her head, refusing to meet his eyes, refusing to let those warm brown depths soften her resolve. Jaxon wasn't having it. His fingers slid along her cheek, guiding her face back to his until she couldn't look anywhere else.

"Did you hear me?" he asked quietly. She nodded. "And will you promise to do as I asked?"

Her lips curled into a defiant smile, soft, stubborn, daring.

"I'll make no such promise."

Jaxon exhaled hard, frustration palpable... along with the heat settling thickly between them.

"So... Jaxon and Cash know now?" Robyn's eyes widened with worry as she looked at her best friend. Leah nodded, rubbing her temples. "How did they find out?" Robyn pressed.

Leah let out a breath. "I accidentally dropped my wigs through a crack in the hayloft. I went to the stables to get my horse so I could take them to you, but then I overheard Milton and Jack talking. I stopped to listen."

"And that's what exposed you?" Robyn blinked.

"Not exactly." Leah grimaced. "Our new cowboy found me eavesdropping, dragged me into the cabin, and, well, that's how everything came out."

Jaxon chose that moment to step closer, folding his arms with a grin that made Leah want to throw a boot at him.

"Don't you want to tell my sister the *rest* of it?" he asked sweetly. Leah shot him a glare sharp enough to split a fence post. Then she shook her head firmly. Robyn looked between them, confused.

"What rest of it? What am I missing?"

Jaxon lifted an eyebrow, savoring the moment.

"Leah ticked him off enough that he threw her over his knee and spanked her backside."

Robyn gasped. "He did *not!*"

"Oh, he did." Jaxon's grin widened. "Didn't he, Leah?"

"Oh, for heaven's sake," she muttered, burning with mortified fury as she marched into the washroom before she strangled him. She grabbed her dry wig and forced it onto her head with far more force than necessary. Behind her, their voices drifted through the doorway.

"I can't believe he—"

"What was she even—"

"He's lucky Cash didn't fire him—"

Leah ignored them as she gathered the two dripping wigs to rinse again and hang by the washroom window. She pushed the curtain aside to open it—and froze. Milton and Jack had just ridden into town. They dismounted in front of the sheriff's office... and a tall man she didn't recognize stepped out and greeted them with a confident handshake.

Leah leaned closer, heart thudding. Then the door opened again. Scott Bailey, Sheriff Bailey, walked out and greeted all three men like old friends. Leah gasped, stumbling back from the window as if burned. Scott Bailey... was a traitor. He was working with the Rowlands.

Her stomach twisted. Spots danced in her vision. If the sheriff was on their side, everything... everything was worse than they'd imagined. She rushed toward the washroom door, ready to tell Jaxon, Robyn, and Chad, but froze. If she went in there, Jaxon would never let her out of his sight again. And she needed to follow the Rowlands *now.*

Leah backed away, pulse racing. She tiptoed back to the window, opened it quietly, and swung one leg outside. A quick glance confirmed they were still in the kitchen, distracted. Without a sound, she climbed out the window, dropped lightly to the ground, and slipped around the back of the house... determined to uncover the truth before anyone could stop her.

"Why is it taking her so long to get that wig?" Jaxon muttered, pacing once before striding toward the washroom. The door wasn't latched, just resting against the frame, but even so, he knocked before nudging it open. The moment it swung wider, his gaze snapped to the open window. His pulse slammed into his throat. The curtain fluttered in the breeze. Jaxon crossed the room in two steps and leaned out the window. His eyes swept the town in a sharp, practiced scan, and then he saw her. Leah.

Sneaking across the back alley. Keeping to the shadows. Slipping around the corner toward the sheriff's office like a fox on the hunt.

"Dang it, Leah," he growled, smacking his palm against the window frame. The sharp crack echoed off the walls. He turned and bolted, storming through the house with such urgency that Robyn and Chad jumped when he burst into the kitchen doorway.

"She's gone," he snapped. "Out the window. She's heading for the sheriff's office."

Robyn gasped. Chad's face drained of color.

"Jaxon—" Robyn began, but he was already reaching for the door.

"Stay put," he ordered, voice low and fierce. Before either of them could speak another word, Jaxon was gone, charging across the yard like a man who knew, with terrifying certainty, that Leah Johnson had run straight into danger.

Leah crept around the back of the sheriff's office, every muscle tight, every step a battle against the instinct to run back to safety. Her heart hammered so violently she thought it might shatter her ribs. She was shaking, not merely from fear but from fury. Betrayal burned hotter than terror, and it pushed her onward even as her legs threatened to buckle. She scanned the wall, desperate for any way in.

Please... please... And then she saw it, a window pushed wide open, as if inviting her. Leah swallowed hard, wiped her sweaty palms on her trousers, and edged closer. She peeked around the corner, and her stomach twisted. Four men sat gathered around a table: Jack, Milton, Wilson... and Sheriff Scott Bailey. Her breath caught in her throat. The sheriff. A traitor. Her fists curled so tight her nails bit into her skin.

Inside, Milton leaned forward, voice tense but triumphant.

"So, our men got the cattle outta the west pasture and are headin' for Eureka?"

Wilson nodded. "Yep. Drove 'em out last night. If all goes smooth, they'll hit Eureka in a couple days."

"Good work, Wilson." Milton slapped the man's shoulder, a smug grin spreadin' across his face. "I'll catch the stage the day they roll in. We'll sell that herd first thing the next mornin', before anybody in Hoopa Valley even knows what hit 'em."

Leah's mouth went dry. Her father's cattle. Their winter income. Their survival. Stolen. Her vision blurred for a moment, rage pounding through her like wildfire.

Scott Bailey leaned back in his chair, folding his hands across his stomach.

"And what d'you want me to do?"

Jack's lip curled into something close to a sneer.

"Soon as Cash starts bawlin' about the cattle bein' gone, you'll ride after the 'thieves.'" His voice turned syrup-sweet, mockin' every word. "Go on, play the hero. Ride out, poke around, pretend you're earnin' that shiny badge you never deserved."

Milton folded his arms, a smirk tugging at his mouth.

"And you're still keepin' up your little performance with Patricia, yeah?"

The sheriff's smile spread slowly, like oil slicking across water, dark, rotten, self-satisfied.

"Oh, I'm keepin' it up just fine. Leah's hatin' every minute of it." He chuckled under his breath.

"Told Patricia we'll be movin' on soon, now that we've got her husband in the ground." He gave a lazy shrug, eyes glittering with cruelty. "But first, I wanna give sweet little Leah a bit more time before we start talkin' about hitchin' proper." Another low laugh. "Makes her think I'm noble."

Leah's entire body went cold. They weren't just after her ranch. They were trying to marry her mother. To control everything. To replace her father. To erase him. A wave of dizziness hit her, and she clamped a hand over her mouth to muffle the gasp threatening to escape. She had to get back. She had to warn Cash. Jaxon. Chad. Someone. But as she slowly backed away from the window, her boot scraped against the loose edge of a stone. It made the faintest sound. Barely more than a whisper. But inside, four heads snapped toward the window at the exact same moment.

She waited until they resumed their conversation. She needed to listen. She needed to hear more. She took a careful step back toward the open window.

An arm snaked around her waist and yanked her off her feet. A strong hand clamped over her mouth before she could scream, and Leah's heart lurched painfully against her ribs. She kicked, twisted, clawed, every instinct screaming danger, but the hold was unbreakable. Her captor dragged her around the corner, behind a shed where no one would hear.

Only when they were completely hidden did the hand drop from her mouth. Leah spun around, breath trembling, and gasped. Jaxon. His face was thunder. His arms, still locked around her slender frame, held her so tightly she could feel every rapid breath he took.

"What do you think you're doing?" he growled, voice low enough to rattle her bones. "Good grief, Leah, I could strangle you sometimes." His eyes raked over her, fear, anger, and something fiercer burning in them, before he finally released her with a frustrated exhale. "I told you to stay away from the Rowlands."

"And I told you I won't," she shot back, eyes blazing. "I make my own decisions."

"Apparently terrible ones," he snapped. "What were you thinking?"

"You had a funeral for my father while I was in Sacramento?" she demanded, her voice cracking. "You buried him without me?"

Jaxon's irritation faltered, replaced by guilt and exhaustion.

"Your mom wanted it done quickly. She and Scott thought it was best."

"Scott Bailey has no right to make decisions for my family." Her voice dropped to a cold, shaking whisper. "He's a traitor."

Jaxon blinked. "You think the sheriff—Leah, that's a serious accusation."

"It's not an accusation," she said sharply. "I heard it with my own ears. He's working with Milton and Jack. They've stolen our cattle from the western pasture, they plan to sell them in Eureka before anyone notices. And Scott Bailey is helping them."

Jaxon stared at her, stunned. The color drained from his face.

"Leah... are you sure?"

"Yes," she breathed. "Wilson, the man they hired, is here. They talked openly about it because they think they've already won. Scott knows everything and doesn't intend to stop it." Her voice cracked, and she turned away, fists trembling. "He betrayed my father. He betrayed all of us!"

"Leah—"

"He's pretending to marry my mother." The words clawed their way out of her. And then, the thought struck like a gunshot. "What if he was responsible for the stagecoach accident?" Her face went white. "No," she whispered. "No, no, no..." Panic surged, and she bolted down the alley, running as though she could outrun the truth clawing at her mind. Jaxon caught up to her in seconds, his boots pounding the ground. He grabbed her hand, spinning her back toward him. She fought him, shoving at his chest. He didn't let go.

Tears spilled over, hot and furious despite her efforts to swallow them back.

"Why?" she choked out. "Why would anyone do that to someone they claim to be friends with?" Her breath hitched painfully, shoulders shaking as she struggled against him.

Without thinking, Jaxon cupped her face gently but firmly between his hands, forcing her tear-filled blue eyes to meet his.

"Listen to me," he said, voice rough but tender. "We don't know the full truth yet. Maybe Bailey's investigating. Maybe he's trying to learn more."

Leah stared up at him, their faces inches apart. His brown eyes, despite the irritation, were soft now. Worried. Protective. Her heartbeat stumbled. He eased her into his chest, wrapping his arms around her in a steady, grounding embrace. She clung for a moment, soaking in the comfort before gently pushing away. When she looked up at him again, her cheeks were damp, her expression remorseful.

"I'm sorry," she whispered. "I didn't mean to fall apart. I just... didn't expect any of this."

"You don't need to apologize," he murmured, squeezing her hand. "Anyone would've reacted the same. Probably worse." His thumb brushed lightly over her knuckles, sending a confusing rush of warmth through her chest. "But," he continued firmly, "I need you to promise me something. No more spying. Let us handle it. Let *me* handle it." He watched her with the intensity of someone bracing for disappointment. And he got it. Because she was already shaking her head.

"No, Jaxon. I owe it to my father to see this through. To protect what he built." She stepped back, steel returning to her spine. "Now let's go. We need to tell Cash about the stolen cattle. We need to leave today."

Jaxon muttered something under his breath that sounded suspiciously like a prayer, or a curse, before falling into step beside her. Because no matter how stubborn Leah was... he wasn't letting her face this alone.

"Leah, what's wrong?" Cash's voice broke the long stretch of silence. He had been watching her for miles now, her stiff shoulders, her blank stare, the way her jaw tightened whenever her thoughts drifted too far. They'd been riding for several hours, and she hadn't spoken once since she and Jaxon returned from town with the devastating news.

Only five of them had left the ranch: Jaxon, Cash, Leah, McKay, and Chad. A small group, intentionally so. They didn't want Milton or Jack realizing she had overheard everything at the sheriff's office. Surprise was their only advantage.

Leah kept her gaze ahead, her back straight in the saddle.

"Nothing is wrong. I'm fine." She nudged her horse into a brisk trot, as if sheer speed could outpace the conversation. Cash followed easily.

"I can see from a mile away that you're not fine," he said gently. "You can roll your eyes all you want, but that won't change a thing."

Leah did exactly that, rolled her eyes, then sighed, long and trembling. But still, she didn't speak.

"Will you please tell me?" Cash pressed, soft but firm. Finally, she turned her face toward him, anger simmering beneath the surface.

"I don't know what you want from me, Cash." Her voice cracked like a whip. "Do you want to hear how furious I am that Milton and Jack stole our cattle? Or are you asking because you know I learned, from a traitor's mouth, no less, that Mom held a funeral for Dad while I was gone?"

Cash exhaled slowly. Yes. That was the wound still bleeding.

"I don't understand why she had to do that," Leah continued, voice sharper now, cracking around the edges. "She told me she was trying to get someone to return his body. I thought that would take weeks. Why didn't anyone contact me? You all knew where I was. I could have come back."

"I'm sorry," Cash said softly. "Truly. We tried talking her out of it. Jaxon, Ruby, even Robyn tried. Your mother refused to listen. She and Scott planned everything without telling a soul. We only found out the night before the service."

Leah's expression twisted, pain and fury, raw and tangled.

"And that makes it worse," she whispered. "Mom acts like she's the only one who lost him. Like she's the only one hurting." Her throat tightened. "She never acted like she cared that much when Dad was alive. They didn't even sleep in the same room."

Before Cash could answer, Jaxon rode up beside them.

"I think we should set up camp," he said, looking at the darkening sky. "Clouds are rolling in. It's going to rain."

Both Leah and Cash nodded. Within minutes, they found a sheltered spot off the trail. The air had turned cold and sharp now that the sun had dipped behind the hills, shadows stretching long across the ground. A narrow cave sat tucked into the hillside, dry, empty, perfect for shelter. Jaxon and McKay immediately gathered firewood as the first icy gust swept down the pass. Leah and Cash went to find a stream to refill their canteens, while Chad stayed behind to tend the horses and lay out sleeping rolls near the cave's mouth.

Camp bustled with quiet efficiency, but beneath the motion, tension clung to the air, Leah's grief, her anger, her exhaustion wrapping around all of them like a storm waiting to break.

Leah kept to herself for the rest of the afternoon. She barely touched her supper, pushing the food around her plate until she couldn't stand sitting anymore. With a quiet exhale, she slipped away from the fire and headed toward the trees where the creek murmured softly. She found a fallen stump and sank onto it, elbows on her knees, thoughts heavy and tangled. She had barely drawn a calming breath when footsteps crunched behind her. McKay. Of course.

She straightened, bracing herself as he approached with that infuriatingly confident stride.

"Why are you following me, McKay?" she asked sharply, letting every ounce of irritation color her tone. He only gave her a lopsided grin.

"I came to see if you're still sore at me for this mornin', Miss Leah."

Her brows shot up. "It's still *Miss Johnson* to you. And no, I haven't. Now please leave me alone." She stood, intending to walk away, but McKay stepped closer, grin still in place.

"Aw, don't be like that," he urged. "A gal as lovely as you ain't meant to stay riled up. I didn't harm you."

"You still had no right," she snapped. "You made a judgment based on what you saw, and I defended myself."

His eyes widened. "You sunk your teeth in my hand and gave me a good kick for my trouble."

"What else was I supposed to do? It's not like I can fight you like a man."

He huffed a laugh. "Fair enough," he said with a slow nod. "Look... I'm sorry. Truly." For once, his gaze softened, earnest and unguarded. "Please forgive me for haulin' you over my knee and tannin' your backside. I shouldn't've done it."

Her cheeks flamed. She crossed her arms, attempting to cling to her dignity. McKay reached for her hand without warning, and she startled violently.

"Hey now, I'm sorry," he blurted, hands dropping away. "Didn't aim to scare you none."

Leah retreated a few steps toward the creek. She could feel his gaze on her like heat. Finally, she faced him.

"Why do you keep staring at me?"

McKay didn't even pretend otherwise. His eyes swept over her, carefully, appreciatively.

"I was just admirin' how well men's clothes suit you," he drawled. "You look mighty... attractin' in those trousers."

Leah's jaw dropped. Heat rushed up her neck, into her cheeks, all the way to the tips of her ears. His grin widened, pleased with her reaction.

"I know you're trying to pay me a compliment," she managed, chin lifting with forced composure, "so I'll let it slide. But I suggest you keep remarks like that to yourself."

"Why's that?" he challenged with a tilt of his head. "Ain't a man meant to be forward when he's speakin' truth?"

"There's a fine line between honesty," Leah countered, "and being inappropriate. Compliment a woman's face. Not her body, especially when she's dressed as a man."

To her surprise, McKay blinked, caught off guard. His mouth opened, ready with another retort, when a harsh rattling sound sliced through the clearing. Leah froze. McKay's head whipped toward the sound. A massive rattlesnake, coiled, tense, ready, lifted itself from the brush not three feet from her boots. She didn't even have time to gasp. McKay lunged.

His arm locked around her waist, yanking her backward with such force her boots left the ground. He pivoted, pulling her away from striking distance just as the snake hissed, tail buzzing louder. Leah found herself pressed against McKay's chest, breathless and stunned, his grip iron-strong, his breath warm against her ear, while the rattlesnake shifted its weight again, preparing to strike.

Leah had been watching the rattlesnake with rigid, focused stillness. Terror seized her for a split second, unwelcome memories of Colt's own snakebite flashing like lightning through her mind, but she shoved the fear aside. Not now. Not with danger right in front of her. Her hand crept toward her revolver, slow and deliberate, ready to draw the moment the serpent lunged. But before she could take even one careful step back, McKay moved. He charged forward.

The abrupt motion sent the rattlesnake into a frenzy. It coiled tightly, hissed, and struck. Leah fired. The shot cracked through the trees, echoing down the creek bed. The snake dropped limp, and the recoil knocked both Leah and McKay backward onto the ground.

She heard Cash and Jaxon shouting their names, voices tight with alarm, but Leah sprang to her feet before either man reached her. Fury surged faster than adrenaline.

"You—fool," she snapped, spinning toward McKay. "Why did you have to scare the snake? It would still be alive if you hadn't jumped like an idiot!"

McKay blinked up at her, stunned. He had clearly expected gratitude, not a verbal lashing.

"I was tryin' to save your hide," he blurted. "Didn't know you were packin' iron, and I dang sure didn't know you could shoot like that!"

Leah's jaw dropped. "That I could hit a target? Who do you think you are?" Her blue eyes sparked like fire. "How dare you say that? I grew up on a ranch, McKay. I'm inheriting this place one day. You must be the most insensitive, chauvinistic, prejudiced man I've ever met!"

"Leah—" he tried, but it was useless. Once her temper blew, it blew.

"I'm well trained with multiple weapons. I know how to shoot, ride, rope, and break horses better than half the men you've ever met, I'll wager. I just saved our lives, and *that's* your response?" She threw her hands up, incredulously. "I can't even, why would anyone say something like that?" Her voice rang through the clearing just as Cash and Jaxon burst out of the trees, breathless.

"What happened?" Cash demanded. "We heard a gunshot!"

"Why don't you ask Mr. Prejudice over there?" Leah snapped, cutting a furious glare at McKay. "I'm sure he'd love to give you a colorful explanation."

She turned on her heel and stomped toward camp before either man could stop her, her boots crunching hard across the ground. Behind her, McKay called out, sounding genuinely remorseful.

"I—I'm real sorry, Leah! Didn't mean no offense. You just knocked me back on my heels, that's all."

She didn't look back. She scoffed instead, marching on with her spine rigid and her wounded pride blazing hot enough to light the whole valley on fire.

"Alright, McKay," Cash said, folding his arms as Jaxon disappeared after Leah. "What did you do this time?"

McKay rubbed the back of his neck and blew out a breath.

"It was—" He winced. "It was a dumb misunderstanding. On my part." He scrubbed his hand over his face. "I really gotta stop underestimatin' that girl." He shook his head, half in awe, half in disbelief. "She's like a volcano, eruption sittin' just under the surface, waitin' to blow."

Cash raised a brow. "That bad, huh?"

McKay nodded, then relayed everything, how he'd jumped at the snake, how she'd shot it, what he'd said afterward, and the spectacular explosion that followed. By the time he finished, Cash had a broad, knowing grin.

"Oh yeah," Cash chuckled. "You've gotta be careful around her. Leah's a spitfire, always has been. Every time you put your foot in your mouth, son, you add another stick of dynamite to an already blazing fire."

McKay groaned. "I swear, I wasn't meanin' no insult. She's just... well, she's different. Didn't expect a girl like her."

"Leah's full of surprises," Cash agreed. McKay glanced toward the path she'd stormed down.

"Lookin' at her mama, you gotta wonder if they're even related. The gap between those two is somethin' fierce."

Cash's grin softened, turning fond. "Leah takes after her father's side. Heart, grit, stubbornness, every ounce of it straight from Mitch Johnson. Patricia..." He sighed. "She's wired differently."

McKay nodded thoughtfully. "Well," he muttered, "looks like I've burned through my day's supply of blunders."

Cash laughed and clapped him on the back.

"Around Leah? Trust me. You haven't even scratched the surface."

"Leah, what happened between you and McKay?" Jaxon's voice was low, steady, too steady. It slid right under her skin.

"Absolutely nothing you need to be concerned about," she snapped, still boiling from anger and embarrassment. Her pulse hadn't settled since the snake, or since McKay's idiotic comment, or, if she were honest, since Jaxon had been following her like a shadow.

His brow furrowed, jaw tightening. Leah turned away, ignoring it, but he reached out and clasped her arm before she could take another step.

"Let go," she demanded, but her voice softened despite her intention. Jaxon pulled her toward him, not roughly, but firmly enough that she stumbled straight into his chest. Leah gasped.

Suddenly all she could hear was the pounding of her own heartbeat, and the slow, deliberate inhale he took. He smelled like leather and warm cedar, dust and sunlight, dangerously familiar. Her stomach flipped, then twisted, then somersaulted all at once.

"Why won't you tell me?" he murmured, his breath ghosting across her forehead. His arms had come around her almost instinctively, strong, warm, unyielding. He wasn't restraining her. He was holding her. Too close. Far too close.

Leah swallowed hard and fixed her gaze somewhere near the collar of his shirt instead of meeting those impossibly intense brown eyes.

"It was nothing of importance," she managed, though her voice shook just enough to betray her. "We handled it. That's that."

Jaxon didn't move. For a long moment, he simply held her there, studying her face as if he could read her thoughts through her heartbeat.

"You're shaking," he murmured.

"No, I'm not." She absolutely was. His thumb brushed her arm, small, unthinking, devastating.

She forced herself to lift her chin, but that was a mistake too. Because now their faces were inches apart, and something warm, dangerously warm, softened his gaze.

Finally, slowly, he released her. The sudden absence of his touch left her breathless. Leah stepped back too quickly, face burning so hot she was certain it had turned crimson. Jaxon's mouth quirked into a knowing smirk that made her want to either stomp away or throw her hat at him. She chose stomping.

Without another word, she spun on her heel and strode into the cave, ignoring the furious pounding of her heart. She sank onto the blankets with a huff, arms crossed tightly. Behind her, she heard Jaxon chuckle under his breath. That only made her blush harder.

McKay and Cash appeared at the cave entrance seconds later. The moment McKay spotted Leah sitting stiffly by the fire, his whole posture tensed. He looked ready to march straight toward her with an apology, another explanation, or another argument already burning in his eyes. Cash caught his arm before he could take a single step.

"Don't," he warned, low and firm. "Trust me, it's best to let her cool down."

McKay blinked, surprised. His gaze slipped toward Leah again. She sat with her back to them, arms wrapped around herself, chin tilted stubbornly as she glared into the flames. Even from this distance, her pride and fury radiated like heat from a forge.

"She's a spitfire," McKay muttered, rubbing the back of his neck. "I just wanted to—"

Cash exhaled, almost a laugh. "Son, trying to fix things with Leah when she's in a temper is like trying to out-wrestle a grizzly. Best give her room unless you're ready to lose a limb."

McKay huffed but didn't argue. Cash clapped him on the shoulder, steering him to the opposite side of the fire.

"She'll talk when she's ready," Cash murmured. "And if she's not ready... you'll know." He arched a brow knowingly. "Believe me."

McKay followed his gaze to Leah, small, fierce, glaring at the flames as if daring them to challenge her. He swallowed.

"Yeah," he murmured. "I believe it."

They caught up with the cattle thieves in the early afternoon, the sun hanging low enough to cast long shadows across the ridgeline. From their concealed vantage point, tucked behind scrub oak and scattered boulders, they watched the group below.

Cash crouched low, counting under his breath.

"Ten of them," he murmured. "Looks like numbers are on their side... but not experience."

Most of the thieves appeared barely past boyhood, their movements jumpy and unsure. A few handled their reins with confidence, but the rest shifted nervously, glancing over their shoulders as though expecting trouble. Reckless, desperate boys were often more unpredictable than seasoned rustlers, which made Cash even more cautious.

Leah crouched beside him, steady as stone. She had already sighted her rifle and tested her angle twice. Cash didn't have to say it. She was the best shot among them. She could hit a pinecone at a hundred yards if she wanted to, and everyone knew it.

"We'll move in fast," Cash whispered. "No time for them to scatter or get brave. Leah, stay tucked in those bushes. You'll have the whole clearing in your sights. If any of them get clever, you make sure they regret it."

Leah nodded, calm and certain, though her pulse thrummed with focus. She shifted deeper behind the brush, high enough for a clean line, hidden enough to vanish from sight. Chad swallowed hard beside her. He wasn't built for a fight, and they all knew it. Cash placed a reassuring hand on the young man's shoulder.

"Take the horses and circle wide," he instructed quietly. "Keep them safe and stay out of sight. We'll signal when it's done."

Relief and embarrassment flickered across Chad's face, but he obeyed without argument, slipping away with the reins.

With the horses gone and the plan set, Cash, McKay, and Jaxon exchanged a last glance, tight, determined, wordless. Then they began their descent, moving like shadows along the rocks. Below, the thieves laughed, oblivious. Above them, Leah lifted her rifle and drew a slow, steady breath. The hunt was over. The reckoning was about to begin.

The men were struggling to keep the stolen cattle steady. Dark clouds rolled in from the west, the sharp metallic scent of rain drifting across the clearing. The animals sensed it, shifting restlessly, snorting and stamping.

Leah crouched low in the brush, revolver at her hip and shotgun within reach. Her focus had narrowed to a razor's edge. Outnumbered or not, she knew they could take these men. She studied the thieves with a hunter's eye, eight barely out of their adolescence, the remaining two older, grizzled, and clearly the ringleaders.

Cash, Jaxon, and McKay stayed well-hidden as they crept forward. When Cash gave the signal, all three sprang from behind the trees, guns leveled with chilling precision.

"You're surrounded!" Cash barked. "Surrender peacefully and no one gets hurt."

One of the older men didn't hesitate. He yanked his gun free and aimed straight at Cash. At the same moment, two of the younger cowboys charged him. Leah's rifle cracked. The bullet tore into the tree bark inches from the older man's face. He jerked back, startled, eyes darting wildly in search of her, an impossible task with how well she was concealed. Leah allowed herself a quiet, satisfied breath.

Cash slammed one charging cowboy to the ground, sending his gun skittering. The second rustler drew his weapon, but Leah was already aiming again. The next shot sheared the hat clean off the boy's head. He nearly fainted where he stood. Cash tackled him before he could think twice.

Meanwhile, Jaxon and McKay moved like lightning, dragging two cowboys from their saddles and tying them up in seconds. Cash took off after yet another young cowboy, snaring him neatly with his lasso and yanking him hard out of the saddle.

Leah's attention snapped to the remaining ringleader just in time to see him fire into the herd. Two cattle dropped instantly. A hot wave of rage seared through her. She fired. The man screamed and toppled from his horse, clutching his shoulder where her bullet lodged. Gunfire sent the remaining horses into a panic. Two thieves were thrown violently to the ground. They scrambled up and fled on foot, poor choice, considering Leah was in her element now.

McKay and Jaxon sprinted after them, but Leah decided to have a little fun. She sighted the first runner. One perfect shot later, the sole of his boot separated from the upper, sending him stumbling and face-planting into the dirt. McKay skidded to a stop, staring back at Leah in open-mouthed disbelief. She only grinned. Her attention shifted to the second rustler, foolish enough to run straight toward her. She fired once. His belt snapped clean through, his trousers fell to his knees, and he tripped immediately, arms flailing, before crashing to the ground in a tangle of humiliation. Jaxon doubled over laughing.

Minutes later, every rustler was tied to a tree, cussing up a storm, until Leah stepped from the bushes. She removed her hat, letting her long hair spill free. A few young thieves whistled, realizing she was the one who'd taken them down. The older two glared with bitterness.

"Let a girl do your fightin', did ya? Pitiful," one sneered.

"No," McKay shot back. "What's pathetic is how this girl dropped you boys flat." He tipped Leah a grin. "Ain't seen shootin' like hers in years."

Leah turned to Cash. "What are we doing with them? It'll be hours before we reach Eureka."

"We make camp," Cash decided. "They're tied tight enough, and I already warned them the next man who cusses gets gagged. The four of us will take turns on watch."

Leah nodded. "I'm going to check the cattle. One of the cows should calve any day."

"I'll go with you." Jaxon fell into step beside her.

They located the cow quickly. She was already in labor—and struggling. They stayed with her as the light faded, doing everything they could to keep her calm, but the birth wasn't progressing.

By the time McKay returned with a torch, night had settled.

"Can you keep her steady?" Leah asked Jaxon. "I think the calf's stuck. I'm going in."

He soothed the cow with a low murmur as Leah rolled up her sleeve. The animal flinched at her touch but was too exhausted to resist. Leah worked carefully until she found the problem, a small hoof bent at the wrong angle.

"There you are," she whispered to the unborn calf, gently guiding the limb back into place. Within minutes, the calf slid free, landing safely in the grass. The cow rose shakily and began licking her newborn clean, soft grunts rumbling from her chest. Leah stepped back, watching in quiet wonder as the calf, legs wobbling, made its first attempts to stand. It took several tries, but finally the tiny creature found its balance under its mother's warm breath.

A small, tired smile tugged at Leah's lips. After everything the day had brought, new life felt like the sweetest victory.

15
Caught Beneath the Hooves

"Mornin', Heber. Marcus and the cattle showed up yet?" Milton Rowland had barely swung out of the saddle before firing off the question. Impatience edged his voice sharply, making Heber straighten reflexively.

Heber shook his head. "No sign of 'em."

Milton's jaw tightened. "And why not?"

"I was waitin' outside the post office earlier," Heber said, droppin' his voice low.

"Heard the sheriff and his deputy jawin'. They got a wire from Hoopa Valley—said some o' the Johnson Ranch hands found their cattle stolen. Rode after the thieves soon as they saw the tracks."

Milton's expression darkened. "And Marcus still hasn't shown his face here in Eureka..."

"That's right," Heber confirmed. "'Less he took some fool detour, I'm thinkin' the Hoopa boys caught up to him."

Milton sucked in a sharp breath, muttering curses under it. The wind carried the bitterness of his pacing steps.

"And what's the fine sheriff plannin' to do about it?" he demanded.

"He's gatherin' a posse," Heber said. "Wants to track 'em down before they disappear into the hills."

Milton barked a humorless laugh. "Then we're already behind."

"Sir... maybe we ought to hold off until—"

"No." Milton slashed a hand through the air. "We leave at once. I won't let a pack of upstart cowboys from Hoopa Valley ruin months of planning." His eyes narrowed, cold and calculating. "Find the horses. Tell the men to saddle up. Time, we deal with those pesky cowboys once and for all."

Heber swallowed and hurried off, urgency pressing on the morning air.

"Where's Leah?" Cash demanded, irritation sharpening his words as he scanned the tree line. It was past time to leave, and she should've been saddled with the rest of them. Jaxon tipped his hat.

"She went to check on the herd. Wanted to be sure that cow and her calf are fit enough to travel."

Cash grunted but didn't argue. If anyone knew cattle, it was Leah. The rustlers, bound, miserable, and mounted for transport, shifted uneasily. McKay strode back from the creek, canteen dripping. Then the valley split open with gunfire. One shot. Then another. Then several more in rapid succession. The peaceful hush of morning shattered.

Cash froze. Blood ran cold. His head snapped toward the sound, past the trembling cattle already stumbling and tossing their heads in fear.

"Leah," he breathed, fear replacing irritation in an instant. He scanned the far side of the valley, heart thundering. Where was she?

A thunderous explosion ripped through the valley, so violently the earth itself seemed to jump. Dust shot upward in a plume, and Jaxon's head snapped toward the sound just in time to see Leah swinging into her saddle.

"Leah!" he shouted, but his warning was drowned out as a second blast detonated, closer, harder, shattering the air and rattling the ground beneath them. The already-nervous cattle lost all control. In a single, terrifying instant, the herd surged into a full stampede, hooves pounding like rolling thunder. Leah's horse reared violently, eyes wide in fear. She grabbed the reins, but the animal twisted, panicked beyond reason, and she was thrown hard into the dirt, directly in the path of the oncoming cattle.

Cash let out a strangled gasp, every drop of color draining from his face. But before he even registered his own movement, Jaxon's instincts kicked in. He slammed his heels into his gelding's sides, the horse leaping forward with explosive speed.

"McKay! Chad! Stay with the thieves!" Cash barked as he tore after Jaxon, his voice tight with fear. Both men rode as if their lives depended on it, but it was Leah's life hanging by a thread. The cattle were already sweeping toward her in a tide of panic and muscle, the ground trembling beneath the sheer force of hundreds of hooves. Dust clouded the air. The roar of the stampede swallowed everything.

Cash's heart hammered against his ribs. McKay's horrified expression mirrored his own. They all knew the truth: no cowboy in his right mind would ever willingly fall beneath a stampede. Even the strongest men rarely made it out alive.

And Leah... Leah was lying helpless, half-buried in dirt, with a wall of frenzied cattle closing in around her. If Jaxon hadn't reached her in the next few seconds, she wouldn't stand a chance.

"Leah!" Jaxon shouted, his voice nearly swallowed by the chaos, bellowing cattle, thundering hooves, and the sharp crack of gunfire erupting somewhere nearby. Bullets whistled past, striking the ground and ricocheting off rocks. Whoever was shooting wasn't just aiming at the herd.

Panic clawed up Jaxon's throat with every passing second. If he didn't reach her soon, if she didn't lift her head, cry out, something, he feared he might lose his mind. His horse danced beneath him, snorting and tossing its head, trying to bolt from the madness. But Jaxon kept a white-knuckled grip on the reins, forcing the animal to hold steady as he pushed deeper into the stampede.

Cash reached him moments later, his face bleak and carved with worry. Their eyes met, and no words were needed. Both men shared the same terror. They urged their horses forward, crowding through the stampeding animals until, through the swirling dust, they finally caught sight of Leah, a small, motionless form half-buried in dirt.

Jaxon's heart nearly stopped. Without hesitation, the two men forced their horses into the tight cluster of cattle, creating a pocket of space around her. As soon as they drew near, Cash swung low in the saddle, reaching for her. Jaxon leaned down at the same time, and together they lifted her, but Jaxon's grip held firmer. He pulled her carefully into his arms and settled her across his lap before turning his horse sharply away from the stampede.

Leah whimpered, low, broken, agonized, and the sound tore straight through him. He tightened his hold protectively, trying to shield her from further jostling as they rode for safety. Once they cleared the chaos and reached a stretch of open grass and trees, Cash dismounted in a heartbeat. Jaxon slid from his saddle with Leah still in his arms, but Cash stepped in gently, lifting her from him and lowering her to a patch of soft ground. The world around them roared with distant shouts, gunfire, and the lingering rumble of hooves, but neither man looked up. Their entire focus was on the battered young woman before them.

Jaxon dropped to his knees beside her. "We need to get her to a doctor, fast," he said, voice tight. Cash nodded grimly. But as soon as he touched Leah's arm, she cried out, her body curling instinctively from the pain. Her left leg lay at an unnatural angle. Her shoulder bulged forward, clearly dislocated. Deep, ugly gashes striped her arms, and a thin stream of blood trickled from a cut at her hairline. The sight made Jaxon physically sick.

"Leah," he whispered, struggling to keep his voice steady, "you need a doctor right away. We have to get you back to camp."

She shook her head weakly, tears slipping down her dirt-streaked cheeks.

"I... I can't move," she whispered hoarsely. "The pain is too much. Please... just leave me here." She gasped as another wave of agony hit her. "Go... go check on the calf. The herd will trample it... if nobody helps..."

Jaxon stared at her, horrified. "Leah, we are not leaving you."

But she squeezed her eyes shut, trying to fight the pain.

"Please. Just go," she cried, her voice breaking. Jaxon's composure finally cracked. He looked at Cash, panicked, raw and unrestrained.

"Goodness... how are we going to get her to a doctor? Cash, she's—she's in no shape to be moved."

Cash scrubbed his hand over his face, breath shaking.

"We might have to do it ourselves."

Jaxon snapped his head toward him. "We can't do that, Cash! Setting bones, fixing a dislocated shoulder, one wrong move could kill her."

"What choice do we have?" Cash shot back. His voice wasn't angry; it was desperate. And the worst part? Jaxon knew he wasn't wrong. The closest doctor was miles away. Leah was broken, bleeding, and barely conscious. If they didn't act, she wouldn't survive long enough for help to arrive.

"Are you Doug Cashley?"

Cash's head snapped up at the unfamiliar voice. A group of riders had just reached McKay, dust swirling around their horses' legs. At the front rode a man with a badge glinting on his chest.

"No, he's right over there," McKay answered, pointing Cash's way. "But these fellas? They're cattle thieves. Go on and arrest 'em."

The sheriff gave a curt nod. With a swift motion of his hand, he ordered two deputies and several armed townsmen forward. They moved quickly, pulling the bound thieves from their saddles and securing them with practiced efficiency. Only once the criminals were dealt with did the sheriff turn his horse and ride hard toward Cash.

"Doug Cashley?" he called again. Cash rose from where he'd been kneeling beside Leah, dust coating his clothes. He nodded.

"That's me."

The sheriff dismounted in one fluid motion, boots hitting the ground with authority.

"Sheriff Thomas Jones, from Eureka," he said, extending a steady hand. "We received word of your trouble and reckoned you might need help haulin' these men in."

"Appreciate that, Sheriff," Cash replied. His voice was steady, but exhaustion and fear clung to the edges. "Any chance you brought a doctor with you?"

"Ain't ridin' with us," Sheriff Jones said, shakin' his head. "But one's close behind. We brought a doctor and a nurse out from the Eureka infirmary. They're comin' by carriage, so they'll be a mite slower, but they ain't far." His gaze slid toward

Jaxon and softened. "Looks like you've got someone needin' tendin' to right quick."

He walked closer, following Cash's line of sight to where Leah lay on the ground. When he caught sight of her bruised face and blood-matted hair, he froze. His expression changed instantly, from professional detachment to sharp, startled compassion.

"Heaven forbid..." he breathed. "Did the thieves do that to her?"

Cash shook his head grimly. "No. Stampede got her. Explosions spooked the herd, and she was thrown right in the middle of it."

Sheriff Jones let out a slow, pained exhale. "Poor girl..."

Jaxon was still kneeling beside her, murmuring reassurances that neither of them fully believed. Leah tried to hold herself still, tried to muffle her cries, but her trembling gave her away. Every breath seemed to hurt. The pain etched itself into her features despite her fierce attempt to hide it. It was heartbreaking to watch. But Cash forced himself to stay steady. Falling apart wouldn't help her, not now.

"She's tough," he said quietly, more to himself than to the sheriff. "But she needs that doctor fast." Sheriff Jones nodded. "We'll get him here. Just hold on."

All three men hovered close, eyes fixed on Leah, willing her to keep breathing, keep fighting, keep holding on until help arrived.

The doctor and his nurse arrived just as Sheriff Jones and his men were preparing to ride out. The posse had spent the last half hour scouring the surrounding hills, hoping to track the men responsible for the explosions. All they found were the splintered remains of dynamite sticks, deep scorch marks in the dirt, and several dead cattle—the calf among them. Sheriff Jones's jaw tightened as he surveyed the carnage.

"Whoever pulled this stunt knew damn well what they were about," he growled.

"And I swear, I'm gonna get to the bottom of it."

The doctor, a young man with earnest eyes and sleeves hastily rolled to his elbows, hurried to Leah's side. The moment he caught sight of her injuries, his face drained of color.

"Good heavens..." he whispered. "How long has she been like this?"

"Not long," Cash replied. "But she's fading fast."

The doctor knelt beside her, assessing her with swift, practiced movements. Leah whimpered as he touched her broken leg, and he exchanged a grim look with his nurse.

"We have to move her," he said immediately. "Her pain is extreme, but that's not the worst of it. A break like this, combined with shock, can turn dangerous quickly. We need to get her to the infirmary as soon as possible."

Meanwhile, McKay and Chad mounted up again and began working their way through the valley, gathering the scattered cattle. The stampede had driven animals in every direction, and it would take hours to round them all up.

Sheriff Jones stepped over, placing a hand on Cash's shoulder.

"I'll leave four of my men with you. They'll help with the cattle and keep watch in case the folks who set off that dynamite are still nearby." He glanced toward the thieves being loaded onto horses. "I'm takin' these men to Eureka. The sooner they're behind bars, the better."

Cash nodded his thanks, though his eyes never left Leah. She lay pale, trembling, and barely conscious as the doctor worked quickly beside her. Each soft moan from her lips made Cash's heart twist painfully. They had saved her from the stampede... but she was far from safe yet.

"Miss Johnson," the doctor said, kneeling beside her with practiced calm, "I'm Dr. Mark Matthews, and this here is my wife and nurse, Jane. We're going to move as quickly as we can, but I won't lie, this is going to be extremely painful."

Leah clenched her jaw, breathing in sharp, shallow bursts. Sweat beaded along her brow. Dr. Matthews continued, voice low but urgent.

"You've got a dislocated shoulder and a broken leg. Under normal circumstances, I'd use chloroform, but I don't have any with me. And we can't wait until we reach town. A break like this..." He glanced at the swelling above her boot. "It can cause internal bleeding or permanent damage. We must set it now."

Leah shut her eyes, a soft whimper escaping. Still, when she forced the words out, her voice held its familiar, stubborn steel.

"Just do it," she gasped, tears spilling despite her best effort to hold them back.

Jaxon knelt beside her, taking her hand in both of his.

"Let it out, Leah," he murmured, squeezing gently. "Don't hold back."

Dr. Matthews looked up toward Cash. "Are you this young woman's father?"

Cash shook his head immediately. "No. But I work for the Johnsons, and Leah..." He swallowed hard. "Leah's like a daughter to me."

"I see." The doctor nodded once. "In that case, I need you to help me. Someone strong should hold her steady while I fix her shoulder and leg. Do you think you can do that?"

The question landed like a physical blow. Cash hated this, hated the thought of causing her more pain, hated that she was suffering at all. But she needed him. And he had never once shirked a responsibility, especially not when Leah was involved. His voice was rough when he answered.

"Yeah. I can do it." He lowered himself beside her, sliding an arm carefully behind her back and lifting her into a position that offered support without putting pressure on her injuries. Leah whimpered at the movement, her fingers digging into his hand.

Jaxon suddenly stood, breathing hard as if the weight of what was coming pressed against his ribs. Without a word, he swung onto his horse, tension stark in his shoulders.

"I'm going to help McKay, Chad, and the sheriff's men with the rest of the cattle," he said quickly, avoiding Leah's gaze.

Cash didn't blame him. Watching this next part, listening to Leah's screams, would break a weaker man. Even Cash doubted his own strength.

"Go on," he said quietly. Jaxon didn't wait to be told twice. He wheeled his horse around and galloped off, leaving Cash to steady the girl he cared for while the doctor prepared to do the most painful work of all.

Leah forced her eyes open, just for a moment. Through the haze of pain, she found Cash's face above her, steady, calm, unshakeable. But she saw the truth in his eyes: worry, fear, helplessness.

"I'll be all right, Cash," she whispered, though her voice trembled. She wasn't sure if she was reassuring him or herself. With her uninjured hand, she clung to his arm, her fingers shaking as she closed her eyes again. Dr. Matthews gently lifted her injured arm.

"Miss Johnson... are you ready?"

Before Leah could answer, Nurse Jane leaned in. "Mark, perhaps she needs something to bite down on—"

Leah shook her head sharply. "Just—just get it done. I don't want to wait."

Cash felt her grip tighten on his sleeve. He anchored her against his chest, bracing her.

"Deep breath for me," Dr. Matthews instructed. Leah inhaled, and the doctor pulled. The shoulder slid back into place with a sharp, sickening click.

Her scream tore from her throat before she could stop it. Her entire body arched in agony, every muscle seizing at once. Cash held her tighter, whispering soft reassurances even as his own chest constricted painfully. Her cry felt like it split him down the middle. She clutched his arm harder, desperate for something, anything, to hold on to as the pain swallowed her.

Dr. Matthews moved quickly, securing her arm in a sling to immobilize the shoulder. Nurse Jane dabbed sweat from Leah's forehead, then cleaned the blood from her temple and cheek, cooing soft encouragement, while Leah gasped through the lingering pain.

Meanwhile, the young physician gathered what he needed for the next, and far worse, task. He selected two thick, straight sticks for splints and laid the bandages across his medical bag for easy reach. He knelt at Leah's side again and spoke gently.

"Miss Johnson... this will be the worst of it. The break needs to be realigned before it can heal right."

Leah nodded weakly, swallowing hard. She didn't have the strength to speak. Cash tightened his hold around her waist, and she gripped his arm as though it were the only thing tethering her to the world. The doctor took a deep breath—and pulled. The sound of bone grinding against bone was muffled beneath Leah's second scream, sharper, rawer, even more agonized than the first. Her body convulsed, her breath shuddering in and out as she fought not to pass out. Then... it was done. The pain didn't vanish, but the intensity ebbed enough for her to slump against Cash's chest, trembling violently.

Cash squeezed her hand and leaned down, pressing a gentle kiss to her forehead.

"That's it, sweetheart... you did it."

Dr. Matthews checked her pulse, then carefully palpated her abdomen and ribs. "No signs of internal bleeding," he murmured with relief. "She's lucky."

Nurse Jane worked swiftly but gently, stitching the gashes along Leah's arms and tending to the cut on her head. Leah winced but didn't fight it. After what she'd endured, the sting of a needle was nothing at all. She lay still, eyes half-open, breathing unsteadily, but alive. And Cash didn't let go of her once.

16
Words That Can't Be Taken Back

"We need to get her to the infirmary as soon as possible," Dr. Matthews said, wiping his hands on a clean cloth. "The worst of it is behind us, but her wounds and injuries must be monitored closely. Infection sets in fast out here."

Leah's breathing was still ragged, but she forced herself to ask, "Can I return home after you've checked my injuries?"

The doctor shook his head firmly. "No, Miss Johnson. You'll need to stay at the clinic until you're properly healed. And even after you're discharged, you will not be returning to ranch work right away."

"But—"

"No, Leah," Cash cut in, lifting an eyebrow at her in a no-nonsense way she knew far too well. "You're going to listen to the doctor. And there will be no sneaking out of the infirmary either."

His stern tone didn't fool her for a second. She heard the faintest hint of teasing beneath it, and despite her pain, a tiny smile tugged at her lips. Cash winked at the physician as he helped ease her into a sitting position, supporting her carefully.

Dr. Matthews chuckled. "I'm glad I brought my wife along. Miss Johnson will need help with basic tasks for the next few weeks, and, well, unless that young man from earlier is her husband, the men here shouldn't be the ones tending to her."

Leah flushed instantly, heat rushing to her cheeks. Cash's grin spread from ear to ear, far too pleased with the doctor's implication.

The doctor continued with innocent curiosity, "So, is he your husband?"

"He is not my husband," Leah muttered, staring intently at the ground as if it might open and swallow her. Dr. Matthews blinked in mild surprise.

"No? Then are you engaged? Because it was clear as day, he was beyond worried about you."

Leah's head snapped up, irritation flaring through the embarrassment.

"He's a friend. Just a friend." Her tone made Cash's grin grow even wider. Jane Matthews joined the conversation with a warm, knowing smile.

"Oh, honey... I doubt that young man sees you as just a friend. Mark is right. The look on his face when he saw you hurt? That kind of fear usually comes with strong feelings, feelings like being in lo—"

"Okay, wow, please stop," Leah interrupted, mortified, her voice rising slightly. "Jaxon and I are friends. Just friends. We are not in love, and we are not getting married." Her face must have been the darkest shade of red humanly possible. The defensiveness in her voice only made her blush deepen.

She shot Cash a glare, but he had conveniently turned away, shoulders shaking as he clearly fought back a laugh. Leah narrowed her eyes. And then she caught the doctor's lips twitching too, as if he was trying very hard not to smile. Leah groaned softly and closed her eyes. This injury was turning out to be painful in more ways than one.

"I should get Miss Johnson washed up and changed before we discuss the next steps," Jane said more professionally. She gestured toward a cluster of trees a short distance away. "Could one of you carry her over there? If we hang a few blankets, we can make a private space."

Cash nodded immediately. With careful hands, he lifted Leah once more. She winced but tried not to show it. He carried her to the shaded grove, and Dr. Matthews and Jane quickly helped him drape several blankets between branches, forming a makeshift tent of privacy. Once they were satisfied, Cash mounted his horse again.

"I'll help gather the rest of the cattle," he said, tipping his hat to Leah before riding off. Jane turned back to her with a reassuring smile.

"All right, my dear. Let's get you comfortable."

The next hour was slow, gentle work. Jane washed dirt, sweat, and dried blood from Leah's skin with careful hands, pausing whenever Leah winced. When it came time to change clothes, the problem became immediately apparent: Leah had only men's trousers in her saddlebag.

"We'll make do," Jane said with a thoughtful nod. From her own belongings, she produced a simple skirt in a soft, dusty blue. "This should fit, and it'll be far easier on your leg."

To Leah's shock, it fit as though it were made for her. Since Leah couldn't raise her left arm, Jane helped her slip into one of her clean shirts, gently guiding the fabric around the sling Dr. Matthews had tied earlier. When the shirt was settled properly, Jane pulled a warm shawl around her shoulders and buttoned it closed for extra support and modesty. Then Jane stepped back, and a slow, mischievous smirk appeared on her face.

"Well, despite everything you've been through, you look lovely," she declared. "I can only imagine that young man's face when he sees his...*friend* looking like this."

Leah stared at her in disbelief. "Why does everyone think—?"

But Jane only laughed softly and began brushing out Leah's tangled hair, letting the clean, loose strands fall past her shoulders. It felt strangely comforting. When she finished, she called out for her husband.

Leah looked completely lost in thought, staring at nothing, her hands folded weakly in her lap. When the blankets were suddenly drawn aside and Dr. Matthews stepped through, followed closely by Jaxon, she startled. Her face went up in flames instantly. Not pink. Not red. A burning inferno.

It was obvious to anyone with eyes that if she'd had even a shred of strength left, she would have leapt up and run straight out of the camp—and kept running.

Jaxon didn't hesitate. He was at her side within moments, dropping into a squat in front of her. His presence filled the little space, warm and overwhelming in a way that made her pulse skitter. He gently took her uninjured hand in his callused one, his touch warm and steady.

"How are you feeling, Leah?" he asked softly. His voice was careful, almost too careful, and yet the concern in it was impossible to miss. Leah tried to keep her gaze fixed on her lap.

"Better than before," she murmured. "Doc Matthews gave me something for the pain. The worst is over now."

Jaxon sensed the way she avoided looking at him. Slowly, almost hesitantly, he lifted her chin with one finger. Their eyes met. Her blue eyes were guarded, but she shivered... not from cold. He knew that immediately.

"You cold?" he asked anyway, his tone deliberately gentle, trying to give her an out, trying to soothe her. Leah shook her head quickly, trying to drop her gaze again, but he didn't let her look away. Not when everything in his chest tightened at the sight of her flustered face.

"Did I do something wrong?" he asked quietly. The earnestness in his voice nearly undid her. She shook her head again, too fast.

"I'm fine. And no, you didn't do anything wrong." Her voice trembled at the end. Jaxon heard it. So did the doctor. Leah wished the ground would swallow her entirely. She scrambled for a different topic, any topic.

"Did you find the calf?" she asked quickly. "Did his mother survive?" That finally made her lift her eyes. She knew it would. She did it purposefully. The change of subject was about as subtle as a runaway horse, and Jaxon saw straight through it.

He sighed softly, realizing she wasn't ready to talk about whatever she was feeling.

All right, he thought, *if she needs space, I'll give it.* He pretended not to notice her attempt to dodge the question that mattered most.

"Unfortunately, no," he said gently. "Neither the cow nor the calf made it. We found them both... not far from where we found you." His hand tightened around hers just a little. It wasn't the calf he was grieving at that moment. It was how close he'd come to losing her.

Leah tried to steady her breathing, but her heart refused to calm. Jaxon's nearness, his warmth, his scent of dust and horse and something distinctly him, made her pulse stutter. His face was much too close, his eyes far too intent. Heat crawled up her neck before she could stop it. Tears welled again, unbidden. She swallowed hard.

"I just... I just hope those thieves get punished. And I pray the Rowlands are arrested soon too. They've caused enough misery."

Jaxon's expression hardened with quiet determination.

"They will be," he assured her. "Sheriff Jones is already looking into it." His voice softened as he shifted closer. "Let's get you closer to the fire. I'll carry you. You're freezing."

She didn't argue when he slid his arms beneath her and lifted her effortlessly. Even injured and worn down, Leah felt a strange sense of safety settle around her the moment she left the ground. Jaxon held her as though she weighed nothing, as though she mattered more than he dared admit.

"We managed to round up all the surviving cattle," he explained as he walked, keeping his hold steady. "But whoever fired those shots and set off the explosions killed quite a few. We moved the carcasses farther off so predators will go for them, not us."

He didn't seem to notice the way Leah clung to his shirt, or how she tried not to focus on the solid muscles flexing beneath her cheek. Every step jostled her closer to him, and her embarrassment warred with an undeniable awareness of how strong he was, how warm.

Reaching the campfire, Jaxon eased himself onto a sturdy log without ever loosening his hold around her. Leah found herself settled securely in his lap, his arms wrapped protectively around her, shielding her from the cold night air. For a long moment, she fought the instinct to lean into him. Pride battled exhaustion... and lost.

Jaxon's heartbeat thudded steadily beneath her ear, strong, grounding, unexpectedly comforting. Slowly, tentatively, Leah let her head rest against his chest. His arms tightened just a fraction. Not enough to frighten her, just enough to make her feel safe. Safe in a way she hadn't felt in a very, very long time. Her eyes fluttered shut.

Despite the pain, the fear, and the humiliation of the day, Leah finally allowed herself to drift into sleep cradled against him, listening to the steady rise and fall of his breath and praying he didn't hear how quickly her heart, beat for him.

The group set out at first light the next morning. Leah lay bedded in the back of the buckboard, cushioned as best as possible by folded blankets and straw. Even so, every jolt of the wheels, sent a fresh wave of pain through her leg and shoulder. The constant shaking, rattling, and uneven terrain turned the journey into a slow, relentless agony. She bit down on her lip more than once to keep from crying out.

By the time they finally reached the infirmary, the sun had nearly disappeared behind the mountains, bathing the small town in a muted amber glow. Exhaustion tugged at Leah's mind, her thoughts blurring from fatigue and pain.

Cash didn't wait for instructions. He lifted her gently from the wagon, cradling her as though she were made of glass, and carried her inside. Warm lamplight flooded the narrow hallway, and another nurse immediately stepped forward to take over.

Jane and Dr. Matthews quickly pulled aside the small staff, explaining Leah's injuries in thorough detail—her broken leg, dislocated shoulder, the stitched wounds, and the constant risk of infection. Their voices were calm and efficient, but everyone listening wore expressions of concern.

Dr. Matthews returned to her bedside after a moment.

"Miss Johnson," he said kindly, "is there a parent or guardian we should contact about your condition?"

Leah swallowed hard and shook her head.

"No... my mother would only worry herself sick." Her voice wavered. "But my godfather lives in Sacramento. You can let him know."

"Of course," the doctor said gently.

Cash and Jaxon stepped forward then, both visibly reluctant. Dirt streaked their shirts and faces from the long ride, but their worry for her overshadowed everything else.

"We'll be back tomorrow," Cash said, brushing a stray lock of hair from her forehead. "After we sell the cattle, and before we start back home."

Jaxon nodded, trying to keep his voice steady.

"We don't like leaving you here alone, Leah. But the doctor says you're in good hands. And you'll be safe."

Dr. Matthews and Nurse Jane both nodded with reassuring smiles.

"We'll watch over her," Jane promised. "She won't be alone."

Leah managed a small, grateful smile, even as her eyes grew heavy with exhaustion.

"Thank you... both of you."

Cash squeezed her hand before stepping back, and Jaxon lingered a moment longer, watching her with a look that warmed her cheeks before he finally forced himself to turn away. As they walked out, their boots echoing softly down the hallway, Leah let out a shaky breath. She was in pain, frightened, and alone in a strange place, but somehow, knowing they would come back made everything feel just a little less terrifying.

Heber lingered in the shadows beneath a stand of trees, his jaw tight, his fists balled so hard his knuckles turned white. He watched with simmering fury as the two cowboys, Cash and Jaxon, walked out of the infirmary and headed back toward the livery. He still couldn't believe what he'd seen earlier: the group riding into town, not with some injured ranch hand, but with Leah, the girl he had unfinished business with. The girl who had humiliated him. The girl who had cost him everything.

His rage churned hot and bitter in his gut. Milton Rowland had hired the cattle thieves specifically to get Heber out of prison. Once freed, Heber had followed the Rowlands' plan, head to Eureka while the rustlers drove the Johnson cattle toward Eureka. His task was simple: make sure the sale went smoothly once the livestock arrived, ensure everyone was paid, and then disappear before anyone could trace the scheme back to them.

But the cattle never arrived. The thieves had been caught. And Heber had nearly bolted the moment he realized their whole operation had turned to dust. Then he'd seen them. Cashley. Finlay. And Leah, lying on a physician's wagon, bruised and bloodied but still alive.

A cruel smile twisted across his mouth. Milton wasn't back in Hoopa Valley yet, but Jack Rowland was. Heber had already sent a telegram, letting the Rowlands know that little Leah Johnson had decided to 'play cowboy' and gotten hurt. He could practically feel Jack's outrage thrumming through the wire.

And now... now he had an opportunity. Leah was here. Hurt. Alone in the infirmary. And the two men who cared most about her had just left. Heber's pulse quickened with dark anticipation.

"Ain't nobody gonna help you this time, Leah," he muttered, disappearing deeper into the shadows. "Not once I get my hands on you." He slipped away from the trees, already plotting exactly how, and when, he'd strike.

A loud, forceful knock rattled the door, jolting both Jaxon and Cash awake. They had barely lain down, exhausted from the long, brutal two days, but instinct kicked in instantly. They were on their feet before the echoes faded. Cash pulled open the door.

"Sheriff Jones," he said, alarm sharpening his voice. "Has something happened?"

The sheriff's expression was grim, shadows etched deep across his face. He gave a tight nod.

"I'm afraid so," he said. "Got a wire from Hoopa Valley not an hour ago." He exhaled sharply.

"And a few days back, Kneeland's sheriff sent word that one of their prisoners escaped, with help from a pack of unidentified men." He held up the folded slip of paper. "This telegram came in for you, Mr. Cashley."

Jaxon felt a jolt of dread shoot straight through his chest. He stepped closer, looking over Cash's shoulder as the foreman accepted the telegram with tense hands. Cash unfolded the paper and read aloud, his voice turning cold: "Cash, I just received a telegram from Heber Thatcher, and it is addressed to Jack and Milton Rowland. If you know where Leah is, let her know that he escaped."

Jaxon's stomach dropped. Heber. Loose. Aware of Leah's whereabouts. And Leah, injured, helpless, lying in an infirmary with no protection. Cash snapped the telegram shut, eyes blazing.

"We need to get to the infirmary. At once."

There was no hesitation. Both men dragged on their clothes with frantic urgency, boots thudding against the wooden floor as they rushed out the door. Sheriff Jones was right behind them, hand already hovering near his holstered weapon. The night air hit cold and sharp as they sprinted across the street. If Heber was anywhere near Leah... they were already running out of time.

The clinic was quiet, too quiet. Shadows stretched across the walls, and the faint glow of a lantern in the hallway barely slipped under the door. The nurse had given Leah a dose of laudanum to ease her pain and help her sleep, but it hadn't worked the way she'd hoped. Her shoulder throbbed relentlessly. Her leg pulsed with sharp, unyielding pain. Every position hurt, and exhaustion only made her more aware of it.

She lay still, listening, counting the distant sounds, clinging to them as a distraction. A creak from the hallway. Footsteps somewhere far off. The soft rustle of sheets from the nurses room. Then... the door to her room opened. Slowly. Quietly. Wrong. Leah froze. Someone was coming inside.

The nurses always knocked. Dr. Matthews always spoke before stepping in. Cash and Jaxon wouldn't return until morning. This person moved differently, too soft, too deliberate. Something cold prickled at the back of Leah's neck. Her heart slammed against her ribs. She couldn't see anything, the room was drenched in darkness, but she felt it. A warning. A pressure in the air that made her breath catch. Someone dangerous was in her room.

Refusing to wait for whoever it was to reach her bed, Leah groped blindly for anything she could use. Her fingers hit the plate and teacup left from earlier. Without hesitation, she grabbed both and hurled them toward the sound of the approaching footsteps. The sharp crash of shattering dishes exploded through the room, followed by a startled curse from the darkness, low, furious, unmistakably masculine.

"Someone is in my room!" she shouted, her voice breaking in fear. Another door in the clinic flew open. Leah heard startled voices, footsteps rushing toward her, the scrape of boots against the floorboards. Before she could shout again, gunfire erupted. One shot. Then another. Then several more. The deafening cracks echoed through the quiet clinic, and Leah's scream was swallowed by the violence tearing the night apart.

Cash and Jaxon burst through the doorway, the instant the gunshots rang out. Neither hesitated, both drew their colts in a single, fluid motion, aiming toward the dark corner where the shots had originated. A nurse rushed in behind them, clutching a lamp, with shaking hands. Its sudden glow cut through the shadows and illuminated the silhouette of a man crouched near Leah's bed. Both cowboys fired.

The intruder jerked violently and collapsed to the floor. For one suspended heartbeat, the world went silent. Sheriff Jones barreled in next, weapon raised. He crossed the room quickly, but one glance told him everything, Heber Thatcher lay motionless, eyes wide and glassy. Dead. The nurse lifted her lamp higher, casting the light across the room, and everyone gasped. Leah's bed was soaked in blood. But she wasn't on it.

"Leah?" Jaxon choked out, terror seizing him. A soft, ragged gasp answered him from the floor. They found her beside the bed, curled weakly against the wall. She had thrown herself off the mattress to escape the bullets, an act of desperate instinct, but the price had been steep. Three grazing shots had torn into her already-injured shoulder, her arm, and the side of her leg. And in the fall, several of her newly stitched wounds had ripped open again, leaving fresh blood streaming down her skin.

"My word, Leah..." Cash dropped to his knees beside her, horror flooding his face. Leah trembled violently, pain etched into every line of her body.

"I—I tried to get down," she whispered, breath hitching. "I didn't want him to s-shoot me..."

"You did the right thing," Jaxon said, voice rough as sandpaper. "You did everything right."

"Get her on the spare bed," the nurse ordered, regaining her composure with a snap. "Now."

Cash and Jaxon didn't wait for a second instruction. Together, they lifted Leah, gently but as quickly as possible, and carried her across the room. Leah whimpered, clutching at their shirts, but they held her fast, murmuring reassurances.

Once she was settled on the only other bed in the infirmary, the nurse hurried back to strip the blood-soaked bedding and replace it with fresh linens, her hands moving with a practiced speed that belied their trembling. The room buzzed with frantic motion and choked fear, but one truth echoed louder than all the chaos: Leah had survived, but only by a hair's breadth.

Dr. Matthews rushed into the room the moment the gunfire ceased, pushing past the sheriff and dropping to Leah's side. His voice was calm but urgent as he barked instructions to his wife, who was still in the hallway, and the other nurse. Together they worked over the young woman's now unconscious, blood-soaked form.

Cash, Jaxon, and Sheriff Jones stepped outside to give them room to work, though neither cowboy truly left, they hovered just beyond the doorway, listening to every sound, every command. Worry etched deep lines into their faces.

A few minutes later, McKay and Chad burst into the clinic, out of breath and wild-eyed.

"What in blazes happened?" McKay demanded. "We heard gunshots all the way over at the hotel!"

"Is Leah—?" Chad didn't finish the sentence. He didn't have to.

Cash raised a hand, trying to steady their panic.

"She's alive. She's hurt again, but alive. Doc's in there patching her up."

The younger men sagged with shaky relief, though fear still flickered in their eyes. When everyone finally quieted enough to breathe, Cash spoke again, voice low and tight.

"We can't leave Leah here by herself. Not now. I doubt Milton and Jack meant for Heber to strike tonight, but they're the ones who broke him out. That means they're coming for her one way or another."

Jaxon grunted, jaw clenching hard. "So, what do we do? One of us stay behind?" He met Cash's eyes. "Or do we hire someone to guard her?"

Everyone could see it, neither man wanted to leave her side. The thought of walking away after almost losing her twice in a single day felt impossible.

"I'll contact David Smith tomorrow," Cash said at last. "He'll know what can be done. He'll have resources and men we can trust."

"I can stay with her," Chad offered suddenly, his voice surprisingly steady. "Until we find a better solution. I'll keep watch day and night."

Cash nodded slowly. "That's probably our best option for now. You've already been pretending to be her brother. No one will question you hanging around."

But Chad's expression shifted to one of concern.

"What if Milton already knows? What if he figured out, she's not Lucas?"

Cash exhaled sharply. "If the telegram Heber sent said what I think it did... then Chuck wouldn't have passed it to

Jack or Milton." His eyes darkened. "He would've given it to Scott instead."

The room went silent. They all knew what that meant. If Milton got his hands on Heber's telegram, then the attack tonight might be only the beginning.

"She's awake again," Dr. Matthews said as he stepped into the hallway. Relief washed over every man standing there. Cash gave a curt nod, and the four of them filed quietly into Leah's room.

Leah opened her eyes at the sound of the door. She looked exhausted, pale as linen and clearly in pain, but she was alive. Fresh bandages wrapped her shoulder, arm, and leg, and the stitches from her earlier wounds had been redone. Despite everything, she managed a faint, fragile smile.

"Who was the attacker?" she whispered.

Cash cleared his throat, his voice gravelly. "Heber Thatcher."

Leah's expression didn't change much, almost as though she had already expected that answer.

"Is he back in prison?"

"No need," Cash said gently. "He's dead."

Leah let out a soft, shaky breath, her whole body sinking slightly deeper into the pillow in relief. Jaxon moved to her bedside then, unable to hold back any longer. He reached for her hand, carefully, reverently, and wrapped his fingers around hers. Leah looked up, and their eyes locked. Something unspoken passed between them, the kind of moment that made the air feel suddenly warmer, closer, more intimate. Cash pulled a chair up beside the bed and sat down with a sigh.

"I'll be staying with you tonight," he said firmly. "You won't be left alone again. Not after this."

Leah opened her mouth to protest, but Cash lifted a hand, stopping her.

"I'll send a telegram to David first thing in the morning. He'll tell us how to handle things from here. But until we've got a clear plan, Chad will stay behind to keep watch over you."

"But—"

"No, Leah," Jaxon cut in, his tone surprisingly stern. He squeezed her hand gently, grounding her. "It's already decided. Milton might not know you were the one injured tonight... but we're not gambling with your safety." He leaned closer, his voice dropping to something softer but far more intense. "I won't."

Leah swallowed, her cheeks warming despite the pain.

"Jaxon's right," Cash added, giving her a firm, fatherly glare. "Heber might not have been ordered to come after you tonight, but Milton and Jack Rowland are unpredictable men. We won't risk you getting kidnapped again." The word *again* settled heavily in the room. Leah's fingers curled more tightly around Jaxon's. For the first time since the attack, she felt her fear ease, just a little. With Cash watching over her, and Jaxon refusing to leave her side, she finally believed she might make it through this nightmare alive.

17
Untangling a Cowgirl's Heart

Shortly after McKay and Chad had gone for the night, Cash and Jaxon began rearranging the room with quiet determination. They dragged two armchairs over to the space beside Leah's bed, while the nurse waited, then led them to the nurses' room where two more armchairs were waiting. They wedged them together to form a makeshift cot. It wouldn't be comfortable, not by a long shot, but it would keep them close enough to hear every breath she took.

Once they settled in, they didn't immediately try to sleep. Jaxon reached for Leah's hand and held it gently in his own, before closing his eyes. His deep breathing followed shortly after. Cash watched Leah rest, his elbows braced on his knees, his hands clasped tightly as though he were holding himself together. Her breathing had fallen into a steady rhythm, deep, slow, and heavy with exhaustion, and for the first time since the attack, her face looked peaceful. But even in rest, she seemed fragile, her lashes resting against cheeks still too pale, her injured arm wrapped snugly in its sling. Cash's chest tightened painfully.

The poor girl had endured more in the past few weeks than most folks bore in a lifetime. Kidnapping. Terror. Watching

Colt die in front of her. And now... this. He had known Leah since she was a small child, knew her stubborn streak, her grit, her fire. He also knew that if she hadn't carried that stubborn spark inside her, that fierce little flame that refused to go out, she wouldn't still be breathing. A gentler girl would've broken. A softer one might have stopped fighting.

But Leah... Leah was a spitfire. Tough as rawhide, fierce as any cowboy he'd ever known. It was that fire, the same fire that had worried, exasperated, and amazed him all these years, that had kept her alive tonight. Even so, seeing her like this... bruised, bandaged, battered, it twisted something deep inside him. He wished he could shoulder some of her pain, take just a portion of it so she could rest without hurting so much.

Cash let out a breath he hadn't realized he'd been holding and leaned back in the two pushed-together chairs.

"I got you, girl," he whispered softly into the quiet room. "Ain't nothin' gonna touch you tonight. Not while I'm here." Then he settled in for a long night, keeping vigil over the spitfire who had survived one more battle because she refused to give up.

Chad arrived early the next morning, taking the chair beside Leah's bed just as Cash headed out to sell the remaining cattle. Leah was awake, though groggy, and she managed a faint smile when Chad entered. He sat with her, talking softly and keeping her distracted while the hours passed.

Cash, Jaxon, and McKay returned shortly after noon. They looked tired but relieved.

"Got a fair price for the herd," Cash told Chad quietly. "Considering what we lost, I'll take it." Then he pulled a folded telegram from his pocket. "David responded." They gathered around as Cash read it aloud.

> *"I have friends in Eureka. One is a retired U.S. Marshal. I will contact him and have him sit in front of her room during the night. Chad can do the day shift. Hug Leah for me. —David."*

Leah blinked in surprise, emotion tightening her throat. David had always looked after her like a second father, even from afar. Cash tucked the telegram back into his vest.

"Well, sounds like we'll have proper protection in place soon." His tone softened as he turned to her. "He asked me to give you a hug, but... we'll wait until the doctor says you're ready for squeezing."

Leah let out a small laugh, weak, but genuine. "Tell David thank you."

Chad nodded. "You'll be safe, Leah. I'll be staying right here. Day and night, unless Dad's friend can take on the night shift."

For the first time since the attack, she let herself relax against the pillows. Not because the pain was gone, far from it, but because she finally felt protected again. Surrounded. Watched over. Not alone.

Cash looked down at Leah, taking in her pale face and the brave little smile she offered him. His chest tightened.

"I wish we could stay with you," he said quietly. "Truly, I do. But we've been gone longer than planned. Folks back home will be wondering where we are."

Leah nodded, though her eyes softened with gratitude.

"With Chad here, and Uncle Dave's friend guarding my room at night, I'll be all right." A wry smile tugged at her lips. "I'll be bored out of my mind, and my imagination will probably invent every worst-case scenario for what's happening at home... but there's nothing I can do from here."

Cash chuckled softly, though he didn't fully hide his concern. Leah continued, more serious now.

"Just make sure the money from the cattle sale goes into the account Dad opened in his, yours, and my name at the beginning of the year. Good thing I transferred most of the funds from our family account before going to Sacramento. If Milton hasn't already, he'll pressure Mom into giving him access to everything."

Cash exhaled through his nose, nodding gravely.

"I'm wondering why they haven't left yet," Jaxon said, frowning. "Don't the Rowlands have a home to go to?" He looked from Cash to Leah, and both shrugged. Leah sighed, frustration creasing her brow.

"I wish we could force them off our property. Why doesn't Sheriff Bailey remove them? Is it because he works with the Rowlands?"

Cash jerked his head toward her, surprised. "Why in the world do you think Scott Bailey works with the Rowlands?"

"Leah," Jaxon interjected gently, "I told you already, he's probably investigating all this."

Leah shook her head. "We don't know that, Jaxon. Something feels wrong. I'm not sure he's trustworthy anymore."

Cash looked between them, bewildered. "What are the two of you talking about?"

Leah sighed and recounted the conversation she had overheard back at the ranch, the words spoken, the tone, the suspicions it raised. Cash listened intently, then shook his head with conviction.

"Scott Bailey's an exceptional sheriff. He takes his job seriously. He's friendly with criminals because that's how you get information out of them. That's his style, always has been."

Leah wasn't convinced. "Then explain why he hasn't removed the Rowlands from our land."

Cash exhaled sharply. "As long as your mother allows them to stay, Scott's hands are tied. He can't physically remove them unless they hurt someone. And so far, they're avoiding that line." His eyes hardened. "At least for now."

Leah scrunched her nose, irritation coloring her tone.

"I still hate the engagement between Mom and the sheriff. I don't care what anyone says. And I know for a fact that it isn't even a real engagement, not from Scott's side." Her voice dropped to a frustrated whisper. "But will that stop them from actually getting married?"

Cash shook his head at her stubbornness, choosing not to argue anymore.

"We need to head out now," he said instead. "Chad, send a telegram if you or Leah need anything. And let us know instantly if something happens."

Chad nodded firmly. Cash leaned down and enveloped Leah in a fatherly hug, careful of her injuries. Leah closed her eyes and breathed in the comfort of it, her throat tightening. When he stepped back, he gestured for Jaxon to come forward.

Jaxon hesitated at the foot of her bed, his eyes sweeping the room as if hunting for excuses to stay. His posture was tense, his jaw clenched, as though he were at war with himself. At last, he drew a breath.

"Could I... have a moment alone with Leah?" he asked, voice low. Cash studied him for a heartbeat, then nodded.

"Of course." He stepped out with the others, closing the door softly behind him. The room fell quiet. Just Leah. And Jaxon.

When the door clicked shut behind Cash, McKay, and Chad, the room fell into a heavy stillness. Jaxon moved closer, his boots soft on the floorboards, until he stood right beside her bed. He reached for her hand, slowly, almost reverently, and when his fingers closed around hers, Leah's breath caught. His touch felt too warm. Too steady. Too certain.

She lifted her gaze just long enough to see the intensity in his eyes, and her stomach flipped violently. Butterflies erupted, fluttering nervously beneath her ribs. She immediately looked away.

"Leah," he murmured, his voice low and roughened by emotion. "I need to finally tell you—"

"Please don't," she blurted, panic flooding her. "Please don't say something you'll regret later." Her voice shook. "I don't want to lose your friendship. Let's just... carry on as we always have."

"I can't do that anymore," Jaxon said, the words breaking out of him like a confession held too long. He gently tugged her hand, urging her to look at him. "Leah, I love you. Not as a friend. Not as a ranch buddy. I love you, and I want a place in your life that's more than—this."

Her chest tightened painfully. "Jax... please don't do this to us." Tears blurred her vision. "What if it doesn't work? What if we try and fail and lose everything? I can't risk our friendship. I—I need you in my life too much to gamble with it."

His jaw clenched. "You'll never lose me, Leah. Ever. I'll always be your friend. I promise."

"You don't know that!" she cried, voice cracking. "Friendships change when the heart gets involved. People get hurt. What if I break your heart so badly you never want to look at me again? What if—what if that becomes the only way forward?"

For a moment, neither of them moved. Then he leaned in, swift, determined, and framed her face in his hands.

"Jaxon—"

But he didn't let her finish. He kissed her. A long, fierce, soul-stealing kiss that wiped the world away. His lips were warm and trembling with pent-up longing, and for a suspended second, Leah forgot to breathe. Sensation flooded her, heat, shock, an ache so deep it terrified her. Her entire body went weightless, dizzy, trembling. When he finally drew back, she was gasping, and crying.

"Why are you torturing me?" she whispered brokenly. "Why are you trying to change everything between us?" She shook her head in anguish. "You haven't even given other girls a chance! Jaxon, I'm not the right one for you."

"What about you?" he whispered, ignoring what she had just said. "Do you love me too? Please, Leah... be honest." His brown eyes pinned her in place, seeing too much, demanding more than she could give. Leah lowered her gaze as fresh tears spilled.

"I love you," she said softly, "but not that way."

His eyes hardened with disbelief. "I don't accept that. I know you're attracted to me. I know you felt something when I kissed you. You're just searching for a reason to push me away, because you're scared."

"I'm not scared." She swallowed her sobs as anger rose in her belly. "Don't you ever say that to me again."

He looked like he was fighting a smile, infuriatingly gentle, heartbreakingly fond.

"Leah... I think that's exactly why. You're afraid to let yourself feel anything real. Afraid to lose control. Afraid of what loving someone means."

"That's ridiculous."

"No, it isn't." His voice dropped, warm and unyielding. "Maybe during these next few weeks... while you heal... you should look inside yourself. Really ask your heart what it's hiding from."

Her irritation sharpened into indignation.

"It won't change anything," she snapped. "Just—go home, Jaxon. Give the girls in town a chance. I know some of them are hoping you'd notice them, and many of them are beautiful." Her voice trembled. "Stop wasting your time on me."

"I don't want any of them," he said simply. "I want you. I've loved you for years. You're the only one I want in my life."

Leah's breath broke. "Well, I'm sorry... but you can't have me. I don't feel that way." Her lips tightened into a hard, thin line, but the tremble in her chin betrayed her. Jaxon exhaled, long and heavy.

"I hope you stop repressing your feelings and finally allow yourself to love, Leah. And I hope you do it while I'm still here... before it's too late." He leaned in and pressed a soft, lingering kiss to her forehead, so tender it hurt worse than his passionate kiss earlier.

Then he turned and walked away. The door closed behind him. And Leah collapsed into sobs. Deep, wrenching sobs that tore from her soul. Because the moment the words had left his lips, she knew the truth: this conversation had already begun to break their friendship. Words had been spoken that could never be taken back. And she didn't know if she would ever be able to face him again... not without feeling that kiss, not without hearing the ache in his voice, not without feeling the pieces of her heart crumble.

"Where on earth have you been, Cash? I haven't seen you in days." Patricia stood on the front porch, her arms folded protectively over her chest. Milton and Jack flanked her like vultures waiting for something to die. Their eyes followed Cash with thinly veiled suspicion as he rode up with Jaxon and McKay.

Cash gave a subtle nod to the two younger men. They understood immediately, wheeled their horses around, and disappeared into the stables without a word. Cash dismounted, dusting off his hat.

"I'm sorry I left without a note," he said calmly, "but we had business to attend to, and no time to notify anyone."

Patricia frowned. "What business?"

"A group of livestock thieves stole some of our cattle," Cash stated plainly. "They were driving them toward Eureka. We tracked them down, caught them, and had them arrested before they reached town."

Milton stepped forward, eyes narrowing. "So, did you haul them cattle home?"

Cash met his stare without blinking. "No. We sold them in Eureka."

Milton's face snapped like a whip. "You done *what*? You ain't got no authority to be makin' that kinda call."

"Actually," Cash said evenly, "I do. I am the foreman." He took one step closer, making sure there was no room for misunderstanding. "And Mitch made me his business partner for a reason. Leah and David Smith also signed a legal document granting me full authority over ranch operations... especially when Leah is away."

Jack stiffened. Milton's jaw twitched. Cash didn't waver.

"Now," he added, "if you're done questioning things that aren't your concern—"

Patricia cut in, eyes wide with worry.

"Do you know where Leah is? I'm worried sick. What if something happened to her?"

Cash softened just slightly. "Leah will be back when she's ready. The last time I spoke to her, she assured me she was fine. Said not to worry." He reached into his vest. "Speaking of which... Sheriff Bailey handed me a letter from her while we were riding through Hoopa Valley. No idea how he got it, but he asked me to pass it along." He offered the folded paper to Patricia. Her hands trembled as she took it.

Cash tipped his hat and turned to leave, but Milton's voice barked after him.

"Mr. Cashley," he called sharply, "if you've sold cattle, you've collected money. I'd appreciate you handin' it over."

Cash turned back slowly, a dangerous calm settled over him.

"The money belongs to Leah and the ranch," he said. "Not to you. And it's already been deposited in the proper bank account in Hoopa Valley."

Milton's face darkened. Jack's fists clenched at his sides. They were both seething, simmering fury barely contained beneath their polished exteriors. Cash smiled, a slow, knowing grin, and tugged the brim of his hat.

"Good day," he said. Then he walked away, leaving the Rowlands fuming on the porch while Patricia clutched Leah's letter to her chest like a lifeline.

Milton exploded the moment Cash disappeared around the corner. Rage surged through him like wildfire. He swung his boot at the nearest object, an empty metal bucket, and sent it clattering across the ranch yard with a ringing crash. Patricia flinched at the outburst but said nothing. Instead, she sat down on a rocking chair on the porch, hands trembling as she broke the seal on Leah's letter. Milton stepped in close, looming behind her like a storm cloud, while Jack stood off to the side, arms folded, jaw tight. Patricia unfolded the letter and read:

Mom,

Please don't worry about me. I'm fine and will return to Hoopa Valley soon. Be careful around Milton and Jack. They are not to be trusted. I found out that some of our cattle had been stolen. One of the new cowboys Cash, hired, got severely injured while they were trying to retrieve the animals and is now recovering with his family.

The cattle thieves weren't the only ones trying to harm our men. Someone shot at the herd and killed several animals. Then an explosion caused by dynamite started a stampede, which injured the poor boy even more. To be honest, I wouldn't be surprised if the Rowlands were behind all of it.

But don't worry. I'm on top of things and in constant contact with Uncle David. I love and miss you, but I know we can win this fight. The Rowlands will have to return empty-handed, if they don't end up in jail first.

Leah

A beat of stunned silence followed. Then Milton leaned in, reading over Patricia's shoulder. He almost didn't register her sharp inhale before fury tore through him. He cussed loud enough to rattle the windows.

"That little brat," he spat. "Either she's as naïve as a newborn calf, or she ain't got the brains God gave a fencepost. Or," his eyes narrowed to slits. "...she wrote it bold as brass, knowin' damn well we'd read it standin' beside her ma."

Jack's face hardened. Patricia paled, clutching the letter to her chest as though it could shield her. Milton paced, boots stomping deep imprints into the dirt.

"She's foolin' with fire," he snarled under his breath. "Callin' us out... accusin' us of things she's got no right even whisperin' about." He whirled, rage lighting his eyes. "She'll pay for that. For the nerve. And for every damn lie she wrote."

Jack smirked coldly. "She ain't half as tough as she pretends," he muttered. Milton snapped his fingers sharply.

"We need to pay Sheriff Bailey a visit. See what he knows about Leah's little adventure—and why she's flappin' her gums accusin' us of anything at all." His smile went thin and cold.

"If she's stirrin' trouble..." He let the unfinished threat hang in the air. It didn't need completing.

Patricia's hand shook harder around the letter. Milton and Jack exchanged a look, dark, calculating. Then Milton grinned, slow and venomous. "...then we'll just have to cook up a little trouble ourselves."

A few days after Cash and the men had left, Leah received surprise visitors. She had just finished lunch when Robyn and her mother, Lisa Finlay, stepped into her room. Chad had gone into town to contact his father and take care of several errands.

"Robyn! Mama Finlay!" Leah exclaimed, lighting up with a genuine smile. "What are you two doing here?"

Both women leaned down and gathered her into careful, affectionate hugs.

"We heard you were laid up in the infirmary," Lisa said warmly, brushing some loose strands of hair from Leah's forehead. "We figured you could use some company. And," she added with a grin, "I have a good friend here in Eureka who's a seamstress. We're working on a little business arrangement, more customers for me, and I'll help with some of her larger orders."

Leah's face softened. "Oh, that sounds wonderful. You deserve that, Mama Finlay. No one works harder than you."

Lisa patted her cheek fondly. "You're such a sweetheart, Leah. Listen, I'm meeting my friend for about an hour, but I'll be back later. Robyn will stay with you as long as you like."

Robyn hugged her mother goodbye, then she and Leah watched her leave before Robyn sank into the chair beside the bed.

"Goodness, Leah, how did this even happen? We only saw Cash and the others for a minute when they got back, but they didn't tell us what went on."

Leah sighed, a tired, heavy sound, and recounted everything that had happened since discovering Milton had hired thieves to steal their cattle. Robyn listened in stunned silence.

"Oh my," she breathed. "Do you know who caused the explosion? Who killed the animals?"

"Heber Thatcher was involved for sure," Leah replied. "And I wouldn't be surprised if Milton played a part."

Robyn's brows shot up. "Leah, you need to stay away from Hoopa Valley. This is getting dangerous, and fast."

"Yes, but they didn't know it was *me* with the ranch hands," Leah insisted. "To whoever fired those shots, I was just another cowboy."

Robyn's expression softened, though worry creased her forehead.

"And what happens if you get killed? Your father is gone. If something happens to you... who gets everything?"

Leah swallowed hard. "I don't know. Dad and Uncle David showed me the will last spring, after I turned eighteen, but I never read it in detail. I need to ask Uncle David what it actually says." Her brows drew together. "And I really don't understand why the Rowlands think they should get the ranch. They're lazy as can be and couldn't manage the workload for a single week. If they took over, every one of our cowboys would quit. They all despise them."

Silence settled for a moment. Then Robyn's eyes brightened.

"You'll never guess what happened last night. My brother came home after work, cleaned himself up, and went into town to see Mia Collins. He asked her on a date."

Leah's stomach clenched. She hid it quickly, but not quickly enough. Robyn's eyes narrowed, studying her reaction.

"I thought for sure you and Jaxon would end up together," Robyn said bluntly. "Mia isn't right for him. Did something happen between you two?"

Leah nodded, tears gathering. "Everything I didn't want to happen... happened. Before Cash and the boys left Eureka, Jaxon told me he was in love with me. I begged him not to say it, but he did. And he kissed me again."

Robyn's mouth fell open, then tightened in annoyance.

"And you just blew him off? Leah, why didn't you at least give him a chance? You two are perfect for each other."

"I don't feel that way about him," Leah whispered.

"Hogwash." Robyn crossed her arms. "I don't believe that for a single second, Leah Johnson. You're scared. Scared to love him. Scared of what might happen. Meanwhile, Jaxon practically worships the ground you walk on. Honestly, you're being selfish."

Leah stared at her, shocked, wounded. She and Robyn had disagreed before, but nothing like this.

"This has nothing to do with selfishness, Robyn Finlay," Leah snapped. "I can't pretend to love someone when I don't. Sure, I could have said yes, but what if my feelings never change? I'd hurt him more in the end."

"You already broke his heart," Robyn shot back. "Now I understand why he went after Mia. He's trying to pretend he isn't shattered to pieces. He's been acting strange ever since he returned from Eureka, you crushed him."

"I tried to tell him—"

Robyn cut her off. "You know what? You're more like your mother than you realize. Everything's always about *your* feelings. Never about the man who loves you."

"You are out of line, Robyn."

"Am I?" Robyn folded her arms. "My brother has done everything for you. Comforted you, protected you, stood by you no matter what. And this is what he gets?"

"What he gets?" Leah echoed incredulously. "I never asked him to do any of that. He did it because he cared, at least that's what I thought. If he only did it to earn my love, then maybe that says more about our friendship than about me."

Robyn scoffed. "So, who is it you want? McKay? Or are you eyeing Chad?"

"Chad?" Leah stared at her, stunned. "Why would you even say that?"

"Oh, I don't know," Robyn said bitterly. "Maybe because I like him, and now you're suddenly interested too?"

Leah's jaw dropped. "I would never go after someone you like."

Robyn shook her head. "I'm not sure I believe that anymore. You're being foolish, Leah. Stop being afraid of your feelings. Just admit that you love my brother!"

Leah's breath shuddered. She felt something in her chest twisting, anger, pain, heartbreak all tangled together.

"What do you know about my feelings?" she shot back. "Nothing. Jaxon said the same thing to me, like he knows me better than I know myself." Her voice broke. "I am so sick of everyone telling me how I should feel. Stop it!"

Robyn stepped forward, angry tears in her eyes.

"Then admit it. Admit you love him! You've mourned your father long enough. You can't hide behind grief forever."

Leah's temper snapped. "You are not inside my heart," she said, her voice shaking with fury and hurt. "So, stop acting like you have the right to tell me what's inside it. My heart is mine, and I'll feel what I feel, whether you approve." Tears streamed down her face. "If my feelings only matter when they match your expectations, then leave."

Robyn blinked, stunned. "Leah—"

"Just go," Leah whispered, exhausted and trembling. "I don't want you here anymore. You don't have to keep me company. I'll be fine on my own."

Robyn froze, staring into Leah's tear-bright eyes. The anger there was unmistakable, sharp, wounded, deeply betrayed. And in that instant, Robyn felt her own breath catch. She had gone too far. The realization struck her hard: her accusations, her assumptions, the things she'd flung at Leah out of frustration rather than compassion. Guilt rose quickly, prickling beneath her skin. She opened her mouth, her voice trembling at the edges.

"Leah, I—"

But Leah's gaze hardened again, her spine straightening despite the pain. She lifted her chin, tears streaking down her cheeks, and the hurt in her voice cut deeper than any shouted insult.

"Get out," she whispered. Robyn blinked, stunned. Leah's voice strengthened with the next words, low, fierce, trembling. "Leave. I don't need anyone."

The finality in her tone was unmistakable. It slammed into Robyn's chest like a blow, stealing the apology from her throat. For a heartbeat, they stared at one another, two friends who suddenly felt like strangers. Robyn swallowed hard, her eyes glistening, but Leah's expression didn't soften.

"Okay, you two, that's enough." Lisa Finlay's voice cut through the tension like a whip crack. She swept into the room with wide, alarmed eyes, stopping directly between the two young women. Leah and Robyn stared at her, stunned, as if she'd materialized out of thin air. "I heard the two of you fighting all the way down the hall," Lisa continued. "Robyn, sit back down. Now."

Robyn's mouth opened, then closed. She obeyed, lowering herself stiffly into the chair. Lisa turned to Leah, her expression softening instantly. She crossed the room and gathered Leah gently into her arms. The moment Leah felt that motherly embrace, the kind she had been starving for, something inside her broke. A sob tore out of her, sharp and aching, and she clung to Lisa as tears streamed freely. Behind them, Robyn's voice trembled.

"Mom, what are you doing? Leah broke Jaxon's heart." Her lips quivered. "I can't believe you would comfort her before me."

Lisa drew back and looked at her daughter with a mixture of sympathy and sternness.

"Leah did not break your brother's heart, Robyn. She only spoke honestly about her feelings, and she has been honest from the beginning."

Robyn flushed with indignation and jumped to her feet.

"I can't believe you're taking her side!"

Lisa's eyes narrowed, just a touch, but the steel there was unmistakable.

"Sit. Down."

Robyn stiffened, startled by the tone. It had been years since her mother used that voice. She sank back into the chair, folding her arms in silent frustration. Lisa took a seat beside Leah again, her expression calm but firm.

"I didn't hear everything the two of you said, but I heard enough. Leah is right, you and Jaxon don't know what she feels. You were incredibly unfair to her."

Robyn dropped her gaze, chastened. Then Lisa inhaled deeply, as if preparing to reveal something weighty.

"I need both of you to listen. I think I know something about your past, Leah, that you may not know... or may have forgotten."

Leah wiped her cheeks, quieter now, curiosity flickering behind her exhaustion. Lisa squeezed her hand.

"As you know, we moved to Hoopa Valley after my husband lost his job due to his gambling and drinking. Hoopa Valley was looking for a seamstress, so I applied. It was right around the time Cash and Ruby's parents passed away, and Ruby moved to your ranch to help your mother as a housekeeper."

Leah nodded faintly. She remembered Ruby always being there, steady, cheerful, dependable.

"Ruby was young," Lisa continued. "Only twenty. And very much in love with Scott Bailey."

Leah's eyes widened. "Wait, Ruby and Sheriff Bailey courted?"

"They were more than courting," Lisa said gently. "They were engaged."

Leah stared at her. "But isn't Scott closer to my father's age?"

"Scott was a bit older," Lisa agreed. "But Cash and your father were his close friends, so Ruby saw him often. And they fell in love." She paused, eyes softening with old sympathy. "Unfortunately, Scott wasn't ready to commit. He broke off the engagement a week before the wedding."

Leah winced. "Ruby must've been devastated."

"She was," Lisa said simply. "Heartbroken. Bitter. And she talked about it constantly. Unfortunately, she shared that bitterness with... well, everyone who would listen."

Leah shifted uncomfortably. Lisa nodded knowingly.

"Yes. Including you."

"What?" Leah whispered.

Lisa continued gently, "Your grandmother was living with you at the time. Her first marriage had ended badly, her husband divorced her while she was pregnant with your father's older brother."

Leah's breath caught. "I didn't know."

"It broke her," Lisa said softly. "She remarried a wonderful man later, someone who adored her, someone who helped her heal. But when he died suddenly, all that old hurt came roaring back. Everything she'd buried resurfaced. She became bitter. Angry with God. Angry with the world." Her gaze deepened with sorrow.

"And Ruby... your grandmother... your mother, they fed off one another's bitterness. Instead of helping each other heal, they kept stirring the wounds. Your home became..." Lisa hesitated, searching for the right word. "Heavy. Shadowed. A place filled with old pain no one ever dealt with."

Leah sank back against her pillows, a knot forming in her stomach.

"And you," Lisa continued gently, "a sensitive, observant little girl... were caught in the middle of it all." She let out a slow, pained sigh. "You were only five, Leah. You had no siblings to distract you, no playmates to pull you away from the adults. And because you were such a good listener, quiet, thoughtful, always taking things in, they poured their heartbreak into you without even realizing what they were doing."

Leah's eyes widened, horrified.

"We didn't know," Lisa said softly. "None of us realized the things they were telling you, not until two years later. Your teacher contacted your father after you wrote an essay for school. It was..." She shook her head. "It was full of sadness and bitterness, things a seven-year-old shouldn't even understand."

Leah swallowed hard. "What did my dad do?"

"He and Cash put a stop to it," Lisa said firmly. "They laid down the law. Your father forbade your mother and grandmother from discussing their past around you. Cash did the same with Ruby. And after that, the men stepped in and made sure you were surrounded with balance, love, and stability. Ruby changed, too, she faced her heartbreak, learned from it, and eventually became the bright, cheerful woman we know today."

Robyn crossed her arms, still defensive.

"But what does any of this have to do with Leah and Jaxon?"

Lisa exhaled slowly, almost patiently.

"I'm getting there." She turned back to Leah, took her hand, and held it gently. "For two solid years," Lisa explained, "Ruby repeated, without malice, that falling in love with your best friend only leads to heartbreak. Your grandmother echoed it. Your mother agreed. It became a theme in your home, a warning spoken regularly in your presence."

Leah drew a sharp breath.

Lisa nodded. "Even after everyone stopped talking about it, after your father and Cash stepped in, your mind had already absorbed it. Children don't forget something they hear repeatedly. I don't think you were aware of it, Leah. But when you realized Jaxon might have romantic feelings for you..." She paused, letting it sink in. "That buried warning woke up. And it terrified you."

The room went quiet. Even Robyn's anger dissolved into quiet concern.

Lisa leaned forward. "Every time someone suggests you might love Jaxon, or that Jaxon might love you, you panic. Not because you don't care about him, but because some old, buried part of you believes, that falling in love with your best friend will end in disaster. That you'll lose him forever."

Leah's throat tightened as she absorbed that truth. It made sense, too much sense. And yet, she still wasn't sure what to do with it.

"So..." Leah whispered, voice trembling, "you think my fear is the problem. And because of that, you think I should marry Jaxon?"

Lisa smiled gently. "As much as I'd love to someday call you my daughter-in-law, that's not what I'm saying." Her expression softened further. "I think your heart is tangled up in fears that aren't yours. Fears that were planted in you before you were old enough to understand what love really is." She squeezed Leah's hand. "Give yourself time to untangle that. Time to look at the years you've spent with Jaxon, not through fear, not through what you've been taught to believe, but through what your own heart feels when it's not scared. Only then will you know if what you feel is friendship... or something deeper."

Leah nodded slowly, letting out a shaky breath. "Thank you, Mama Finlay."

"Oh sweetheart," Lisa murmured, pulling her into a warm, enveloping hug, "I want you happy, whatever that looks like for you. I want you to make a choice without pressure, from anyone. Not from me, not from Robyn, not from Jaxon." She kissed Leah's temple. "And I won't tell Jaxon any of this. That part of your heart belongs only to you."

Leah closed her eyes, leaning into the comfort. For the first time in days, she felt something inside her shift, not quite clarity, not yet, but understanding. And perhaps... a place to begin.

Robyn cleared her throat, eyes red and remorseful.

"Leah... I'm so sorry. For everything I said earlier. I was completely out of line. I shouldn't have attacked you the way I did."

Leah nodded slowly. "No, you shouldn't have. But... you didn't know about my past. And he is your brother."

Robyn swallowed. "Yes, but I'm also your best friend. And I acted like anything but. I didn't consider your heart at all. I guess... that makes me the selfish one, doesn't it?"

18
Watching Him Ride Away

Leah truly enjoyed the company of Robyn and her mother over the following days. Their presence made the long hours in the clinic far more bearable. Robyn's lively chatter kept her spirits up, and Mama Finlay's gentle warmth brought comfort Leah didn't realize she'd been craving.

Chad also seemed to enjoy Robyn's company, more than he tried to show. They spent a great deal of time talking, laughing, and exchanging shy glances when they thought no one noticed. Leah hid a smile each time she caught them. They weren't officially courting yet, but she knew it was only a matter of time. They looked good together, balanced, steady, and happy.

A few days before Leah's expected release from the infirmary, Jane and Dr. Mark Matthews were guiding her through a set of careful shoulder exercises. The joint was still stiff and tender, but she was healing faster than anyone expected. Just as Leah winced through another stretch, the doorway filled with the soft rustle of skirts. A nurse stepped inside, looking pleasantly flustered.

"Miss Johnson, you have a visitor. Since it's a gentleman, I thought it best to check with you first."

Leah blinked. *A gentleman?* The only man she expected to see was Chad, and he was in town. Curious, she nodded. Nurse Jane helped her slip into her dressing gown and settle back against her pillows. Once Leah looked presentable, the nurse returned to escort the visitor. And when he stepped through the doorway, Leah lit up.

"Uncle Dave?" she exclaimed. "What are you doing here?"

David Smith crossed the room in two long strides and sat carefully on the edge of the bed. Then he pulled her into a warm, fatherly embrace, holding her as if she were ten years old again and back from her first big fall off a horse.

"I'm here to see my favorite goddaughter, of course," he said, kissing the top of her head. "And to take you home. Chad has been released from protection duty. I'll be filling in until you get back on your feet. He's packing his bags as we speak."

"Really?" Leah asked, stunned and touched. "Uncle Dave, you didn't have to—"

"I did," he cut in firmly. "I don't trust Milton or Jack Rowland as far as I can throw them. And with Thanksgiving only weeks away, I've decided to work out of Hoopa Valley for a while."

Leah's eyes softened. "Will Aunt Brooke be joining us?"

"Of course she will," he said with a proud grin. "We'll all spend Thanksgiving together this year."

"That's wonderful." She rested back against the pillows. "Have you heard anything new from home? Has Cash gotten in touch with you?"

David's expression changed slightly, still calm, but edged with seriousness.

"His last telegram said the Rowlands are still on the ranch. He's keeping a close watch." He hesitated, then added, "But I did receive a telegram from Joseph Hicks."

Leah straightened. "Our banker?"

He nodded. "Yes. It seems Milton made quite the scene at the bank. Your mother gave him permission to withdraw funds from the family account whenever he wanted. But when he and Jack went to transfer money, they discovered the account almost empty."

Leah tried not to smile. "I told Mom to leave the finances alone. I knew Milton would try something."

David continued, "Milton was furious when he learned you'd transferred most of the money to the other account. He demanded Joseph tell him whose name was on it. Joseph refused."

Leah grinned. "Good."

David chuckled. "Milton then asked whether the cattle-sale money had also been deposited there. Joseph again refused. Milton got so angry he nearly got himself arrested after threatening the man."

Leah shook her head, though satisfaction warmed her chest.

"I'm sorry Joseph had to deal with that, but I'm relieved to know he's trustworthy."

David waved a hand. "Joseph is perfectly fine. He's tougher than he looks, and he's not about to be intimidated by any Rowland. He handled the situation just fine."

Leah let out a breath she didn't know she had been holding. She felt... safe. For the first time in weeks. Her godfather was here. Her friends cared for her. Milton's schemes were crumbling. Her ranch was still standing. She had a long road ahead, but she wasn't walking it alone.

"Leah, you're finally home. Goodness, child, why would you put me through that?" Patricia Johnson swept her daughter into her arms, holding her tight. The embrace startled Leah. Her mother was not known for affection. For a moment Leah allowed herself to lean into it, into the softness, the worry, the flicker of maternal love she so rarely felt.

"It had to be done," Leah said quietly. Then she straightened. "How is everything? Are Milton and Jack still here?"

"Course we are," Milton said, stepping into the room with a cold, near-triumphant glare.

Jack trailed after him, his face even darker. "Truth is," Milton went on, his voice cutting, "I ain't got the foggiest idea how your pa ever figured you for an heir. Soon as things get tough, you go runnin' and hidin' like a scared rabbit."

Leah scoffed. "Hide? Oh, please. I stayed on top of everything while I was gone. Just because you can't be trusted doesn't mean the people who live and work here can't. And it is more than time for you to leave."

"We ain't budgin'," Milton growled. "Not till you give us what's owed."

Leah nearly laughed. "Owe you? I owe you nothing. You're lazy, greedy parasites who think you can get rich off the hard work of others."

Milton sneered. "Keep your blasted ranch. Just hawk whatever's worth a penny and fork over the coin."

"And tell me why I would ever do that?"

"'Cause you owe us, that's why," Jack growled. "Your ma worked herself near to breakin'. She's due her share."

Leah stared at them as if they'd sprouted horns.

"You're both delusional. My father worked hard. Ruby worked hard. Cash and the cowboys worked hard. But Mom?" She shook her head. "Dad hired Ruby to run the house because Mom couldn't do it on her own. Everything was too much for her. Mom has lived well and will continue to do so. And even if she had earned what you think she should have, it has absolutely nothing to do with you."

"How dare you spit talk like that about your ma," Jack barked, lurching forward like a rattlesnake ready to lash out.

"Oh, don't you dare lecture me on disrespect," Leah shot back, fire rising in her veins. "You abused her for years. You terrorized her. And now I'm the rude one?" She scoffed. "You're both hypocrites."

Jack's jaw twitched. Milton gave a humorless chuckle.

"So that's the tale Patricia spun for ya?" Milton sneered. "We never touched her."

"Sure," Leah snapped. "And you two are harmless angels who wouldn't hurt a fly." Her voice hardened. "You're liars. Pathetic liars."

Jack's hand shot up, rage blazing in his eyes, he was seconds away from striking her. But just then, the front door burst open. Cash, Sheriff Scott Bailey, David Smith, and Aunt Mildred strode inside. Jack and Milton froze, hands dropping immediately. They took several steps back as if caught doing something far worse.

"Cash!" Leah exclaimed and limped straight into his arms, relief flooding her. Cash held her tightly.

"What's goin' on with that leg o' yours?" Milton demanded, eyes darting over her like he owned the right.

"None of your blasted business," Leah snapped. She moved next toward Aunt Mildred, who swept her into a warm, perfumed hug.

"You need to stop scaring us, darling," Mildred said with a playful wink. "I swear I've sprouted three gray hairs since you left. Your mom has been beside herself with worry."

Leah huffed softly. "Sorry, Aunt Mildred. But as long as Mom keeps certain... company, I can't promise anything." She pivoted toward Scott Bailey. "Sheriff, can you please send these men away? They're trespassing."

Scott shook his head with a sigh. "Ain't nothin' I can do, Leah. Your ma's givin' 'em leave to stay, and the law can't shove 'em out."

Leah inhaled sharply. She studied him for a moment, searching for the truth, for loyalty, for something deeper, but this wasn't the moment to challenge him.

"Fine," she snapped. "Then I won't stay here while they're under this roof. I'll live in town."

"I don't want you to leave, Leah," Patricia said, her voice surprisingly firm.

Leah's eyes narrowed. "Then ask the Rowlands to leave." She held her breath, waiting. Patricia said nothing. Not a word. Leah's lips tightened. She rolled her eyes, shaking her head in bitter disappointment, and turned toward the stairs.

"Then I'll go," she said flatly. She limped up the steps one slow, painful stride at a time, her heart aching but her resolve unshaken. She packed a small bag, clothes, personal items, a few keepsakes. Leah knew Milton and Jack wouldn't dare follow her upstairs with Cash, Scott, and David waiting below. But she also knew this: She would not sleep under the same roof as men who wanted to destroy her. And if her mother chose them over her? Then Leah would choose herself.

"Please stay, Leah," Patricia pleaded as her daughter limped toward the front door, bag in hand. Her voice trembled, not with authority, but with desperation. Leah didn't slow. She didn't even glance back.

"No, Mom." Her tone was firm but laced with hurt. "I don't understand why you refuse to stand up to Jack and Milton, especially when you're surrounded by people who would protect you without hesitation." She finally turned, meeting her mother's eyes with a mixture of disappointment and sorrow.

"You know Scott Bailey would protect you," Leah continued quietly. "Cash would fight for you. Uncle David would too. You're not alone, and you haven't been for a long time."

Patricia's face crumpled, as though the words struck deeper than Leah intended. But Leah pressed on.

"The Rowlands can't hurt you, not with all of us around." She shook her head, her resolve hardening. "But I won't stay under the same roof as men who've threatened our family and tried to steal from us. I'll be close by. I'll help on the ranch. But I won't live here. Not like this."

Patricia took a tiny step forward as if she might reach for her, but Leah lifted a hand, not harshly, but definitively.

"I need to feel safe," she said simply. "And right now, I don't."

"Don't worry, Patti," Aunt Mildred said as she stepped beside Leah, looping an arm around her shoulders in solidarity. "I'll keep an eye on her while she's in town. And I'll make sure she doesn't get herself into too much trouble."

The attempt at humor softened the tension only marginally, but it gave Leah the strength to open the door. She stepped outside without looking back, with Aunt Mildred by her side and the knowledge that, for once, she was choosing her own safety over everyone else's expectations.

Leah felt a flutter of excitement as she crossed the ranch yard toward the stable. It had been weeks since she'd seen her horse, and the moment she stepped inside, the familiar scent of hay and leather wrapped around her like a welcome-home embrace. Her mare lifted her head, ears pricking the instant she recognized her. A soft whinny escaped the animal, and Leah's heart melted.

"I missed you too, girl," she whispered, running her hand along the horse's neck. The mare nudged her shoulder carefully, almost protectively, and Leah smiled. She wasted no time saddling the horse. Though her shoulder twinged with the effort and her leg still protested each step, she worked as quickly as she could. She had plans, important ones. The Finlays wanted to gather everyone at their home to discuss what came next, and Leah had no intention of being late.

Just as she led her horse out into the open yard, Chad and McKay rounded the corner of the barn. Both stopped short. Both grinned wide. Chad was first to reach her. He wrapped her gently, careful of her injuries, into a warm, brotherly squeeze.

"It's good to see you again, Leah," he said, stepping back with a relieved smile. "Looks like you're back to normal?"

Leah laughed softly. "Not quite. My shoulder still gives me fits if I move it too much, and my leg isn't fully healed, but..." She patted her horse's neck. "I'll get there."

McKay approached next, slow, appreciative, unmistakably taken aback.

"Well, would ya look at you," he murmured, eyes traveling from her boots clear up to the curly waves at her cheeks. "You look downright beautiful in that dress."

Heat rushed to her cheeks. She opened her mouth to respond, but before she could, McKay stepped closer, placed his hands lightly on her hips, and lifted her effortlessly into the saddle. A startled gasp slipped from her lips, her hands catching the pommel.

"Easy now," McKay said with a soft chuckle, making sure she was seated safely. When she looked down at him, he was already watching her with a spark in his green eyes that sent butterflies tumbling through her stomach.

"Listen," he said, his voice turning earnest. "There's a dance in town this weekend..." He met her eyes, not looking away for a second. "I'd be mighty honored if you'd go with me."

Leah's breath caught. Butterflies became a storm. Her cheeks warmed even more, and she wasn't sure she trusted her voice, so she simply nodded. McKay's smile deepened, slow and warm, the kind that did dangerous things to her insides. He tipped his hat to her, stepping back as if giving her room to escape before he changed his mind and kissed her.

"You look lovely, Leah," he added quietly. "I'll see you Saturday."

Chad clapped him on the shoulder, both men watching her ride off. Leah guided her horse toward the road, her heart fluttering wildly beneath her ribs. And for the first time in a long while, she felt something light, sweet... and full of possibility.

Leah hadn't gone far when a lone rider crested the hill ahead. Her breath hitched. Jaxon. He rode with his usual confidence, the afternoon sun glinting off his dark hair, his posture tall and sure in the saddle. Leah's pulse quickened, her heart beating like a frantic drum the closer he drew.

She couldn't look away, not from him, not from the familiar set of his shoulders, not from the way he always looked like he belonged on horseback more than anywhere else.

When he finally reached her, their horses slowed to a halt. His brown eyes met hers, warm, steady, and still so devastatingly handsome that her breath caught in her throat.

"It's good to see you back, Leah," he said softly. The words should've comforted her, should've felt like coming home, but his tone was guarded. Careful. Distance woven into the gentle greeting. He just looked at her... nothing more. No smile. No spark. No flicker of the closeness they once shared. Her heart dropped.

"It's good to be back," she managed, offering him a bright, hopeful smile. "I heard... you started courting?"

He nodded once. "Yes. You were right. There are some nice, pretty girls in Hoopa Valley."

The words sliced through her like a blade. Nice. Pretty. Girls. Every one of them, everyone but her. Leah forced a smile, but inside she felt herself crumpling. Jealousy clawed at her chest, sharp and raw, but she shoved the emotion deep down where it couldn't betray her.

"I'm staying with your mom and Robyn for now," she said, her voice tight but steady. "At least until we figure out how to get rid of the Rowlands."

"Mom told me," he answered flatly. For a moment she just looked at him, searching, hoping, desperate for some fragment of the bond they used to share.

"Will you... come by sometime?" she asked softly, timidly, almost pleading without meaning to. He shook his head.

"I don't think so. With you gone, we've had to work harder. Jobs are taking longer."

"Oh." The single word slipped out, small and aching. "I'm sorry I was away so long," she whispered. "They wouldn't let me leave. And even now... I'm not supposed to do much."

His reaction, calm, distant, hurt more than the injuries she'd survived. Jaxon softened only slightly.

"I'm not trying to make you feel guilty, Leah. I know you were hurt. I know you're still recovering. Please... listen to Dr. Matthews. Be wise."

She swallowed the knot rising in her throat. She could only nod, unable to form words past the hurt pressing against her chest. He cleared his throat and adjusted his reins.

"I'd better get going before Cash chews me out for being behind. It was good to see you." A final nod, polite, impersonal, and he rode past her. Not even a backward glance.

The moment he was far enough away, Leah's composure shattered. Tears spilled down her cheeks, hot, steady, merciless. She had known this might happen. Lisa's talk, the past, the buried warnings, none of it mattered now. Maybe Ruby had been right. Maybe falling for your best friend did end in heartbreak. Jaxon had promised she'd never lose him... and yet here he was, colder to her in five minutes than he'd ever been in their entire friendship.

Leah swiped at her tears, but they only fell faster. With a choked sob, she nudged her horse sharply and urged her forward. The mare leapt into a fast gallop, wind whipping at Leah's hair, the world blurring around her. She rode hard and fast, hoping the speed would dry her tears. Hoping it would drown out the feeling that she had just lost something she didn't know how to live without.

Cash wanted to pace. Every muscle in him begged for it. But Leah already looked tense enough, her jaw tight, her lips pressed thin, her shoulders trembling ever so slightly every time her hand drifted unconsciously toward the sore spots on her leg and shoulder. Cash refused to add to the heaviness in the room.

Leah's eyes flashed like blue fire as she glared at the men gathered around the sitting room.

"So, tell me, how do we get rid of those vultures? They've been in my home far too long, and I'm sick of it."

David exhaled tiredly. "There isn't much we can do right now. They haven't broken any laws we can prove. And like Scott already told you, as long as your mom allows them to stay, his hands are tied."

Leah clenched her teeth. "What are they trying to accomplish with all this? What's their end goal?"

Cash took a deep breath. "For one thing, they didn't expect you to be a problem, Leah. They hadn't seen you in years. They thought you'd be timid, easy to manipulate, easy to scare." His eyes burned with irritation. "They weren't prepared for you to fight back, and they definitely weren't prepared for you to disappear for weeks. And today, when you told them you wouldn't be living under the same roof as them anymore... well, that threw them again."

Leah lifted her chin, her expression was still fierce.

"And the kidnapping? We can't use that against them?"

Scott and David both shook their heads. David reached over and squeezed her uninjured hand.

"There's no evidence. Heber knew exactly what he was doing when he destroyed that letter. Without proof, it's his word against yours."

Lisa Finlay let out a worried breath. "Then what are they waiting for?"

David's expression grew grim. "They want Leah alone. Without Cash, without Scott, without any of us. That's when they'll force her into whatever scheme they've planned."

Robyn gasped softly. Lisa wrung her hands. Leah rolled her eyes hard.

"Well, they're going to have a long wait. And now Milton is claiming we owe him money. He actually had the audacity to say Mom worked hard all these years and deserves compensation." Her voice sharpened. "I've never wanted to slap someone more."

Lisa looked close to fainting from stress.

"So... how do we protect her?"

"For now?" David sighed. "We watch. We wait. I'll be here in town until Thanksgiving collecting as much information as I can. And I'll be visiting your mother, Leah."

"You shouldn't go there by yourself," Leah warned.

"I won't," he assured her. "Scott or Cash will be with me." He stood and looked around the room. "And if any of you hear anything, anything at all, tell me at once."

The meeting began to break apart as the men prepared to leave. Cash paused, leaning down toward Lisa and speaking in a low tone, quiet, but not quiet enough. Both Robyn and Leah heard every word, and their eyes widened before they turned toward each other with matching, delighted grins. The three women followed the men outside to see them off. Cash turned toward Leah, ready to give her a gentle goodbye embrace, when he caught the unmistakable sparkle of mischief in her eyes. He narrowed his gaze suspiciously.

"I suggest you keep that sass in check, young lady."

"What sass?" Leah asked sweetly, blinking up at him with an innocence that fooled exactly no one. He arched a brow. She reddened. Cash began to turn away. But Leah rose on her toes, leaned in close, and whispered in his ear, "Oh, you mean the part where you finally asked Lisa if you could court her?" She didn't wait, she spun, squeaking with laughter as she tried to flee. Cash caught her before she made it more than two steps. With a surprised yelp, Leah found herself thrown over his shoulder like a sack of grain.

"Cash! That's not fair, put me down!"

"You should be grateful it's cold," he warned, amused. "Otherwise, you'd be in that water trough over there."

David, Lisa, and Robyn all paused at the spectacle, grinning widely.

"For what?" Leah demanded.

"For your sass," Cash growled, shifting her slightly. That's when several men walking across Main Street stopped to stare. Among them was Hoopa Valley's young doctor, Riley Carter. He ambled over with a raised brow.

"Cash, why is Leah Johnson over your shoulder?" Riley laughed. "What'd she do now?"

"Just giving me some sass," Cash said. "You know how the young ones get. Always begging for attention and a lesson or two."

Leah's entire face flamed as Riley laughed louder.

"You're cruel, Cashley," she hissed. "I whispered my sass for only you to hear, and you embarrass me in front of the whole town?"

Cash smirked. "Would good, old-fashioned discipline be better in your eyes?"

He set her down, slowly, carefully, mindful of her injuries, but kept a gentle grip on her arms to steady her.

"I'm a woman, not a child," she shot back. "So, you can't exactly threaten me with that kind of discipline anymore."

"Oh really?" Cash smirked. "Funny, you somehow managed to get that discipline from McKay, didn't you?"

Leah's face went scarlet. "We are not using McKay as an example. He shouldn't have done that. And he isn't exactly a nice guy."

"No?" Cash drawled. "Hmm. Interesting. He told me you agreed to go to the dance with him this weekend." He lifted an eyebrow, smirking as her blush deepened to a blazing inferno. Leah sputtered helplessly. Robyn looked thrilled. Lisa looked like her heart was melting. And Cash looked just a little too pleased with himself.

"I didn't want to be rude when he asked me," Leah muttered, playing with a loose thread on her sleeve as if that required her full concentration.

"I see," Cash drawled, studying her more closely than she realized. "And you don't find him even a little attractive?"

Leah's cheeks warmed. She lowered her gaze to her boots.

"Maybe a little," she admitted, barely above a whisper.

Cash lifted an eyebrow. "Hmm. I'm surprised you aren't going with Jaxon. I was certain you two would end up together. Can you tell me why he's taking Mia instead of you?"

The name hit her like a fist to the chest. A sharp, unexpected ache stabbed beneath her ribs, and tears rushed so fast to her eyes she had to blink hard to keep them from spilling. Why did her heart always revolt at even the smallest mention of Jaxon?

They had always gone together. Always. But now... Leah forced her face into a mask of indifference, one she had no strength for, but she tried anyway. She didn't want Cash reading the storm inside her.

"I don't know," she said quickly, waving a hand as if brushing away dust. "Maybe he likes her or something."

"And you're... all right with that?"

Leah's throat tightened. Her heart throbbed painfully, and she could feel Cash watching her with that quiet, fatherly concern that always unraveled her defenses.

"It has nothing to do with me," she whispered.

"Are you sure about that?" Cash asked softly, his tone gentle but probing. Leah's frustration surged.

"Why are you interrogating me about this? Jaxon asked a girl to the dance. That's it. There's nothing to talk about."

"Leah—"

"Please," she choked out. "Just drop it. I don't want to talk about this right now." Her voice cracked, so thin, so fragile, that Cash knew she was seconds away from breaking. He reached out and gently lifted her chin, urging her to meet his eyes. The moment she did, the dam burst. The sobs she'd been fighting, sobs of heartbreak, confusion, fear, jealousy she didn't dare name, ripped through her. She spun away, unable to face him, and bolted across the yard, desperate to find a quiet place to cry where no one could see her fall apart.

"Leah!" Cash called, already moving. Her limp made her slower than usual, and Cash caught up within moments. He didn't touch her at first, he knew better, but he shadowed her steps, close enough to catch her if her knees gave out, determined not to leave her alone in her pain.

Leah stopped with her back toward the house, shoulders trembling, sobs bursting out of her, her face buried in her hands. She looked so small, so breakable in that moment, that Cash's heart squeezed painfully in his chest. Without a word he stepped next to her then, wrapped his strong arms around her, and pulled her firmly against him.

The moment she felt his solid warmth, she shattered completely. A deeper wave of sobs tore from her, muffled into his shirt as she clung to him. Her fingers twisted in the fabric at his waist, holding on as if he were the only steady thing in a world that suddenly felt tilted and uncertain. Cash said nothing. He simply held her, one hand cupping the back of her head while the other rested between her trembling shoulder blades. He knew she didn't need advice right now. She needed a safe place to fall apart.

Only when her crying softened, slower breaths, quieter tears, did he speak.

"You love him, don't you?"

Leah hesitated... then lifted her face. Tears streamed freely down her cheeks, carving glistening lines across her skin.

"I don't know," she whispered, her voice raw. "I want to say yes... but I'm not sure." She swallowed and continued, her words trembling like fragile glass. "While I was in the infirmary, Lisa told me everything Ruby went through, her heartbreak with Scott, and how my mom and grandmother used me as their sounding board. Lisa thinks I grew up hearing that loving your best friend ends in pain. She said maybe I'm scared to let myself love Jaxon because I'm terrified of ending up like them, broken." Leah's eyes filled again. "And she told me to take time… to look inside myself. I'm trying, Cash. I really am. But the fear won't go away. And now…"

Her gaze drifted toward the horizon, where the sinking sun painted the sky with streaks of gold and rose.

"…now I feel like I've already lost him."

Cash blinked, taken aback. "Why would you think that? Jaxon adores you."

"We passed each other today," Leah murmured, voice tight. "He'd just come back from town. He looked at me like I was… like I was someone he barely knew. He's changed. I can feel it." Her voice cracked. "Before you guys' left Eureka, he told me he loved me. I panicked. I told him he needed to find someone else, someone who wasn't me. That was before Lisa told me everything. Before I understood what was happening inside of me." She wiped a tear with the back of her hand. "But now… knowing he's courting Mia Collins, actually courting her, it… it hurts. So much."

"Sounds like jealousy to me," Cash said gently.

"I know," she whimpered, leaning back into the comfort of his chest. "But the fear is still there. My feelings are pulling me in two opposite directions, and I don't know which one is right. How can I be sure?"

Cash stroked the back of her head, his voice low and steady.

"Have you told Jaxon any of this? About what you're sorting through?"

She shook her head hard. "No. And I don't want to. I don't want to give him hope if all this confusion means he isn't the right one for me."

Cash breathed out slowly. "Maybe you should start praying about it. Ask God to clear the fog."

"I have," she whispered. "I pray every night. Every morning. Sometimes in the middle of the day when I can't stop thinking about it. But the confusion won't go away."

"Then be patient," Cash murmured, lifting her chin so she had no choice but to meet his eyes. "Keep listening to your heart. Keep praying. Maybe God wants to see if you'll be brave enough to face the truth, whatever it is. Maybe He's already answered, but fear has drowned it out." He leaned down and pressed a soft kiss to her forehead, tender and protective. "But sweetheart... if you and Jaxon are meant to be, nothing in this world will stop that. Not fear. Not confusion. Not even a Mia Collins."

Leah closed her eyes, letting his words sink deep. For the first time that day... she allowed a flicker of hope to rise.

19
Breathless with Heartbreak

The rest of the week passed faster than Leah expected. Since she still wasn't allowed to do any physical ranch work, Cash brought her every piece of paperwork that needed handling before the end of the year. She organized receipts, balanced ledgers, sorted invoices, and even corrected several mistakes Milton had made in the account books, mistakes she strongly suspected were intentional.

She met with Joseph Hicks, the banker, several times. He was a kind, calm man with a quiet sense of humor, and he patiently answered every one of her questions. Together they made sure the ranch's finances were in perfect order and that every bill had been paid under her direction, not Milton's.

Leah saw Jaxon ride into town a few times throughout the week, but he never stopped at his mother's house. Not once. Each time she spotted him from a distance, tall in the saddle, brown hat low over his eyes, her heart squeezed painfully. She missed him more than she could bear. His laughter. His companionship. His warmth. Even his terrible jokes. And it gutted her to think he might be avoiding her.

At least Robyn had something to smile about. When Chad asked her to the dance, Robyn practically floated for the rest of the day. It wasn't a secret they'd liked each other since meeting in Sacramento, and Leah was genuinely happy for her friend. They suited each other beautifully.

But as the days crept closer to Saturday evening, Leah's anxiety worsened. She wasn't looking forward to the dance, not one bit. The thought of walking into the hall and seeing Jaxon with Mia Collins on his arm sent a hollow ache through her chest. She didn't even feel like dressing up. If she'd been on her own, she probably would have canceled entirely.

But McKay had asked her so kindly, even lifting her into the saddle with that charming grin of his, and she didn't want to disappoint him. And her father had always taught her: *You can't run away from your problems. Face them, or they'll only grow larger.* Still... her stomach knotted every time she thought about stepping into that room.

On the afternoon of the dance, she and Robyn headed upstairs to dress. The moment their bedroom doors opened, both girls froze. Two beautiful dresses lay spread across their beds. Robyn's delighted squeal echoed through the upstairs hallway.

"Mama! Oh, Mama, it's perfect!" she cried before running to find her mother. Leah could only stare at her own dress. Dark blue satin, with delicate stitching along the waist and neckline. Breath catching, she reached out and let her fingers skim the fabric. It was lovely. Elegant, but not too elaborate. Exactly the kind of dress she would have chosen for herself, if she ever allowed herself such luxury.

She took her time getting ready, slipping into the gown with care. It fit as if it had been tailored just for her. The shade made her eyes appear even bluer than usual, and for a moment she simply studied her reflection, stunned by the transformation. Lisa's soft knock went unheard. Leah was too lost in her thoughts, wondering what Jaxon would think if he saw her like this, wondering if he'd even look at her. She nearly jumped out of her skin when Lisa's warm voice floated from behind her.

"Do you like it?"

Leah spun around, hand over her heart.

"Mama Finlay, you scared me." Then she laughed softly. "It's beautiful. Thank you so much." She crossed the room and hugged the older woman tightly. Lisa squeezed her back, proud and comforting all at once.

"I thought a special dress might cheer you up," Lisa said, brushing a stray curl from Leah's face. "You've had more than your share of trouble lately. Tonight, should be about joy. About feeling young and lovely, and forgetting everything at home for just a few hours."

"You shouldn't have gone to so much trouble," Leah murmured, touched beyond words.

"It was no trouble at all," Lisa insisted. "And I trust Chad and McKay won't leave you or Robyn alone for even a minute." Her eyes sparkled with excitement, just like a matchmaker who knew exactly what she was doing, before she excused herself to change, leaving Leah staring after her with a soft, grateful smile.

The dress truly did make her feel different. Stronger. Braver. Maybe... ready to face whatever waited for her at the dance.

Even if that *whatever,* had brown eyes and a girl named Mia on his arm.

"Leah, you look gorgeous," Robyn gasped the moment her best friend stepped out of the room. Her eyes widened, roaming over the dark-blue gown as if she'd never seen Leah in a dress before.

"My word, I knew Mama picked something lovely, but Leah, you look like you stepped out of one of those fancy magazines in Sacramento."

Leah laughed softly, touched by the awe in Robyn's voice.

"Well, look at you," she countered warmly. "Chad won't have eyes for anyone but you, tonight."

Robyn's cheeks flushed a rosy pink, and she bit back a huge smile.

"Do you really think so?"

"I know so," Leah said, nudging her gently. "When he sees you in that dress, he's going to forget how to breathe."

Robyn squealed, excitement bubbling over. She grabbed Leah's hands and gave them an eager squeeze. The two girls shared a glowing, breathless moment, equal parts nerves and anticipation. Tonight was going to be unforgettable... one way or another.

Lisa had barely stepped out of her room, radiant in a soft lavender dress, when a firm knock sounded at the front door. The girls exchanged a nervous glance before Robyn hurried to answer it. Three men stood on the porch, all of them looking far more polished than usual. Chad wore a crisp shirt and vest, boots newly shined. Cash looked almost regal in his dark coat and hat. And McKay, tall and broad-shouldered, seemed carved from confidence itself. For a heartbeat, the three women simply stared.

Robyn's mother recovered first, offering a warm smile. Chad and Cash stepped forward at once, each offering an arm to the lady they had come for. Cash looked impossibly proud with Lisa on his arm, while Chad blushed bright pink when Robyn slipped her hand into his.

McKay lingered a moment longer in the doorway, his gaze fixed entirely on Leah. She swallowed hard. The intensity in his green eyes made her suddenly aware of every inch of the dark-blue dress, the soft shawl, the curls Robyn had painstakingly arranged. He stepped toward her and offered his arm with a little bow, surprisingly charming for a ranch hand who usually teased her to no end.

"Leah... you're downright stunnin'," he said low, the warmth in his voice rare and real.

"I knew you were pretty the moment I figured out you weren't a boy, but somehow, you just keep gettin' prettier."

Heat flooded Leah's cheeks so fast she felt lightheaded. No one had ever looked at her like that, not even Jaxon, and it startled her enough that she hesitated before placing her hand on his arm. McKay's smile deepened, pleased by her reaction.

Together, the two couples and Cash and Lisa, headed down the steps toward the boardwalk. Lamps flickered to life along Main Street, casting soft golden light across the dust and wooden walkways. Music drifted faintly from the saloon, fiddles warming up, boots shuffling across the floor.

Leah's heart thudded harder with each step. McKay's presence beside her felt steady... safe... but her thoughts were already tangled with what, or who, waited for her inside that dance hall. And whether she was truly ready to face him.

They joined a long table near the back wall, where the lantern light was warmest and the music pleasantly loud. Robyn sat close to Chad, fingers shyly laced with his under the table, while Cash and Lisa shared quiet smiles that spoke volumes. A few minutes later, David arrived and pulled up a chair beside them, giving Leah a reassuring wink.

Before she could catch her breath, McKay was already asking for the first dance. And the second. And the third. Leah found herself whirled across the floor in his strong, confident arms. He was surprisingly light on his feet, leading her smoothly through each turn. He twirled her playfully, lifted her once just to hear her gasp and laugh, and for a brief while, Leah forgot the heaviness in her heart.

When the musicians struck up a slow, elegant waltz, McKay released her with a charming bow. Cash stepped forward before anyone else could claim her.

"May I?" he asked, offering his hand. Leah smiled, bright and grateful, and placed her hand in his. Cash guided her to the center of the floor with the quiet protectiveness of a father escorting his daughter. Their steps matched easily, and she followed his lead without effort.

He had just finished twirling her when the saloon doors swung open. Jaxon and Mia stepped inside. The sight hit Leah like the ground had vanished beneath her feet. Her vision blurred for a second, and her balance gave way, she would have fallen if Cash hadn't tightened his hold immediately, steadying her against his chest.

"Easy," he murmured. But Leah didn't hear him. Her eyes were fixed on Jaxon. He looked... breathtaking. Freshly shaved, wearing his best shirt, posture proud. And Mia, smiling, glowing, clung to his arm as if she belonged there. Jaxon guided her to a table, leaning down to say something that made Mia's cheeks flush pink. He didn't glance once toward Leah. Not even a flicker.

A cold ache rippled through her chest, sharp enough to steal her breath. Cash felt her stiffen, and lowered his head slightly, trying to catch her gaze, worry etched across his features. She forced herself to look up at him, but she knew her eyes betrayed her, begging him silently not to speak, not to ask, not to pity her.

"Please excuse me," she whispered, voice tight and fragile. Cash hesitated for only a heartbeat, then nodded solemnly, understanding far more than she wished he did. Leah didn't look back as she left the dance floor or as she slipped through the saloon doors into the cool evening air. But she didn't have to. She could *feel* Cash's gaze following her, heavy with concern.

And she knew that if anyone approached her, McKay, Robyn, or even Jaxon, Cash would be right behind them... ready to step in if her heart shattered any further.

The cool night air hit her like a slap, and she ran. She ran, boots pounding the boardwalk, skirts gathered in her fists, until she reached the quiet street leading to the Finlay home. She didn't go inside. She couldn't. Her heart felt too raw, her breath too tight in her chest. Instead, she slipped around the side of the house and followed the narrow path toward the small grove of trees behind it. Moonlight filtered through the branches, softly illuminating the worn wooden bench beneath them.

Leah collapsed onto it. And then she broke. Not the quiet tears she tried so hard to hide. Not the controlled sniffles she forced upon herself inside the dance hall. But real sobs, deep, heaving, unstoppable. Her entire body shook as all the pain she had bottled up for weeks burst out at once.

"Leah?" McKay's voice came from behind her, rough, worried, breathless, as if he had run the whole way too. She lifted her tearstained face. His expression was startled and full of concern, the kind a man wore only when he truly cared. He reached for her, trying to pull her into his arms. She turned away.

"Don't. I'll be okay."

But McKay wasn't the kind to be brushed off. He stepped forward again and drew her gently but firmly against his chest. Leah pushed back, slipping from his hold and stumbling into a run. She wasn't fast, not with her injured leg, and she barely made it ten steps before McKay caught her. This time his arms wrapped around her securely, anchoring her trembling body. She sagged against him, drained and heartsick. McKay didn't ask any questions. He didn't demand explanations. He simply held her.

Eventually, after what felt like forever, Leah's sobs eased. Her breathing steadied. McKay guided her back to the bench and sat with his arm still around her, offering quiet solidarity.

"Do you want to talk about it?" he finally asked, voice gentle.

Leah shook her head. "There are no words for this right now. I'll be okay. It just... takes time."

She looked up at him with red, puffy eyes and managed a small, grateful smile. "Thank you." She gave his hand a quick squeeze, then moved to sit on her own. That was when they both heard it, a rustling behind them in the grove of trees.

McKay's head snapped up, eyes narrowing. Before Leah could turn to look, he reached for her, pulled her closer, and suddenly his lips were on hers.

The kiss shocked her. At first, she froze, stunned. But McKay deepened it, his mouth demanding, urgent, far too heated, far too much. Leah's heart jolted in panic, and she shoved him hard. He stumbled back, breath unsteady. Leah opened her mouth, outrage and confusion tangling on her tongue, but an angry voice cut through the night.

"So, that's why you rejected me."

Leah and McKay whirled around. Jaxon stood several yards away, moonlight turning his brown eyes into dark, burning embers. His jaw was clenched so tight it looked painful.

"Have you been seeing McKay longer than just tonight," he demanded, voice trembling with fury, "or do you let every man who takes you to a dance kiss you like that?"

McKay immediately stepped between Leah and Jaxon.

"Don't go sayin' somethin' you'll regret, Jaxon. I kissed her without askin'. She didn't have a thing to do with it."

"Oh, of course," Jaxon snapped. "Completely innocent. That must be why she kept kissing you until it got out of control. Right?"

Leah's breath hitched. "Jax—"

He stopped her cold with a raised hand, never taking his eyes off McKay.

"Don't go actin' stupid," McKay growled. "I surprised the girl. She didn't expect—"

Jaxon scoffed loudly, the sound full of bitterness and hurt. Then he turned his gaze finally, unforgivingly, on Leah.

"Well," he said tightly, "it's a good thing I listened to you earlier. I did exactly what you told me to do. I started courting." He stood straighter, shoulders squared. "I care about Mia. I want to marry her. Her family is moving to Eureka in a few weeks, and we'll likely marry there."

Every drop of blood left Leah's face. She felt herself sway, the world tipping. Something inside her broke so loudly she was certain they had all heard it. Before she could speak, before she could *breathe*, McKay grabbed Jaxon by the front of his shirt and yanked him forward.

"What the hell are you doin', man?" McKay snapped. "Why're you bein' such a damn fool? Can't you see this girl's in love with you?"

Jaxon's laugh was bitter and humorless.

"Loves me? That must be why she was kissing you, right?"

"Jaxon," McKay snapped, fire in his eyes, "don't push me, I'll knock the damn foolishness right outta you. I kissed her—she froze like a spooked filly. Didn't kiss me back once. Your pride's makin' you blind as a bat."

Jaxon jerked free of McKay's grip.

"Whatever," he spat. "She can kiss you all she likes. I don't care anymore." He turned sharply and strode away, disappearing into the shadows of the grove.

Leah stood frozen, breathless, trembling, shattered, his words echoing through her chest like gunfire. *I don't care anymore.* They struck deeper than any wound she had ever suffered.

McKay turned back to Leah, but the sight of her instantly stole his breath. She was gasping, sharp, shallow, panicked breaths that made her entire chest heave. Her hands trembled violently, clutching at the fabric over her heart as though trying to hold herself together. Tears streamed down her cheeks, but she made no sound, not a sob, not a whimper. Only the frantic, ragged pull of air as she tried to breathe.

"Leah?" McKay stepped toward her, worry tightening every muscle in his body. She shook her head as if trying to push away the pain, but her breaths only grew quicker, more desperate. Her knees buckled. McKay lunged forward, catching her just before she hit the ground.

"No, no, no, look at me," he urged, one hand cupping her cheek, the other holding her upright. "Slow breaths. Leah, breathe with me. In... and out... nice and slow."

But she couldn't. Her lungs refused to cooperate. Each inhale became shorter than the last, her chest fluttering like a trapped bird. Her vision blurred. Her body shook so violently he had to tighten his grip to keep her from slipping through his arms.

"Leah, sweetheart, stay with me," he murmured, panic creeping into his voice despite his efforts to sound steady. Her eyes rolled slightly, her body sagging as she teetered on the brink of losing consciousness. Footsteps crunched along the path behind them.

Without turning, McKay shouted over his shoulder, voice raw with urgency, "Get Doc Carter! Now! We need him right away!" His arms closed protectively around Leah as she struggled for every breath, the night suddenly far too quiet except for the frightening sound of her hyperventilation and McKay's desperate attempts to keep her anchored to consciousness.

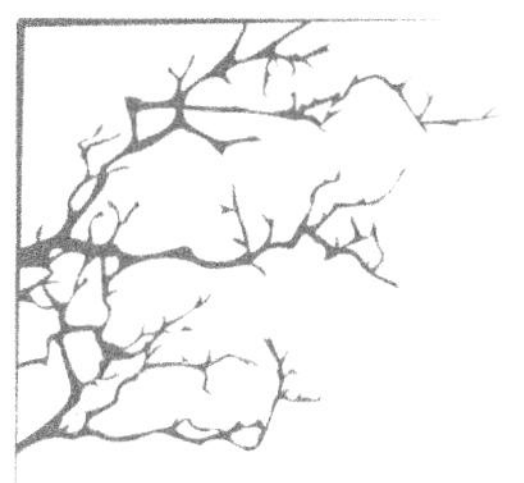

20
Just Gone

Chad took one look at Leah's condition, her gasping breaths, trembling limbs, wide, terrified eyes, and spun on his heel, sprinting back toward the saloon as fast as his legs would carry him. Robyn rushed forward at the same time, skirts flying behind her.

"What's happening?" she cried, dropping to her knees beside her friend. "Leah? Oh, sweetie, please... try to breathe slowly. Stay with us." Her voice trembled, tears gathering in her eyes, but she forced herself to remain steady. She cupped Leah's face gently, brushing sweat-soaked strands from her forehead, murmuring soothing words despite her own fear.

Within a minute, though it felt like an eternity, Cash and Lisa burst through the trees. One glance at Leah and Cash's entire expression changed. Fear, fury, and fierce protectiveness all crashed through his features at once. He didn't hesitate. He was at her side in a heartbeat, gathering her shaking body into his arms just as her eyes fluttered closed. Leah went limp, collapsing against his chest.

"She's fainting," Lisa whispered, voice tight with fear. Cash lifted Leah as though she weighed nothing, holding her close. Her head lolled against his shoulder, her breaths shallow and uneven.

"Get the door," he ordered, voice rough, already striding toward the house with long, urgent steps. Lisa and Robyn hurried ahead. Tears slipped down their cheeks as they pushed the door open and stepped aside so Cash could carry Leah inside. Behind them, McKay followed. His chest rose and fell rapidly, guilt twisting his features, panic tightening every muscle in his jaw. His eyes never left Leah's pale, unconscious face.

"I—" His voice caught. He swallowed hard and stepped closer, though he couldn't bring himself to cross the threshold. "She broke down cryin' outside. Then Jaxon came along, thought he'd seen somethin' he hadn't." McKay scrubbed a hand through his hair, jaw tight.

"Jealousy hit him hard. He lit into her. Said he was fixin' to marry Mia and didn't give a damn about Leah anymore... then stomped off like a bloody fool." He shook his head slowly, pain carving deep lines into his expression.

"And Leah... she just crumpled. Fell clean apart." He shook his head, pain settlin' deep.

"I ain't never seen hurt like that. She tried to breathe, but it only made things worse." His voice broke. "I never shoulda kissed her. She didn't want it, and she was already shaken. I just made it worse. Pushed her right past her breakin' point." His shoulders sagged in defeat. "I'm so sorry."

But Cash wasn't listening. His entire focus, his whole heart, was on Leah as he carried her up the steps of the porch, praying with every step that she would be all right.

At the doorway, Robyn clutched Lisa's hand. Both women trembled as they watched Leah's limp body disappear inside the house, knowing something had broken inside her tonight. Something that would be very, very hard to put back together.

"She's awake again, but she's in a bad place," Riley Carter said quietly as he stepped into the parlor, where Cash, Lisa, Robyn, Chad, and McKay waited with pale, anxious faces. "She's asked to be left alone for the rest of the night. She said she doesn't want to see anyone."

Robyn's hand flew to her mouth. "Oh, Leah..."

Cash rose from his chair, jaw tight. "Is it safe to leave her by herself right now?"

Riley hesitated. "I gave her something mild. It should calm her nerves and help her sleep. She's exhausted, emotionally and physically." He glanced toward the guestroom door. "I'll check on her again in a few minutes, and once she's asleep, someone should sit with her. She shouldn't be alone long."

Everyone nodded, but the worry in the room only thickened. Silence settled, heavy, suffocating, as each of them replayed the night. Five minutes passed. Then ten. Riley finally stood.

"Let me make sure she settled." He hurried down the hallway, footsteps quiet but determined. The others strained to hear any sound, movement, a voice, anything, but the house remained unnervingly still. Moments later, Riley's voice rang through the house, sharp, alarmed.

"Cash! Lisa! Someone, come quick!"

Cash tore down the hallway so fast the others barely had time to react. Riley stood frozen in the doorway of the guestroom, staring into the dimly lit space. The bed was empty. Sheets rumpled. Pillow askew. And the window, wide open, curtains fluttering like ghostly fingers in the night breeze.

"She's gone," Riley said, shock draining the color from his face. Robyn let out a strangled cry. Lisa pressed her hand to her heart. Chad ran a shaking hand through his hair, whispering a prayer under his breath. Cash staggered forward, gripping the windowsill as if he could will her back into existence.

"She's gone," he whispered, fear and fury tightening every word. "Leah is gone."

McKay, Cash, Chad, and Dr. Carter launched into action. They scattered across the property without hesitation, searching behind the barn, along the creek, through the grove of trees, and around every corner of the Finlay home. But there was no sign of Leah.

"Leah!" Cash bellowed, his voice raw with fear. Only silence answered him. Riley sprinted around the back of the house while Chad checked the road leading toward town. McKay tore across the yard, his eyes scanning the ground for any clue. Cash rounded the side of the house and stopped cold. On the patch of dirt beneath the window, he found footprints. Large ones. Much larger than Leah's. Deeply imprinted... meaning whoever had stood there was heavy. Or carrying someone. His stomach dropped like a stone.

"Cash?" Chad called, breathless. "Any sign?"

Cash crouched down, fingertips brushing the edges of the prints, dread spreading through him like ice.

"She didn't climb out on her own," he said quietly, his voice hoarse. "Someone was here. Someone took her."

Riley and Chad froze, horror washing over their faces. McKay came running from the front yard.

"What did you find—?"

Cash pointed at the prints. "A man stood right here. Recently. He was waiting for her."

Robyn, who had followed at a distance, let out a strangled sob and covered her mouth with both hands. Lisa wrapped an arm around the girl, eyes wide with terror. McKay clenched his fists until his knuckles went white.

"I'm getting the sheriff," he ground out. "Right now." Without another word, he vaulted onto his horse and took off down the dark street at full gallop. Cash watched him disappear into the night, then turned back toward the house, his heart pounding with a single, terrifying thought: Leah was gone, and someone had stolen her right out from under their protection.

"So, after the breakdown, Leah was in her bed, but when you checked on her a few minutes later, she was gone?" Sheriff Scott Bailey asked, his jaw tightening as he looked at the young doctor.

Riley Carter nodded grimly. "Gone. Window wide open. Not a trace of her."

Cash dragged a hand through his hair, pacing a short line before facing the sheriff again.

"Do you think Milton and Jack are behind this?"

Scott exhaled through his nose. "It's possible. But I doubt they did it themselves. They're cowards. They'd hire someone to do the dirty work."

"What about that Wilson guy?" Robyn asked suddenly.

Cash turned to her, confused. "Wilson guy?"

"Yes. Leah mentioned a man named Wilson. She overheard Milton talking about him."

"Sheriff?" Cash pressed, brow raised. Scott looked genuinely puzzled.

"That's news to me. But as I said, it's possible."

"News to you?" Robyn snapped, her voice sharp as a whip. "Leah said she saw you meeting with the Rowlands and that Wilson man. She isn't a liar." Her eyes flashed with fury, her entire body trembling with adrenaline and fear.

Scott blinked, stunned. "I think you're misunderstanding—"

"No." Robyn stepped closer, fists clenched. "I remember exactly what she said. Are you hiding something, Sheriff? Are you working with them?"

"Robyn," her mother said sharply, gripping her daughter's arm. "You need to calm down. Throwing accusations around isn't helping Leah right now."

"How am I supposed to calm down?" Robyn cried, tears filling her eyes. "My best friend is missing, and the sheriff might have something to do with it!"

Cash stepped between them, raising both hands in a calming gesture.

"All right, enough. Everyone needs to breathe for a minute. Lisa's right, turning on each other doesn't solve anything." He turned to Robyn, his voice softer. "I know you're scared. We all are."

Robyn pressed her trembling lips together, her anger mingling with panic. Just then, the front door flew open. Jaxon stepped inside, his hat still in hand, chest rising fast as if he'd been running. Robyn spun toward him in an instant.

"You!" she shouted, storming across the room. "Why did you attack Leah like that? Why did you let your jealousy get the best of you?"

Jaxon recoiled, eyes wide with shock. "What are you talking about?"

"McKay told us everything," Robyn burst out, tears welling again. "Leah had a breakdown because of you, and now she's gone."

Jaxon's face drained of color. "Gone? What do you mean gone?"

"Someone kidnapped her," Robyn said, voice cracking. "She was in her room, trying to recover, and when Dr. Carter checked on her again, her bed was empty and the window was open. Leah is gone, Jaxon."

The words hit him like a gunshot. His knees nearly buckled. And around them, the room fell into a heavy, terrified silence, because in that moment, every single person knew: whatever fractures had formed between them... whatever hurt had passed between Leah and Jaxon... it no longer mattered. Only one thing did. Leah was missing. And they had to find her.

It was hours before Leah and Wilson finally reached a hunting cabin. Neither of them had spoken much on the ride, and Leah was grateful for the silence. She was exhausted, bone-deep exhausted, but fear and the events of the night had her nerves vibrating like taut wire. Whatever Doc Carter had given her to help her sleep wasn't working. Not tonight.

She recognized the area the moment the small structure came into sight. This was one of her father's cabins, one she had visited as a child. If she wanted to escape, she could. She knew the land, the trails, the ridges. But she also knew what hunted the forests at night... and she wasn't stupid enough to limp through miles of wilderness, half-crippled, in the pitch-dark with wolves and mountain lions prowling nearby.

Wilson dismounted, yanked her off the horse, and hauled her inside. He tied her to one of the beds with practiced efficiency before heading back out to tend the horses. Escape didn't even occur to her, not tonight. She was too worn out. Too heartsick. Too emotionally shredded to even pretend to have strength left.

When Wilson came back in, he cut away the ropes, then lit several candles and built a fire. The glow illuminated his features. He was younger than she originally guessed, early thirties, maybe. Not unattractive, though his eyes held a hardness that made her wary. Leah wrapped her arms around herself and went to the fireplace, sinking into one of the large armchairs. She shivered from the cold, and from everything she refused to let her mind replay.

Focus on now, she reminded herself. Not what happened. Not who said what. Not the pain sitting like a burning coal behind her ribs. Wilson rummaged through his bag and set out beans, meat, cheese, and bread.

"You hungry?" he asked. Leah shook her head. "It's been a long day for you," he said calmly.

"A little food won't hurt none." He offered her hot peppermint tea. She hesitated before accepting. It was warm, and she needed that much at least.

"So," she said quietly. "What do you want from me?"

"You'll find out soon enough."

"I'm not stupid." Her voice sharpened. "I know you're working for Milton and Jack."

Wilson grinned, amused. "Oh? And how d'you know that?"

"I overheard you three talking with Sheriff Bailey."

He let out a low whistle. "Didn't see that comin'. Looks like we done underestimated you."

"Clearly." Her tone was sharp. "And where exactly will you be sleeping? Because if you think I'm sharing a cabin with a strange man—"

Wilson chuckled. "You ain't got a choice. But settle down, I ain't gonna lay a hand on you."

"And I should believe you because...?" she challenged. He raised a brow, studying her, clearly recognizing that she wasn't meek, naïve, or scared of him in the way he might have expected.

"I done told you," Wilson shrugged. "I'm here to keep an eye on you, nothin' more."

"Oh, wonderful," she muttered. "Because criminals are so trustworthy."

Wilson laughed again.

Her glare sharpened. "Glad you find this amusing."

Before either of them could say more, a knock rattled the door. Wilson got up and opened it.

Leah's breath left her lungs. McKay stepped into the cabin. Her stomach dropped.

"Anyone trailin' you?" Wilson asked.

"No," McKay said. "They're worried near sick. Search'll start come dawn."

"Good job tonight," Wilson praised.

"Just doin' what needed doin'," McKay responded quietly. Leah rose slowly, fury blooming so hot she felt dizzy.

"So, all that flirting... all your courting talk... the kiss... all of it was just to use me?" Her voice rose, sharp as broken glass. "I knew I shouldn't have trusted you. After what happened on the ranch, after you ambushed me, I knew you were trouble."

McKay only smirked.

"You ambushed her?" Wilson asked.

"Hell no," McKay snorted. "Girl was skulk'n around dressed as a boy. I grabbed her, she sunk her teeth in me and kicked like a mule. So, I tanned her backside a couple swats. Didn't please her none." He smirked. "But she forgave me, didn't ya, sweetheart?" He reached out to touch her cheek. Leah slapped his hand away, her eyes blazing.

"You must be very proud," she spat. "Targeting a woman. Helping thieves. Embarrassing me in front of Jaxon just for fun. You humiliated me deliberately!"

His smile faded. "That part wasn't supposed to happen," he muttered. "Milton and Wilson were crouched behind them trees. I didn't want you layin' eyes on 'em. So, I kissed you, just to throw you off. Had no idea Jaxon'd come stormin' in and—"

Leah laughed, humorless and cutting.

"Right. So, I'm just a pawn. My feelings are a joke. Good to know." She turned her glare on Wilson. "And you, don't think for one second I'm afraid of you. You both are cowards. If kidnapping a girl makes you feel powerful, you need help." She got louder. More furious. More unhinged from exhaustion and heartbreak.

Wilson sighed and rubbed his temple.

"Goodness... make her shut up."

McKay moved in a flash, grabbing her face and crushing his mouth against hers. Leah's fury exploded. She shoved him, claws out, trying to twist away, but he held her until he chose to release her. When he finally stepped back, her chest heaved. Tears burned her eyes, but not from heartbreak this time. From rage. From humiliation.

Without a single word, she stumbled to the bed she had been tied to earlier, climbed under the blanket, and buried her face in the pillow. She didn't want them to see her cry. She failed. She sobbed anyway, quiet, strangled, broken sounds she despised herself for making.

The men talked in low voices. Planning. Plotting. Ignoring her tears. She was grateful for that much. She had nothing left in her to fight tonight. Her world had been unraveling piece by painful piece since her father died. She had clung to strength for so long, pushing through trial after trial, but now? Now she felt hollow. Like the last pieces of her were crumbling. And the emotional blow with Jaxon, the look on his face, the words he'd thrown at her, had split her wide open.

Was this Milton and Jack's plan? To break her heart first, weaken her spirit, then strike? If so... they were succeeding. She felt herself slipping. Losing hope. Losing fight. And alone, in the dark corner of her father's cabin, Leah wondered if she had anything left to give at all.

When Leah woke, the sun was only beginning to brush the mountaintops with pale gold. A thin strip of dawn light cut across the wooden floorboards, dust motes drifting lazily through the quiet cabin. Her body ached, her eyes were swollen, and her throat felt raw from everything she had let out... and everything she still held tight.

Wilson was sprawled across the other bed, boots still on, snoring softly. McKay had slumped sideways in one of the armchairs, his hat tipped over his eyes, his chest rising and falling in slow, even breaths. For once, both men looked deceptively harmless.

Leah stared at them for a long moment, her heartbeat unsettled but steady. The heaviness in her chest pressed sharply, and tears threatened again, hot, insistent, familiar. She swallowed them back with effort. She had cried enough the night before. More than she wanted anyone to know. If she let herself unravel again... she might not find the strength to pull herself together.

No more crying, she ordered herself silently. *Not now.* Very slowly, she pushed the blanket aside and rose from the bed. Her body protested, stiff, sore, exhausted, but she forced herself to stand tall. She moved quietly, careful not to wake either man. She wasn't ready to face them yet. Not after everything. When she lifted the latch, the door gave a soft creak, and she winced. Neither man stirred.

The morning air hit her the moment she stepped outside, crisp and cold, carrying the scent of pine, earth, and distant snow. She closed her eyes and breathed it in deeply, letting it cool the heat still burning in her chest. The forest stretched behind the cabin, peaceful and untouched. She could hear the faint trickle of the little stream that ran behind the property, one she remembered from childhood trips with her father. Back then it had been a place of wonder, where she collected smooth stones and dipped her feet in icy water on summer afternoons. Now it felt like the only place she could breathe.

Wrapping her arms around herself, she stepped off the porch and walked through the grass toward the sound of running water. Each step loosened the tightness in her lungs, as though the earth itself was urging her forward.

She needed a moment, just one quiet moment, to wash her face, clear her mind, and remind herself she was still Leah Johnson… not the girl who had fallen apart last night, not the broken heart Jaxon had crushed, not the trapped daughter being used as leverage. Just Leah. And she needed that before she could face whatever came next.

The moment Leah stepped back into the cabin, the door clicking softly shut behind her, both men bolted upright as though gunfire had gone off. Wilson lurched halfway out of his bed, and McKay shot to his feet so fast he nearly tripped.

"Where in blazes you been?" McKay barked, voice sharp with adrenaline. His eyes swept over her as though he expected to see blood. Leah arched a cool eyebrow.

"I ran home last night but decided I couldn't do that to your ego, so I came back," she quipped with a dry smirk and one of her signature death glares. McKay's jaw tightened.

"This ain't somethin' to joke about, Leah. There's wild critters out there, mountain lions, wolves—"

"Oh really? Is that what lives in the mountains?" she shot back with exaggerated innocence. "Strange, I thought I grew up here." She crossed her arms. "And don't pretend you were worried about me. The only thing you were panicking about is having to tell Milton I escaped."

McKay opened his mouth. "Leah—"

"I don't want to hear it." Her voice iced over. "Your entire act is done, McKay. The flirting, the dancing, the sweet words, you can keep it all. I won't believe another thing that comes out of your mouth."

His face tightened, irritation and something else flickered there, but before he could respond, hoofbeats thudded outside. Heavy. Decisive. Leah rolled her eyes and sat on the bed with all the grace of someone utterly done with the stupidity around her. The cabin door swung open. Milton Rowland strode inside without a word to either McKay or Wilson. His eyes locked on Leah like she was prey, he'd already claimed. He walked straight up to her, his boots scraping the floorboards.

"I reckon a night in these woods taught you somethin'—you ain't no match for us, not by a long shot."

Leah gave an exaggerated shiver.

"Oh yes, I'm absolutely petrified." She rolled her eyes again, slow and deliberate. Milton's face flushed with anger. She could almost hear the blood boiling under his skin.

"Best watch yourself, girl," he spat. "We been patient as saints, but if it takes force to cure that mouth o' yours, we'll go that route." His eyes burned with hatred. Leah stood to her feet in a flash, meeting him eye-to-eye, shoulders squared, chin high.

"I don't care about your threats, Milton." Her voice was cold steel. "Sure, you can hurt me. You can try to break me. But if you think I'll crumble easily, you truly don't know who you're dealing with." She stepped closer, defiant. "And you won't kill me. Not until you think you've wrung every penny and ounce of power from me. So no, I'm not scared of you."

She sat back down, deliberately turning her shoulder to him. The three men stared at her, thrown off by her composure, her fire, her total refusal to cower. The silence stretched thick. Finally, Leah tilted her head, eyes landing on Milton again.

"So, tell me, how long do you plan on keeping me here?"

He blinked, as if snapped out of his stupor.

"However long it takes to break you." He sneered. "I'll be back in two days. You'd better be ready to fall in line." He jerked his head. "Let's go, McKay."

Both men left. The door slammed behind them.

Wilson exhaled sharply and dragged a chair over, dropping into it beside her. For the first time, something like respect, or reluctant admiration, glimmered in his eyes.

"Ain't never seen a girl with guts like that," he muttered. Leah stared into the crackling fire, her voice low and steady.

"It's not fearlessness. It's having nothing left to lose."

Wilson frowned slightly, but she continued.

"They had my father killed," she whispered. "They've terrified my mother. They've taken over my home like parasites and believe they can bully their way into owning everything Dad built." She looked at Wilson then, truly looked at him. "My dad put the ranch in my name for a reason. He trusted me. He believed I'd fight for what was right when it counted." Her voice didn't shake. "No matter the outcome, I will fight until I have nothing left. If I give up now, I dishonor him, everything he sacrificed, and the will he left behind."

She lifted her chin, the firelight glinting in her eyes.

"And that," she finished, "will never happen."

"Have you found anything?" Cash demanded, his voice rough with worry as he swept his gaze over Chad and Sheriff Scott Bailey. Both men shook their heads.

"Nothing," Chad said grimly. "No tracks we can follow, no broken branches, no sign of a camp. It's like the earth just swallowed her up." His jaw tightened in frustration. "Do you think they left the area?"

Scott exhaled sharply. "If they left, we'd have seen tracks headed out of the valley. There's been no movement on any of the main trails, north or south." He shook his head. "No. They're close."

Cash paced a few steps, then stopped, staring toward the dark tree line as though sheer willpower could force answers out of the shadows. His fists were balled so tightly his knuckles were white.

"She's still somewhere around here," he said, voice low but brimming with controlled fury. "They want money from her, and that means they have to stay in Hoopa Valley. They need access to the bank, access to her accounts." His throat tightened. "They can't risk taking her far."

Chad nodded, though fear flickered in his eyes.

"Then they're hiding her somewhere local. Somewhere they think we won't look."

Scott crossed his arms, scanning the quiet streets as early morning light crept over the rooftops.

"We'll find her," he said firmly. "I'll bring in more men. Check every shack, every trapper's cabin, every abandoned building within a fifteen-mile radius. They can't hide her forever."

Cash swallowed hard. His voice cracked with something raw and personal.

"They'd better pray we find her before them."

"This ain't a game, Leah. You don't give in, I'll put hurt on someone you care about." Milton's voice thundered through the tiny cabin as he slammed his hand onto the table so hard the wood rattled. His face was flushed an ugly, mottled red, the veins at his temples bulging, his eyes narrowed into something dark and menacing.

Leah didn't flinch. She only pressed her lips together and shook her head, refusing to give him a hint of fear, though her heart pounded painfully inside her chest. The man in front of her looked seconds away from losing control entirely.

"That's it," Milton snapped, jabbin' a finger at the door. "McKay, git to it. You know what needs doin'."

McKay's jaw tightened. He nodded once and strode out of the cabin. Milton paused in the doorway, sending one final icy glare toward Leah.

"I'll be back come nightfall," he spat. "And you damn well better have changed your mind."

The moment he disappeared, the air inside the cabin felt lighter, but only barely. Wilson exhaled, shoulders sagging slightly. He walked toward the small stove and began setting water to boil, but before he could strike a match, Leah let out a sharp, startled squeal and practically vaulted onto the nearest armchair.

Wilson spun around. "What—?" His eyes tracked where hers were fixed, and he spotted the large spider skittering across the floorboards. When he looked back at Leah, she was clinging to the back of the chair, eyes wide with horror. Wilson burst out laughing. Her death glare should have killed him where he stood.

"That is not funny," Leah snapped, voice breathless. "Please remove that thing."

"Leah Johnson, scared of a speck o' a spider?" Wilson teased. "You're facin' Milton, girl. He's the one you oughta fear."

"That is not tiny," she hissed. "That thing is big enough to eat a child."

Wilson shook his head, chuckling as he stepped closer to her, big mistake.

"How 'bout I make the introductions? Might be real interestin'," he teased, reaching out as if to take her hand.

Leah bolted backward with a yelp. The armchair tipped dangerously, and before she could crash to the floor, Wilson lunged. His arms wrapped around her, catching her mid-fall and lifting her clean off her feet. For a heartbeat, they froze like that, her breath caught, his arms locked around her, their faces inches apart. His grip was firm but gentle, his expression softened unexpectedly.

"Well now," he murmured, a crooked grin tugging at his lips, "look at me, rescuin' a pretty girl from a fearsome man-eatin' spider. Reckon a fellow deserves a kiss for such bravery?"

Heat flooded Leah's cheeks. "Wilson, don't you dare—"

But he was already leaning in. His lips brushed hers, quick, warm, startling, before he set her back down on the solid, upright chair. Leah stared at him, stunned, speechless, completely thrown off guard. Without another word, Wilson crossed the room, trapped the spider in a tin cup, and carried it outside.

Leah remained frozen, legs curled beneath her, so they didn't touch the floor. Wilson was her kidnapper. Her enemy. Yet he had just caught her mid-fall, teased her, kissed her, and escorted a spider out like some absurd gentleman. She didn't know whether to scream, sob, or throw something at him.

Leah was still perched on the armchair when Wilson stepped back inside. Her knees were drawn up, skirts tucked beneath her, as if the wooden floorboards were made of fire instead of pine. Her eyes swept the cabin anxiously, checking every shadow for more spiders. Wilson grinned, brushing dirt from his hands.

"Intruder's taken care of. You're safe to come down now, darlin'."

She only shook her head stubbornly. "I don't think so."

He huffed an amused breath and crouched before her, taking both her hands gently in his. Leah stiffened, breath catching as he looked up at her from beneath his lashes.

"You're awful cute when you're spooked," he murmured. Leah's cheeks burned. He stood slowly, leaning in as he brushed a loose strand of hair away from her face. She pressed herself back against the chair as if she could disappear into the upholstery.

"What are you doing?" she demanded, voice trembling. "Why are you messing with me?"

His breath stirred a lock of hair near her cheek as he paused just inches from her mouth.

"I ain't messin' with you."

"The kiss earlier," she pushed out. "Why did you do that? You kidnapped me, Wilson. You work for Milton Rowland. I doubt he'd approve of you... taking a fancy to the hostage."

One corner of his mouth lifted.

"Milton don't need knowin' everything. And I can't rightly be blamed if the hostage happens to be a beautiful girl." His gaze dipped to her lips. Leah panicked, shoved him hard, and darted off the chair. But he caught her easily. His arms wrapped around her waist, firm but not forceful, just enough to prevent her escape.

"Easy now, sweetheart," he murmured quietly. "You don't gotta be afraid. I won't ever hurt you."

"That's exactly what I thought about McKay," she shot back, glaring up at him. "And look how that turned out. Another traitor. Another liar."

Wilson's brows knit slightly, but he didn't release her. Leah searched his face desperately for something, truth, deceit, anything she could hold on to.

"You still haven't answered my question," she pressed. "Why did you kiss me earlier?"

A faint smile touched his lips. "'Cause I wanted to feel them pretty lips of yours against mine."

Her outrage flared instantly. "How dare you?" She tore herself free and backed away, fury sparking in her eyes. "I knew you were just playing with me. Tell me, Wilson, do you treat every girl like a toy for your amusement? Or am I just the entertainment you kidnapped for the week?"

For the first time, he looked genuinely taken aback. "Leah—"

"No." She sliced the air with her hand. "Men think there's no harm in kissing a girl just for fun, don't they? Well, believe it or not, I'm not interested in being used or added to some collection of conquests. I want to be kissed because someone loves me. Not because of my lips." Her voice cracked. She turned her face away, blinking fast as unwanted memories of Jaxon and McKay twisted in her stomach.

Wilson stood still for a moment, watching her. Then, more quietly than before, he said, "Leah… I never aimed to use you. Might've spoken like a fool, but I sure as hell didn't kiss you for sport." He stepped closer, cautiously, as if approaching a skittish wild mare. "Truth is… I'm beginnin' to fall for you."

Her heart jumped, but she forced her expression to remain cold. His hands found her arms again, pulling her gently back toward him. She swallowed hard, her pulse hammering against her ribs.

"There's no future for us," she whispered. "You're a criminal. You work for an even bigger criminal."

Wilson's voice dropped, the edge of it strangely earnest.

"What if I ain't as bad as you reckon I am?"

21
From Kidnapper to Protector

Leah drew in a breath to answer Wilson, though she wasn't even sure what she meant to say when the cabin door burst open. McKay strode inside first. Robyn stumbled in behind him, wrists bound, cheeks streaked with tears.

"Leah, thank goodness," Robyn choked, rushing forward. She flung her arms around Leah, trembling so violently that Leah had to steady her. Leah's heart dropped. Terror crashed through her so fast she nearly swayed. Her gaze whipped to McKay, sharp, murderous.

"What is she doing here?" Leah demanded, fury trembling through every word. McKay didn't even bother to look ashamed.

"You weren't cooperatin'," he said, voice dead calm. "Milton ordered me to haul her in. He'll be here any minute."

Leah stared at him in disbelief. "How—how did you even get back so fast? The cabin is three hours away from town."

"Snatched her durin' the night and stashed her in a small cabin close by." McKay answered without remorse. Robyn made a small, broken sound. Leah stepped in front of her instantly, protective as a lioness.

"Robyn has nothing to do with this! You let her go, right now."

McKay only crossed his arms.

"Milton wants proof he ain't bluffin'. So, I'd start bendin' if I were you, Leah... 'cause your little friend's life is runnin' out fast."

Leah's entire body went cold. She turned desperately to the only person in the room who hadn't openly threatened murder.

"Wilson, you can't let them do that. Please—"

"Ain't no call for you to look at Wilson, Leah." The chilling voice came from the doorway. Milton Rowland filled the frame, shoulders squared, eyes glittering with cruel delight. He stepped inside slowly, savoring the fear rippling through the cabin. Leah immediately pushed Robyn behind her again.

"Let her go, Milton," she said coldly. "She isn't part of this."

"That right there," Milton said, grin slicing wide, "that's what makes it so damn fun."

Before she could react, he lunged. His hand clamped around Robyn's arm and yanked her up beside him. Leah tried to reach for her, but McKay seized her from behind and held her back. Robyn whimpered, terror choking her voice. Milton leaned close to Leah, eyes burning with twisted satisfaction.

"You've got 'til sunup," he drawled. "Robyn's ridin' out with me. If that paper ain't signed by then..." He tipped his head, eyes glinting. "You'll never see her again, 'cept maybe in a pine box."

Leah shook with fury. "You are a foul, disgusting creature, Milton Rowland! Let her go!"

He only laughed, a cold, satisfied sound that made Robyn flinch.

"Here," he said, tossing a folded document onto the table. "Sign it now, or sign it come mornin'. But if I ride back and it ain't signed..." He leaned in, the smile draining clean off his face. "I'll stand right beside you while you make your mark. 'Cause by then?" His voice dropped to a cold rasp. "I'll be done playin'."

Leah's breath hitched. Her eyes darted to Wilson, pleading, desperate. She didn't care what happened to herself, but she would not let Robyn pay the price for her defiance. Milton noticed the glance. His grin stretched, oily and poisonous.

"Well, ain't that sweet. You bondin' with your kidnapper?" he cooed in a cruel sing-song. "Adorable." His smile dropped like a blade. "Don't get cozy, girl," he spat. "Wilson's the one who sent that stagecoach into the lake. He's the bastard that murdered your pa."

Everything inside Leah stopped.

"No," she whispered, voice hollow. The blood drained from her face. Her breathing turned sharp and uneven. McKay rushed toward her, but Leah slapped his hands away with a choked cry.

"Don't touch me!" Her chest heaved. Her vision blurred. Her heartbeat thundered in her ears. Milton watched with sick pleasure.

"After makin' us wait so damn long, seein' you hurt feels mighty satisfyin'," he breathed.

"And I hope you ain't sweet on Wilson... 'cause he's the one who made sure your precious father never came up for air."

"Milton." Wilson's voice cut through the air like a blade. Sharp. Furious. Dangerous. Milton turned toward him, but

Wilson had already grabbed his arm and shoved him back through the doorway. "We need to talk," Wilson snapped, practically dragging him outside. The door slammed behind them, leaving Leah in the cabin, alone, shaking, and shattered.

Leah stood frozen for only a heartbeat, her mind blank, before instinct roared to life. *Move.* She snatched the folded document Milton had left on the table and shoved it deep into her pocket. Then she hurried to the back wall of the cabin, where a narrow window sat half-hidden behind a chair. She threw it open, letting the icy morning air rush in, and dropped to her knees.

Her fingers found the floorboard she remembered. She pried it up and retrieved the small brass key hidden beneath. In three quick motions, she replaced the board and scrambled under the bed.

Her fingers trembled, but she forced them to steady as she slipped the key into the nearly invisible slot. A soft click. The trapdoor loosened, and she pushed it open just enough to slide through.

The cold earth beneath the cabin made her gasp, but she didn't hesitate. She dropped down, quietly pulled the hatch closed, locked it again, and crouched in the darkness, heart thundering. Above her, she heard Wilson's boots thudding back inside the cabin. A furious curse exploded from him. Then her name, sharp and echoing through the floorboards.

"Leah! Leah!"

She held her breath, every muscle locking as the floor creaked under his weight. Then she heard him bolt out the back door, mount his horse, and take off at a dead run into the forest. That was her moment. Leah pressed her sleeve to her eyes, just once. She didn't have the luxury of breaking down again. Robyn needed her. Every second mattered.

She crawled through the thicket behind the cabin, pushing past sharp branches, then slipped into the trees. Leah knew every trail on this mountain, every shortcut, every creek bed that hid footprints, every hollow where she could disappear if Wilson doubled back. She grabbed a small pine branch, sweeping behind her as she moved to erase her tracks. Her breath fogged in the icy air. She kept going. *Listen. Run. Hide. Repeat.* She made it to a bend in the trail when a deep, guttural growl vibrated through the trees. A mountain lion.

He stepped onto the trail ahead of her, muscles coiled, tail twitching, golden eyes locked on her. He was massive. Too massive for her to outrun. Too close to climb anything in time. Leah froze. Her heart hammered. Her breath came shallow and fast.

"Easy..." she whispered, not daring to move. "Easy, boy. I'm not here to hurt you."

But he didn't care. His shoulders lowered, preparing to pounce. She darted a glance around her, searching for a sturdy branch, anything she could use as a weapon. Then, gunfire. Three sharp cracks exploded through the forest. The lion snarled and vanished into the trees. Leah didn't need to look to know who fired the shots. Wilson.

She ran, bolting down the trail, skirts flying, lungs burning. She heard him shout her name behind her, heard his horse pounding through the forest. She didn't look back. But he was faster. Wilson pulled alongside her, launched himself from his saddle, and tackled her before she could react. They hit the ground hard, leaves and dirt flying. Leah thrashed, swinging her fists, shoving, clawing, anything to escape his grip.

"Why would you do somethin' so damn dangerous?" Wilson snapped, pinning her wrists to stop her shaking. His voice was ragged, near frantic. "Runnin' off alone like that? You tryin' to get yourself killed?"

"Let me go!" Leah shouted, twisting underneath him. "I don't ever want to see you again! You murdered my father! You killed the other passengers on the stagecoach! I swear I'll make sure you rot behind bars!" She fought him like someone possessed, tears, rage, and heartbreak exploding all at once.

"Leah—stop. Listen to me—"

"No! Get away from me!" She struck him again, breaking his hold for an instant. But he caught her wrists in one strong hand and pressed his other palm gently, but firmly, over her mouth.

"Leah. Enough." His voice broke, not angry, but desperate. "I'm not who Milton said I am."

She screamed behind his hand. But he kept going, voice low and urgent.

"He lied. I never harmed your father. I never harmed anyone. I'm not working for Milton or Jack. I'm working undercover to bring them down. I swear to you, my name is Wilson Taylor. United States Marshal."

Her struggle faltered. Her breath hitched. And very slowly... she stopped fighting. He released her mouth.

"Can you prove it?" she whispered hoarsely. He nodded once, reached into his coat, and pulled out a badge. A solid, gleaming U.S. Marshal badge. Leah let out a long, shaky breath as her fury collapsed into confusion. "What about McKay?"

"McKay Wright is my partner," he said, pulling her gently to her feet. "And he's undercover too."

Leah backed a step away, rubbing her wrists. Her thoughts whirled. Trust didn't come easily to her, especially now, but something in his voice rang true.

"Then why," she demanded, wiping her face with her sleeve, "did both of you have to kiss me? Is that normal behavior for federal officers? Do you flirt your way through every assignment?"

He winced, then gave a sheepish grin.

"Milton wanted us to intimidate you. But you..." He gestured to her helplessly. "You don't scare easily. So, we did the opposite. If we pretended to show interest, romance, charm, Milton thought it might shake you up enough to make you suspicious of us."

"And it worked," Leah muttered darkly.

"Oh, it worked better than we intended," Wilson admitted, rubbing the back of his neck. Then his grin widened. "Although, if I'd known you were terrified of spiders, I would've let them do the intimidating."

Leah's jaw dropped. Heat flooded her cheeks.

"It's not funny, Wilson! That spider was huge."

"Leah... it was hardly bigger than your thumb."

"It had fangs," she snapped. "And it looked like it could eat a toddler."

He burst into laughter. She glared at him until she couldn't hold it anymore, and then her glare softened, just a little.

"Besides," Leah added grudgingly, "I was bitten twice as a child and nearly died both times."

That shut him up. Wilson's eyes widened.

"Wait, you almost died from spider bites? Twice?"

She nodded. "Yes." Then, with a lighter tone, she casually continued, "And because they move so fast, it's nearly impossible to shoot them."

Wilson blinked. "You've... tried shooting a spider?"

"Sure," Leah replied matter-of-factly. "I use anything for target practice."

Wilson stared at her, stunned, and then he laughed again, shaking his head.

"You," he said finally, "are something else, Leah Johnson."

She lifted her chin. "I know." But her voice trembled, because the world around her had just shifted again. And the one man she thought she could safely hate now held the only truth that could save her... or destroy her.

"We still haven't found her." Cash's voice was low and strained as he stepped into Lisa Finlay's parlor. He looked exhausted, dust streaked his clothes, his jaw clenched and worry carving deep lines into his face. Sheriff Scott Bailey stood beside Lisa, his expression grim. But it was Lisa who broke him. She was sitting on the edge of the sofa, hands trembling, her eyes red and swollen. The moment she saw Cash, she stood and collapsed into his arms with a sob.

"Lisa?" Cash wrapped his arms around her, steadying her shaking frame. "What's wrong? What happened?"

"Robyn is gone," she choked out. "My baby, she's gone."

Robyn. The word hit Cash like a blow. Scott's voice came next, tight with worry.

"A few people in town said they saw McKay sneaking around here last night, but when I rode out to Johnson's ranch, McKay was there. Several cowboys swore he'd been working all day."

Cash pulled away from Lisa, his eyes blazing.

"What the devil is going on here?" His voice snapped like a whip, so sharp Lisa flinched. "We've checked every hunting cabin, every cave, every damned hollow inside the ranch border," he continued, pacing now, fists clenched. "Tomorrow we'll expand the search. Mitch had a string of small cabins on the far edge of his land. I didn't think the Rowlands knew about them, but maybe they found notes in Mitchell's office... or maybe Patricia let something slip."

Lisa gasped, pressing a shaking hand to her mouth.

"Cash, what if... what if they kill Robyn?" The tears came harder. "She's just a girl. She's just a baby."

Cash stopped pacing. His expression softened, though anguish still burned in his eyes. He took Lisa's hands gently.

"Listen to me," he said, voice steadier now. "Leah is out there too. And Leah will never let anything happen to Robyn."

Lisa looked up at him, searching his face for something to cling to.

"Leah is one of the cleverest, strongest young women I've ever known," Cash continued. "She'll fight until her last breath to protect the people she loves. Even if it means sacrificing herself."

Lisa let out a broken sob, burying her face against his chest again. Scott Bailey exhaled, rubbing the back of his neck.

"We will find them. Both of them. And when we do, the Rowlands won't see the inside of Hoopa Valley again except through jail bars."

Cash held Lisa tighter, staring out the window into the growing darkness, every muscle in his body coiled like a drawn bow. Leah and Robyn were somewhere out there. And heaven help the Rowlands when Cash found them.

"Where do you think they're keeping Robyn?" Leah whispered, barely daring to breathe. Wilson crouched beside her behind the thick pine, its branches shielding them from view. His eyes were locked on the dimly lit ranch house, studying every shadow, every flicker of movement. From where they knelt, they had a clear line of sight to the back porch and the section of wall where Leah's bedroom sat.

"My guess?" he murmured. "Your room. It's tucked away at the back of the house, far from the barn, far from anyone who might hear her. They want isolation."

Leah's gaze shot upward. Her window was wide open, curtains fluttering gently in the cold night breeze.

"The window is open," she whispered, horror creeping into her voice. "If she screams, the whole ranch could hear her."

Wilson exhaled sharply, the sound low and grim.

"They probably tied her up and gagged her. And that open window? They may be trying to weaken her. Exposure like that, freezing air all night, it could get to her fast."

Leah's breath hitched. "She's only wearing her nightgown." Her voice cracked. "She doesn't even have a shawl." Her fists curled tight, nails digging into her palms. She felt sick. "I'm going up," she said with fierce determination. "I'll climb the tree and check if she's there. If she is, I'll get her out." She turned to him, eyes burning with urgency. "You make sure she gets to safety. That's all that matters."

Wilson shot her a quick look, alarm flashing across his features.

"Leah, that's a pretty high tree." He kept his voice low. "Shouldn't I be the one climbing up there? If she's in danger—"

"I've been climbing this tree since I could walk," she whispered back, already scanning the lower branches. "I'll be fine." The firmness in her tone left no room for argument. "And besides," she added, turning her head toward him, "do you really think she'd trust you after everything that's happened? You did kidnap me. She might not go with you until I tell her who you really are."

Wilson opened his mouth, then stopped. That was a fair point.

"All right," he conceded with a nod, though tension remained stiff in his shoulders. "Just... be careful."

Leah offered a faint, humorless smirk. "Careful is my middle name."

He didn't believe that for a second, and she didn't either, but he let her go. Leah took hold of the lowest branch, her movements quiet and confident. Wilson watched in stunned silence. She moved like someone who'd lived half her life in this tree, steady footing, quick balance, no hesitation. Within seconds she was halfway up, her form blending into the branches. By the time she reached her window, Wilson realized he'd been holding his breath.

Leah peered inside, heart pounding against her ribs. She cupped a hand around her eyes to cut the glare of early sunlight. For a moment she didn't move... then she turned toward Wilson through the leaves and gave a firm nod. Wilson exhaled with relief. Robyn was there. And Leah was about to risk everything to rescue her.

"Leah... how did you get here?" Robyn whispered once Leah had removed the gag, eyes wide with shock and relief all at once. Leah pressed a finger to her lips.

"Quiet," she breathed. "We can't let anyone hear us."

Robyn nodded quickly, trembling.

"I'm here to get you out," Leah continued in a hushed tone. "Do you still remember how to climb the tree in front of my window?"

Robyn blinked, then nodded again. Leah's heart swelled with a bittersweet ache as she remembered the two of them scrambling through those branches as children, hiding from Jaxon or playing outlaws and heroes. Never in her wildest dreams had she imagined climbing that same tree to save her best friend's life.

"Good," Leah whispered, and reached for a warm blanket, wrapping it around Robyn's shoulders. "Now listen carefully.

Do exactly what I tell you. Wilson is below the window. He'll take you back to town."

Robyn's face twisted in horror. "Wilson? Leah, he's the one who kidnapped you! I'm not going anywhere with him."

"You can trust him," Leah said firmly, gripping her friend's arms. "I know how that sounds, but he's undercover, he's trying to bring Milton and Jack down. I promise he won't hurt you."

Robyn hesitated, uncertainty clouding her expression.

"Robyn," Leah whispered urgently, "please. Go with him. Find your mom and either get out of Hoopa Valley or stay somewhere safe. Don't leave whatever building you're in unless you have no choice. I don't want those evil vermin using you as bait again."

Robyn swallowed. "What about you? What are you going to do?"

Leah's jaw tightened. She wasn't sure she had the right words, but the fire in her chest burned bright.

"I'm going to end this," she whispered. "Once and for all. I'm tired of this stupid game. I want my house back. My life back. And I will not let them hurt the people I love anymore."

Robyn's eyes filled with tears. "Leah..."

"We don't have time," Leah cut in gently, already scanning the room. "I don't know when someone will check on you or when Milton might change his mind. You must go, now. I'll follow as soon as I can." She crouched, reaching under her bed until her fingers brushed the familiar handle of her knife, her father's gift, one she kept close even now. In one swift motion, she sliced through Robyn's bindings.

"Come on," she whispered, guiding her to the open window. Robyn climbed out, gripping the thick branch she'd climbed a hundred times in childhood. Leah leaned out, her breath caught in her throat as she watched her friend descend through the branches. Halfway down, Robyn's foot slipped. She let out a tiny gasp and ended up dangling by her hands. The blanket slipped off her shoulders.

Leah froze. Her heart pounded so loudly she was certain the whole ranch could hear it.

"Let go," Wilson called softly from below. "I've got you."

Leah held her breath as Robyn finally released the branch. Wilson caught her easily, steadying her on her feet. Only when he lifted Robyn up onto the horse did Leah finally exhale. Wilson glanced up, meeting Leah's hurried, desperate gaze. She gave a small nod. *Go.* A moment later, he swung onto the saddle behind Robyn, and they vanished into the trees.

Leah stayed at the window long after they disappeared, the early morning air cold against her flushed cheeks. She was alone again. But this time, she wasn't running. This time, she was ready to fight.

22
When Blood Begs for the Truth

Leah drew a steadying breath and crept back toward the door. Every step was silent, every move calculated. She reached it and eased it open, her pulse pounding in her ears. The upstairs hall was empty, no footsteps, no shifting shadows in the lantern glow. But downstairs, she heard murmured voices. Her mother's. Milton's. Low, tense, far too close for comfort. A warning instinct rose in her chest like a cold tide: *Get out. Now.* But another thought pushed in, sharp, insistent, impossible to ignore.

What if her father had known the danger Milton and Jack posed before his death? What if he'd been threatened... pressured... blackmailed? What if he'd left evidence behind? Letters. Names. Dates. Hidden instructions. His diary. Her father had always been careful, almost overly so. And he had shown her his secret hiding place, telling her she was the only person he trusted to know.

Just in case, he'd said with a gentle smile that now broke her heart. If there was ever a time to look... it was now. Leah slipped into her father's room, and the moment the door clicked softly shut behind her, emotion slammed into her like a wave. Tears stung her eyes. She hadn't stepped foot in here since before his trip to Sacramento. The room was still exactly as he'd left it, tidy, warm, faintly smelling of pine soap and tobacco.

Her throat tightened painfully. For a few seconds she couldn't move. She simply stood there, staring at the bed where he used to read before dawn and the worn armchair where he'd sit polishing his boots. The ache inside her was almost unbearable. She crossed to the closet, opened it carefully, and pulled one of his shirts from the hanger. The familiar scent struck her like a blow, comforting and devastating all at once. She pressed the fabric briefly to her chest, fighting the sob clawing its way up.

Later, she told herself fiercely. *You can cry later. You are not safe here.* She tucked the shirt back into place, shut the closet quietly, and forced her breathing to steady. *Focus, Leah.* She hurried to his armchair, braced her hands against it, and gently slid it aside without allowing it to scrape the floor. Then she lifted the corner of the large woven rug. Her fingers searched for the familiar lump beneath the fabric. There, a small key, wrapped in cloth. She snatched it up, tucked it deep into her pocket, lowered the rug, and slid the chair back exactly where it had been. She hurried to the door.

Her fingers had barely brushed the handle when voices drifted closer. Footsteps. Heavy ones.

Milton's. Heart lurching, Leah spun and darted into the closet, easing the door shut behind her. She pressed herself into the farthest corner, holding her breath. The footsteps reached the threshold.

And the bedroom door began to open.

Leah clamped a hand over her mouth, willing herself not to breathe too loudly. Her pulse thundered as footsteps halted right in front of the closet.

"I searched that whole blasted room top to bottom—nothin'," Milton growled. "Mitchell kept track of every damned thing. You'd think he left a diary, a ledger—***something.***"

Leah's stomach twisted. He was hunting for what she had come for. Her mother spoke next, and Leah nearly gasped. The voice was hers, but not *hers.* Calm. Measured. Almost rehearsed.

"I've gone through his room for years," Patricia admitted. "Never found so much as a scrap. Went to the bank, too, asked if Mitch left anythin' in a lockbox or deposit box. Unless he hid money somewhere I don't know about, there just ain't nothin'."

Milton exhaled sharply, pacing. His boots thudded against the floorboards inches from where Leah crouched.

"He had to hide somethin'," he muttered darkly. "Fella never trusted a soul, not even you. There's gotta be a clue. A ledger. Some kind of record."

Leah pressed her back harder against the wall, lungs burning. Every word her mother spoke struck her like a blow. Her mother had searched her father's room? Many times? Gone to the bank? Why? To protect Mitch's secrets? To erase them? To help Milton? Nothing made sense. Her heart hammered as Milton moved even closer, so close she saw his shadow through the thin crack beneath the door.

"I don't buy for one damn second he left nothin' behind," Milton drawled, voice tight with suspicion. "Men like him don't go to their grave without a trail."

Patricia huffed in frustration. "If there is one, Milton, I ain't found it."

He spat a curse. "And if that girl stumbles on it before we do—"

Leah's heart stopped.

Her mother cut in sharply, "she ain't gonna. She's all worked up and ain't thinkin' clear."

Leah flinched at the coldness of it. The tone, flat, dismissive, almost irritated, did not belong to the timid woman she had known her whole life. It chilled her deeper than Milton's threats ever had.

"Can't tell ya how ready I am for this to be over so I can come home again," Patricia sighed. "Been missin' you somethin' awful."

Leah froze inside the dark closet. *Home again? Missed who?* That wasn't meant for Milton.

That was meant for someone else. Someone she didn't know existed.

Milton chuckled. "Been a long spell. You sure did keep yourself tucked outta sight."

"I had to," Patricia said, her voice weighted with a kind of relief Leah had never heard from her before. "Livin' out here all these years... playin' the timid little mouse... pretendin' I gave two hoots about folks in this town or this house… it wore me plumb out."

Leah's knees nearly buckled. Her mother, pretending? Pretending fear? Pretending affection?

Who *was* she?

"Mitchell near smothered me at the start," Patricia went on. "Man was too darn affectionate, clingin' like a burr on a saddle blanket. Weren't till I told him straight I wasn't sharin' no room with him that he finally backed off."

Milton snorted. "Reckon he figured out your marriage was nothin' but a put-on?"

She paused—just a heartbeat. "Yeah," she said at last. "He got suspicious 'fore that trip to Sacramento. Started pullin' back. Acted guarded-like. He knew I wasn't who I was pretendin' to be. Cash and David Smith caught wind of it too, but they never called me on it."

Leah's mind reeled. Her mother had deceived everyone. Played a role. Lied for years. Every comforting story. Every trembling fear. Every excuse. Manipulation. Her mother's next words shattered her.

"When the dust finally quits flyin', I'll be goin' home, back to the life that's mine, back to the family I oughta be with."

A cold wave washed through Leah's body. Her mother had another life. Another family. Everything Leah had ever known crumbled.

"I just wish we could've gotten rid of Mitchell Johnson years back," Milton muttered. "Would've saved us a heap o' trouble."

Patricia let out a scoff. "After Lilian died, puttin' Mitchell in the ground would've been downright stupid. Two sudden deaths in one family? Folks would've started sniffin' around. This way, it looked like a sorry accident... not like she was murdered."

Leah's entire body went rigid. Aunt Lilian... murdered. Her lungs seized. She pressed both hands over her mouth to trap the cry rising in her throat. Why? Why Lilian? Why her father?

Milton blew out a sharp breath. "You reckon Leah's caught on? To any of it?"

There was a pause, long enough to chill the air. Then Patricia's voice, colder than creek ice in January: "She ain't even aware I ain't her real ma."

The world tilted. *Not her real mother.* Leah braced against the wall as her breath came in short, panicked gasps. Spots danced before her eyes. Her entire life, every moment, twisted into something grotesque. The woman she loved, feared, defended... A stranger. A liar. A murderer.

"Everyone told her Lilian was her aunt, not her mama," Patricia went on. "We laid the whole thing out clean. She never thought to question a lick of it."

Milton grunted, pleased with himself. "If those fools back in Virginia hadn't blown our cover, we wouldn't be in this mess. But hearin' about the Johnsons' money, now *that* was a stroke of luck. Once we threaten Robyn right in front of Leah, she'll crack wide open. She'll hand over every last cent. Then we hightail it outta this miserable country."

"To England," Patricia breathed. "At long last."

"England," Milton echoed, near dreamy. "Where we can live like civilized folks. Where we can be man and wife out in the open. No pretendin'. No lies."

Leah heard the soft rustle of clothing, the unmistakable sound of someone being pulled into someone else's arms. Her fake mother. In Milton's embrace. Leah pressed both hands over her mouth again, struggling not to sob. Everything she had ever believed was a lie.

The door burst open so suddenly Leah flinched. Mildred rushed in, breathless and frantic.

"Robyn is gone!" she cried.

"What?" Milton and Patricia snapped together.

"I went to bring her some grub and the room was empty. Ropes're cut clean through. She must've lit out the window, ain't no other way she got loose!"

A beat of stunned silence. Then Milton cursed violently and the three of them bolted toward Leah's bedroom. Their footsteps thundered across the floorboards, doors slamming open, voices rising in panic.

Inside the closet, Leah pressed a trembling hand over her heart as adrenaline surged through her. They think Robyn escaped. They don't know *I* did. Not yet. But soon they would. And when they discovered Leah was gone too, their rage would shake the whole house. She needed to get out. Now.

Leah waited, counting her own breaths, until the house finally fell quiet. The last thing she heard was Milton shouting for McKay, but the voice came from outside, fading toward the barn. Only then did she let herself fold, just a little. A quiet sob escaped her. Then another. She pressed both hands over her mouth, swallowing the pain down hard. She couldn't break now. Not trapped in this house. Not with the truth clawing at her chest like a wild animal.

Get out first. Fall apart later. She wiped her eyes with trembling fingers and forced her breathing to steady. When her legs felt strong enough, she slipped out of the closet and eased the door shut behind her. The hallway was empty. She darted back into her bedroom.

Her knife was still hidden beneath her mattress. She grabbed it with shaking hands. Next came the small pistol she had tucked away weeks ago, wrapped in cloth behind the bed frame. She shoved both weapons into her belt, snatched the little emergency bag, and hurried to the window.

Leah peered outside, scanning every inch of the yard, porch roof, and shadows around the tree. Nothing moved. No voices. No footsteps. *Now.*

She swung one leg out, fingers gripping the familiar bark. She had climbed this tree a thousand times growing up, it had always felt like freedom. Today, it felt like survival. Her mind raced with every step downward, her mother's lies, Milton's threats, the shattering truth of her real parentage. Tears burned her eyes again, warping the branches beneath her feet. Her throat tightened. Her boot slipped. Leah gasped, her hand missed the branch, and she fell.

She hadn't even hit the ground when two strong arms swept around her, breaking her fall. Her breath slammed back into her chest as she found herself pressed against a solid wall of muscle, familiar, steady, unforgettable. She looked up. Jaxon. His face hovered inches from hers, pale with fear, brown eyes wide and frantic as they searched her features.

"Leah, are you hurt?" His voice shook. Her heart nearly stopped. Of all people... of all moments... Jaxon was the last person she could face. Her emotions were too raw, too volatile, too dangerous. She instantly began to struggle.

"No—no, let me go," she gasped, her voice trembling as hard as her limbs.

"Leah, please," he begged, tightening his hold when she nearly collapsed. "Calm down. You're shaking. What happened? How did you—"

"I can't—Jaxon, I can't do this right now." Her breath came in shallow bursts, panic clawing up her throat. "Please... I can't be seen. Let me go."

The fear in her eyes finally reached him. Hurt and confusion flickered across his face, but he slowly lowered her to her feet. Leah tore away from him the moment her boots touched the ground.

And ran.

"Leah!" he hissed, quiet enough not to draw attention.

"Stop, please, stop!"

Branches whipped against her dress as she raced toward the family cemetery. She didn't look back, couldn't look back, but Jaxon was faster. Just as she reached the weathered iron gate, his hand closed around hers. He spun her toward him and pulled her into his arms again, holding her as if she might vanish. She thrashed wildly.

"Let me go! Jaxon, please—please—"

"No," he breathed, arms locked around her trembling body. "Not until you tell me what's happening. You're terrified, Leah. I can feel it. Something's wrong. Terribly wrong."

She froze inside his embrace, pulse pounding against his chest. She wanted to scream. To weep. To collapse. To tell him everything, and nothing. But her body kept shaking, refusing to calm.

Cash and McKay had barely rounded the corner when they saw Jaxon sprinting after Leah, her dress flashing between the trees like a frightened bird. Panic shot through both men, and they broke into a run.

By the time Cash reached them, Jaxon was holding Leah upright, keeping her from collapsing. Her face was ghost-white, her eyes wild with confusion and betrayal.

"Leah—" Cash reached for her, trying to gather her close, but she recoiled violently, slapping his hand away as though burned.

"Don't touch me!" she cried, voice cracking. "Why didn't anybody tell me? Why did you *all* lie to me?"

All three men froze.

"Lie to you?" McKay repeated, stunned. Cash stepped forward again, slow, careful, as though approaching a wounded animal.

"Sweetheart... what are you talking about?"

"Don't!" she snapped again, retreating a step. Her entire body trembled, hardly able to hold itself upright.

"Leah," Jaxon whispered, reaching for her arm, "please—"

"You knew," she choked out, pointing with a shaking hand toward the cemetery stones behind them. "You all knew, and none of you said a word. You let me believe a lie my entire life. How could you do that to me? How can I ever trust you again?" Her voice cracked. She staggered backward, one hand clutching her chest as though her heart were tearing apart.

Cash went pale. "What lie? Leah, *what lie?*"

"That Patricia isn't my mother!" she cried, her voice ripping through the icy air. "That Lilian wasn't my aunt, she was my mother. My *real* mother!"

Her breath hitched. A raw wail tore from her throat.

"And what about Mildred?" she demanded, shaking. "Is she even my aunt? Or is that another lie you all kept from me?"

Jaxon's grip on her arm tightened as her breathing spiraled, shallow, ragged, frantic.

"Leah," he whispered, fear rising in his voice, "breathe. Please breathe."

But she couldn't. Her breaths came too fast. Her knees buckled.

"Leah—!"

Cash lunged, but Jaxon caught her first. Her body collapsed against him, limp, shaking, barely conscious, as he swept her into his arms and carried her toward the wooden bench inside the small, fenced cemetery. He lowered her gently, holding her upright, her head lolling against his shoulder.

Cash swallowed hard, his voice breaking.

"My word... Leah, what did they *do* to you?"

McKay hovered behind them, stunned, realizing that whatever Leah had overheard inside that house... it had shattered her completely. And in the cold mountain wind rustling the pine needles above them, her sobs were the only sound, raw, small, and echoing like the cry of a soul who had just lost her entire world.

23
Too Late to Pretend Anymore

"Patricia... isn't her mother?" Jaxon's voice cracked. He stared at Cash in disbelief, still holding Leah against his chest. His heart hammered painfully, he had never seen such terror and betrayal in Leah's eyes, not even after the kidnapping.

Leah stirred, her lashes fluttering. A soft gasp escaped her lips as she blinked rapidly, confusion giving way to memory. The moment recognition hit, a strangled sound tore from her throat and she jerked upright.

"All right, easy—easy," Cash murmured, reaching to steady her, but she tore herself free, wild and desperate, scrambling off the bench.

"Don't touch me," she snapped, backing away from all three men, her breath coming in rapid, uneven bursts. "You all lied to me my entire life."

"Leah—" Cash rose slowly, hands raised in surrender.

"Don't." Her voice cracked like a whip. "I just found out the woman I thought was my mother is married to the man trying to steal from us. Which means her marriage to my father was never real!"

Jaxon felt the ground tilt beneath him.

"Patricia is married to Milton?" he whispered, horrified. He wanted to pull Leah back, to protect her, but she looked as if she would shatter if anyone touched her again.

She turned her icy gaze on Cash. "Did you know? Did you know she was married to someone else? Were you hiding that too?"

"No," Cash said firmly, stepping forward. His voice was steady, though his eyes were storm-dark with regret. "It wasn't until earlier this year that your father discovered Patricia wasn't Milton and Jack's sister or daughter as they claimed, but Milton's wife."

Leah's breath hitched, but she forced herself still, jaw trembling. Cash took that as permission to continue.

"Not long after he married Patricia," Cash said, "your father found letters in her room. Love letters. Threatening letters. Letters from Milton Rowland." His voice roughened. "They hinted that Milton and Jack might have been behind Lilian's death."

Leah swayed, the world spinning. Jaxon reached instinctively to steady her, but she recoiled and lifted a trembling hand to hold him off. Cash exhaled hard.

"Patricia caught him reading the letters," Cash continued quietly. "She grabbed them, ripped them right out of his hands, and burned them in the fireplace before he could get proof."

McKay cursed under his breath. "This keeps getting worse."

"Believe me," Cash said bitterly, "I wish I were making it up."

Leah's voice shook. "And Mildred? Who is she? And Heber, what did he have to do with any of this?"

Cash braced himself. "Mildred is Lilian's sister. Your real mother's sister." He paused. Leah flinched as if struck. "We don't know why she sided with Patricia and Milton. At first, we thought she only pretended to be Patricia's sister to keep an eye on things, but over the years... too many things stopped making sense."

Leah's pulse thundered in her ears.

"David believes Mildred was the one who knew Heber," Cash continued. "He thinks she helped coordinate your kidnapping."

Leah gasped, a deep, breaking sound. She doubled over, grabbing the edge of the bench, trembling violently. Jaxon took a half-step toward her, but she lifted a warning hand without looking at him. Cash softened his voice.

"Leah... Mitch contacted David as soon as he realized something was wrong. Your godfather started investigating quietly. He uncovered pieces here and there, enough for us to suspect the Rowlands were dangerous. We wanted proof before involving you."

Her eyes flooded, furious, wounded oceans. Cash took another slow step forward

"We didn't tell you because we were afraid Milton would sense something was wrong and hurt you. We thought keeping you believing Patricia truly was your mother would keep you safe. Neither your father, your godfather, nor I ever wanted to deceive you. We only meant to protect you from people capable of murder."

Leah stared at him, tears spilling freely. "Protect me?" she whispered hoarsely. "Protect me... by breaking me?" And as the words left her trembling lips, Jaxon felt something inside him crack, because he knew nothing they said would erase the pain now carved into her soul.

Leah breathed through her teeth, trying to keep herself from exploding. Betrayal seared through her blood like fire. Her fingernails dug into her palms. She needed to hit something, break something, scream until her throat bled. Instead, she turned away.

"Whether you intended to hurt me doesn't change anything," she said, voice shaking with fury she could barely contain. "You lied to me. Everything I ever believed about my mother, my life, was a lie. I don't even know who I am anymore." Tears blurred her vision, but she strangled the sobs clawing up her throat. "I'm done with all of you," she whispered, then shouted, "Every single one of you lied to me. Don't follow me. Don't touch me. I don't need you."

She spun, ready to run, anywhere, but Cash caught her arm gently, turning her back toward him.

"Leah, you must understand—"

"No," she snapped, ripping her arm free. "I don't have to understand anything. Go."

Cash visibly flinched. Seeing the heartbreak in his eyes made her own pain burn hotter. She turned again, only to nearly crash into McKay blocking her path. She recoiled, fury reigniting. She drew a breath to push past him when a new realization slammed into her. She whipped toward Cash, eyes blazing.

"You knew," she whispered, voice trembling with rage. "You knew McKay was a U.S. Marshal." Her voice rose. "You knew Wilson was his partner. You lied about that too."

"I did," Cash said quietly before she could continue. His voice was heavy with guilt. "I'm sorry I couldn't tell you, or Jaxon. The marshals have been tracking the Rowlands for months. Your godfather asked me to keep their identities secret."

Leah's body tightened. "Get. Out. Of. My. Way," she said to McKay, low and deadly. But McKay didn't move.

"Leah, listen to Cash. Let him explain. You can't just run from this."

"Let him explain?" she repeated, her voice cracking. "Explain?" And the dam broke. "How would you feel," she demanded, "if you overheard your mother talking to your uncle, only to realize she wasn't your mother at all? That she was married to the man trying to steal everything your father built?" Her chest heaved.

"How would you feel if you found out your aunt, the woman you trusted, the woman who tucked you in at night, might have helped murder her own sister?" Her voice splintered. "How would you feel if you learned that the woman you thought was your mother had a part in killing your real mother... and might have had something to do with your father's death too?" She sobbed now, helpless, breathless.

"How would you feel," she whispered brokenly, "if everyone you loved... lied to you?" Her legs gave out. She doubled over, gasping. Cash was on her instantly, pulling her into his arms even as she resisted. But the moment his warmth surrounded her, the last of her strength evaporated. She collapsed against him, sobbing into his shirt. He held her as though she were made of glass.

"I can't tell you how much I hurt for you," he murmured, voice rough with emotion. "I understand your pain, your anger. Anyone would feel betrayed."

Leah shook her head weakly, but he continued, steady and soft.

"None of us took lying to you lightly. We hated it. Every moment of it." His breath hitched. "But when Mitch found those letters, when he suspected Patricia of being involved in more than deception, we had to play it smart. We couldn't risk alerting her." He tightened his hold, jaw tense.

"As it turns out, they've been on the run for years. Even before Jack and Milton landed in prison for that bank robbery in Eureka. That's why you hadn't seen them since you were ten. Patricia was waiting... biding her time."

Leah's breath trembled violently.

"We didn't tell you," Cash finished gently, "because if you knew... you would've confronted her. And if you had, they would've run again." His voice thickened. "And we would've lost the chance to expose them for good."

Leah cried harder, her heart splintering inside her chest. And Cash held her, because in that moment, she had nothing else left to hold her together.

As soon as Leah's sobs quieted and her breathing finally steadied, she pulled away from Cash's arms. She didn't look at him, or at any of them. She couldn't. Her heart was too raw, too shredded to let another emotion through without breaking again. But she felt his eyes on her, the weight of his concern, his guilt, pressing against her back like a burden she never asked for. Several tense minutes passed in silence. Only the whisper of the wind through the pines dared to fill the void between them.

Finally, Leah turned. Cash met her gaze instantly, his expression open and wounded. She saw the truth in his eyes. She also saw the ache, the regret of a man who had kept terrible secrets because he believed it was the right thing. And yet... the betrayal didn't vanish simply because she understood it.

Cash must have sensed it all, her turmoil, her anger, her confusion, because he stepped forward again, arms lifting in a silent offering. Instinct told her to recoil, but exhaustion won out. When he wrapped her in his arms again, the warmth was comforting... until she felt herself tense against him. She looked up. He looked devastated. Her heart twisted painfully. She knew Cash loved her like a daughter. She also knew he had held back truths that had shaped her entire life.

Tears filled her eyes again, she hated how easily they fell today, and she blinked them back in frustration. She felt broken, scattered, as though every emotion she'd ever buried had awakened at once. Behind them, Jaxon cleared his throat, his voice cutting softly through the tension.

"Does anyone know why they're so desperate to ruin the ranch?" he asked. He looked at McKay and Cash, but both men shook their heads. Leah swallowed hard, wiped a tear from her cheek, and turned toward him.

"I don't have all the answers," she rasped, "but I heard a lot... when I was trapped in my dad's closet."

They all stiffened. Leah repeated everything she had overheard, every horrifying detail. McKay swore under his breath.

"I need to report this to Wilson and David immediately."

Jaxon rubbed a hand over his jaw, eyes narrowed in deep thought.

"So, they must've done something awful in Virginia. Something that got them run out. I'd bet they even changed their names."

Leah frowned. "But why wait so many years before coming after us? Why now?"

McKay thought aloud. "Because they couldn't risk anyone suspecting them about Lilian. They needed the past to get cold. They stayed quiet while Jack and Milton were in prison. Patricia kept herself safe as Mitchell's wife. And maybe they waited until they thought Leah was old enough to take care of herself... before getting rid of Mitchell, too."

Leah's stomach churned. "But wouldn't they want to kill me, too?"

McKay shook his head. "They need you alive to access anything. And... Patricia may not see you as her daughter, but she has lived with you for years. She might not want you dead. Mildred too, apparently."

Leah pressed her hand to her forehead. Accepting any of this would take time she didn't have.

She exhaled shakily.

"Would you leave me alone now? I need... time. Just time."

Cash and McKay exchanged a glance, then nodded. They mounted their horses and galloped toward the ranch, leaving her alone with Jaxon. He stepped closer, hesitant but determined.

"May I stay?" he asked quietly. "I want to talk to you."

"Jaxon—" she began, but he cut her off gently.

"I just want to talk. I won't pressure you." His voice was soft, hurting. "I promise."

She didn't turn around. She stood facing the headstone of her real mother, the truth still echoing through her bones.

"Why do you want to talk to me?" she whispered. "You said enough at the dance." Her voice was hoarse, trembling. She fought the tears threatening to break free.

"Leah—" he tried.

"It seems you and McKay are fine again," she said, still not looking at him. "So, I guess that means you think the incident was my fault."

"What incident?" His voice was tentative.

"The kiss," she said sharply. "With McKay."

Jaxon sighed. "Leah—"

"You obviously didn't think much of me if you believe I'd kiss just anyone."

He stepped closer. She felt his presence behind her, warm, painful.

"Listen, about that kiss—"

"When are you leaving?" she asked suddenly.

He blinked. "Leaving?"

"Yes. For your wedding." Her voice cracked. "With Mia. You said her family was moving to Eureka. You said you were going to marry her there."

A long pause.

"Mia and her family are leaving this weekend," he said quietly. Leah nodded once, stiffly.

"I'm glad you found someone so quickly. I knew it wouldn't take much." The moment the words left her mouth, she felt sick. All the lies from her mother, from Mildred, from the Rowlands. All the heartbreak of discovering how deeply she'd been fooled. And now this. Her heart felt as if it were splitting open.

"Leah—" Jaxon whispered, but she shook her head.

"Leave it," she said, barely holding herself together. "I have nothing left to fight with. Please... don't make this worse." She finally turned to look at him. His brown eyes were full of pain. "I hope you and Mia will be happy together," she whispered. "Have a great life, Jaxon." Then she turned, slow, hollow, and walked away.

Leah burst into tears only moments later and took off running toward the forest, blindly, her vision blurred by panic and heartbreak. She didn't know where she was going, only that she had to get away. Away from everything. Away from him.

But Jaxon followed. His boots pounded the frozen ground behind her. He called her name, breathless, desperate. She didn't slow until his hand clasped around hers and he spun her back toward him, pulling her straight into his arms. She fought him hard, fists landing against his chest, tears soaking into his shirt.

"Go away!" she sobbed. "Stop torturing me! You lied to me, too! Every single one of you lied to me! I can't trust anyone anymore—I can't—I can't—"

Jaxon stared at her in stunned confusion.

"When was I dishonest with you?" he demanded, breath uneven.

"You promised me," she cried, voice shaking violently. "You promised me that no matter what happened between us, our friendship wouldn't suffer. But the moment you left the infirmary, you were different. You barely looked at me. That's exactly why I said we shouldn't start anything, I knew it would ruin us, and it did." She broke then, tears pouring down her cheeks.

"It wasn't even the fact that you started courting so fast," she whispered brokenly. "It was how you looked at me when I came back. Like I'd done something wrong. Like I was nothing to you."

Jaxon's chest rose and fell sharply.

"Leah... I never meant for you to feel that way. I just needed time to understand my own feelings. I didn't think how my behavior would hurt you."

"It doesn't matter anymore." She shook her head, defeated. "You'll be leaving soon, which means our friendship will never be the same again. I know you will be a good husband to Mia."

She forced a trembling, heartbreaking half-smile. Jaxon didn't loosen his hold. He cupped her cheeks gently, his voice barely a whisper.

"Leah... are you in love with me?"

Her breath caught. Her eyes flew wide. Color rushed into her cheeks.

"Wh—why would you ask me that? My feelings don't matter here," she stammered, looking anywhere but at him. "You found someone who makes you happy. This is about you and Mia."

Jaxon stepped closer until there was barely a breath between them.

"Are you in love with me?" he asked again, more insistently this time. She lowered her gaze, terrified he would see the truth shining through her eyes. But he slipped a finger beneath her chin, lifting her face toward him. His touch made her shiver. His expression, intense, hopeful, full of something she'd longed for, stole the breath from her lungs.

"Are you in love with me, Leah Johnson?" he whispered.

Her heart broke open. "I am," she breathed.

Jaxon's smile exploded with pure joy and relief. Before she could take another breath, his hands slid to her waist, drawing her against him as he bent and kissed her. Not a gentle kiss. Not a hesitant kiss. A kiss full of love, full of passion, full of years of longing he'd kept locked away.

Leah felt the world tilt. Her knees weakened. Her heart thundered. She melted into him, fingers clutching his coat, as though he were the only steady thing left in her shattered world.

When he finally tore his mouth from hers, she gasped for air.

"What about Mia?" she whispered, breathless.

"Mia," he said, brushing his thumb over her cheek, "is engaged. But not to me."

"What?" Leah blinked. He laughed softly, resting his forehead against hers.

"She met someone while you were kidnapped. When I got back from Eureka and asked her on a date, she was completely stunned and asked me about you, and how I felt about you. She told me she'd known for years, you and I were meant to end up together. She was the one who suggested we pretend to court, hoping it would give you the courage to admit your feelings."

Leah's heart flipped. Butterflies fluttered wildly in her stomach. Jaxon's grin softened.

"Her fiancé knows it was an act too. They wanted to keep it quiet, so we did."

Leah opened her mouth to respond, but hurt crept back in.

"But you... you accused me of—"

He covered her lips gently with his hand.

"I trust you, Leah. I'm sorry. I'm so sorry for how I reacted. I saw McKay kissing you and I lost my mind. Jealousy... fear... everything hit me at once, and I said things I can never take back."

Her eyes burned at the memory. "The last few days have been torture," he continued hoarsely.

"Not knowing where you were. Not being able to apologize. I searched for you every spare moment. Just before seeing you climb out the window, I cornered McKay. He told me everything, who he is, who Wilson is, what happened. I was already saddling my horse to get you when I spotted you up in the tree."

Leah swallowed hard. "But... what if this doesn't work? What if you regret choosing me? What if someone else—"

He silenced her fears with another kiss, slow, deep, full of devotion that stole the breath straight from her lungs. By the time he pulled back, she was trembling.

"There will never be a better choice," he whispered. "Not for me. My heart's been yours for years. Stubbornness and sass included." His smile softened. "You stole it long ago. And I'm begging you to keep it."

For the first time in weeks, Leah smiled. A soft, fragile smile, but real. Jaxon breathed a laugh of pure relief, cupped her cheek, and leaned in for another kiss, when a sharp whistle split through the cold air. Both jolted and looked over. One of the ranch hands sprinted toward them.

"Part of the north enclosure fence is down!" the man shouted. "Cattle scattered. Looks like someone cut it!"

Jaxon muttered several very unchurch-like words. He shot Leah an apologetic glance before running toward the cowboy. His horse was already waiting. Seconds later, he mounted and galloped away.

Leah watched him disappear down the ridge. Her heart felt warm... but the moment he vanished, the earlier heaviness returned. She walked slowly back to the family cemetery, the place that felt safest, even now, and sank to the ground before her mother's headstone. She wasn't crying... but the ache was enormous. Why had this happened? Why had the Rowlands destroyed her family? How long had the lies been in place? She needed answers.

Just as she placed a hand on the grave to stand, a rough arm wrapped around her from behind. A gag was shoved into her mouth. A blindfold was thrown over her eyes. Ropes cinched around her wrists, and a heavy sack yanked over her entire body.

She tried to scream. She kicked. She twisted with all her strength, until her foot slipped. She fell hard sideways, slamming into the wooden cemetery fence. Pain exploded behind her eyes. Then everything went black.

Jaxon and Cash stood shoulder to shoulder with half a dozen ranch hands, staring at the mangled disaster before them. The fence wasn't just cut, no neat wire snipped, no simple break. It had been ripped out of the ground, posts yanked free and tossed aside like matchsticks. Jaxon crouched, pressing his palm against the churned-up dirt.

"Why would anyone do something like this?" he muttered, disbelief tightening his jaw. "None of the cattle are missing. Whoever did this didn't try to steal them... they just let them loose."

Cash scanned the tree line, his eyes darkening.

"Has anyone seen anything? Tracks? A rider heading away? Was it the Rowlands?"

The men shook their heads, until one of the youngest cowboys, barely more than a boy, stepped forward. His face was pale. His voice shook.

"I... overheard somethin'," he said, swallowing hard. "Was in town earlier today. Heard Lester Kinney jawin' with Milton Rowland behind the feed store. Milton was fit to burst, said Robyn had lit out. Told Kinney to 'take care of it.'" He drew in a shaky breath. "Didn't know what he meant at the time... but now..."

Cash's breath caught. "Robyn was here? On the ranch?"

The boy nodded. "Far as I heard, they had her holed up in Leah's room... but she... she's gone. Vanished."

Jaxon felt the blood drain from his face.

"This wasn't random. This was a distraction." He looked at Cash with dawning horror. "Maybe they figured out Leah was back on the ranch."

Cash swore loud enough to startle the horses. "Damn it!"

No more hesitation. He and Jaxon vaulted onto their horses in the same breath. Cash barked rapid-fire orders, his voice ringing across the pasture.

"Split into three groups! First group, search for Leah and Robyn. Second group, round up the loose cattle before they wander into the canyon. Third group, start fixing the fence before we lose half the herd!"

"Yes, sir!" the cowboys shouted, scattering at once. Cash pointed a commanding finger.

"If you find either Leah or Robyn, send someone into town immediately. Don't wait. Don't stop."

Jaxon didn't need to hear more. He dug his heels into his horse's sides, and Cash did the same. The two men thundered across the pasture toward Hoopa Valley at full speed, hearts pounding with dread. Because now they knew for certain: This was no longer just trouble. This was war.

24
Braver Than They Bargained For

When Leah came to, the world swayed beneath her. Her stomach lurched. Her head throbbed. The air was cold against her skin, and every jarring step of the horse sent a bolt of agony through her skull. She realized with dawning horror that she was slung over the saddle like a sack of grain, face down, arms dangling, her wrists bound painfully behind her. Warm liquid trickled down her temple and into her ear. Blood.

Her vision blurred. Her hearing muffled. All she could focus on was the pounding in her head and the suffocating gag cutting into the corners of her mouth. It was impossible to know how long they rode. Minutes. Hours. Her senses drifted in and out as consciousness flickered like a dying candle. At last, the horse stopped. Rough hands grabbed her, hauling her off the animal. The sudden shift made her world spin, and she whimpered through the gag. Her captor carried her a few steps before another set of hands took over, stronger, colder, and dragged her through an open window.

She heard whoever had brought her in climb through behind them. The window slammed shut.

Then a mattress creaked beneath her. Someone forced her legs together, binding them at the ankles. Moments later, the sack and blindfold were ripped off. Bright lantern light stabbed her eyes. She blinked rapidly, gasping as the world slowly came into focus. Her throat tightened when she saw where she was. A prison cell. And crouched in front of her, Wilson.

He wasn't smiling now. His face was pale and drawn tight with concern as he inspected the gash on her forehead. Behind him stood Milton. And Jack. And... Sheriff Bailey. Her stomach dropped.

"We oughta fetch the doctor," Wilson said sharply, his fingers brushing the blood at her brow. "That there's a bad wound."

"We ain't fetchin' nobody," Milton snapped, his voice cutting through the air like a whip. "Soon as Joseph Hicks shows up, we're haulin' her to the bank." His eyes locked on her, hatred, greed, triumph all shining like a rattler's eyes before the strike. "Ungag her."

Wilson hesitated, his jaw flexing, but obeyed. He pulled the gag free. The moment Leah's mouth was unrestrained, she spat venom at Milton.

"What do you want from me?" she snapped, giving him a glare that could split granite. His lips curled.

"You know what we want. I ain't playin' cat-and-mouse no more, Leah Johnson. You fall in line... or people're gonna die."

Before she could respond, footsteps sounded in the sheriff's office. A moment later, Patricia walked in as calmly as if she were arriving for tea, followed closely by Joseph Hicks. Leah froze. Where was Mildred? Was she part of this, too? Jack and Milton grabbed Joseph by the arms, but the banker's eyes went straight to Leah. His face drained of color.

"Good heavens, Leah, what have they done to you?"

Milton snapped his head toward Patricia. "How in blazes did you get him here?"

Patricia gave a sweet, syrupy smile that could curdle milk.

"I told him you'd snatched Leah and she was in need of rescuin'."

Leah bit the inside of her cheek to keep from breaking. Her throat burned. Her eyes stung. Patricia, the woman she had loved and defended for years, looked at her now with nothing but calculation.

"I'm fine, Joseph," Leah whispered.

"You're not fine," he argued. "Has anyone gotten Doc Carter? That's a deep wound—"

"Don't worry about it," she murmured, even though her vision kept swimming. Joseph tried to pull free, but Milton shoved him violently to the floor before dragging Jack out of the cell and locking the barred door behind them.

As soon as they were gone, Joseph scrambled to Leah's side. He sat beside her on the narrow cot, hands trembling. But Leah shook her head sharply, not wanting him to say a word. She kept her eyes on the silhouettes moving in the main office. Her pulse hammered.

"Listen to me," she whispered. "As soon as they open that door again, I'm going to cause a distraction. You need to run. Find Cash. Find Jaxon."

"I'm not leaving you with them," Joseph hissed. His voice trembled with fear... and outrage.

Leah turned her head just enough to meet his eyes.

"Yes. You will. If you stay, they'll hurt you to get to me. I won't let anyone die because of me. You're the only one who can get help."

"Leah—"

"Promise me." Her voice was a razor. Her tears threatened, but she blinked them back with steely determination. Joseph cursed under his breath. Then nodded.

"I promise."

Leah exhaled shakily and braced herself. Because she knew, without any doubt, the moment that cell door opened again, she would be facing hell alone.

"So," Wilson said quietly, eyes bouncing between father and son, "how're you figurin' to move ahead?"

Milton paced a tight, angry line across the sheriff's office floor, agitation rolling off him like heat off desert rock.

"We're runnin' outta time," he snapped. "That ship to New York pulls out in two weeks from San Francisco—two weeks." He jabbed a finger at the wall as if the date were carved clear into the boards. "If we miss it, we're stuck in this dustbowl till spring just to reach New York, and after that, who knows how damn long 'til we can catch passage to England."

Jack folded his arms, scowling. "We can't keep layin' low in this valley. Too many folks pokin' their noses where they don't belong. The longer we sit on our hands, the uglier this gets."

Milton jerked a sharp nod—jaw locked like iron.

"Exactly. So, we finish it today." He cut a look toward the cell door, where Leah and the banker waited like pieces on a worn-out chessboard. "We go back in there and force her to open up those accounts."

"And if she still won't?" Wilson asked, though from the look on his face he already knew. Milton's eyes went black and mean.

"Then we keep it simple. We put a bullet in the banker. Right in front of her. She'll cough up every cent once she sees we're done playin' games."

Jack let out a low, vicious chuckle. "Oh, she'll fold. Leah Johnson's stubborn as a mule, sure, but she ain't gonna let a man die on her account."

Milton turned fully toward Wilson, his voice low and chilling.

"Best get yourself ready. 'Cause one way or another, we ain't quittin' this town without that money."

And in that moment, Wilson realized just how little humanity either of the Rowland men had left.

Before the cell door even opened, Leah launched herself into the plan. She spun toward Joseph and began hammering her fists against his shoulders, her expression twisted in convincing fury. The poor man stumbled backward, eyes wide, unsure whether she'd lost her mind or was doing something deliberate.

"Why didn't you transfer the money when I told you to?" she shouted, her voice cracking with manufactured rage. "I specifically told you to do it weeks ago!"

"Leah, your safety is more important," Joseph tried, hands raised in placation, still trying to understand where she was going with this. He flinched when she grabbed the nearest chair and kicked it so hard it skidded across the cell and crashed into the bars.

"Forget my safety!" Her voice boomed through the cramped room. "Those prairie-coal vermin are not getting a single dime that belongs to me!"

From outside, she heard the scramble of boots, then the clank of the key in the lock. Wilson flung the door open just as Leah lunged for the second chair. Everything exploded into chaos at once.

Jack strode forward, barking something at her, but Leah was faster. Despite her tied legs, she hurled herself directly into his chest with the force of a charging bull. Jack yelped, lost his balance, and crashed backward onto the floor.

"Grab her!" Milton roared. Wilson lunged and caught her by the arms, pinning her back onto the bed as she twisted and writhed like a wildcat. Milton grabbed her shoulders while Wilson fought for her wrists.

"Let *GO* of me!" Leah screamed, but when she hissed the last word, she flicked a pointed, frantic glance at Joseph. *Go.* And Joseph, finally understanding, didn't hesitate. Jack was scrambling to his feet, swearing. Sheriff Bailey was stepping forward to intervene, confusion all over his face. But Joseph moved first.

He shoved the startled sheriff aside with surprising strength and darted through the open doorway. The bell above the sheriff's office door clanged hard as he barreled into the front room and burst out into the street. Wilson saw it a second too late.

"Stop him!" Milton bellowed. But Joseph was already gone, racing down the boardwalk, shouting for Cash, for Jaxon, for anyone who could hear him.

And Leah, still pinned beneath Wilson's hands, felt the first tiny spark of hope ignite in her chest.

Milton and Jack bolted after the fleeing banker, boots pounding across the wooden floorboards and out onto the street. But by the time they reached the boardwalk, Joseph Hicks was already in the saddle. He kicked the horse hard, dirt spraying behind him as he shot down Main Street like a man possessed. His figure disappeared between the buildings before either outlaw could so much as aim a gun.

"Damn it!" Milton roared, fists clenched as he skidded to a halt. Jack cursed under his breath, scanning the road as if hoping Joseph would magically reappear. When it became clear the banker was truly gone, and that the entire town would soon hear his warning, they exchanged a dark, panicked look.

"This is bad," Jack muttered.

"This is what happens when orders ain't obeyed," Milton snapped. Rage simmered off him in waves as he stormed back inside the sheriff's office.

Wilson had settled Leah against the cold stone wall of the cell when the door slammed open again. Milton strode in with Patricia clamped against his side. One arm locked ruthlessly around her waist while the other pressed the barrel of a gun to her temple.

"You got five seconds, exactly, 'fore I put a bullet in your ma," he snarled. Leah stared at him, wide-eyed, trembling, but not from fear. Her expression hardened into pure contempt.

"You're a fool, Milton Rowland," she spat. "Do you honestly expect me to believe you'd shoot your wife?"

Milton's jaw dropped. His arm slackened, the gun lowering an inch as shock flashed across his face. Patricia went ghost-white and collapsed into the nearest chair, hands shaking uncontrollably.

"How... how did you find out?" Patricia whispered. Leah's glare sharpened.

"I heard you in my father's room. Now tell me, did you ever love him? Even for a moment? Or was it just his money you were after?"

"Leah—" Patricia tried, voice trembling, but Leah cut her off with a slash of her hand.

"Answer the question. If you want me to cooperate in any way, you'll tell me everything. Every lie. Every secret. My whole life was built on your deceit."

Milton scoffed. "'Course she didn't love your pa. That was all part o' the plan."

"I wasn't talking to you," Leah snapped, never taking her eyes off Patricia. Patricia straightened slowly, as if preparing for impact.

"No," she said flat as a board. "I didn't love your pa."

Leah swallowed hard. "Why pretend you were abused and mistreated?"

A cold, humorless laugh escaped Patricia.

"Because it works, plain as day. Good men just can't resist a gal who seems breakable and scared. Playin' the helpless one opens doors every time."

Leah stiffened. "Always? How many times have you done it?"

"It ain't none of your concern how many times," Milton cut in, voice sharp enough to draw blood. "Now you're comin' with us. If Hicks won't play along, we'll lean on his family till he does. And this time," he added, eyes gone dark, "he ain't slippin' away." He cut the ties on Leah's legs and yanked her arm, but she planted her feet and held firm.

"No. I said I want answers. You'll talk before I go anywhere." Her voice carried so much steel that Milton involuntarily stepped back.

"Fine," he growled. "You want the whole damn story? Lemme spell it out for you." He started pacing, each step full of anger that twisted through every word. "Pa and Ma had a little farm back in Virginia. Weren't much, but it kept us fed, 'til the railroad came through and stole it out from under us. Cheated us blind. Then torched the place to the ground. My ma died from the heartbreak. After that, my pa and I, we made ourselves a promise, revenge on every high-and-mighty railroad family we could lay eyes on."

Leah shook her head. "Did you even know the men who robbed you were truly from the railroad? There are dozens of stories of scammers pretending to represent railroad companies."

"We weren't bothered none," Milton said, voice like ice. "A debt was owed, and we paid it back in kind."

"By murdering innocent families?" Leah mumbled, horrified. Milton's eyes gleamed with sick delight.

"We took their ranches. Put down the ones who fought. Shut their kin in the barns and watched the fire rise. Their screams—"

"Enough!" Leah cried, gagging on the horror in his words. "I asked for answers, not a confession soaked in pride. You're vile. You deserve to rot in a cell for the rest of your life."

"Ain't gonna happen," Milton sneered. "We'll be in England 'fore anyone can lift a finger to stop us. We've already paid our dues."

"Paid?" Leah's voice cracked with fury. "You haven't paid for anything."

Patricia finally spoke again, voice trembling but defensive.

"They've paid plenty. Milton and Jack spent years sittin' in a jail cell up in Eureka for that bank job and takin' them hostages."

"And that's supposed to make me pity you?" Leah shot back. "You committed murder. Arson. Who knows how much else. How could you even associate with men like that, let alone love one of them?"

Patricia's gaze hardened. "Because they saved my life. I lost my folks when I was just a little thing and spent my childhood rottin' away in a miserable orphanage. Ran off when I was fourteen. Jack found me. Took me in. Gave me somethin' that felt like family. And Milton... well, he loved me, in his own way. Married me on my eighteenth birthday."

"And you condoned their crimes?" Leah whispered.

"Easy for you to sit there judgin'," Patricia snapped. "Mitchell spoiled you rotten. Turned you into this—proud, mule-stubborn, self-righteous—"

"Do you think this year has been easy?" Leah's voice exploded, raw with grief. "I lost my father. I was kidnapped. I watched a good man die of rattlesnake bites because of you." Her voice cracked, memories crashing over her. "Dad didn't spoil me. He taught me courage. Honor. Kindness. Things you can't even comprehend."

"The way I reckon," Patricia said, voice like a blade, "anyone who hurt because of us deserved every bit of it, and more besides."

Leah stared at her, blood turning to ice. How had she not seen this? How had the woman she called 'Mom' been hiding this monster behind soft smiles and timid gestures?

"So, what about Mildred?"

Milton's head snapped toward her, irritation flashing hot in his eyes.

"What about her?"

"That's what I'm asking you," Leah shot back, her voice steady but edged in steel. "Is she related to any of you? Or are you just using her the same way you used everyone else to get what you want?"

Milton and Jack exchanged a look, one cold, one amused, before both men burst into harsh laughter. Jack snorted.

"Usin' her? Hell, it's the other way 'round."

Milton smirked. “And no, she ain’t kin to us. She was your ma’s sister.”

Leah’s stomach twisted. “Then what does she have to do with this? I want to know. All of it.”

Her gaze swept from Patricia to Jack to Milton, demanding an answer. For a moment, no one spoke. The air grew thick with tension. Then Milton lunged. He grabbed Leah by the arm, hard, yanking her off balance and dragging her through the small corridor into the sheriff’s office. Before she could right herself, he shoved her into a wooden chair, the legs scraping loudly across the floor.

“Ain’t givin’ you another answer, Leah Johnson,” he snapped. “I’m fed up. You’re just tryin’ to drag this out with your damn questions.”

Leah leaned forward, fury igniting every inch of her.

“Did you think I’d just meekly submit myself to you? Did you think I’d hand over everything my father built without even lifting a finger to fight you?” Her voice rose, sharp, unwavering, fearless. Milton stopped mid-rant, taken aback. For a fleeting second, real surprise flickered across his face, as if the thought had genuinely never occurred to him that Mitch Johnson’s daughter might have inherited her father’s backbone.

Leah stared him down, refusing to blink, refusing to give him even a hint of fear. And for one stunned heartbeat, Milton Rowland had nothing to say at all. They had expected things to go much smoother. In their minds, Leah Johnson was still the ten-year-old they had last seen, a child who had been sassy and, yes, strong-willed, but they certainly hadn’t prepared for the young woman standing in front of them now: forceful, sharp-tongued, and fearless enough to stare Milton down without flinching.

Patricia had written to them over the years, sending letters full of exaggerated sweetness about her 'meek' stepdaughter. But never, not once, had she mentioned the steel in Leah's spine or the fire in her eyes. She had left out entirely the fierce loyalty, the untamable resolve, the stubborn streak that could rival any full-grown cowboy.

Milton and Jack had walked into this plan convinced they were dealing with a gullible girl they could intimidate. Instead, they found themselves facing a woman who refused to break... and who seemed more determined with every threat they hurled at her. Leah Johnson was nothing like they remembered. And nothing like they had expected. If anything, her courage was beginning to complicate their entire carefully crafted scheme.

After a long, simmering moment spent regaining his composure, Milton's face hardened into something cold and murderous. He turned to his father with terrifying calm.

"Pa, ready the dynamite," he said, voice flat as stone. "Let's end this for good."

Jack moved toward the door, but before he could take two steps, Milton lifted his gun and leveled it directly at Leah's head. That was all Leah needed. She sprang from the chair with a burst of desperate strength and slammed into him. The impact knocked Milton backward, his aim jerking wild as he stumbled. The gun clattered against the desk, but he caught himself before he fell. She didn't get far.

Jack lunged, grabbing her by the arms and hauling her back as easily as if she weighed nothing at all. He shoved her down into the chair again, pinning her shoulders with bruising force. Milton was at her side a moment later, rage twisting his features. Together, father and son held her down, their grips like iron.

Leah's breath came fast and sharp. She squeezed her eyes shut, not in fear but in defiance. If this was how it ended, so be it. She had fought with everything she had. She had protected the people she loved. She had refused to bow, refused to betray her father's memory or the home he built. She had resisted every threat, every lie, every game these men had played. If this was the moment her story ended... at least she was facing it with her head high and her spirit unbroken.

Several deafening gunshots exploded through the room, splintering wood, ricocheting off stone, ringing in Leah's ears. Milton howled in pain, his gun flying from his hand as he staggered back, clutching his arm.

Before Leah could draw a breath, the window behind them crashed open. McKay vaulted through first, landing with the focus of a man who had been waiting for this moment. Two U.S. Marshal deputies followed right on his heels, rifles raised, faces set with grim determination. Jaxon came last, eyes blazing, chest heaving, every muscle coiled like he might tear apart anyone who touched her.

Jack raised his gun, fury twisting his features, but didn't get the chance to pull the trigger. Sheriff Bailey and Wilson stormed in from the adjoining office, drawing their weapons in perfect unison. Both muzzles fixed squarely on the Rowlands.

"Drop it," Wilson barked, voice like steel. Jack froze. Rage warred with self-preservation in his eyes, but the sight of four guns trained on him finally broke his bravado. He let his weapon clatter to the floor.

McKay didn't hesitate. He lunged forward, grabbed Leah by the arms, and yanked her away from the chair where she had been pinned. He spun her behind him as if shielding a priceless treasure, and she collided straight into Jaxon's waiting embrace. Jaxon's arms wrapped around her instantly, protectively, as if he'd been holding his breath for days just waiting for her to be back where she belonged. Leah felt his heart hammering against her cheek.

Behind them, deputies forced Milton and Jack to their knees. Handcuffs snapped shut with loud, final clicks. Both men were dragged across the room and shoved into the nearest cell, the clang of iron bars slamming shut echoing like the final punctuation on the nightmare they'd unleashed.

Leah sagged against Jaxon's chest, trembling, but safe. Jaxon's hold only tightened, as though he refused to ever let her be taken from him again.

Patricia spun toward the front door, panic tightening her features, and bolted for her only chance of escape. But she didn't make it two steps. Scott's deputy stepped inside at that exact moment, blocking the doorway with a solid wall of muscle and authority. Patricia skidded to a halt, eyes wide. Behind the deputy came David Smith, face grim with barely restrained fury, and Cash, whose expression alone could have frozen fire. And then, last of all, a familiar figure crossed the threshold. Mitchell Johnson. Patricia went rigid. Every trace of color drained from her face until she was as pale as fresh-fallen snow.

"Mitch," she breathed, voice cracking. "How...?"

But he didn't answer her. Didn't spare her a single word. Mitchell's gaze went straight to Leah, disheveled, bruised, her forehead still bleeding. His chest rose in a shaky breath, something like agony flickering in his eyes as he took in the sight of his daughter. Not the girl he'd left behind. Not the girl he'd hoped to protect. But the young woman who had survived every betrayal, every lie, every danger placed in her path.

Patricia's voice faltered into silence as Mitchell stepped deeper into the room, his focus never wavering. Behind him, Cash hovered close like a shadow, ready to support him if he faltered, ready to break someone if he had to. The room seemed to stop breathing altogether.

And Patricia's knees nearly buckled as she realized her lies... her manipulations... her years of deceit... had finally come face-to-face with the one man she never wanted to answer to. Mitchell Johnson.

Leah heard Patricia's strangled gasp—"Mitch"—and the name slammed into her like a physical blow. She blinked, looked around McKay's shoulder, and nearly crumpled where she stood.

"Dad." The word was barely a whisper, cracked and raw, as if torn from the deepest part of her. Mitchell took a step toward her at once, his face breaking open with relief and aching worry. He reached out. He was so close to pulling her into his arms, but Leah's gaze slid past him, unfocused, trembling. Her eyes found Cash... then David... then Sheriff Bailey. One by one. All men she had trusted. All men who had lied.

Cash saw it, the second the light faded from her eyes. They had pushed her too far.

"Mitchell, wait," he said sharply, stepping in front of the grieving father, blocking him with a firm hand across his chest. Mitch froze, stunned.

"Cash, she's my daughter—"

"I know." Cash's voice was low, steady, heavy with regret. "But right now she feels betrayed beyond imagination. She's not ready. If you touch her, she'll break."

Leah backed away from them all, this final betrayal slicing her open from the inside out. They waited for her temper to explode, waited for her to yell, curse, rage like she always did when pushed too far. But nothing came. She only shook her head, slowly, painfully, as if every heartbeat hurt. Tears spilled over, silently, one by one.

"Leah," Jaxon whispered, stepping toward her, reaching for her arm as if he could anchor her back to the world. But she flinched like his touch burned her.

"Don't," she choked out, shoving him away with surprising strength. Then she turned and bolted. Not toward the door, toward the sheriff's back room. Before anyone could fully register her movement, she threw the door open, crossed the small space in three desperate steps, and shoved the window up.

"Leah!" Jaxon lunged, but he was too late. She climbed out, dropped to the ground outside, and vanished into the freezing afternoon before a single soul could stop her.

Scott Bailey cleared his throat, once, sharply, snapping every man in the room to attention.

"Go," he ordered, his voice firm but not unkind. "McKay, Wilson, my deputies and I will finish things here. You go after her."

Behind him, the deputies were already escorting Patricia toward the cells, her protests dissolving into frantic breaths as the iron door clanged shut behind her. The marshal deputies were cuffing Jack and Milton more securely, but Scott never took his eyes off the men in front of him.

"She won't get far on foot," he added quietly, urgency threading through his tone. "Go. Now."

Cash didn't wait for a second command. He was already pushing through the doorway, David and Mitchell right on his heels. Jaxon shot after them like a man who had finally realized what he stood to lose. The door banged against the wall as the rest of the men followed, boots hammering against the wooden boards.

25
The Making of a Monster

Outside, the cold afternoon slapped them in the face, but there was no sign of Leah. No flutter of skirts. No fading footsteps. Nothing. Just silence.

"Spread out!" Cash barked, climbing onto his horse with a fluid, practiced motion. "Check the alleys, the back road, the path by the creek, anywhere she could've run!"

The men scattered immediately, searching behind the saloon, around the general store, behind the livery, calling her name into the chilling wind. But Leah was nowhere.

"She's not in town," Jaxon muttered, breathless with fear.

"Then she's heading home," Cash replied, already kicking his horse into a gallop. "Ride!"

Within seconds, the group thundered out of Hoopa Valley, hooves pounding like war drums as they tore down the road leading toward the ranch, praying they weren't already too late.

Leah had taken the first horse she could get her hands on. The poor creature wasn't even fully saddled and tore out of town like the ground itself was giving way beneath her. Cold wind lashed her face, but it barely registered. Her skull pounded as if someone were striking it from the inside, and warm blood slid down her temple in steady rivulets.

But she didn't care. Not anymore. Hot tears blurred her vision, spilling faster than she could wipe them away. A strangled cry tore from her throat, then another, and another, raw, desperate screams ripped straight from her chest in a futile attempt to relieve the unbearable pressure building inside her. She had reached the breaking point. Something inside her had splintered so violently that she felt nothing but the instinct to run, to disappear, to be anywhere but trapped between truths that had destroyed her world.

The first gunshot split the air. Her heart lurched as she whipped around. Two men thundered after her on horseback, shadows against the fading light. More shots cracked into the dirt at her horse's feet, spraying earth and sending the terrified animal rearing sideways.

"No—no, no—easy, girl, easy!" Leah cried, trying to steady the reins, but the horse wasn't listening. The repeated crack of a whip sliced through the wind, spooking the mare further. Then the animal bolted. The world blurred. Trees. Dust. Sky. Her pulse hammered as she desperately tried to regain control, pulling on the reins with trembling hands. Panic struck like lightning when she saw the canyon looming ahead.

"Stop!" she shouted, voice breaking. "STOP!" The horse didn't slow, not even a fraction. The riders closed in. One leaned from his saddle, grabbed Leah by the waist, and yanked her from the horse. She hit the earth hard, pain exploding through her body, then momentum carried her toward the canyon's edge. Leah clawed at the ground, fingers scraping for anything to hold onto. She caught a tree root, but it snapped instantly. And she fell. Not a sheer drop, but steep enough to be deadly.

Her body slammed into jagged rocks, loose rubble breaking free and tumbling with her. She rolled helplessly, earth and stone crashing against her ribs, her back, her arms. The world spun in a violent blur until she collided with a massive boulder near the bottom. The impact knocked the breath out of her. A choked gasp escaped her lips, followed by a thin, pained moan. Every inch of her hurt, her skin torn, her limbs throbbing, warm blood trickling from several cuts. She tried to move... and couldn't. She lay there, broken and shaking.

Tears welled again, hotter than before, unstoppable. She cried until her voice was gone, until her vision blurred, until she thought her body might dissolve into the trembling earth around her. Too much. Too much pain. Too much betrayal. Too many lies.

Her father was alive. *Alive.* And everyone had kept it from her. Something inside her cracked wide open at the thought. What else had been hidden from her? What hadn't been a lie? She wasn't even sure she cared anymore. Who would find her here? Who would even know where to look?

Death felt close, close enough that she could almost sense its cold hand reaching for her. And for the first time in days, she didn't fight it. She couldn't. Not anymore. Leah closed her eyes, letting the darkness rise to claim her. Her father was alive. The ranch would survive. She didn't have to. She finally let herself drift, broken, exhausted, surrendering to the darkness creeping in around her.

As soon as the four men thundered onto the ranch, they split off in different directions without a single word needing to be spoken. Horses skidded in the dirt, hooves pounding as they scattered across the property, toward the barn, the corrals, the bunkhouse, the line of trees behind the yard. Every man called Leah's name, their voices echoing across the chilled evening air.

Nothing. Not a single answer. Not even the faintest sign she had been there. By the time they regrouped in the yard, the fear on each of their faces had carved itself into something sharp and unmistakable. Cash ran a shaking hand across his beard. Mitchell's jaw clenched so hard the muscles twitched. McKay scanned the horizon as if he could force her to appear by sheer will. Jaxon's chest tightened painfully.

"Where is she?" he whispered, more to himself than anyone else. Then, louder, "Where would she go? She is hurt. She wouldn't get far."

Cash shook his head. "She's not anywhere on the main property. If she was on foot, we'd have found tracks. If she took a horse, we'd see it missing."

Mitchell exhaled slowly, voice rough. "Heaven help us... I knew she'd run, but not like this. Not without leaving a trace."

A horrible silence settled for a beat. Then Jaxon's eyes snapped up as a terrible possibility struck him.

"Do you think... Mildred found her?" He looked at Cash, then at Mitchell. "If Mildred knew Leah was on the ranch again, if she came back for something, they could have crossed paths." Both older men turned pale instantly.

"That's possible," Mitchell said, voice low and grim.

"More than possible," Cash muttered, his stomach twisting. "If Mildred grabbed her... she wouldn't hesitate to use Leah to save her own skin."

Jaxon didn't wait for further discussion. He was already swinging into the saddle, fury and terror surging through him.

"Let's go," he said, his voice ragged. "Now."

Within seconds, all four men were back on their horses, kicking hard, racing toward the dark tree line, toward the one person left in this nightmare who still had the power to hurt Leah.

It was nearly dark by the time Leah heard the shuffle of hooves scraping against loose rock above her. She didn't bother lifting her head. Her eyelids stayed sealed shut. Her mouth was dry as dust, her skin cold and clammy. She felt half-buried beneath the weight of pain. A familiar voice floated down the slope.

"Is she dead?"

Leah's stomach twisted. Of course. It had been her aunt behind this.

A deep male voice responded, "I don't reckon so. We made damn sure she tumbled down *this* stretch o' the mountain, not off no cliff."

How thoughtful, Leah thought bitterly. Wouldn't want her to die too fast, after all. Better to watch her suffer.

"Leah?" Mildred called again. Leah didn't respond. What was the point? The woman who had held her as a child, brushed her hair, hugged her during thunderstorms, had helped throw her off a mountain. There was no voice left in Leah for her.

"She looks pretty beat up," Mildred remarked, as if reporting on a horse with a lame leg.

Is that right? Leah mocked silently. *Shoved off a mountain, rolled through half the forest, hit a boulder... I'm shocked I don't look refreshed and glowing.* Was she delirious? Was this how the mind protected itself, sarcasm instead of screaming?

"Can you turn her around?" Mildred asked.

"I ain't thinkin' that's wise," he answered. "She's scraped up real bad. Move her wrong, we'll do more harm than help."

Oh, now you care about my well-being. Touching.

"What exactly you aimin' to do with her?" a second deep voice asked.

"I'm not sure yet."

Leah felt Mildred's gaze on her, long, heavy, full of something she couldn't read. When Mildred finally spoke again, her voice was softer.

"I would like to explain why I did what I did."

Leah almost laughed. *Of course. Story time. Because naturally, nearly murdering someone gives you the right to offer explanations.* Her body screamed in agony, muscles throbbing, bones vibrating with pain, every cut burning. Staying still hurt. Moving hurt more. Eventually she turned onto her side with a strangled moan. Mildred stepped closer immediately.

"Leah?"

She didn't look at her. Just tried to breathe through the stabbing pain. Once she had found a position that hurt slightly less, she opened her eyes and faced the inevitable.

"What do you want?" she rasped. Her voice was a mixture of sand and ice.

"So, you are awake," Mildred said softly.

"I'm alive," Leah answered coldly.

Mildred seemed to wait, perhaps expecting gratitude, perhaps expecting tears. Leah offered neither. A long sigh escaped the older woman.

"Listen... I didn't mean for you to get hurt. If I had known your father was still alive—"

"Just tell me what you came to say," Leah cut in sharply. Her patience was nonexistent.

"I don't know where to start."

"Fine," Leah hissed. "I'll ask. Why did you do this? What reason could possibly justify any of it? Why do you hate my family so much?"

"I don't hate you," Mildred whispered.

Leah barked out a humorless laugh. "Right. Because trying to murder people is usually a sign of affection."

"Leah, you don't understand what emotional pain can do to someone."

Leah scoffed loudly.

"I don't understand? Really? Do you have any idea what these last months have been like for me? What you, and the Rowlands, put me through? Kidnappings. Lies. Betrayal. Fear. Watching someone die. If you think pain is an excuse to become a monster, then I should be as evil as any of you by now." Her voice cracked, rage, exhaustion, and heartbreak all tangled together. "So, unless you're going to tell me the truth," she continued, "leave me alone so I can die in peace."

A sharp moan tore from her throat as another wave of pain hit, but she swallowed it down. She would not beg for help. Not from Mildred. The older woman sighed, a sound halfway between regret and irritation.

"You don't know anything about my past, Leah. Horrible things can make people bad. It happened to the Rowlands."

"No," Leah snapped, forcing her eyes open despite the agony. "Don't you dare hide behind that. There is no excuse for hurting or killing innocent people. None. We choose what we become."

Mildred tried to interject, but Leah overrode her.

"Yes, life is cruel. Yes, terrible things happen. I get it. But that doesn't give anyone the right to drag others into their darkness. What you've done, you didn't do it because of your past. You did it because you chose to. You let hate and greed guide you. And you listened to the devil whispering in your ear." Her voice was shaking now, but every word was sharp.

"No matter what you've been through, Mildred... you had the power to stop this. You had the power to be better. You simply chose not to."

Mildred fell silent. For the first time since arriving, Leah sensed a crack, thin, brittle, splintering through the older woman's mask. Mildred's jaw tightened. Her fingers curled and uncurled, her breathing uneven. She hated this. She hated how Leah, battered and bleeding, still managed to sound clear-headed, strong, principled. Hated that Leah sounded so much like...

Mildred inhaled sharply, but when she spoke, her composure shattered like glass.

"You are just like your mother," she hissed, trembling with bitterness. "Lilian was the same way. Always fighting for people who couldn't fight for themselves. Always making herself look kinder, purer, and holier than anyone else. Everyone adored her, and she loved every second of it. That's how she stole Mitchell away from me."

Leah blinked. The words hit her like rocks.

"What are you talking about?"

Mildred's face contorted, pain, anger, and envy twisting together, until she barely resembled the aunt Leah had once trusted. When she spoke again, her voice was cold enough to freeze bone.

"I was in love with your father. I wanted to marry him. I was supposed to be the one he chose." Her nostrils flared. "But then Lilian, pretty, perfect Lilian, walked in and ruined everything."

Leah's stomach turned. Her mother? Mildred had been in love with her father... all this time?

Mildred went on, her words coming faster now, pouring out as if years of resentment had finally snapped free.

"She was only sixteen when we moved to Hoopa Valley. We came from Denver before that, where we met Heber." Her lip curled. "Heber was obsessed with her from the moment they met. Head over heels. But our father forbade it. And Lilian, spoiled little princess, didn't want anything to do with him anyway."

At the mention of Heber, Leah's skin crawled. So, he had been in this even back then. Mildred continued, her eyes burning with an old fury.

"Heber kept following her. Watching her. Our father warned him, threatened him, even. But Heber wouldn't listen. He was jealous of the attention Lilian got. He wanted her. Needed her. And when Lilian rejected him, he became obsessed."

Leah felt a cold sickness spread through her chest.

"Are you saying..." Her throat tightened. "He shadowed her?"

Mildred nodded, her mouth twisting.

"He followed us to Hoopa Valley after our father moved us away. Heber would show up everywhere, near the ranch, in town, behind the church, just to get a glimpse of her. But did Lilian ever think about what that did to me? No. She just kept living her perfect life while I lived in her shadow."

Leah's breath came in short, painful bursts.

"My mother tried to protect herself," she whispered. "That isn't stealing anyone away. That's survival."

Mildred's eyes flashed. "You wouldn't understand. She ruined everything for me. And when she married Mitchell?" Her voice cracked with old grief. "That was the final blow. She took the only man I ever loved."

Leah stared at her aunt, horrified. This wasn't a misunderstanding. This wasn't a moment of weakness. This was decades of festering hatred, jealousy, and twisted longing. And Leah had been living beside it her entire life, without ever knowing the truth.

26
The Cost of Their Silence

Leah listened, though every word twisted deeper confusion and horror through her stomach. Mildred, however, was fully lost in her own rage, her voice gaining momentum, her bitterness spilling out like poison.

"Mitch and I became friends," she went on, her tone sharp with old longing, "but he never tried to court me. I told myself he just needed time. But whenever he tried to court another girl, I made sure she disappeared from his interest. I frightened every single one of them."

There was pride in Mildred's voice, sickening, almost triumphant. Leah's stomach churned.

"When my sister turned eighteen, Mitch was hopelessly in love with her." Mildred's lip curled. "Everyone wanted her. The boys in town, the merchants' sons, they all thought she was so pretty." She spat the word as if it were venom. "Perfect little Lilian with her golden hair and soft smile."

Leah felt the sting of sympathy for a mother she didn't remember.

"Mitch pursued her," Mildred said, "and Lilian... she fell for him. Of course she did. And no matter what I tried, I couldn't pry them apart. When I started feeding lies about Mitch to our father, he believed me, he always believed me, but Lilian rebelled anyway and they eloped." Mildred's fists tightened, her knuckles white.

"My father was furious, but Lilian managed to show him what Mitch was really like. That little beast betrayed me, stole his heart, and stabbed me in the back." She shook, not with sorrow but with vicious resentment. "When my father found out I had lied to him, he sent me back to Denver to stay with my uncle. And my uncle married me off." Her voice hardened.

"Edward, my husband, was a good man. Too good. His family was wealthy. I should have been content, but all I wanted was Mitch. So, I made a plan." Her eyes glimmered with a cold, nostalgic cruelty. "I contacted Heber. He hated our family for rejecting him," Mildred continued. "He wanted Mitch dead. But that wasn't what I wanted. I convinced him that he would never have Lilian anyway, but he could hurt her by getting rid of the man she loved most, our father." Mildred's voice sharpened to a blade.

"He deserved to die. He favored Lilian over me every day of my life. And when he agreed to let my uncle marry me off, I never wanted to see him again. So, I made sure Heber killed him before Lilian's death. I wanted her to suffer."

Leah's breath hitched, sharp, painful. Her mind reeled. Her mother had lost her father because of this woman.

"By then," Mildred continued, "I had met the Rowlands. And once I introduced them to Heber, they agreed to kill Lilian, if I paid enough."

Leah's entire body went still. Her mind screamed. Her heart felt like it was shattering with every sentence.

"So, they murdered Lilian," Mildred said flatly, "and then I needed to get rid of my husband."

Leah gasped. "You killed your husband?"

"No," Mildred said with a shrug. "Not with my own hands. But Heber, he was more than happy to do it. Then everything was set. I planned to return to Hoopa Valley and reclaim the life Lilian stole from me." Her expression twisted again. "But Patricia had gotten to Mitch first. Married him before I arrived. I was furious, but I had to play along if I didn't want the Rowlands to expose me. And since Mitch was no longer available, and Patricia didn't love him anyway, I thought... fine. She'd drive him away eventually, and I would step in to take her place."

Leah felt physically sick. "And my grandparents," she whispered. "What about them?"

Mildred scoffed. "I tried to play the doting older sister to Patricia. I pretended to support Mitch's family. But your father and Cash and David wouldn't let Lilian's death go. They watched Patricia. Watched me. Then one day, I caught your grandfather listening. Eavesdropping on Patricia and me while we argued outside about her leaving Mitch."

"You wanted her to divorce him," Leah said slowly.

"Yes," Mildred snapped. "I wanted her out of the way. But with your grandfather knowing too much? I had no choice but to silence him."

Leah's heart plummeted. "You killed my grandfather?" she choked out. Mildred smiled. It was cold and triumphant.

"Not by my own hand. But yes. I orchestrated it. And once he was gone, your grandmother followed soon after. She couldn't live without him."

Leah's vision blurred. "Don't you dare blame them," she rasped. "Don't you make excuses. They died because of you."

"They shouldn't have listened in," Mildred sneered. "Your grandfather never trusted Patricia. Or me."

"Well, of course he didn't," Leah whispered, trembling. "What father would welcome a woman who tried to destroy his son's marriage?" The words hung heavy in the cold air. Leah felt no fear, only disgust, heartache, and a dawning, icy understanding of just how deep this betrayal went.

Mildred stared at her, eyes narrowing. Leah's refusal to break, her sharp mind, her composure despite the agony, infuriated her. Mildred sucked in a thin breath through her teeth, struggling to keep control of herself.

"As I was saying," she bit out, "I believe the Rowlands had planned to get rid of your father long ago. They needed money. But then they robbed the bank in Eureka, got caught, and ended up in jail. Patricia wanted me to bail them out, but I refused." She rolled her eyes as if the memory annoyed her. "With Jack and Milton behind bars and Heber traveling all over the country doing who-knows-what, I wasn't too worried anymore that anyone would uncover my involvement."

Leah still refused to look at her. Her entire body burned, throbbed, ached, but she wouldn't give Mildred an ounce of satisfaction.

"Then," Mildred continued with a sigh, "I noticed a shift. Mitch and Cash started acting strangely around me. Suspicious. And Patricia, she was terrified Mitch had figured everything out. He'd been moving money into a separate account she couldn't access. He must've realized funds were disappearing and wanted to protect what was left." She paused, studying Leah's battered face. Leah's expression didn't change. She stared past Mildred as though looking anywhere else would keep her heart from collapsing.

"Not long after," Mildred went on, "I discovered David Smith had someone shadowing me. Trailing my movements. Asking questions. That's when I knew I had to be careful. I made sure I was hired at the Hoopa Valley school and pretended innocence." Her lip curled into a proud smirk.

"I created the perfect excuse to travel, tutoring the children of wealthy families. It let me move freely while nobody suspected a thing."

Leah swallowed, the movement scraping painfully down her throat.

Mildred continued, "I needed answers. I needed to know how much they knew about me. So, I traveled to Sacramento and broke into David's office. I found nothing." A smug smile tugged at her mouth. "But I became very skilled at searching rooms without leaving a trace."

Leah's jaw tightened. She fought the urge to retch at the woman's self-satisfaction.

"Unfortunately," Mildred said with a scoff, "Patricia lacked that skill. She grew desperate. Looked everywhere for any way to access Mitch's accounts again. She wanted to get Jack and Milton out of prison sooner, but she couldn't do anything without proof or leverage."

Leah stared at her, bitterness slicing through her chest.

"Then Patricia admitted that one of Milton's letters had gone missing. A letter that mentioned me." Mildred exhaled sharply. "She assumed Mitch took it, and that he'd begun putting the pieces together. The Rowlands hated him. Heber hated him. And I... well, I couldn't afford to have Mitch discover the truth. So, I paid to free Jack and Milton. And when Heber was arrested after kidnapping you, I paid to get him out as well."

Leah's voice cracked when she spoke.

"So now you expect me to forgive and forget because you weren't physically involved these past few months?" Her eyes blazed. "Because technically you didn't tie me up yourself? You were still behind it all."

"I didn't take part in the day-to-day chaos," Mildred argued, lifting her chin in offense. "I only freed the Rowlands. And paid to get Heber out of jail."

"You funded the monsters who tortured me," Leah spat, her voice shaking with white-hot fury. "You paid for the nightmare. You made every single one of these horrors possible." She stared at her aunt with so much disdain it burned. "You are as innocent as a rattlesnake."

Mildred scoffed loudly. "Oh, spare me. It won't matter for long. I doubt you'll survive the night. Blood attracts predators, you know." Her voice grew colder. "Perhaps I'll blackmail Mitch into marrying me in exchange for your life. And once he agrees, we'll tragically discover your dead body. Such a pity."

Leah's heart lurched. Not from fear, no. From staggering disbelief.

"How do you know my father is still alive?" she rasped.

Mildred smirked. "I have eyes and ears everywhere. I saw him earlier when he entered the sheriff's office." Her smile twisted into something sinister. "It was quite the shock. But really, it's perfect. Because now I can make him pay for choosing Lilian over me." She chuckled softly, coldly. Her gaze drifted toward the darkening horizon, as though imagining her triumph painted across the sky.

Leah lay still, broken and bleeding, but a spark, faint, trembling, yet alive, flickered in her chest. There was no forgiveness for this. But perhaps... there could still be justice.

"You're a heartless, evil monster, Mildred. I can't believe I saw you as a loving aunt all these years." Leah forced her head to lift despite the agony shooting down her spine. She stared up at the woman who had once braided her hair, baked her pies, hugged her when she cried. There was nothing left of that woman now, nothing but a cold, twisted stranger wearing her face. How had she concealed this darkness for so long? Mildred's expression didn't flicker.

"Goodbye, Leah. I'll check back in the morning to see if you're still breathing." She leaned in slightly, eyes gleaming with calculated cruelty. "Unless you'd like to beg me to take you to Doc Carter now... and agree to be my hostage until I have Mitch eating out of my hand. Then I might consider keeping you alive a little longer."

Leah pressed her lips together, refusing to give that monster a single tremor of fear.

"Tch." Mildred shook her head. "Just what I thought. Too hard-headed and prideful to show you're weak."

A bitter breath escaped Leah, half laugh, half exhaustion. She didn't intend to speak again... but something tore free from her throat anyway.

"I wish you a long life, Mildred."

Her aunt chuckled darkly. "A long life in prison?"

"If that's what God has planned for you, then yes. It would be fair." Leah swallowed hard, fire burning through her injuries. "But that's not what I meant. I wish you a long life, so you never forget the legacy you've chosen. You had innocent, defenseless people murdered. Yet some of them died as heroes, protecting those they loved. Can you say the same?"

Mildred's laugh twisted into a furious shriek.

"Everyone but you, Leah. Were you able to protect Colt?" Her tone was cruel, deliberate. A stab straight into Leah's deepest wound. Leah's breath stuttered, pain trembling through her. But slowly, painfully, she steadied herself.

"You're right," she whispered. "I couldn't rescue him. Colt died protecting me, and I'll carry that regret for the rest of my life." Her eyes burned, but her voice held strong. "But I did rescue Robyn. So at least one innocent person didn't die because of you."

Mildred's entire face went rigid. She sucked in a gasp.

"You rescued Robyn?"

Leah nodded, weak but unbroken. "I did. I might die here with guilt in my heart... but at least I prevented one soul from being slaughtered by your hands."

The silence that followed was ice-cold and razor-sharp. Then Mildred snapped. With a scream, she lunged forward and began kicking Leah's battered body. Hard. Over and over. The two men with her scrambled to drag her back, both shouting, but Mildred fought them like a wild animal. Leah bit down on her lip until she tasted blood. She refused to cry out. She refused to give Mildred the satisfaction.

"You are not worth another thought, Leah Johnson!" Mildred shrieked, her voice so warped with fury she barely sounded human. "I hope wolves or mountain lions find you and tear you apart while you're still alive!" With one last scream, she jerked free, marched to her horse, and mounted in a violent motion. Her hired men followed quickly, spooked by her madness.

A moment later, they were gone. The forest swallowed their hoofbeats until there was nothing but the lonely whisper of wind and the slow, shallow sound of Leah's own breathing. Silence fell around her like a heavy, merciless blanket. Leah closed her eyes.

When they reached Mildred's house, an eerie stillness hung in the air. The curtains were drawn tight, the door closed, and not a single lamp burned inside.

"Nobody's home," Cash muttered, scanning the yard. The silence felt wrong, too deliberate. Mitchell's jaw tightened as he dismounted.

"She's up to something. She wouldn't leave that fast unless she had help."

David agreed with a grim nod.

"Then we split up. Someone had to bring horses for her, and that means they can't be far. If we track whoever she's working with, we might find Leah."

The group made quick decisions. David and Mitchell led their horses behind the small shed at the far end of the property where the shadows were deepest. They tethered the animals low to the ground so the silhouettes wouldn't be seen from a distance.

"If Mildred comes back," David said quietly, "we'll be waiting."

Mitchell didn't reply. He stood rigid, scanning the tree line, fury and dread etched into every hard line of his face. His daughter was out there somewhere, hurt, alone, and in danger, and the thought nearly undid him. Jaxon and Cash exchanged a quick look before turning toward the woods.

"We'll sweep the forest," Jaxon said, already pulling his rifle free. "She can't have gone far, not if she's hurt."

Cash clapped him once on the shoulder.

"Keep your ears sharp. If Mildred or those men left tracks, they'll lead somewhere."

The two slipped into the trees like shadows, moving swiftly and silently between pines and undergrowth, listening for anything, a snapped twig, a cry, hoofbeats fading in the distance. Behind them, Mitchell stared into the growing darkness with a father's fear tightening his breath.

Hold on, Leah, he prayed silently. *We're coming.*

It was fully dark when Mildred slipped off her horse and handed the reins to the sleepy stable boy at the livery. The two men riding with her didn't dismount. They would need their mounts ready if they planned to free the Rowlands under cover of night.

"I'll make you some supper before you ride out to the prison," Mildred murmured, glancing around the quiet street. "Just wait here. And don't let anyone see you." She kept her voice low, cautious, watchful, the way someone behaves when every shadow might hide an enemy.

But the real danger stepped out of the shadows before she even touched her front steps. Mitchell and David appeared beside her, silent, sudden, immovable. Mildred froze, startled only for a moment before slipping back into her practiced mask.

"Mitchell?" she gasped, voice full of false warmth. She lifted her hands as if to embrace him, but Mitchell seized her wrists before she could touch him.

"Don't," he growled. "Don't even pretend you didn't know I was still alive. Now, where is Leah?"

Mildred blinked innocently, her eyes wide. "Leah? I—I don't know. Why would I know? Have you checked your house? Patricia and her—"

"You can stop lying through your teeth," David cut in sharply. His eyes were cold. "We're done listening to your stories."

Both men grabbed her arms, pulling her away from the stairs to the front porch. Mildred stiffened, panic flashing across her face.

"What are you doing? Let go of me!" she hissed, struggling. "Alfred? Easton!"

The two men who had accompanied her sprang into action at once, lunging toward Mitchell and David. Fists flew. Shouts cracked through the still night. But Mildred didn't wait to see who won. The moment the men attacked, she tore free and bolted toward town, skirts whipping around her legs. She didn't get far. McKay and Wilson barreled into her path from the direction of the prison yard. Mildred tried to pivot, but McKay caught her by the arm. She screamed, fought, clawed at his vest, but the marshal had reached his limit.

With a frustrated huff, he threw her over his broad shoulder and carried her, kicking, shrieking, demanding, to the sheriff's office. By the time he dumped her into the cell beside Patricia, she was breathless with fury.

"What are you doing?" she roared, grabbing the bars. "You have no right to keep me in here!"

She turned on Sheriff Bailey the moment he approached. "Scott, let me out this instant! Why are you arresting me?"

Scott didn't flinch. "I think you already know," he said evenly. "It took David months to piece everything together. Years, actually. Tonight, while you were gone, we searched your house." His expression hardened. "And we found enough evidence to bury you."

Mildred's face contorted. "How dare you—how dare you—!" Her voice rose to a hysterical pitch, echoing through the small jailhouse, but no one paid her tantrum any mind. Scott locked the cell with a final clang and stepped back.

"Don't worry," he said calmly. "You'll get a fair trial. Just like the Rowlands." His gaze turned steely. "But make no mistake, Mildred, justice is coming. And you will answer for every crime you helped to commit." He turned away, leaving her gripping the bars, white-faced and furious, while the rest of the room fell silent.

Alfred and Easton never stood a chance. By the time the struggle in the dark yard was over, both men were flat on the ground, wheezing, bleeding, and completely overpowered. Mitch had Alfred pinned, before the outlaw even understood what hit him, and David had Easton face down in the dirt. Jaxon and Cash arrived seconds later, breathless and ready for blood.

"Where's my daughter?" Mitch barked, his voice raw with terror. Alfred clenched his jaw, refusing to look at him. Mitchell's fear snapped into something vicious. He slammed Alfred's head into the ground with a bone-rattling crack. "Tell me where my daughter is!"

Still, the man said nothing. Cash stepped in, grabbed Alfred by the shirtfront and throat, and hauled him upright as though he weighed nothing. His eyes burned with fury.

"Listen carefully," Cash growled, tightening his grip until Alfred choked. "We don't have a problem beating it out of you. So, you can either talk now, or after we break a few bones."

Meanwhile, Jaxon had Easton subdued. He flipped the man onto his stomach, shoved a knee between his shoulder blades, and twisted his arm behind his back. When Easton continued to grit his teeth in silence, Jaxon yanked the arm higher, slowly, deliberately. The outlaw screamed.

"Talk, you piece of prairie coal," Jaxon snarled, "or I swear I'm breaking your arm clean in two!"

Easton writhed, panting, sweat dripping down his temple, but he still fought against the pain. Jaxon shifted his grip, twisting harder, and this time Easton broke.

"All right—ALL RIGHT!" he hollered. "I'll take ya to her! We left her where Mildred said—just stop—STOP!"

Jaxon released him just enough for him to breathe. Easton collapsed against the dirt, trembling.

Scott Bailey arrived at that moment, took one look at the scene, and dragged Alfred away by the collar. The sheriff tossed him into the same cell as the other captured men, slamming the iron door shut with a satisfying clang.

The rest of them, Mitch, David, Cash, Jaxon, McKay, Wilson, grabbed torches and lanterns, their fury merging into one focused purpose.

"Lead the way," Jaxon ordered coldly, shoving Easton ahead of them and toward his horse. No one spoke as they followed him into the night, every man carrying the same prayer in his chest: Let her be alive. Let us not be too late.

Leah waited… waited until the last hoofbeats faded, until the voices disappeared into the night, until even the wind seemed to stop listening. For a while, she had truly wanted to give up. Let the cold take her. Let the darkness swallow her. Let the pain finally end. But the moment Mildred rode away, leaving her to die alone like a wounded animal, something inside Leah snapped back into place. That woman wanted her weak.

Wanted her broken. Wanted her erased. Not tonight. Not like this.

Leah lifted her head, her breath trembling. The world blurred, then steadied. She looked around the ravine, trying to find a place less brutal than the patch of rocks slicing into her ribs. She spotted a small clearing, a thin stretch of grass glimmering faintly in the moonlight. It wasn't far, but it might as well have been a mile with the way her body screamed.

Still, she rolled. Inch by agonizing inch. Every movement tore a whimper from her throat, but she refused to let it become a scream. By the time she reached the grass, sweat mingled with blood on her skin. She let her head fall into the softness and, just for a moment, allowed unconsciousness to pull her under like a merciful tide.

When she woke again, she didn't know how much time had passed. The stars had shifted. The air was colder. She blinked slowly, letting her senses return one at a time. Pain. Cold. Loneliness. Resolve. She remained still until she could draw a full breath without blacking out. Then, trembling, she forced herself upright. The world tilted hard, and she dropped to one knee before steadying herself. Everything ached. Her ribs. Her legs. Her arms. The gashes across her body burned like fresh fire.

But staying here meant dying. And she refused to give Mildred that victory. Leah dragged herself upright again, gritting her teeth, and searched the ground for something sturdy. After a moment, she spotted a long, fallen branch. She leaned her whole weight against it, grateful for the crude stability it offered. One step. Another. Slow, shaky progress, but progress, nonetheless.

She took the long way out. She had no choice. The canyon walls here rose too steep and jagged to climb directly, so she traced a narrow, winding path that sloped gradually toward higher ground. The moon, bright and full, blessed her with just enough light to keep from stumbling blind. She forced her mind away from the physical misery clawing at her. Instead, she let the truth she had learned earlier pour through her veins. Her father was alive. Her mother had never been her mother.

Her aunt, her trusted aunt, was a murderer and had orchestrated nearly every tragedy of her life.

The betrayal cut deeper than any wound her body carried. The emotional agony fueled her steps, but it also made tears spill freely down her cheeks. They fell hot onto her chilled skin, tiny sparks of grief that refused to be ignored. Her breathing grew ragged as she climbed, leaning heavily into her makeshift cane. Her strength bled away with every step. By the time she reached the section of trail where Mildred's men had forced her horse toward the drop, her body gave a violent shudder. The world swayed. The shadows deepened. Her vision blurred at the edges, darkening like ink spreading across parchment.

Not yet... not yet...

But her knees buckled. Leah caught herself on the stick, barely staying upright. The canyon spun around her, and she felt consciousness slipping, like sand spilling between her fingers. She wasn't done fighting. She wasn't done telling the truth. She wasn't done taking her life back. But her body... her battered, beloved body... had reached its breaking point. And as the darkness finally closed over her, she whispered a single promise, to herself, to her father, to everyone who had taken her life from her: *I'm not finished. Not yet.*

The men had been riding in grim, focused silence, the only sounds the pounding of hooves and the low hiss of their torches. Then, almost at the same moment, Jaxon, Mitch, and Cash recognized the curve of the trail. The steep ridgeline. The drop into shadow below. All three men went pale.

"Where is Leah?" Cash barked, his voice cracking with terror. "Did you kill her by pushing her into the canyon?"

Easton stiffened, shaking his head quickly.

"No. Alfred shoved her over, but it wasn't a cliff, just a steep slope."

Mitch cursed low and savagely through his teeth. Cash spat a furious oath into the darkness. Jaxon didn't waste a single breath. He kicked his horse forward and tore up the trail, his heart hammering so hard he could barely breathe. The others raced after him.

They were almost to the spot Easton had described when faint, uneven footsteps echoed somewhere ahead, a soft, dragging shuffle that didn't sound human so much as ghostly. Everyone froze. Torches lifted. And then they saw her. Leah. Barely upright. Barely conscious. Her clothes were torn and soaked with blood. Her face pale beneath streaks of dirt and scarlet. She swayed like a dying flame. Her eyes lifted toward the sudden light. And she crumpled.

Jaxon reached her before her body hit the ground, catching her against his chest. The other men were beside him instantly, dismounting in a blur of panic.

"My word..." David whispered, horrified.

Mitch's breath broke as he dropped to one knee. "My girl..."

Cash turned away for a moment, wiping his face with the back of his sleeve before the others could see the tears welling in his eyes. But his voice trembled when he spoke.

"We need to take her to Doc Carter, now."

Jaxon scooped her into his arms, cradling her as though she were made of glass. She was limp... cold... her breathing shallow and unsteady. Seeing her like this, so broken, twisted something deep in his chest until he thought it might shatter him from the inside.

"We're losing time," Jaxon choked out. "She's barely holding on."

The men snapped into action. Mitch and Cash mounted again, their torches guiding the way back. David checked for any further threats, his jaw rigid with fury and grief.

Behind them, McKay and Wilson hauled Easton back toward their horses. The outlaw didn't bother resisting. One look at Leah had drained the fight from him.

"We'll ride ahead and alert Doc Carter," McKay called to Jaxon. "He'll be ready the moment you arrive."

"Go!" Jaxon barked, already swinging into his saddle with Leah held tightly against him. With that, the men surged down the mountain, racing the night, and racing death, to bring Leah home.

"Nurse Esther, keep a close eye on her. I don't want her waking up anytime soon." Riley Carter's voice was low, tight, dangerously close to breaking. His jaw clenched so hard the muscle in his cheek twitched. He had spent years tending gunshot wounds, trampling accidents, and every sort of ranch disaster Hoopa Valley could produce... but he had never seen anything quite like this.

Criminals had pushed Leah Johnson, barely more than a girl, down a canyon like she was refuse, to be discarded. They hadn't just tried to kill her. They had tried to shatter her. To torture her. To humiliate her. Riley's fists curled until his knuckles whitened, and Nurse Esther shot him a cautious glance over her shoulder. The doctor wasn't merely angry. He was seething, a quiet, simmering fury he was struggling to keep contained.

"It's all right, Doctor," Esther whispered as she adjusted the blankets around Leah's still, pale form. "We'll take care of her."

But Riley didn't answer. Couldn't. His eyes were glued to the bandages wrapped around Leah's ribs, her arms, her hands. The deep gashes along her back. And worst of all—the vicious, jagged wound across her forehead, still seeping faintly, even after all the pressure, stitches, and poultices he could apply.

It had taken over an hour, an excruciating, relentless hour, just to clean the blood and dirt from her skin. Another to treat, stitch, and bandage every torn, bruised, or broken part of her. By the time they finished, Riley Carter's face was damp with sweat. Some from effort. Most from fury. Her head injury was the worst, bleeding, severe, dangerously close to fracturing the skull beneath. She had lost far too much blood. Her pulse was thready. Her breathing shallow. She was young. Strong. A fighter. But even fighters had limits.

Esther brushed back a stray lock of Leah's hair, her voice soft with compassion.

"She's safe now."

Riley exhaled shakily. Safe. For the moment. But the rage burning in his chest promised one thing: Whoever did this would answer for it.

Nurse Esther had just begun cleaning the instruments, quietly dropping bloody cloths into a basin and setting used tools in a pan of steaming water, when a faint sound made her pause. A breath. A soft groan.

"Dr. Carter..."

Riley spun around instantly at the note of alarm in Esther's voice. Leah's eyelids fluttered, her face pale and drawn beneath the lamplight. He was by her side in a heartbeat.

"Leah," he said gently, scanning her face, her pulse, the rise and fall of her chest. "How are you feeling?"

She let out a weak, humorless chuckle. "Like I was pushed down a mountain."

Esther cracked a brief, relieved smile, and Riley huffed a quiet laugh through his nose.

"Well," he said dryly, "that would be because you were. And you're lucky they found you when they did. Your body was starting to go into shock by the time they carried you in. With the injuries you've suffered..." He shook his head. "It'll be a miracle if none of those wounds get infected."

Leah swallowed, her throat tight, then looked straight into his eyes.

"Who found me?"

Riley hesitated, not because he meant to hide anything, but because he saw the storm already building behind her gaze.

"Jaxon," he said quietly. "Your father... Cash... and David Smith."

Her entire body went rigid. Even the muscles in her jaw clenched, her eyes darkening with a familiar, raw hurt. Riley sighed inwardly. He had expected that reaction—and dreaded it.

"They would like to see you," he continued cautiously. "They want to explain—"

"No." The word was sharp, immediate.

"Leah—"

"I don't want to see anyone," she whispered, but the pain beneath it was unmistakable. "Not right now."

"They're all waiting out front," he said gently. "Worried sick."

She turned her face away from him, eyes burning, voice cracking.

"Tell them to leave me alone." She swallowed hard, her breath trembling. "I've heard enough lies to last me a lifetime."

The room went silent, except for the soft clatter of Nurse Esther setting down another instrument, and the distant murmur of men waiting anxiously in the hall.

Riley Carter's gaze flicked toward the door, the crack of light beneath it, the shadow of someone lingering just outside. Leah noticed it too. Before she could demand that everyone stay out, a knock sounded. And then Cash stepped into the room. Her stomach twisted. She turned her face away instantly, but she could still feel his eyes on her, heavy, aching, full of remorse.

"Leah," Cash said softly, his voice rough. "I'm so sorry you had to go through so much this year."

She didn't even let him finish. "Don't pretend you care now," she snapped, glaring at the wall instead of at him. "You've been nothing but a liar."

Cash flinched as if she'd slapped him. Before he could answer, another voice came from the doorway, one she knew too well.

"Leah," her father said as he stepped inside, his expression weighted with pain. "Please... please let us explain. You need to listen—"

"No!" The word tore from her with raw force. "I won't listen to anything anymore." Her voice trembled, but she pushed on, fury and heartbreak pouring out of her in waves. "This entire year has been nothing but one nightmare after another. I was thrown from one hell to the next, and all because of you... and those criminals. None of you stopped for even a moment to think about how I might feel." She swallowed a sob. "You all just thought, 'She's Leah, she can handle it.' Well, I can't. Not anymore." She pressed a shaking hand to her eyes, tears spilling through her fingers.

"I'm tired. I'm exhausted. And I'm so hurt I can't even think straight." Her voice cracked into a painful whisper. "I never thought the men I love most could betray me like this. Not in such awful, unforgivable ways." Her breath hitched. "My heart has been shattered into so many pieces... I don't think it can ever be mended."

She finally broke, sobs wracking her bruised and bandaged body. Cash took a step toward her. Her father did the same, reaching out instinctively. But Leah jerked back, shaking her head fiercely.

"No," she gasped. "Don't. Don't touch me."

They froze.

"Get out," she whispered. Then louder, broken and pleading: "Just... get out. I want to be left alone."

Riley didn't have to say a word. Cash and Mitch exchanged a devastated look, then quietly backed out of the room, closing the door with the softest click, leaving their daughter and friend to weep in the dim, lamplit silence.

Dr. Carter stepped out behind them and eased the door shut, firm enough to grant Leah privacy, gentle enough not to echo through the clinic. The moment the latch clicked, Jaxon and David moved toward him in a rush.

"How is she?" Jaxon asked, breath tight with worry. "Were you able to take care of her injuries?"

Riley nodded. "Physically, yes. She's bandaged, stitched, and stable for now. But she's going to be in a tremendous amount of pain for days." He exhaled and turned toward Mitch and Cash, who both looked like men bracing for judgment they feared they deserved.

"Listen to me," Riley began, lowering his voice. "I may not know every detail, but McKay and Wilson filled me in on enough."

The two older men stiffened, guilt written in every strained line of their faces.

"I understand why you want to talk to her," Riley continued, "why you want to explain yourselves. But you must give her time." He paused, searching their expressions to be sure the message landed. "She was severely injured tonight. Her body is in shock, she's lost blood, she's exhausted, and on top of all that, she's reeling from a lifetime of lies unraveling in a single day. She can't absorb anything right now. If you push her, she's only going to break further."

Mitch's jaw clenched. Cash looked at the floor.

"You all know how she is," the doctor said, softening just a little. "Leah forgives easily, more easily than most people I've ever met. But this?" He shook his head. "This betrayal cuts too deep, even for her." He let the silence settle before he went on: "Try again tomorrow morning. Let her sleep. Let her breathe. Let her come to terms with the fact that her father is alive... and that Patricia isn't her mother. Let her process the pain without all of you standing over her, waiting for absolution."

David swallowed hard. Jaxon looked toward the closed door as if listening for a cry.

"Nurse Esther and I will be with her all night," Riley reassured them. "If she wakes, if she needs someone, if she wants to talk, she won't be alone. But right now, she needs space more than anything."

None of the men moved. Not at first. They stood like pillars cracked at the foundations, torn between wanting to rush back inside and knowing they would only make things worse. Finally, with reluctant nods and eyes heavy with regret, they accepted the truth in Riley's words. And they stepped back, each man carrying the weight of guilt, fear, and hope that morning might bring even the smallest chance of redemption.

"How was the night?" Mitch asked the moment he stepped into the clinic, his voice tight, as if bracing for a blow. Dr. Carter set down the chart he'd been holding. His expression told them everything before he even spoke.

"Leah is still very, very hurt," Riley said quietly. "You can try approaching her, but don't push. She didn't want to talk to us, not even Nurse Esther, and she's still in a tremendous amount of pain. She might not want to talk to you at all yet."

Mitch looked from Riley to the men beside him, desperation creeping into every line of his face.

"Isn't there a way for us to make her listen? Even a little? I just want her to understand—"

"No." Cash's answer came first—firm, steady, leaving no room for debate. He stepped closer, placing a grounding hand on Mitch's arm.

"It won't be easy," Cash went on quietly. "Mitch... everything we kept from her, for years, and everything she's endured these last few months... it all hit her yesterday at once. Her entire world collapsed and burned right in front of her." He paused, letting the truth sink in.

"You showing up alive," Cash continued, his voice low, "was the very tip of the iceberg. The final shock she wasn't prepared for. After she overheard Milton and Patricia talking, I thought about telling her you were still alive, but she was already so upset, so raw... it would've pushed her over the edge.

I even thought maybe she'd be so happy to see you that it would outweigh everything else, but... I was wrong."

Mitch swallowed hard, emotion rising in his throat. Guilt, fear, helplessness, everything he'd been holding in, flickered across his eyes. Cash softened his tone.

"Let Jaxon and me handle this for now. She's angry. She's hurt. And she deserves to let that anger land on us, not on you." He squeezed Mitch's arm gently. "Give her time to breathe. Time to feel. Time to come back to you on her own."

Jaxon nodded in agreement, his jaw tight with determination.

"We'll try to talk to her," Cash said. "As much as she'll let us. We'll explain everything, piece by piece, until she's calm enough to think instead of just feel." He offered Mitch a small, reassuring smile. "And when she's ready, truly ready, she'll give you that hug she's been longing to give since the day she thought she lost you."

Mitch nodded slowly, but the effort it took him was visible. Every part of him wanted to run down the hall, sweep his daughter into his arms, and beg for forgiveness. But he stayed where he was, shoulders slumped, heart aching, trusting his oldest friends to help mend what he feared he had broken.

Nurse Esther had just brought Leah a warm, carefully prepared breakfast, but Leah refused even to touch it. Esther tried gently, urging her to take at least a few bites, but Leah only shook her head. Her stomach was twisted in knots. She couldn't force down a single crumb. She watched the nurse leave through the side door and exhaled shakily. She longed for solitude. For silence. For a moment when no one expected anything from her. No more explanations. No more revelations tearing her heart apart.

The sudden knock at the door made every muscle in her body tense. She had agonized over everything through the long hours of the night, pain, confusion, betrayal, and she still had no idea how to process any of it. Why couldn't they leave her alone? Why did they keep reopening wounds that hadn't even begun to heal? She pushed herself upright.

"Go away. Just leave me alone."

But the door opened anyway. Leah instinctively tried to leap from the bed, driven by panic and exhaustion, but her battered body couldn't handle sudden movement. She collapsed, her vision blurring, and Jaxon lunged forward, catching her before she hit the floor. She lost consciousness only for a heartbeat, but waking up in Jaxon's arms made her heart stutter painfully. Then her gaze drifted to Cash, her fatherly friend, her protector, and the anger that had been simmering inside her erupted again. She tried to pull away, but Jaxon held her firmly, not in restraint, but in grounding.

"Leah," he murmured, tightening his hold just enough to steady her. "Give Cash a chance to explain. We know you're hurting beyond anything right now, but you need to let them apologize. You deserve answers."

She looked up at him, at his soft, pleading expression, and something inside her wavered. His gentle smile, the warmth in his eyes, and the light brush of his lips against hers, softened her tension for a brief, fragile moment. When he pulled back, he lifted her onto the bed with great care, keeping one strong arm wrapped around her waist as if shielding her from the whole world. His muscles coiled protectively, and she found herself leaning into him despite herself.

Jaxon nodded at Cash. Cash inhaled deeply, guilt etched into every line of his face.

"Please believe me, we never intended to hurt you or break your heart. You're right. We didn't think... not about how this would crush you." His voice cracked. "Our focus was on the Rowlands, on getting justice for Lilian. We weren't thinking clearly. We didn't think about you the way we should have."

Leah stiffened at the mention of her mother, and Jaxon felt it. He glanced at Cash.

"Why was Mitch gone for nearly a year?" Jaxon asked quietly. "Just to get to the Rowlands?"

Hearing her father's name shattered whatever fragile strength Leah had left. Tears pricked her eyes again, and she buried her face against Jaxon's shirt, seeking refuge from the truth, from the ache. She couldn't look at Cash.

He sighed heavily. "When David found out Milton and Jack were being released after nine years in prison, we had to act fast. David was convinced they would kill Mitch the moment they got the chance, maybe even convince Patricia to do it for them. And then he learned Heber had been hired to finish the job."

Leah trembled.

"So, we planned the fake stagecoach accident," Cash went on. "We made Mitch disappear. It was never supposed to be for so long. But the Rowlands took their time. They acted like they weren't in any rush to finish what they'd tried to start years ago. We had no choice but to wait."

Jaxon held her a little tighter.

"We suspected Mildred was tied into all of it," Cash continued. "David wanted her, and Patricia, to feel safe enough to make a mistake. When it became clear they weren't moving, we asked Scott to play along and pretend he wanted to marry Patricia. It opened doors. Made them careless."

Leah finally lifted her face, though she didn't push away from Jaxon.

"Where was Dad all that time?"

"He stayed with David in Sacramento."

"He wasn't there when I visited the Smiths," she whispered.

"No," Cash said gently. "During that time, he lived in a hotel. He stayed in touch with us, making sure everything was going well and you were safe. It nearly broke him to leave you behind, Leah, but he chose pretending to be dead over actually being dead. And when you were kidnapped... Mitch nearly came undone. He wanted to rush back home. He almost rode with David the day we found you. But he had to stay behind in Eureka. We couldn't risk the Rowlands spotting him."

Her tears finally spilled, and Cash leaned forward, pulling her into his arms despite her initial hesitation. He kissed the top of her head like he had done since she was a little girl.

"We all love you, Leah," he whispered fiercely. "Everything we did, every lie, was meant to protect you and end this for good."

She lifted her gaze to his, her eyes shimmering.

"Do you know how my real mom died?"

He nodded. "Lilian went into your room after your nap... and found rattlesnakes surrounding your crib."

Leah choked on a sob. "Just like Colt," she breathed. "That was Heber's doing."

Cash nodded solemnly and continued, his voice faintly trembling.

"She must've known she couldn't save herself, but she could save you. I believe she grabbed you the moment she saw the danger, ran toward the door... but the snakes were already striking. Lilian pushed you through the doorway and slammed the door shut behind you, blocking it with her own body so the snakes couldn't escape. She trapped them inside... with her."

Leah broke. Cash wrapped her tightly against him.

"Mitch and I found you crying outside the door," he whispered. "I've never seen your father more horrified, more broken, than the moment he realized... she sacrificed herself to keep you alive." He swallowed hard, and Leah's arms curled around him in raw instinct, comforting him even through her pain. When he steadied himself, he lifted her chin so she would look at him.

"We knew it wasn't an accident. But it took years to uncover Patricia, her husband, her father-in-law... and Heber. When we realized the danger wasn't over, your father agreed to disappear until the Rowlands were dealt with once and for all."

Silence filled the room, heavy, aching. Jaxon gently pulled Leah back into his arms.

"Are you ready," he asked softly, "to welcome your father home?"

Leah looked from him... to Cash... to the doorway. Then she nodded. Jaxon took her hand, grounding her.

Cash stepped to the door and called softly, "Mitchell. David. She's ready to see you now."

27
The Hug She Dreamed Of

Leah instinctively leaned back and hid behind Jaxon's shoulder, needing the shield of his presence, just enough space to gather herself, to steady her racing heart. Jaxon felt her tremble and subtly shifted closer, pulling her gently into his arms, giving her both protection and room to choose.

David and Mitch approached slowly, as if afraid to startle her. Mitch's eyes never left her face, not for a single heartbeat. Every step he took toward her carried a mixture of awe, regret, love, and longing so profoundly it nearly knocked the breath from her lungs. Jaxon released his hold on her, stepped aside, gently letting her decide the moment for herself.

Leah lifted her gaze to her father, unsure, overwhelmed, but yearning, and in an instant Mitch crossed the last distance between them. He gathered her into his arms with a fierce, trembling tenderness, lifting her slightly off the bed as if anchoring her to him so she would never slip away again.

The moment Leah felt his strength, his warmth, his familiar scent, the last wall inside her crumbled. A broken sob tore from her, then another, and she buried her face against his shoulder. Years of loss, months of fear, days of betrayal, all of it rushed out in waves she could no longer hold back. Mitch held her tightly, one hand cradling the back of her head, the other locked around her waist.

"I've got you, sweetheart," he whispered into her hair, voice thick with emotion. "I've got you. Let it out."

She clung to him, gripping his shirt with trembling fingers as though afraid he might vanish again. He didn't move, didn't loosen his hold, simply let her cry, finally, freely. Only when her sobs quieted into soft hiccups did he ease his embrace, lowering her gently back onto the clinic bed. His hands framed her face as he lifted her chin. His thumb traced soothing circles over her cheek, brushing away the last of her tears. Leah gave him a small, beaming, wobbly smile, fragile but real.

Mitch's breath hitched, emotion tightening his throat, though he mastered himself quickly.

"I'm so sorry, Leah," he said softly. "For everything we put you through this year. But I never stopped thinking about you. Not for a single day. I love you more than I can ever say." He glanced at David and Cash. "We all do."

David stepped forward and wrapped Leah in a gentle, paternal embrace. His arms were warm, steady, apologetic.

"You're my goddaughter, sweetheart," he murmured. "I'd give my life for you. Please don't ever doubt that."

Leah's heart swelled and ached all at once. She knew healing wouldn't come in a day. Trust needed to grow back slowly, carefully. But being back in her father's arms... it felt like breathing properly for the first time in months.

When she finally lifted her eyes, they drifted to Jaxon. He stood a few steps back, giving her space, but the look on his face, raw, gentle, overflowing with love, sent her heart into wild, dizzy flutters. Her breath caught. She remembered the way he had held her earlier... the way his arms had steadied her, sheltered her, loved her. And for the first time, she could not fathom why she had ever fought her feelings for him at all.

Riley Carter checked Leah's wounds one more time, his brows drawn tight with concern.

"You really should stay another night," he said gently. "Your body needs rest, Leah. No riding, no walking long distances, no heavy work. Promise me."

"I promise," she murmured, though exhaustion alone made her long for her own bed more than the cot in his clinic. He sighed but didn't argue further. "I'll come by tomorrow to make sure you're healing properly."

When they stepped through the front door of the ranch house, Ruby froze mid-step—torn between the instinct to pull Leah into her arms and the sheer horror of what had been done to her. Then her eyes widened, shimmering like fireworks against the night sky, as Mitch Johnson, very much alive, walked in behind Leah.

"Mitch?" she whispered before her face turned crimson. He wrapped her in a warm, grateful hug, and Ruby nearly sagged with shock and relief.

After supper, Leah settled into the sitting room with Cash and her father. The house felt different tonight, warmer, safer, finally complete again. When Mitch patted the seat beside him, she hesitated only a moment before sitting. His arm came around her shoulders, steady and familiar. After a heartbeat of uncertainty, she let herself snuggle against his chest. Cash watched them with a soft, satisfied smile, his best friend home, his goddaughter safe, the family whole again.

Once Leah relaxed, Mitch gently cleared his throat.

"So," he said, a teasing glint in his eyes, "you and Jaxon, huh? I can't pretend I'm surprised. I've seen that coming for a long, long time."

Heat rushed into Leah's face so fast she thought she might spontaneously combust. Everyone else had seen it... except her. Or maybe she'd been fighting it too hard to notice. Mitch tipped her chin up, making her meet his eyes.

"You love him, don't you?"

Leah swallowed and nodded. "It took me a long time to accept it. I've always been afraid of ruining our friendship. And even now... the fear's still there."

Cash leaned forward a bit. "What are you still worried about, Leah?"

She shrugged helplessly. "I guess... I'm scared he'll regret never courting anyone else. Or that he'll realize he wasn't in love with me, just the idea of me. And then..." Her voice broke just a little. "Then I'd lose him entirely."

Mitch and Cash exchanged a look, one part amusement, one part disbelief, before chuckling softly.

"Leah," Mitch said, smiling wide enough to crease the corners of his eyes, "that boy has never looked at another girl the way he looks at you. Jaxon loves you with a fierceness I've only seen a handful of times in my life. He'd move mountains for you. And if it came to it..." Mitch chuckled. "He'd kill for you."

Leah groaned softly. "But what if I'm too much for him? He has complained about my stubbornness before. Maybe someone less... me would be better for him."

This time both men burst out laughing.

"No way," Cash said, shaking his head. "He loves all of you. Stubbornness included. You two grew up, side by side. If he had a problem with your hardheadedness, he'd have run for the hills years ago."

Mitch nodded. "Instead, he kept coming back."

Cash added with a grin, "And I'll tell you something else: Jaxon knows exactly what he's signing up for. He wants the spitfire. He wants to marry... you."

Leah sputtered. "Marriage? Okay, let's not get carried away. We only just started courting. It'll probably be ages before—"

Cash snorted. "That boy has been waiting years for you to open your eyes. Now that you have?" He winked. "He's not going to be dragging his feet."

Leah hid her burning face against her father's chest, mortified and secretly, deeply thrilled. Knowing Jaxon, Cash was probably right. As Mitch and Cash drifted into easy conversation, two old friends reunited after too long, Leah let the sound of their voices wash over her. Safe. Familiar. Home. Her eyes fluttered closed, and it didn't take long before sleep claimed her at last.

Cash gave Mitch a small nod of reassurance, and Mitch returned it with a grateful smile. With infinite gentleness, he shifted Leah in his arms and rose to his feet, lifting her as though she were still the little girl he used to carry around the ranch. She curled instinctively against him, her head nestling against his chest. Mitch held her tighter, his jaw flexing with emotion as he felt the slight weight of her, alive, safe, home.

He carried her slowly up the stairs and down the hall to her bedroom, careful not to jostle her injuries, his steps soft but sure. When he reached her room, he nudged the door open with his shoulder and crossed to her bed.

Tenderly, he lowered her onto the mattress, easing her down as though she were made of porcelain. He pulled the quilt up around her shoulders, tucking it beneath her chin with the same familiar care she hadn't felt since childhood.

Leah blinked drowsily, her lashes fluttering, and for a brief second, she looked up at him, her eyes soft, fragile, and filled with aching love.

Mitch leaned down and pressed a lingering kiss to her forehead, his hand brushing her cheek as he whispered, "Rest, sweetheart."

Her eyes drifted closed, exhaustion finally overtaking her battered body. But right before sleep claimed her, her lips parted in a faint, breathy whisper.

"I love you, Dad."

Mitch's breath caught. He cupped her cheek, his voice trembling as he murmured back, "I love you too, my angel. More than anything." He stayed there a moment longer, watching her breathing even out, the tension easing from her features, finally, finally at peace.

Robyn couldn't help the soft giggle that escaped her when Leah finished talking. She had known for years, long before either of them would admit it, that her best friend and her brother belonged together. Watching Leah finally overcome her fear of losing a friendship and instead gain a man who cherished her with his whole heart filled Robyn with nothing but joy.

The two young women were nestled in the hayloft, legs dangling over the edge, the scent of hay and warm wood surrounding them like an old, familiar blanket. It felt like stepping back in time, back to the days before Milton and Jack had ever cast their shadows over the ranch.

Much had changed since then. Chad had proposed to Robyn, and she hadn't even let him finish the sentence before saying yes. They planned to celebrate Thanksgiving and Christmas in Hoopa Valley with everyone they loved, then move to Sacramento so Chad could begin work with his father as an attorney. Robyn was glowing with excitement, and Leah couldn't be happier for her.

"Do you think Cash will propose to your mom before the year is over?" Leah asked, twirling a piece of hay between her fingers. Robyn shrugged, though her eyes sparkled.

"Who knows? But I can absolutely see that happening soon." She nudged Leah with her shoulder. "How are your dad and Ruby getting on?"

"They're taking things slow," Leah replied. "Ruby is definitely more than ready to marry my dad, she's been patient with him for years, but he's still working through everything with Patricia. He wants to make sure he's doing the right thing."

"I still can't fathom how Patricia got away with all those fake marriages," Robyn said with a disgusted shake of her head. "You'd think someone, anyone, would have noticed something sooner."

Leah nodded. "Dad made sure their marriage was annulled immediately. They didn't even have to go through a divorce, since technically she should never have been allowed to marry him in the first place."

Robyn kicked her heels lightly in the hay.

"And what about you and Jaxon?"

"What about us?" Leah asked, turning to her with a furrowed brow.

"You know... future plans. Marriage. Where you'll live. All that."

Leah's cheeks burned bright red. "Robyn..." She looked around as though making sure Jaxon wasn't hiding behind a hay bale. "Nothing like that is happening anytime soon."

"I know my brother," Robyn said, smirking. "He'll want to secure you the second he thinks you might slip away. Have you two talked about where you want to live?"

"No!" Leah squeaked, then cleared her throat quickly. "I mean... no. He hasn't even proposed yet. So no, we haven't discussed any of that."

"But don't you already have ideas?" Robyn pressed, grin widening. "Are you still hoping to live in that little house down the creek?"

"The homestead from my grandparents?"

Robyn nodded eagerly.

Leah softened. "I *would* love that. But it would need to be completely renovated. Nobody's lived there in years. I can't ask Jaxon to do all that work."

"You know he'd do anything for you," Robyn said gently.

"I know," Leah admitted, fiddling with her sleeves. "But it would take so much time and money to bring it back to life. Maybe someday we could turn it into a cabin or something, but... I don't know. It might not be worth it."

"It would be perfect for newlyweds," Robyn teased.

Leah groaned, hiding her face in her hands.

"Can we please talk about something else before I spontaneously combust?"

Robyn giggled, then paused when she heard footsteps below. Someone entered the barn. A moment later the ladder creaked, and Jaxon climbed into the hayloft. The instant his eyes landed on Leah, his entire face lit up, bright, warm, unmistakable. Robyn watched the way her best friend blushed, pink flooding her cheeks, and felt her heart squeezing with happiness. Leah Johnson, bold, confident, fearless Leah, reduced to an adorably bashful mess simply because her man had walked into the room. Robyn hid her grin behind her hand.

Oh yes, she thought. *These two never stood a chance.*

"Robyn," Jaxon said, though his gaze never once left Leah's face. His voice was warm, distracted, almost amused by how clearly smitten she was. "Chad is looking for you. He said you two were supposed to meet David and pick up Brooke from the stagecoach."

Robyn's eyes widened. "Oh, dang it—that's right!" She scrambled to her feet so quickly she nearly kicked hay into Jaxon's boots. "See you later, Leah!" she called over her shoulder, flashing a knowing grin that made Leah's cheeks turn an even deeper shade of pink.

Robyn hurried to the ladder, climbed down with practiced ease, and a heartbeat later her footsteps faded toward the barn doors, leaving Leah alone in the hayloft with Jaxon, his warm gaze, and the sudden, breathless flutter in her chest.

Jaxon crossed the loft in a few long, purposeful strides, his eyes locked on Leah as if she were the only thing in the world worth looking at. Before she could even catch her breath, he took her hands, tugged her gently to her feet, and gave her a smile so warm and devastating her pulse tripped over itself.

"Hi," he murmured, soft, teasing, far too confident for her fluttering heart. Leah barely had time to form a thought before he slid an arm around her waist, drew her flush against him, and lowered his head. His lips found hers in a kiss that stole every ounce of air she possessed.

28
Will You Marry Me, Leah Johnson?

Heat shot through her, dizzying and sweet, and her knees nearly gave way. Luckily, Jaxon's arms wrapped around her, strong, sure, holding her as if she were the most precious thing he'd ever touched. He smelled like pine, warm leather, and something uniquely him, something that made her toes curl in her boots. The kiss deepened, slow and unhurried, the kind that made the world tilt and vanish. Leah clung to his shirt, feeling his heartbeat pounding against hers, and let herself melt into him.

He was just sliding a hand along her back, sending a shiver racing straight down her spine, when a thunderous voice exploded through the barn.

"Who's up there?" Cash roared. "I thought I told you to clean out the stables!"

Leah jerked back, breathless, cheeks flaming. Jaxon didn't move an inch. He just grinned, wide, wicked, and not even remotely sorry, before leaning in to steal one last quick kiss from her stunned, crimson lips.

"Well," he whispered, "looks like we've been caught."

Jaxon shot Leah a wicked little wink, lifted a finger to his lips in a *don't-you-dare-say-a-word* gesture, then sauntered toward the loft's edge as if he were the picture of innocence. He leaned over the railing, arms casually folded, and flashed Cash a grin far too big to be trustworthy.

"What's the matter, Cash?" he drawled. "Lose something? Or someone?"

Cash's eyes narrowed immediately.

"What are you doing up there, Jaxon?"

Before he could answer, Mitch wandered up beside Cash, folding his own arms as he looked between the two with barely concealed amusement. Cash, however, remained as stern as a preacher on Sunday.

Jaxon shrugged, all ease. "Does it matter? It's just a hayloft. Not much trouble a man can get into up here."

"Oh, it matters," Cash fired back. "It matters a whole lot if you're sneaking around with your pretty girlfriend."

Leah, hidden safely out of sight, covered her face with both hands, wishing she could disappear into the hay. Jaxon's grin only widened.

"Sneaking around?" he repeated, sounding highly offended. "Cash, that makes it sound like I'm doing something improper." He pressed a hand dramatically to his heart. "Surely you're not implying the woman I love would ever let me do anything questionable."

Cash and Mitch exchanged a look, then cracked identical, knowing grins.

"Boy," Cash said, shaking his head, "I think that depends entirely on how fast you climb down from that loft."

Jaxon laughed and glanced over his shoulder at Leah with a dangerous glint that made her pulse skitter.

"Leah," Cash called up a moment later. Her heart jolted so hard she wondered if the rafters shook with it.

Absolutely not, she thought. *There is no way I'm poking my head over that edge looking like a tomato fresh off the vine.* She cleared her throat, forcing her voice to sound steady.

"What is it, Cash?"

"I'd like to speak to you," he replied. "Face to face."

"Well, I don't want to speak to you right now," she fired back, rolling her eyes so hard she was surprised Jaxon didn't hear it. "Why are you wandering around bothering people? Robyn and I come up here to talk, you know."

Below, Mitch chuckled, and Cash muttered something that sounded suspiciously like, *"Heaven help that boy..."*

Jaxon smirked and whispered softly, "You're adorable when you panic."

Leah shot him a murderous glare, her face burning all over again.

"So, Robyn is up there with you?" Cash called loudly, winking at Mitch as though they shared a secret. Even Jaxon bit back a grin, clearly enjoying himself at Leah's expense. Silence. A long, suspicious silence. Finally, Leah's voice floated down, tight, clipped, and far too high-pitched to be innocent.

"No."

Cash's brows shot up. "So... you and Jaxon are *all alone* up there?"

There was a thump, a shuffle, and the violent rustling of hay, as if someone had just kicked an entire bale in sheer indignation. A moment later, Leah appeared at the edge of the loft, her face blazing scarlet. Her eyes, however, were pure molten fury.

"You know what, Cash?" she snapped, her voice trembling, not with fear, but with the effort of not yelling. "I am a grown woman. I do not have to explain myself to you. If you don't trust me enough to be alone with Jaxon, that sounds like *your* personal problem. And I find it extremely sad that you'd judge me so harshly and accuse me of things I would never do."

She folded her arms across her chest and leveled him with the most wounded, wide-eyed glare imaginable, dramatic enough to win an award. Her bottom lip even pushed out in a slight pout. Mitch turned away, pretending to cough, but his shaking shoulders betrayed him. He was laughing. Cash crossed his arms and let out a slow, deliberate breath.

"I see you're using womanly tactics now, trying to make me feel guilty just for looking out for you." He raised a brow. "Impressive effort, though."

"Ha!" Leah huffed. "Don't flatter yourself. You are *not* looking out for me. You have an obsession with knowing exactly what I'm doing every second of the day. Are you planning to keep that up even when I'm married?" The words slipped out before she realized what she'd said. Her eyes widened.

Jaxon's grin stretched into something downright smug. Cash froze, only for a second.

"*Married?*" Cash barked. "Dang it, Leah, why didn't you tell us Jaxon already proposed?" He threw his hands up dramatically. "That's something worth celebrating!"

"Cash—" Leah tried to break in, her face blazing so hot she was sure the entire barn could feel it. But Cash, thoroughly delighted, turned toward the house, clearly ready to shout the news to every soul within forty miles.

Oh no he didn't. Leah scrambled down the ladder so fast she nearly missed the last rung and lunged for his arm, grabbing it with both hands.

"Don't you *dare*! Cash, I swear—"

She didn't get another word out. Cash spun, scooped her up like she weighed nothing, and tossed her over his shoulder.

"What are you doing!?" she shrieked, pounding at his back, though it didn't make the slightest difference. Cash was built like the barn itself.

"I want to make sure," Cash announced loudly, "that you can't hide, sprint off, or jump in the creek when I share this wonderful news with everyone!"

"CASH!" Leah kicked helplessly, her entire world upside down, literally and emotionally. "Put me down!"

He didn't even wobble. He was enjoying this enormously. Luckily for her dignity, Jaxon finally took pity. He came down the ladder in three long steps, strode over, and peeled Leah off Cash's shoulder like he'd been rescuing damsels his whole life. The moment her feet hit the ground, he pulled her straight into his arms. He held her tight, steadying her with a low chuckle rumbling in his chest. Cash turned around with the grin of a man who had just accomplished a great deed.

"You're welcome," he declared. Leah glared up at him, cheeks nearly incandescent.

"You are *truly* mean sometimes." Her lips formed the most dramatic pout known to mankind. Cash put a hand over his heart.

"I'm just teasing you."

"There is teasing," she corrected sharply, "and then there's public humiliation disguised as teasing."

Jaxon's lips twitched. He took her hand gently, brushing his thumb over her knuckles in a way that sent a warm shiver down her spine.

"Come on," he murmured. "Let's go for a walk before Cash decides to parade you through the entire valley."

She nodded, still glaring at Cash for good measure as she let Jaxon guide her toward the back of the ranch house.

They had barely reached the side of the house when Cash's voice boomed across the yard, echoing off the barn walls: "JAXON CAN'T PROPOSE UNTIL HE TALKS TO YOUR FATHER!"

A cluster of cowboys burst into laughter, some tipping their hats, others outright hooting. Leah spun around, ready to unleash a fiery comeback powerful enough to send Cash straight into repentance, but she never got the chance. Jaxon caught her by the waist, pulled her flush against him, and *kissed her*. Just kissed her. Deep. Slow. Confident.

Her gasp melted into his mouth. Her fingers curled into his shirt as her knees nearly gave out. Butterflies erupted in her stomach, fluttering wildly. The world dissolved until nothing existed except Jaxon, his breath, his warmth, his lips claiming hers with sure, breath-stealing certainty.

When he finally drew back, he whispered against her lips, "Ignore him."

Her heart pounded so hard she was sure he could feel it. She rested her forehead against his chest, breathless. She'd never known love could feel like this, fire and comfort, passion and peace. Jaxon had always been her friend... but now? Now her heart was his. Completely. Forever.

"I have a surprise for you," Jaxon whispered, brushing a loose curl from her cheek. "Would you join me on a buggy ride?"

Leah's breath caught. His smile, the one that made her whole chest warm like a sunrise, was impossible to resist. She nodded, heart fluttering. It was the afternoon before Thanksgiving, and the air had turned crisp, sharp enough to nip her nose. Jaxon had clearly prepared: thick fur covers warmed the buggy seat, and he wrapped a woolen blanket snugly around her before climbing in beside her. His body radiated heat, and she instinctively leaned closer.

"I need to blindfold you," he said.

She recoiled slightly. "Why?"

"Because," he murmured, eyes twinkling like he held all the mysteries of the universe, "this is a very special surprise."

Leah raised a skeptical brow. He answered with a slow, heart-melting grin.

"Do you trust me?" he asked softly. His warm brown eyes held hers, steady, earnest, breathtaking. She hesitated only a second before nodding. He wrapped a long scarf gently around her eyes, careful not to tug her hair, then tucked her close beneath his arm.

The buggy jolted forward. As they rode, she snuggled into his side, feeling the heat of his body, the steady rhythm of his breathing, the light brush of his thumb over her arm. She could have stayed like that forever.

Soon the buggy stopped. She felt his arms slip around her as he lifted her easily out of the seat.

"Jaxon—!" she gasped, half startled, half laughing.

"Trust me," he murmured, carrying her up a few steps. A door creaked open. Their footsteps echoed softly inside. He set her down gently. She reached for the blindfold, but he caught her hand.

"Not yet," he teased. "Be patient."

She let out a dramatic sigh, earning a soft chuckle from him. She listened: his boots moving, a blanket being spread, a door opening then closing, his steps returning. Then, warm hands cupped her face. A breath. And then his lips found hers in a deep, breath-stealing kiss that made her knees go molten. As she melted against him, he untied the scarf and let it fall. She blinked, and gasped.

They stood inside a beautifully restored room with polished wooden floors and a stone hearth where a fire crackled merrily. Flickering firelight bathed everything in gold. Before the hearth, Jaxon had placed a thick blanket, fur covers, and a picnic basket filled with unknown wonders.

Leah turned to him, heart thudding. "I had no idea you could be so romantic."

He grinned, hands sliding around her waist.

"Well, when I was just your friend, I didn't have to romance you. But now..." He pulled her closer, so close she could feel his heart beating beneath her palms. "Now everything's different."

His warm brown eyes held hers, and the world fell away. Only when she finally tore her gaze around the room again did recognition strike.

She inhaled sharply. "You... renovated my grandparents' homestead?"

He nodded proudly. "Not just me. Your father, Cash, half the cowboys. Everyone helped when they could."

Her jaw dropped. "How did you even know about this place?"

A faint blush crept up his neck. "I listened to more of the conversations you and Robyn had as teenagers than I'll ever admit."

"You remembered?" she whispered.

"Every word."

Emotion surged through her. Leah threw her arms around his neck and gave him a quick, breathless kiss. It wasn't enough for him. His arms tightened, pulling her flush against him as he kissed her back, deeper, warmer, more boldly. Fire raced through her. Finally, she had kissed him first, and Jaxon responded like he'd been waiting years for this moment. When his lips grew insistently passionate, she tore back, pressing her hand firmly over his mouth, breathless.

"Stop," she gasped. "You're taking my breath away, and we're alone."

"But we're just kissing," he murmured against her fingers.

"Dad always said kissing can lead to... more," she stammered. "And we do *not* want to go there."

His brows knitted adorably. "Go where?"

Leah nearly combusted. Her cheeks turned volcanic. She opened her mouth, nothing came out. He watched her flounder for a beat before grinning like the devil.

"Oh. *There.*"

"Jaxon!"

He stole a quick kiss, then rested his forehead against hers. His voice dropped into a warm, tender murmur.

"I'm teasing you. And you're right, we wait until after we're married."

Relief, and butterflies, washed over her.

"Now," he said, excitement flickering in his eyes, "there's something you need to see. Over there." He took her hand, guiding her across the room. When they reached the window, he placed his hands lightly on her hips, gently turning her into position. His warm grip sent a shiver racing up her spine. She looked out... and saw nothing unusual.

"What am I supposed to be looking at?"

He didn't answer.

"Jaxon?" she asked, turning, and froze.

He was on one knee. Her breath fled her. Her heart tripped, stumbled, then pounded with a force that stole her voice. Jaxon took her trembling hand, his expression open and overflowing with love.

"Leah Amelia Johnson," he began softly, "you have made me happier than I ever thought a man could be. You've captured my heart, completely, and I can't imagine my life without you. I want to share everything with you. Every sunrise. Every fight. Every kiss. Every dream. I will never let you go again. Will you marry me?"

Her throat closed. Tears brimmed. She swallowed hard—and nodded. Jaxon let out a breath that was half relief, half joy, and surged to his feet. He swept her into his arms and kissed her like a man claiming his future. Passion filled the room, the fire crackling behind them, warmth pulsing between them. He pulled back only when neither of them seemed capable of stopping.

"I love you, Leah," he whispered against her lips. She cupped his face with a trembling hand, eyes shining.

"And I love you."

Dark clouds had gathered thick and low over the mountains by the time Leah and Jaxon settled in front of the newly lit fireplace. The wind picked up, rattling the shutters and sending the trees outside swaying like restless shadows. The flames crackled warmly behind them, but the world beyond the windows was turning wild and stormy. Jaxon glanced outside, frowned, then jumped to his feet.

"I'd better get the horse into the barn behind the homestead. It isn't renovated yet, but it'll keep him dry enough. I think there are still some old blankets in there, too. Might come in handy if we get stuck for a while."

He was already halfway through the door when Leah called after him, voice raised above the howl of the wind,

"Make sure the blankets don't have any unwelcome creepy crawlers in them!"

Jaxon burst out laughing, the sound warm and deep, echoing off the bare walls. Leah grinned triumphantly, until his head poked back through the doorway, eyes sparkling with mischief.

"Oh, I will," he said. "And speaking of creepy crawlers, Wilson told me about the giant intruder at the cabin. He couldn't believe Miss Leah Johnson, the girl who throws punches at outlaws, was terrified of something the size of my thumbnail." He smirked. "He said it was refreshing to see you had girly moments, too."

"Girly moments?" Leah practically sputtered. "What do I look like to him, a man?"

Jaxon chuckled. "Of course not. You are very much not a man." His gaze dipped for a half-second, bold enough to make her blush, subtle enough to pretend innocence. "But you are fearless... for a girl. It's nice to see something that lets us pretend we're heroes now and then. I may or may not have used that weakness against you when we were younger. You know... to rescue you." A grin cracked across his face. "Or to make you jump into my arms."

Leah gasped. Her eyes widened, then narrowed dangerously.

"You did not."

Jaxon didn't answer. Didn't dare. He just grinned like a scoundrel, spun around, and sprinted into the rain before she could get off the blanket and wring his neck. His laughter drifted back to her through the doorway, carried on the wind.

Leah glared at the empty doorway, but a smile tugged at her lips anyway.

"Oh, he is going to pay for that," she muttered, but her heart was fluttering like it wanted to leap out of her chest and chase after him.

Since she knew he'd be gone several minutes, Leah took the opportunity to wander through the homestead. The small house was simple but charming: two cozy bedrooms, a tiny washroom, and one large open room that served as kitchen, dining area, and sitting space. Even stripped bare, the place felt warm. Hopeful. Full of promise. She traced her fingers along the window frame, imagining curtains. A rug. A rocking chair near the fireplace. A family gathered around a Christmas tree.

Our family, her heart whispered before she could stop it. The thought made her pulse jump. She hurried back to the front room the moment she heard the door bang open. Jaxon stumbled inside, dripping wet, shivering, covered in rain and hail. His hair clung to his forehead, and his shirt was plastered to his skin.

"Goodness, you're soaked," Leah gasped. "Let me get one of the blankets, it'll be warm from the fire." She rushed to grab one, but when she returned, Jaxon had already yanked his shirt off and tossed it aside. Leah froze mid-step. Heat exploded across her face, and she spun around so fast she nearly tripped.

"Jaxon!" she squeaked. "Couldn't you have waited until I was somewhere, anywhere, else?"

Behind her came the unmistakable sound of a grin in his voice.

"Why?"

"Because," she snapped through mortification, "it is not appropriate to show yourself... not fully dressed!"

"We'll be married soon," he said lightly.

Her head whipped toward him, instinctively, before she remembered he was half-naked and squeezed her eyes shut again.

"You did that on purpose, didn't you?" she accused, storming deeper into the room and away from him. "Why do you enjoy making me uncomfortable? I thought you and I agreed about what we should and shouldn't do before marriage. Am I the only one trying to hold the line? Because if so—"

Suddenly arms wrapped around her waist. She yelped. He'd moved silently despite being dripping wet and now pulled her gently back against him. Leah tried to wriggle away without looking at him, but he held her easily. He turned her around, but she kept her eyes squeezed shut.

"Why aren't you looking at me?" he murmured, amusement rich in his tone.

"Because I shouldn't."

"I'm dressed, Leah."

Her eyes flew open. And sure enough, he stood fully clothed, dry shirt, dry pants, giving her that infuriating grin that made her want to both strangle him and kiss him senseless.

"I, uh... had a change of clothes here," he admitted. "Left them from when I was working on the place."

The sheepish note only made her glare harder.

"We should go home," she insisted, flustered. "We shouldn't be here any longer." She made it two steps toward the door before he caught her hand and tugged her back into his arms with an effortless laugh.

"We can't go home. The storm is turning fierce. The rain's freezing, the wind's worse. The whole road's one big mud slide. We'd risk breaking a wheel... or a limb. Or the horse." He lowered his head, so their foreheads almost touched. "I'm afraid," he said softly, "we'll have to stay the night."

Her breath stalled. "Jaxon," she whispered urgently, "we can't. My father will be worried sick, and people might think—"

He cupped her face in both hands, his voice warm as late-summer honey.

"No one who knows you would ever question your character, Leah. You're pure. Kind. Good. Those who matter know that. And your father, he knows exactly where I took you today. He'll put two and two together when we don't return." His thumb brushed her cheek, steadying her even as her heart raced.

"You can trust me," he went on gently. "I won't push you. I won't cross a line. I want to wait just as much as you do. I love kissing you." He smirked. "And I love teasing you even more, but I want our first time to be after we're married. Properly. The way God wants it."

Leah's blush deepened, but this time her heart swelled with gratitude instead of mortification.

She flung her arms around his neck and pressed her face into his shoulder.

"Thank you, Jax," she whispered. "For being so wonderful... and understanding."

"And handsome?" he teased.

She giggled despite herself. "Yes. Very handsome."

He dipped his head and captured her lips with a warm, passionate kiss. Leah kissed him back—but pulled away breathlessly when the butterflies in her stomach became an entire stampede. They shared a radiant smile. Then Jaxon laced his fingers through hers and led her back toward the blankets by the fire, his thumb brushing her knuckles with quiet affection.

"Come on," he murmured. "Let's get warm."

And for the first time, Leah wasn't sure whether he meant the fire... or the way he looked at her.

Leah curled against him, her cheek finding the steady rise and fall of his chest as naturally as breathing. Within minutes, her body softened completely, surrendering to sleep in the safety of his arms. The firelight flickered across her peaceful face, and Jaxon felt something inside him settle, something that had been restless for years. He pressed a slow, reverent kiss to the top of her head. His arms tightened around her instinctively, protectively, as if he were holding the most precious thing God had ever placed in his keeping. And in truth, he believed he was. His heart felt whole. Full. Complete.

"Thank You," he whispered into her hair, his voice barely audible over the crackling fire. "Thank You for her." Gratitude swelled through him, deeper than words could touch. God had brought this girl, this brave, stubborn, tenderhearted girl, into his life, and Jaxon knew with unshakable certainty that his world would never be the same.

He brushed one more kiss against her temple, then rested his cheek lightly on her hair, holding her as the storm raged outside and peace wrapped itself around them both.

When Leah woke, the world was wrapped in darkness. The storm still howled outside, wind rattling the shutters and rain pelting the roof in relentless sheets. But inside the little homestead, everything was warm and still. She lay cocooned in blankets, the soft fur covers beneath her, another blanket tucked gently around her shoulders, and Jaxon's arm was draped securely over her waist, holding her as if even in sleep he couldn't bear to let her go.

Leah shifted just enough to look at him. His face was relaxed, softened by sleep, the firelight casting a faint golden glow along his jaw and cheekbones. He looked so peaceful. So safe. So completely hers. A swell of gratitude rose in her chest, warm and overwhelming. She was thankful for him. Thankful for his strength. Thankful for the way he always seemed to know exactly what she needed, even before she did.

She listened to the storm's fury outside, the wind's low roar, the rumbling thunder, the relentless drumming of rain, but none of it stirred fear in her. With Jaxon beside her, the world could rage, and she would still feel protected, still feel loved.

Leah tucked herself a little closer, fitting perfectly into the curve of his body. His arm instinctively tightened around her even in sleep, and the simple gesture made her heart ache in the sweetest way. Wrapped in his warmth, lulled by the quiet crackle of the dying fire, Leah let her eyes drift closed again. Safe. Cherished. Home. She fell back asleep within moments—held securely in the arms of the man she loved.

29 Behind Those Blue Eyes

Ruby, Brooke, Lisa, and Robyn were already bustling around the kitchen when Leah and Jaxon returned, pots simmering, pies cooling on the counter, and the scent of roasting turkey filling the entire house with the unmistakable promise of Thanksgiving. Laughter and the clatter of dishes floated through the air, creating the kind of cozy chaos Leah had always loved.

Cash spotted the couple as soon as they stepped through the door. His eyes gleamed with mischief, clearly ready to unleash an avalanche of teasing about them spending the night at the homestead together. But before he could open his mouth, Jaxon caught his wrist and tugged him aside.

"Don't," Jaxon whispered firmly. "I know you're dying to tease us, but Leah was horrified when she realized we couldn't make it back. She worried all night about what people would think, about her reputation, about us, about everything." His voice softened. "She's sensitive about the intimacy between us, Cash. If you make a joke out of it right now, it'll crush her."

Cash blinked, then nodded slowly, his expression shifting from playful to protective.

"All right," he murmured. "No teasing. Not today." But then a broad grin crept across his lips, unable to be contained much longer. "Did you propose?"

Jaxon's answering nod was so full of pride and joy that Cash let out a low whistle.

"I figured," Cash chuckled. "You're practically glowing. And Leah..." He glanced toward the young woman across the room. "She looks like she swallowed a sunbeam."

Leah had just thrown her arms around her father's neck in a warm embrace before slipping toward the kitchen to help the other women. She didn't get far. David suddenly sprang out of the armchair where he'd been lounging, practically exploding upward like a startled jackrabbit.

Leah gasped and nearly dropped the bowl she was carrying. David caught her hand midair and pulled her straight into a tight hug, laughing. Everyone around them burst into smiles as Leah clutched her chest, trying to calm her racing heartbeat. David only squeezed her tighter, grinning like a delighted guardian who'd just won the world's greatest prize.

After drawing in a steadying breath, Leah finally found her voice again.

"What was that for? Why would you scare me like that?" She gave David a reproachful glare, though it clearly had no effect whatsoever. David only crossed his arms and raised an eyebrow, unimpressed.

"Where were you this morning? I looked all over the ranch for you."

Leah felt heat rush up her neck instantly.

"Why were you looking for me? Did something happen?" she asked, studiously avoiding his eyes.

"No, nothing happened." David tipped his head, pinning her with a knowing stare that made her squirm. "I simply wanted to ask about your plans."

"My... plans?" she echoed weakly.

"Yes," he repeated, drawing out the word just to torment her. "Your plans with a certain young man you are very fond of. I believe said gentleman owes you a proposal."

Leah gasped—but caught herself immediately. She straightened her spine, took a deep breath, and prepared to tell him *exactly* what she thought of that comment when David burst into loud, unabashed laughter.

Leah's brow wrinkled. "What? Why are you laughing at me?"

"It amazes me," David said, wiping the corner of his eye, "how your pretty blue eyes are a complete window. You've got a great poker face, but those eyes betray every emotion. They give you away."

She blinked. "Give me away?"

"Oh, absolutely." His grin deepened. "Every reaction, every thought, every stubborn declaration, you might as well speak them aloud."

Before she could respond, Cash wandered closer, clearly enjoying himself.

"Your eyes express everything you're feeling," he agreed. "We can see the storm brewing when you're about to lose your temper. They show your stubbornness coming through like sunrise over the mountains, and when you love someone?" Cash nodded with mock reverence. "It shines brighter than a bonfire. Behind those blue eyes are fire and water, love and loyalty, and a heart big enough to shame the Rockies. It's something to watch."

Leah pursed her lips, trying not to smile.

"Fine, Uncle Dave. What exactly were my eyes telling you when I reacted to your statement?"

David clasped his hands behind his back, smug as a fox.

"Well... first, frustration at being ambushed." He laughed when her cheeks turned pink. "But most importantly, they showed your outrage at the idea that Jaxon owed you anything. You were about two seconds away from telling me, quite fiercely, that the man you love is not in your debt at all. Am I right?"

Leah's blush deepened, and she ducked her head with a soft smile, confirming his assessment without a single word. Cash jumped back in, grinning wide.

"McKay and Wilson learned that the hard way," he said. "McKay told me he started checking your eyes before he said anything after you bit his head off about that target comment."

Leah groaned.

Cash winked. "He said he learned not to underestimate you ever again."

Just then Mitch approached, slipping an arm around his daughter's shoulders.

"You get that fire from your mama," he said warmly. "She had the same fierce temper. And yes, her eyes gave everyone fair warning when teasing her wasn't smart."

Leah lit up. “Really?”

“Really,” Mitch chuckled. “You’re a lot like her. She wasn’t quite as dynamite-laden as you are.” Cash and David snorted. “But if someone pushed her too far, she’d explode quick enough.”

“Was Mom pretty?” Leah asked quietly, her gaze soft, hopeful. The men around her exchanged tender smiles. Her love for Mitch always showed, bright as day. Mitch’s face softened instantly.

“Your mama was beautiful,” he said, voice thick with memory. “She turned heads everywhere she went. When your grandparents, my brother, and I first moved to the homestead, Lilian was one of the first people I noticed. I think I fell in love with her right there.”

Cash mildly rolled his eyes. “We all did.”

David nodded. “Scott too.”

Leah’s eyes sparkled. “Oh? Did you all fight over her affection?”

Across the room, Jaxon leaned against the wall, arms crossed, wearing a grin that said watching Leah charm an entire room full of grown men was his new favorite pastime. Cash shook his head with a fond smile.

“No. Your mama made it clear from the very beginning she only had eyes for your father.”

Mitch chuckled softly, memories lighting his expression.

“Lilian and I just... clicked. Mildred tried to pursue a friendship with me first, she was older and very determined, but the moment I got to know Lilian, everything changed.” His smile grew distant and warm. “Your mom had a way about her.

Gentle, but strong. Sweet, but firm. I fell for her faster than I could blink." He exhaled, his voice softening.

"She also picked your name, you know. She wanted all our daughters' names to start with L, like hers. And the boys would all have M names." He chuckled. "She had it all planned before we were even married. Determined woman, your mama. Once she set her mind on something, nothing could budge her."

Leah's chest tightened at the affection in his tone.

"That's why we know," Mitch continued gently, "without a shred of doubt, that she didn't think twice about risking herself to save you. You were her pride and joy. She loved you fiercely, Leah, more than life." He paused, clearing his throat as emotion threatened to spill over.

"You were heartbroken for a long time after she passed, even at only two years old. Nobody could soothe you the way she did. You knew... somehow, deep down, that she wasn't coming back."

Leah swallowed, blinking rapidly.

"It was Ruby," he said with a grateful smile, "who slowly brought your smile back. She was only seventeen, but she helped me in ways I still can't fully express, held you when you cried, rocked you to sleep, sat up with you when nightmares woke you." His voice softened further. "When I met Patricia and married her, Ruby stopped coming around. And it broke your little heart all over again."

Leah stared at her hands, her voice barely above a whisper.

"Well... she was probably already in love with you and couldn't stand that another woman had taken her place..." The second the words left her mouth, her eyes widened and she slapped a hand over her lips. "Sorry, I didn't mean to say that out loud."

All three men burst into loud, unrestrained laughter. Leah turned the color of fresh strawberries and looked like she might dive under the nearest piece of furniture. Mitch wrapped an arm around her shoulders and pulled her into a warm hug.

"Just like your mama," he said with a smile thick with love. "She had a gift for reading people. Always knew who needed comfort, who needed teasing, and who needed a good dose of truth. And she had a habit of blurting things out without meaning to." He kissed the top of Leah's head. "You're so much like her it hurts sometimes."

Leah smiled through the shy pink dusting her cheeks. Hearing about her mother, *really* hearing about her, warmed her heart in ways she hadn't realized she desperately needed. And knowing she carried so much of Lilian within her filled her with both pride and peace.

They had an exceptional Thanksgiving celebration that year, one unlike any they'd ever known. The air around the Johnson Ranch felt lighter, warmer, and fuller. So much had happened, so much had nearly been lost, and each person seemed to carry the same swelling sensation in their chest: hearts overflowing with gratitude.

A few days later, Chad and Robyn were married in a joyful ceremony filled with laughter, music, and tears. They surprised the family afterward, standing arm in arm beside David and Brooke, announcing that they were all moving to Eureka.

David's older children were scattered across the West Coast, and Sacramento no longer felt like home. But Eureka, with all its family ties and fresh beginnings, called to them. David and Chad had plans to open a law firm together, and the entire family rejoiced at the news.

Not long after, Cash finally proposed to Lisa in the middle of the kitchen while she was elbow-deep in cookie dough, much to everyone's amusement. Their wedding was set for spring. And in the quiet, steady way of two people who had been meant for each other all along, Mitch and Ruby began courting. The spark between them grew into something deep, tender, and certain.

But the moment everyone had been waiting for with eager hearts arrived a week before Christmas. Leah and Jaxon were married. It was a breathtaking winter morning: crisp, white, peaceful. The little homestead, once abandoned and weary, was now fully furnished, glowing with warmth and charm. Jaxon had renovated the barn behind it and, with the help of every able-bodied man on the ranch, built small sheds filled to the brim with firewood in case they were snowed in their first winter as husband and wife.

By the time the newlyweds left the ranch for their little house, gentle flakes floated from the sky. But halfway there, the snowfall thickened, swirling in heavy curtains until it became a full winter storm. Laughing, breathless, radiant, Jaxon carried his bride through the front door. Leah squealed and clung to him as he crossed the threshold, then gasped when he nearly stumbled on purpose, just to hear her shriek and cling tighter.

He finally set her down with a soft kiss before heading back outside. He put the horse into the barn, made sure the animal was warm and dry, then stored the buggy beside it. But by the time he returned to the house, he was drenched, hair plastered to his forehead, shirt clinging to him before he stripped it off entirely.

Leah had already laid warm clothes for him near the fire, wanting everything to be perfect for their first night. She stood in front of the window now, wrapped in soft lamplight, watching their world disappear beneath the blizzard's white fury. The snow howled against the glass. Inside, though, the fire crackled, and the room glowed with golden warmth.

Jaxon stepped up behind her, quietly, reverently. Then his bare arms slid around her waist. Leah inhaled sharply. Warm skin. Hard muscle. Her husband, shirtless, soaked, and entirely too close.

"J-Jaxon..." Her voice trembled, half scolding, half breathless. He chuckled softly against her hair, his breath warm at her ear. "I'm not cold anymore," he murmured, his tone low and undeniably seductive. "You're better than any fire."

Leah froze, unsure whether to melt or flee. She could feel every inch of him, strong, solid, chest and arms, very much not clothed, and her cheeks flamed hotter than the hearth.

"Y-you should... get dressed," she managed, keeping her gaze locked firmly on the storm outside. "You'll catch your death."

"Hmm," he hummed, pulling her closer, "I think I'm in more danger from my beautiful wife refusing to look at me."

"Jaxon!" she protested, voice cracking adorably. He laughed quietly, the sound deep and full of affection.

"I'm teasing," he whispered, pressing a soft kiss to her temple. "But you're so easy to fluster... and it's charming. Really charming."

She elbowed him lightly, which made him laugh harder.

"Go get dressed," she ordered, still refusing to turn around. "Before I die of embarrassment."

"But we *are* married now, Leah," he said softly. His voice dipped into that low, velvety register that always, always, made her knees feel unreliable. "It isn't improper anymore."

Before she could gather a single coherent protest, he was already moving. His arms slid around her waist, warm and sure, pulling her gently back against him. Leah barely had time to gasp before his lips found hers, slow, confident, devastatingly tender at first... then deepening with a passion that stole the breath straight from her lungs.

When he finally drew back, his breath brushed her lips, warm and unsteady.

"Improper," he murmured, his forehead resting against hers, "is the last word I'd use for kissing my beautiful wife."

Leah's cheeks flamed scarlet, but she didn't try to pull away. Not this time. Her fingers curled into the fabric of his shirt, holding on as though she might float away without him.

"Still..." she whispered weakly, breathless and dazed from his kiss. "Go, put a new shirt on."

Jaxon chuckled, low and sinful, and pressed one last fleeting kiss to the corner of her mouth.

"As my lady commands."

Jaxon watched her with that familiar spark of amusement dancing in his eyes, a look that somehow managed to be both teasing and reverent at the same time. Before Leah could even decide whether to flee or nudge him away, he slid his hands around her waist, turned her toward him, and gently but firmly guided her with him as he dropped onto the sofa in front of the fireplace. She landed across his lap with a soft gasp, his arms locking around her in one smooth motion.

"Jaxon!" she whispered, half scandalized, half breathless. He only grinned, boyish, smug, completely smitten, and without giving her a chance to recover, he captured her lips in a kiss so passionately it stole the air from her lungs. She melted against him at once, her fingers curling into his dry shirt as he drew her closer.

When he finally pulled back, it was slow... reluctant. Leah blinked up at him, dazed and flushed, trying to catch her breath. His gaze held hers, warm as the firelight dancing across the room, deep as midnight, and filled with something tender. She tried to speak, but all she managed was a soft, trembling smile, the kind that made his own eyes soften and his chest tighten.

Jaxon inhaled slowly, his gaze sweeping over her face with quiet awe.

"That smile..." he murmured. "I swear it could melt snow faster than this fire."

Leah blushed fiercely, but her smile widened, brightening her entire face and melting his heart all over again.

In that moment, with the blizzard raging outside and the warmth of the fire flickering behind them, Jaxon held his wife as though she were the most precious thing he had ever been given. And Leah felt it. Felt all of it—the love, desire, safety, and joy. She rested her forehead to his, her fingers threading through his hair, her voice barely above a whisper.

"I love you."

His answering smile was slow, breathtaking, and full of emotion.

"And I love you... more than life."

And then he kissed her again, deep, slow, and tender.

30
True Love Always Wins!

The snow didn't let up for days. Thick drifts climbed across the windowsills, the wind howled around the corners of the little homestead, and the world outside disappeared beneath a blanket of white so heavy it felt almost enchanted. The cold was bitter enough to freeze breath in the air, but neither Jaxon nor Leah minded a bit. They had everything they needed. Plenty of food. Stacks of chopped firewood and buckets of coal. And, most importantly, each other.

They slipped into a rhythm as natural as breathing. Their favorite place became the warm, glowing patch in front of the fireplace, where the flames cracked and danced and painted the room in golden light.

Jaxon had outdone himself with the furnishings he'd chosen. The soft sofa, the cozy armchairs, the braided rugs, and hand-carved table... everything whispered warmth, comfort, and home. Leah had never felt more at peace, or more cherished, than within those walls.

Whenever she curled up with a book on the sofa or sank into one of the armchairs, she felt his eyes on her. And without fail, Jaxon crossed the room, sat beside her, and tugged her gently, sometimes playfully, onto his lap.

"Come here," he'd murmur, his voice low and irresistible. Leah would pretend to protest, her cheeks warming, but she always melted against him instantly. It became their new routine, one neither had any intention of breaking.

Leah fit perfectly in his arms, head resting against his broad chest, wrapped securely in the circle of his strength. Jaxon held her as though she belonged there, because she did. His hand would slide up her back, warm and steady, and he'd press a kiss to her temple or the curve of her jaw. And somehow, every time, it made her breath catch.

Sometimes she'd whisper a teasing comment about him distracting her from her book, but he only tilted her face toward his and kissed her until the words faded into a soft, helpless sigh. Those days became a world of their own: snowfall, firelight, stolen kisses, shared laughter, and the quiet, unshakable joy of being newly married and utterly in love. And as the storm raged on outside, Jaxon held Leah close, grateful for every moment, every soft breath, every smile, every kiss that left her breathless in his arms. They were snowed in, and neither of them would have traded it for anything in the world.

The night before Christmas Eve, the cold deepened with a sharpness neither of them had expected. The temperature dropped so drastically that even both fireplaces, the one in the main room and the small one in their bedroom, struggled to keep the little homestead warm. Frost crept across the windows like delicate lace, and the wind outside wailed against the eaves.

Jaxon stirred sometime after midnight, the chill brushing against his skin. The moment he shifted, he realized Leah was trembling beside him. A soft, involuntary shiver rippled through her, and Jaxon reacted before she could even blink. He gathered her instantly into his arms, tucking her tightly against his bare chest as though shielding her from the very cold itself. His palms swept up and down her back in brisk strokes, trying to rub warmth into her chilled skin.

Leah instinctively curled into him, seeking heat and comfort. Her small, ice-cold hands brushed against his ribs, and he jerked slightly at the shock of cold that shot through him.

"You're freezing, sweetheart," he murmured, touching his lips to her forehead. Her shivering didn't stop right away. Her whole body trembled with the deep cold that had settled into the house during the night, but slowly, steadily, he felt her begin to soften and thaw in his embrace. His body heat wrapped around her like a living blanket, and with one arm he pulled the covers more securely around them while the other held her firmly against his chest. Safe. Warm. His.

Jaxon didn't let go, not even for a moment. He kept her tucked tightly against him, protective and steady, his chin resting atop her head. When he finally felt her breathing slow into the soft, sweet rhythm of sleep, he relaxed just enough to press another gentle kiss into her hair.

"I've got you," he whispered, though she couldn't hear him. Only when he was certain she was warm and safe did he allow himself to drift back to sleep, his arms still wrapped around his wife, holding her close against the winter night.

It was snowing again when Leah woke the next morning, the world outside their windows blanketed in soft white. Christmas Eve had arrived, and both their families were expected for dinner, followed by Christmas dinner the next day. The thought both warmed and worried her. She slipped quietly from the bed so as not to wake Jaxon, wrapped herself in her dressing gown, slid her feet into her slippers, and padded into the big room.

Snowflakes drifted lazily past the window, swirling in the gentle breeze. Beautiful, yet the steady fall made her worry her family might not be able to travel through the drifts. She stood there, lost in thought, when suddenly strong arms wrapped around her waist. A moment later, Jaxon's lips captured hers in a fierce, hungry kiss that made her knees turn to water. She squeaked and pulled away, slipping out of his arms with all the determination of a startled deer.

"We—we need to get ready for our dinner guests," she stammered, trying, and failing, not to get distracted by the bare-chested, half-awake man behind her. Jaxon took one slow, purposeful step. Then another. He wasn't even trying to hide the amusement in his warm brown eyes.

Leah turned to escape, but not fast enough. In the next breath, she was back in his arms, and his lips were on hers again, stealing the air from her lungs.

"Jaxon," she gasped between kisses, pushing a hand weakly against his chest. "You are incredibly unfair."

He drew back only enough to grin at her, irresistible and smug.

"And why is that?"

"Because you use your strength against me, and your handsomeness!"

"Is that so?" He arched a brow, thoroughly entertained.

"Yes," she insisted. "Not to mention that you smell far too good for a man who just rolled out of bed."

He laughed softly, deep, warm, and devastating. Then he pulled her flush against him again, lowering his face until their noses brushed.

"And are you certain that's my fault?" he murmured. "Because I could say the same of you. You're so beautiful it's impossible to stand beside you without wanting to steal a kiss, or ten."

Her cheeks caught fire. She tried to hold onto her indignation, but his eyes, dark with affection and a little mischief, made it very hard.

"Are you implying," she said dramatically, "that I am beguiling you?"

"I'm implying," he countered, lips twitching into a smirk, "that you tempt me more than is reasonable or fair."

She closed her eyes for a moment, trying to gather the scattered pieces of her composure.

"I think it's time," she said firmly, "that you get dressed for the day. Our families will be here this afternoon, and I have a great deal to prepare."

Jaxon's lips curved into a slow, mischievous smile.

"You don't like it when I'm shirtless?" he teased.

"I didn't say that," she muttered, mortified enough to stare at the floor. "I'm merely stating that it's improper. If my father ever thought I was entertaining guests with my husband half-dressed—"

Jaxon outright laughed. "You are adorable when you're flustered."

She shot him a warning glare, but before she could escape again, his arm shot out, pulling her back.

"Jaxon—!"

In one smooth motion, he lifted her clean off the floor and slung her over his shoulder. Leah shrieked, pounding his back with her small fists.

"PUT me down!"

But he only carried her toward the sofa by the fireplace. He dropped onto the cushions with her in his lap and wrapped both arms around her. Then he kissed her. A deep, consuming kiss that swept away every coherent thought she had. By the time he slowed the kiss, her fingers were curled in his hair, and her indignant protest was long forgotten. Jaxon leaned his forehead against hers, breath warm on her lips, and gave her the softest, most sheepish grin.

Leah rolled her eyes, because that was safer than admitting she wanted to kiss him again, but she didn't try to leave his lap. His arms tightened around her, holding her against his warm chest. He pressed a tender kiss to her temple.

"I love you," he murmured. "More than I've ever loved anything. And I will never stop being grateful that you're mine. No one will ever take your place in my heart."

Leah's breath caught. Her pulse skipped. And though she tried to hide her smile against his shoulder... Jaxon felt it anyway. But Leah felt the same way he did, deep in her bones, in the quiet place where fear and hope lived side by side. For so long she had dreaded the idea of risking their friendship, terrified that one wrong step could shatter the bond she treasured most. But now, resting within the circle of Jaxon's strong arms, she knew with absolute certainty that stepping forward had been the right choice.

Love didn't erase hardships. It didn't guarantee they would never argue or face moments of frustration. But the love they shared, steady, intentional, fiercely loyal, would give them strength to weather the storms together instead of alone.

She curled closer, letting the rising warmth of his body chase away the last of the chill. Her eyes drifted shut, and two quotes slipped into her mind, words she had read repeatedly during the hardest moments of the past year. The first was from Jane Austen, her newly discovered favorite author, a confession spoken with raw honesty: *"In vain have I struggled. It will not do. My feelings will not be repressed. You must allow me to tell you how ardently I admire and love you."*

A small, soft smile touched her lips. How many times had she pretended she didn't feel exactly that way? The second quote rose in her thoughts like a warm light, familiar and comforting, the scripture she had carried with her throughout every trial:

"Love is patient, love is kind. It does not envy, it does not boast, it is not proud. It is not rude, it is not self-seeking, it is not easily angered, it keeps no record of wrongs. Love does not delight in evil but rejoices with the truth. It always protects, always trusts, always hopes, always perseveres."

Those words soothed her heart in ways nothing else could. Because she knew she was loved. Truly loved. Despite the wounds, despite the betrayals, despite the unbearable moments that had nearly crushed her this past year, she was surrounded by people who cared for her. By a father who adored her. By friends who would give their lives for her. By a husband whose love burned so deeply it left her breathless.

And above all, by a Heavenly Father who had watched her reach her breaking point yet gave her strength when she felt she had none left. She had grown. She had been tested, stretched, pushed to the edge, and somehow, she had come out stronger. She had learned that loving someone meant forgiving them. It meant risking pain. It meant showing up again and again, even when it would be easier to shut down.

But she also knew this truth now: Love could heal what had been broken. Love could rebuild what had been shattered. Love could conquer anything, if both hearts chose to keep fighting for it.

Held safely in her husband's arms, Leah finally understood that she hadn't just survived the year. She had become someone braver. Someone wiser. Someone capable of loving with her whole heart—and being loved in return. And for the first time in a long time... her soul felt completely at peace.

The End

A Note from the author...

Dearest Reader,

Thank you so much for choosing Behind Those Blue Eyes *as your recent read. I hope you enjoyed it as much as I did while writing it. If this is your first time picking up one of my books, allow me to share a bit about myself, my writing style, and the characters you'll meet throughout my stories. You may soon notice a familiar pattern, though each book has its own unique tale, there are themes I return to again and again.*

I am a hopeless romantic at heart, but I also adore suspense, drama, playfulness, and emotional depth. I love blending these elements and strive to make my stories as believable as possible. Of course, they are fiction, but I want readers to feel that the adventures could *happen and that the characters* could *step right off the page.*

When it comes to my heroines, I gravitate toward strong, spirited women who fight for their rights and stand up for others. Because I predominantly write historical fiction, women's rights and the early feminists who paved the way are subjects dear to my heart. Those women fought for basic human rights with extraordinary courage. Today, much of modern feminism often looks different from those original battles, and I deeply admire the determination and grit of the women who came before us.

I am also a devoted advocate for protective alpha males, men who cherish and shield the women in their lives, especially in the context of the past. While I adore writing independent, fiery heroines, history shows there were realities they simply could not face alone, and there is nothing wrong with relying on the strength of a good man. I struggle with how masculinity is often portrayed today. Yes, there is such a thing as toxic masculinity, and harmful men do exist, but harmful women exist as well, and most men are not that way.

So yes, my books are filled with strong women from history and men who love them fiercely. You'll find stolen kisses and simmering tension, the kind you see in old novels or classic films. I love protective, powerful masculinity, and I'm not afraid to write it.

Rebecca Lange

Did you love *Behind Those Blue Eyes*? Then you should read *Not His To Kiss*[1] by Rebecca Lange!

[2]

She's not the girl he was sent to protect. But she might be the one he can't let go. Riley Hastings's world shatters when she discovers her entire life has been built on lies. When she uncovers the devastating truth—that her parents faked their deaths to escape the law and that she was never their daughter to begin with—she vows to uncover their secrets and make them pay. To keep her safe, her aunt and uncle arrange for her to leave Boston and travel west to Oregon. But when her escort

1. https://books2read.com/u/bzGnwj

2. https://books2read.com/u/bzGnwj

cancels, a rugged stranger arrives in his place… and greets her by the wrong name.

Adam McCall thought he was doing his best friend a favor by escorting a reluctant bride-to-be across the country. But the woman he's meant to protect is nothing like he expected. Instead, he finds himself entangled with a fiery, unpredictable, secretive woman who upends every expectation. With every mile, the danger deepens and the misunderstandings multiply. Sparks fly and feelings begin to stir between two people who were never supposed to fall in love.

About the Author

Rebecca Lange is a devoted romantic at heart. Though she has explored a variety of genres throughout her writing journey, her deepest passion lies in historical fiction—particularly stories set in the 1800s American West and the Regency era.

A passionate advocate, Rebecca uses her stories to raise awareness of abuse, human trafficking, and the devastating impact of drug and alcohol addiction. These themes are not woven in for suspense alone, but as a reminder that such struggles are tragically real—and that victims are never to blame.

She is also a firm believer in women's rights, inspired by the courageous women of the 1800s who fought to prove they were not the property of their husbands but their partners and equals. Rebecca upholds the conviction that violence has no place in relationships or marriage.

Originally from Germany, she was born and raised there before moving abroad in 2002 to serve a mission for her church in Scotland. A member of The Church of Jesus Christ of Latter-day Saints, she now lives in Utah with her husband, their two sons (ages 18 and 20), and two lively Yorkie puppies.

Her writing motto is: *Never Smut, Always Sizzling Kisses, Consistently Closed Door.* Rebecca delights in weaving passion and tenderness into her stories, offering what she calls "sweet and diet spice" romance. Diet spice—what is that, you ask? It's the thrill of longing gazes, passionate kisses, and close embraces that build anticipation without ever crossing into explicit territory. For her, the most powerful love stories are those that remain tasteful and teasing, proving that romance can be both heart-stirring and wholesome.

Read more at https://authorrebeccalange.wixsite.com/bookstolove.

www.ingramcontent.com/pod-product-compliance
Lightning Source LLC
LaVergne TN
LVHW020646110826
845149LV00012B/1927

9781957089256